In

Wolf's

Clothing

Niall McOmish

www.fertileblack.scot

A
Fertile
Black
publication

First published in paperback in 2020

No claim is made as to the accuracy of any historical, geographical,
geological, botanical or sociological references in this novel.

This is a fable

A CIP catalogue record for this title is
available from the British Library.

Paperback ISBN 9780953546527
EBook   ISBN 9780953546510

Printed and bound by CPI Group (UK) Ltd, CR0 4YY

www.fertileblack.scot

To Richie, who liked a good western.
And Ina.
They loved and put up with each other for fifty years.

One

It was a night for lovers. If they could have been persuaded to look up. For after the pale, delicate starlight had finally flickered and danced its romantic way to earth – it was lost; either devoured by those weird shapes of darkness which lurked ominously at street level or simply eclipsed by the criss-crossing shafts of bright yellow and white light that shone harshly from the un-shuttered windows and sawn-off doorways on Maple, seemingly fuelled by the raucous merry-making within.

The young couple who stood on the sidewalk were almost invisible. But their urgent whisperings would have carried clearly to any passer-by. The Lieutenant had his strong arms wrapped around the girl, talking softly to her now, coaxing her along.

"C'mon, honey," he said, leading her gently off the sidewalk and into the mouth of the dark alleyway, "we can talk down here."

It would be reasonable to assume that even if the Lieutenant had managed to drag his eyes away from the girl, the undeniable beauty of the starlight would have been completely lost on him, since this particular young man would have thought it romantic if he found himself at the bottom of a mine shaft ... as long as he was making out down there.

Carrie drew back a little, a vague anxiety causing her to hesitate. "I don't know, David. You know what he's like. What if he's missed me? Suppose he's out looking for us?"

The Lieutenant took a firmer grip of Carrie's arm, pulling her reluctant body forward. "We'll have come to a decision by then," he reasoned. "We'll be able to face him together."

"David!" Carrie was indignant, and a little scared. "You're hurting me."

"Sorry, Hon." The Lieutenant eased his grip slightly, his placating smile fading as he looked nervously over his shoulder.

Misinterpreting the source of her growing fear, Carrie allowed herself to be enveloped by that slightly different shade of black that marked the opening of the alleyway.

It takes a lot to halt the clamouring babble of conversation in that smoky, unhygienic haunt called McGarvey's; but it stopped at the sight of Judge Perry brandishing a handgun.

It started up again, in slight amazement, when it was realised that the object of his wrath was to be found amongst those seated at the troopers' table. He was yelling at them, his face contorted with rage.

"You! Sergeant. Where is he? Tell me." It was half plea, half screaming demand, "Tell me."

Sergeant McVey dropped his poker hand. "For christ's sake, Judge, calm down."

It was the wrong approach to take.

"I'll blow your damn head from your shoulders. He's with my daughter."

McVey spread his hands. "I don't know where he is."

The Judge pulled the hammer back, deadly serious.

McVey looked at the gun, a foot from his face. "Judge, I don't know."

"Sarge." The word was spoken tentatively, reluctance dragging out the single syllable.

All eyes swivelled to trooper Hendrix, who was making a meal out of his lower lip, his own eyes fixed squarely on McVey, not daring to look at the Judge.

"I ... eh, saw them just bef..."

"Where?" The question exploded from the Judge, slicing through Hendrix's hesitancy, forbidding him to embellish on the information he was about to give, then quietly, even more commanding of succinctness. "Where?"

"Back at Johnston's. You know that alley at the side..." Hendrix stopped speaking since the Judge was already half way out the door.

He turned apologetically to the rest of the troopers at the table and, speaking mainly for the benefit of Corporal Bailey who had sent a certain winning hand crashing to the table and who was now staring disgustedly in his direction, said, "They wis only talking."

McVey snapped out of it and charged outside after the Judge. McGarvey himself was only seconds behind, leaping over the bar to lead the rush. This was bound to be good. Nobody was going to miss this.

The single, high-pitched scream stopped Judge Perry dead at the mouth of the alley. McVey brushed past him and continued at a blind run into dark space. It was not much lighter at the back of Johnston's either, but enough to see by. And what he did see stopped the Sergeant in turn.

He almost laughed. But his brain told him it wasn't funny. Then the sight of the Lieutenant, with his pants crushed down on his boots, his bare ass heaving rhythmically, held him in fascination. The girl was almost naked, her head thrown back, her neck taut, inviting; her

3

arms splayed wide, one hand tangled in her long, blonde hair.

She was unconscious. But still he stood, frozen; his eyes lingering on her exposed breasts, his mind eager to fill in those gaps in the erotic image which the poor light was unable to capture.

He did not have the chance to see anything else. Perry hurled past him, sending the Sergeant crashing heavily into the timber wall. The Judge was screeching in uncontrollable rage, completely gone.

When McVey looked up, the Lieutenant was almost on the other side of the enclosure, vainly trying to get to his feet, panic making the task of sorting out his pants from his boots impossible. The Judge was only yards away, bareheaded now, his hat lost in the collision, getting his balance back.

McVey started towards the girl.

Then stopped. "Judge. Wait"

The first bullet burst through the Lieutenant's right hand and into his thigh. He screamed; a cut-off, frightened squeal, and whipped his left hand over to cover them both.

"Scum! Bastard scum." Judge Perry's hand was shaking as he lined up again on the Lieutenant.

McVey took an involuntary step backwards, resuming the onlooker role. He was vaguely aware of the people who were now milling around him. The first arrivals had spilled into the yard but had stopped after only a few feet, resisting the pressure of the horde behind them. You do not crowd in on bullets.

The second and third shots both missed.

"Filth."

The fourth bullet smashed into the Lieutenant's left forearm. The fifth took away his right ear. The Lieutenant wailed. A fearsome animal wail. He did not have enough hands to cover his wounds.

The sixth shot kicked up dirt between his legs.

The Judge had stopped now. The Lieutenant had stopped screaming. He sat there, squat and grotesque, the blood leaking steadily from his shattered ear dripping down his side to merge with the sticky mess oozing from his thigh, together forming a dark pool in his groin.

The pain had gone, replaced by a sickening sensation of reality. His bulging eyes tried to make sense out of the scene in front of him, latching onto the presence of his Sergeant.

McVey. McVey would help him now. At least get him away from this madman. Give him a chance to explain. To tell them how it was.

Judge Perry was trying to reload his revolver, but he would not take his eyes off the Lieutenant, lest the man escaped him, and his fumbling fingers kept missing the chambers.

McVey woke up. "Judge, see to your daughter. For god's sake, Judge," the Sergeant implored him. "Your daughter."

"Yes. My daughter. He did this to my daughter." With only three shells in, Judge Perry impatiently snapped the revolver shut.

"Shit," breathed McVey. He pulled his own side-arm out as the Judge fired. The bullet tore into the Lieutenant's stomach and he gave a heaving grunt, his head coming forward to look at his belly.

The Sergeant took slow, careful aim and his gun boomed just before the Judge could let loose again. McVey's bullet made a neat hole at the very top of the Lieutenant's forehead, snapping his whole upper body backwards, his arms going wide, knees up, dead.

Judge Perry fired again. Then twice the hammer came down on empty chambers. His arm dropped and he stood quietly, staring at the mutilated corpse, reluctant to let go of his revulsion, his anger and his despair.

McVey called over his shoulder at the blue shapes behind him, "Hold those people back." He recognised the instinctive, routine command for what it was; a vain attempt to bring some order and sense to the chaos he knew he now faced. Fuckin' moron.

He went over to the Judge and gently prised the firearm from his hand.

The troopers at the front of the mob became soldiers again and half-heartedly began to push against the crowd, their own heads swivelled round to take in the naked form of the girl and the Lieutenant's bullet-ridden body.

"Can you make some way there? Let me pass. Let me through, will you?" The insistent voice of Doctor Brady carried above the excited murmuring of the crowd, and, finally, he broke through, heading straight for Carrie who was still unconscious.

"George. George, come over here," the Doctor commanded, while he removed his coat and ineffectively covered the girl. The Judge went slowly over and knelt beside his daughter.

"Use your coat to cover her," Brady tugged at the Judge's sleeve. "We have to get her inside, George."

But the Judge's only answer was to put his hands gently under his daughter's head and pull her to him. He put his face down into her hair, letting the tears fall as he rocked her, soothing her, telling her it would be all right.

Doctor Brady looked around, seeking help. The light from the lanterns that had appeared helped him pick out a bearded face on the fringe of the crowd. "Garve! Garve, give me a hand here."

McGarvey brushed a trooper aside and came forward. He didn't have to be asked twice.

6

"Take her to the Hartford house."

McGarvey nodded and lifted the girl easily; her father yielding his precious possession without protest. McGarvey hefted her once, feeling the coolness of her thighs against the coarseness of his hand and set off with purpose and pride.

"I'll be right with you." Brady leaned over and touched the Judge on the arm. "George, we'll go with her. Let's go with your daughter, George."

McVey was over at the Lieutenant, giving the young officer some semblance of dignity by pulling up his pants, satisfying himself that nothing could be done. He looked up. "Bailey, make some room there."

The crowd fell back as the troopers went to work, some viciously swinging their gun butts, righteously clearing a path for McGarvey and the girl.

As the Judge was being led away by Doctor Brady, he suddenly stopped and turned on McVey, his misery making his voice go unnaturally high. "Sergeant. You get your dirty little band out of this town."

McVey stood up and walked over. "Alright, Judge," he said quietly, "we'll head out in the morning."

"Tonight! You'll go tonight," the Judge screamed. "If you're still here in the morning, I'll have you hanged."

The Sergeant felt his own anger rising at the stupid threat and couldn't stop the words. "Have you forgotten it was you who asked us to come here?"

"Did I ask you to rape my daughter?"

The grief-stricken question brought home the futility of the argument. "Bailey, go and round up the rest of the squad."

Judge Perry was still shouting as Doctor Brady dragged him off down the ghoul-filled alley. "And don't leave that filth there. Take it with you."

"Sarge," Bailey's tone of voice was very reasonable, as it always was when he was about to query an order. "it'll take hours to get the men together. They could be anywhere."

McVey was keeping his eyes fixed on the Judge's retreating back. "Just do it," he told the Corporal. "We leave tonight."

★

The sun had been at work for an hour but already the lone horseman crossing the open plain was sweating uncomfortably under its hot glare. Not quite six feet, he sat easy, at home in the saddle, his body swaying with the rhythmic movements of his mount. His dark face was weather-beaten and the fuzz of several days growth curled on his chin.

Reckoning by this, his worn, green jacket and faded, sweat-stained shirt, this man had ridden hard and long.

Only the working cowboy would have noticed his lack of 'oneness' with his horse. But the item which really distinguished him from any other Wyoming ranch-hand was the colt .44, snug in a black leather holster, within easy reach at his side. Not that the gun itself made the difference, rather the way it was, as if part of him, belonging there.

The horse was moving at an easy trot. Now the flat, grassy plain was beginning to develop into shallow gullies and slight rises. Here and there they passed scattered groups of grazing cattle, munching in the darker coolness under the shade of the cottonwoods.

The cows turned their lazy attention on them, idly surveying this break in their luxurious monotony. Now there were fewer stands of cottonwoods and more mountain aspen and bush. The rider was continually losing and regaining sight of the high peaks of the Rocky

Mountains, far on the western horizon, as he traversed basin after basin, moving ever deeper into the foothills.

The rider reined up beside a fast-flowing, trickle of a stream and climbed down from his horse. He let the reins dangle and moved over to the tiny brook, following it down to where it formed a small pool, nestled in the lush prairie grass. He knelt and took off his hat and buried his head in the life-reviving liquid.

Satisfied, he filled his hat with cool, clear, spring water and fetched it back to his horse. But the buckskin had not had the manners to wait and was already lapping at the thin flow of sweet water bubbling down to the pool.

He dumped the hatful between the buckskin's ears and thought he recognised a gleam of appreciation in the horse's left eye, but couldn't be sure.

He clamped the hat back on his head, enjoying the dampness. He shrugged off his jacket and jammed it under his bedroll. The buckskin had had his fill and started to graze, so he sat back against a grassy mound and stretched out, feeling his muscles. He allowed them both a couple of minutes but resisted the urge to talk to his horse.

Wearily, he took up the reins, drew them over the buckskin's head and swung into the saddle. Getting into deep conversation with your horse was not an uncommon pastime for lone riders whose only companion was their transport.

A few miles further on he hit a faint trail coming from the north and swung south on to it. The narrow trail, abundant with curves and bends, wound its way gradually down, forever descending. The sunlight was dappled as it slipped between the lattice of leaves and branches overhead, gleaming in staccato bursts when it was reflected off the silver birch and the pale bark of the quaking aspens.

Presently, the rider pulled the buckskin up for the

second time that morning, letting his eyes wander over the scene ahead, taking in the details as the town of Limon spread itself out before him.

About half a mile ahead, settled in a tight, oval valley Limon looked peaceful enough. The rider was looking down on the town from his high vantage point to the north, and the wide street he could see stretched out for two hundred and fifty yards or so, before splitting, one fork curving out of sight to the south east, the other to the west, following the base of a low, high-grass butte.

To the left, lay a long, deep row of irregularly sized buildings, thrown up in a confused mixture of timber and some brick, behind which the vegetation was battering against a line of back yards. From there the greenery banked away up the flank of the east ridge until it couldn't compete with the scree, leaving sagebrush clumps to sneak through the gaps in a dilapidated, wooden snow-barricade, which ran parallel to the street, about sixty feet below.

There were several side streets branching out to the right, but, aside from the west peak which dominated the surrounding landscape, his view was mostly restricted by the dense foliage growing at the side of the trail. Easing his horse forward, he went on down.

Presently, the narrow trail gained some width and he emerged into a small plaza, set back on a spur off the bend on the main drag, with a public well as its centre point. An oasis. With an armed guard.

A precious resource for everyone. Free to fetch. Just queue up; but don't pollute or we'll shoot you.

The Plaza was doubling as the town meeting place for those thirsty and grateful citizens queuing patiently to fill their water buckets; happy to exchange gossip and laughter while they waited. On the business side of the well, a flatbed wagon with 'LW&I' stencilled on the side was

10

loading barrels from the cascade pouring down from the swing arm of the duel pump.

He skirted the well and pulled up at the junction, getting his bearings. He had to pull up. Because contrary to the impression it gave out at a distance, Limon was bustling. People were on the move, even at this early hour; wagons were being hauled; stores were open and already well into their business day.

He eased the buckskin back further as a freight wagon swayed perilously round the curve, the teamster deliberately locking the wheels into the deep ruts to sweep his cargo safely around the bend; a creaking consignment of felled timber destined for the sawmill at the very edge of town. Feltman's eyes followed the high-spirited team as they pulled valiantly away to his right, veering around the construction debris at the bottom of a huge water tower.

Beyond the stacked piles of cut lumber in the sawmill, the road continued on, providing the main route out of town to the north west.

He eased carefully into the traffic, his wandering eyes seeking out the detail. Ahead, on the corner at the first side street, he picked out a sign; *'Ma Kelly's'.* The smells wafting across the street as he drew level confirmed it was a chow house, the kind of place a working hand could get a big plateful of cheap grub - without removing his hat.

The juices in his stomach started to get excited but he pushed on down the street, the buckskin prancing his way through the heavy ruts while he kept his eyes open for a livery barn.

More than one set of eyes registered the stranger's entry into town. But none were more professional than those of the old man lounging in a rickety chair in the sun outside Sammy's saloon.

He did it for a living, literally. His surveillance of all that moved in Limon was his only reason for getting up in the morning. He had picked up the stranger as soon as he had come within range of his failing eyesight, drinking in the detail, assessing, guessing, releasing him reluctantly only when the rider's image blurred and became indistinct as he rode on through the town.

The uninspiring names of the side streets, which gave the town a great deal of depth to the west, came back dully at Feltman from weathered boards. 'Grant' and 'Lincoln.'

He registered them as he passed. He had to be riding down 'Main.' But something was inspiring the busy residents of Limon because the signs of prosperity were obvious and everywhere; glass-fronted stores, plaques announcing the services of physicians and lawyers; the chaos and noise of a Chinese laundry and bathhouse coming at him through a veil of steam; well-maintained double-storied buildings with balconies. Twin banks, glaring at each other in competition from opposite sides of the street.

And, in a commanding position, directly opposite Lincoln, on the east side of the main drag, an imposing, brick build, three-storied structure; the 'Limon Hotel' a well-painted sign proclaimed.

At the third, and what looked like the last major junction, beyond which the main street carried on for a couple of blocks before diverging out of town, he saw what he wanted and turned down the broad, unnamed street.

Wide, but the opposite of salubrious; and sleepy. This was saloon alley and business would not pick up again until the excesses of the night before had dissipated, or a payday wave of cowboys hit town.

'The Purple Pit' ; 'McGarvey's'; mostly just den after den, interspersed with the odd store and a barber shop. And a 'Silver Hat', still with some glazing intact.

All open, but quiet.

He pulled up level with the livery and stood in the stirrups, swinging in the saddle to take in the view behind him, checking it out once again. He settled back, satisfied his eyes had not deceived him.

Beyond the livery stables the whole demeanour of the street changed. Two different streets, split by the long frontage of the corral and livery barn on one side and a strategically placed undertakers on the other.

He had found where the rich people lived.

It was a scene straight out of a merchant's avenue back east. This section of the street pointedly merited a sign, *'Maple.'* A long narrow stand of trees had been left to form a shaded green island in the middle of the road and the prim and proper properties formed a proud, elongated arc around it. Stone walls and picket fences defined the tended gardens; cut stone paths leading to the ornate porches. The houses themselves were more painted timber than stone and brick; and no metalled road – but there were no deep ruts here, a welcome relief to the bone-shattering buggy rides as the residents crossed the threshold into their private world, a satisfying indication that they had arrived home.

The raw realism at the end of their street must make their stomachs heave. They'd want them gone.

He moved the buckskin into the corral in front of the barn and reined to a halt as an indistinct figure emerged from the shaded opening.

The liveryman, a small, wiry looking guy with a mean mouth, peered up at the stranger through eyes that were almost screwed shut in defence against the sun.

"Through there," he directed, barely opening his mouth wide enough to let out the words.

The rider nodded and, dismounting, led his horse into the spacious stables. Light and airy, they extended all the way back to the high, wide, open double doors which led on to a yard and more corrals fronting on Lincoln. There had to be upwards of fifty stalls in the huge airy barn and most of them were full.

He found three empty stalls near the end and nudged his mount into the middle one. First the stranger removed his canteen and saddle-bags; bedroll and the shabby jacket, then lifted the moleskin covered Springfield from its scabbard. Leaning the barrel of the rifle against the back wall, he dumped the rest of his gear in the corner and started to loosen the cinches. He heaved the saddle and blanket from the buckskin's back and draped them over the side of the stall. The liveryman watched in silence, grudgingly admiring the newcomer's taste in horseflesh.

"Think you might manage the bridle?"

The liveryman remained unmoved.

"I'll leave the roll an' bags with the rig. I'll expect them to be here when I get back."

Again, the liveryman said nothing.

"Rub him down well, an' feed an' water him." The stranger gently slapped his horse's neck, communicating his thanks for the journey, and reached down to pick up his rifle.

"Sad livery that didn't feed an' water a horse," the liveryman spoke matter-of-factly. "A dollar a day plus fodder." And when the new customer showed no sign of coughing up, added, "That would be up front"

The stranger paused and reached between the two bottom buttons on his shirt. He dug out a dollar from his money belt, spinning it at the liveryman, who caught it with practised nonchalance.

He slung his saddle bags behind his rig and hefted his rifle. He walked out through the high doors into the sunlight, issuing a mild warning as he went, "Bear in mind,

I know how much that horse can eat." Only with a little effort had he prevented his face from flinching at the robber rates.

Outside, he stood for a moment, deliberating. The pangs of hunger now constant in his belly signified his urgent need of food. Yet his sweaty, sticky body cried out for a wash. The last time he had bathed, or had even felt remotely clean, had been back at the Platte. The extra rumble across his midriff and the sight of the horse trough on the far side of the corral seemed to solve his problem.

He made for the trough and, for the second time that morning, buried his head in cool – if not clear – water.

"That, Mister, is fir the horses." Squint eyes had followed him out. "I'd be outta business if'n my customers' nags kept droppin' out from under 'em cause their innards wis poisoned."

Slowly, the stranger stood up. Still with his back to the liveryman, he loosened the grey band of cloth at his throat and began to wipe his face and hands. He tied it back and reached behind him to pull up his hat. All this to give the words time to lose their needle. It might not be too clever to beat up what could be a respected member of the community - and at those prices he had to be. He did not want to fight with anybody; not even a grave-ambitious liveryman. Not yet.

When he turned round, he was smiling, pleasant. "Do you have a forge?"

"I got a smith who works with me."

"He needs reshod. All four" He retrieved his rifle and started to make his way out of the corral.

"Hey!"

He stopped. And turned. "Yeah?"

"I ain't a mind reader."

The stranger waited patiently.

"So, if you don't want to swap that buckskin for a donkey, you'd better tell me your name."

The stranger smiled. Nosey bastard. "Feltman," he said. And followed his stomach across the street.

He had emerged at a cross-street between Lincoln and Grant and stepped up on to the eastern sidewalk, following it along on the shady side of the street. He enjoyed the walk; stretching his muscles; dodging his fellow pedestrians and drinking in the atmosphere of the town.

There was a lot to take in. Not least the hustle and bustle in front of a huge ice-house on the opposite side of the street. Large blocks of ice were being unloaded on to rollers at one end of the 'Limon Water & Ice Co' and dispatched, cut and crushed, in barrels out the other.

When he got to the corner of Grant, he caught sight of the weathered cross-street sign. *'Stonewall'*. This town had a sense of humour. Or somebody was looking for a fight.

Which reminded him. He slipped the Springfield out of its cover and tucked the moleskin into his belt. Not the weapon for a street fight, but it was time it had some air.

He turned right into Grant and felt the warmth of the sun on his body. By the time he had finished walking the long diagonal to reach Ma Kelly's, the dampness on his shoulders and neck had evaporated, taking most of the muscle tension with it.

The double doors on the corner were both open and he passed through into the restaurant. Maybe not quite as rough as he had imagined. It was big, clean, and it had cloths on the tables.

The place held ten circular tables that would take about five or six. In addition, there were four high-backed booths ranged either side of the corner entrance doors, butted tightly against the windows, which were clean enough to allow a decent view of the comings and goings out in the

16

streets; and it was crowded with the late breakfast trade.

No one was behind the counter. A grizzled old man was moving briskly between the tables, taking orders, while a stern-faced matron was busy stacking and clearing plates.

A central table only had two guys at it so Feltman moved to join them but changed his mind when he saw an empty spot at one of the windows and altered course to approach the booth.

"You gents mind if I join you?"

Of the three men already occupying the table, the one in the window seat diagonally opposite ignored the polite inquiry completely while the other two mumbled something incoherent.

Feltman sat down anyway and put his rifle on the bench seat between himself and a weedy looking man with a pock-marked face, leaning the barrel against the back of the booth. The two men opposite were much of a kind, except the one at the window had cultivated a neat, brown moustache. Both were reasonably well dressed; looked like pen-pushers. Their eyes never left their plates as they devoured their breakfasts. But that might have had a lot to do with the food, which looked good.

He turned his attention back into the room, seeking out the old-timer. But he was distracted when a server broke through the curtain at the rear of the counter. As she emerged, Feltman caught a glimpse of another matron tending to the stove behind her, shaking her huge ass to help stir something in a pan in the steamy kitchen. Ma Kelly in the flesh, he supposed.

He hoped she was not the mother of the server. That would be a sad future, because this girl was stunning. Her fresh, bright face was framed by a blue-black bob of hair; her lips full, sensuous. The apron did nothing to disguise her womanly shape and the cut-off men's pants she wore only served to draw every male eye up her long legs to her achingly desirable butt. Even allowing he would have found almost any woman appealing right then, she was definitely a cut above.

It wasn't just the cooking that kept this place crowded.

His watch on her progress was cut short when a dirty white apron drifted across his line of sight. Looking up, he was confronted with a set of rotten, black teeth.

"Eggs 'r all out. We got belly, steak, fried tats 'n chilli beans. Do yah?" the old man asked cheerfully.

"No beans. I've been livin' on beans. An' hot coffee."

"Do you mind, Mister? Those things scare me."

Feltman turned quickly at the sound of the whine, meeting the awkward eyes of the weed. The barrel of the Springfield had slid along the back of the booth and was resting on the guy's shoulder.

"Sorry," Feltman apologised. He retrieved the rifle and slid it under the table, resting the stock against his thigh.

The old waiter shot past again, dumping a tin mug of steaming coffee in front of him. He took a long taste. It was good. But lacked sugar.

On his next circuit, the old man appeared with his steak but as he was clattering down the eating irons, three dusty, young cowboys came in and moved past him on their way to the vacant seats at the central table. One of them clapped a big hand on the oldster's shoulder. "That looks good, Grandpa. Bring it over here. It'll do for starters." They moved on and seated themselves around the table.

The old man hardly hesitated. Just scooped up the cutlery and went over and placed the hot food in front of his grandchildren.

Feltman's natural inclination was to let the old man do things his way. But he supposed it wouldn't do any harm to leave a calling card.

18

The rest of the cowboys' orders were made, accompanied by a fair amount of laughter, in which the old waiter joined. His route back to the kitchen took him past the frustrated diner. As he went by, Feltman reached out and grabbed him by the belt, pulling him firmly back.

"Old man, that was my steak you gave away," he reprimanded mildly.

"Son, it ain't your steak untils I puts it in front o' yuh." You could hardly claim that the old boy was intimidated. "Anyhow, it don't make sense to get yersel all upset when I kin get yuh another in seconds flat"

"Does Ma approve of the way the help treats her customers?"

"Yep. I sure do."

It took a few seconds.

"You're Ma Kelly?"

"Yeah, he's Ma Kelly." One of the tough, lean young men had appeared at the old man's side. "This drifter givin' you a hard time, Grandpa?"

"Hell no, Jimmy," the old man soothed. "We wis only discussin' the way he liked his steak."

"You hear that, boys?" The boys heard. Now there were three, tough, lean, young men gathered protectively around Grandpa. "See what a nice old man he is. He'll even defend a saddle tramp; a bum, givin' him abuse."

The three young cowboys turned their fond gazes from their Grandpa and looked smilingly down on the saddle tramp, who smiled warmly back. The old man smiled self-consciously. And there they all were, smiling together.

Jimmy was the first to stop smiling. He felt the surge of nausea as the tablecloth was thrust forward, deep into his gut. The air was forcibly expelled from his lungs and his body jack-knifed, sending his head crashing violently into the table. His protective arm around the old man became a desperate grab to try and remain upright as his legs buckled underneath him.

Feltman was half standing as he wrenched the rifle out from under the table. His weedy breakfast companion arched his body away in a frantic attempt to avoid the backswing, trying to force his head into the window. But no luck; and he let out a high-pitched squeal as the foresight caught him across the mouth.

Feltman's closed fist crashed sideways into the throat of the nearest young cowboy, sending him sprawling backwards, gasping for breath.

Too late, the last young man realised that he had been wasting time trying to keep Jimmy on his feet. He looked up to meet the forward swing of the Springfield and howled in agony as it scythed viciously into his cheek, laying open the bone and spraying blood when he twisted away, clawing at his face.

A few frenzied seconds. Feltman surveyed the scenic residue, checking it out for further action. But it seemed to be over. When he turned, the guy at the window opposite was leaning over the table, vainly trying to stem the flow of blood from the Weed's face, who was manfully keeping his whimpering to a minimum.

"What happened to him?" It was only polite to ask.

Your rifle caught him in the mouth," answered the moustache. "I'd better get him to the doc."

As the Pen-pusher directly opposite Feltman shuffled out of Moustache's way, he decided that, since he had to move anyway, he might as well help and reached round to grab hold of the Weed, carefully easing the unfortunate soul out of the bench seat; happy to help, but not to the extent of getting blood on his coat.

With Moustache taking up station on the other side, they negotiated the stricken cowboys and headed for the door, the innocent victim mouthing off under cover of the blood-stained handkerchief.

"What's he sayin'?" Feltman was curious.

The Pen-pusher glanced back. "Wants to buy you a drink."

"The cowboy with the busted face stumbled after them out the door, almost colliding with a couple of fellows on their way in.

The first of these men was coming in backwards, his attention drawn by the bleeding Weed and his escort. He stopped just over the threshold when he saw Jimmy and friend lying on the floor, his eyes flickering to the stranger in the booth.

As his partner moved ahead into the room, his companion caught at his sleeve and motioned that they should give breakfast a miss.

The change of mind was not lost on Ma. "What's up, Colby? Too rough fur ye."

Colby smiled, "I like a bit of peace an' quiet with my breakfast."

Ma was wearing a disgusted look as he stepped over Jimmy to clear up the mess. "Hell o' a fuss over a piece of goddamned beef," he grumbled.

Feltman sat back down. "Think you could put some sugar in the coffee this time?"

"Love to, son. But, right now, there ain't enough sugar in this town to sweeten up the state virgin, let alone you."

Feltman let his eyes wander over the room again, picking out the girl. The ruckus did not seem to have disturbed her working rhythm any. She certainly was not doing any of the expected womanly things like rushing round with a pan of hot water and an armful of clean towels and mopping up bloodied faces. But then, the stern-faced matron hadn't missed a beat either.

Meanwhile, after a certain amount of trial and error, Jimmy and the other young cowboy had discovered the exact angle of lean required to keep their counter-balanced bodies upright for more than a second at a time and were making a sorry lurch for the door when Jimmy's legs folded, bringing his friend down with him as he veered sharply to his right and went crashing against the legs of a table near the exit.

There were four burly members of a grading crew sitting round that table. And they were trying to eat.

"Mother 'o Christ!" And one hefty, pissed off Irishman, eyes to heaven, fork slammed to the table, stood up. He reached down and hoisted the two unfortunate young men up by the back of their pants, testing their weight in his hands before stomping for the door.

The cowboy with the sore throat was recovering and looked a little apprehensive, but Jimmy could not have cared less. It was help and he clutched at the big Irishman's arms and suspenders while he was being half dragged, half carried outside and dumped on the sidewalk.

The disgruntled grader came back in and settled himself down once again to the pleasures of uninterrupted eating, sparing the time to cast a meaningful glance at the stranger in the booth. Feltman looked out the window.

He felt the tugging of the table covering and looked round to see the sour-faced matron pulling the debris of the interrupted breakfasts towards her, aiming to wrap them in the blood-splattered cloth as an efficient way of hauling the mess into the kitchen..

He retrieved his rifle, furtively wiping off the clot of blood clinging to the foresight as he removed its weight from her load.

She didn't thank him. Feltman patted the walnut stock in slight apology for having used such a beautifully tooled weapon as a club and slid the rifle back into its moleskin cover.

Since the girl had disappeared into the kitchen, he spent the time waiting for his breakfast trying to sort out the relationship between sugar and state virgins. Feltman had a reasonably tidy mind and the old man's descriptive refusal to sweeten his coffee had nagged at him and now failed to stand up under even minor scrutiny.

Because, if a girl was a state virgin, then, by definition, she had to be famous for having rebuffed every known tactic, plea and wheedle in her suitors' armoury. And so no amount of sugar whatsoever would have any effect on her. Now common, everyday virgins did not usually need much sweetening at all to bring about a change in their status – assuming they were not in training to become a state virgin.

So Ma should have said, 'There ain't enough sugar in this town to sweeten up an everyday, common, willin' virgin."

Feltman admitted defeat. State virgin sounded better. And he got the gist. He wasn't getting any sugar.

There was more disappointment when it was the stern matron who placed his food in front of him. But the girl soon reappeared, and he spent a very pleasant fifteen minutes watching her slender, sensual shape move enticingly amongst the tables while he drank the hot, bitter coffee and eased down the well-cooked steak.

She was efficient, turning away from one table and, almost in the same motion, gliding up to the next. When she receives the odd bit of sass, she plays it straight back. Then again. This time, she laughs it off. Nobody ignored; holding politeness via laughter. The quiet smile; the single, reproachful 'Ha!'. The friendly chuckle at a much-repeated joke.

Finished, Feltman pushed away his plate and sat back,

deliberating on whether he should try or not. He had always hated the uncertainty of the initial approach. Especially if it mattered to him. And he could feel that it mattered now.

Ma swept down on hm. Feltman looked up. "That was good."

"Yeah? Well, I heard hands claim roast shit was good when they wis as hungry as you."

Feltman sighed. Platitudes were obviously out. "What do I owe you?"

"A dollar twenty-five," the old man answered. "See Rach at the counter. She does the money."

Please let 'Rach' be the young one. But a dollar twenty-five?

The old man interpreted the look correctly. "That's what it is. An' these guys," he made a short sweep with his hand at the booth, "forgot to pay."

Having quelled the rebellion, Ma moved on.

Timing was the essence of all good contacts so Feltman waited until the girl was heading back behind the counter before he got up. He was halfway there when he realised that he had left the Springfield behind.

By the time he had retrieved the rifle she was away, in amongst the tables again. There was nothing else for it. He went to the counter and waited. He stood there for a full minute, every second of which made it harder for him to retain his decorum, pessimistically aware that 'Rach' could yet turn out to be the 'Matron.'

He began to fidget.

'Rach' came round eventually, flashing her customer smile at him. Bad sign.

Feltman had the coins ready, placing them carefully on the counter. "Hope none of those cowboys meant anything to you?"

That was personal. That got rid of it. The smile.

"Yes, they all did." The girl was wary now, prickly, unsure what was coming next. "We like to think all our customers are our friends."

Feltman winced inwardly as she swept the coins into the cash drawer and slapped down his change. He flashed his easy grin at her, pretending he wasn't hurt. "Keep the change," he said, gallantly. "For the trouble."

The girl looked down at the seventy-five cents. Then back up, flicking her hair out of her eyes. "Do you know how much trouble it is to get blood out of a tablecloth?"

Feltman laughed. "Look, I'd hate to have you mad at me." She made to say something but Feltman ploughed on, "I was hoping, maybe ..."

"You're a little pushy, aren't you, Mister ...?" The girl forced the interruption, back in control again, smiling.

"Feltman." He let his own grin widen at the opening she had left for his name. "Michael."

"Well, Mister Feltman ..."

"Michael," he insisted.

"Michael," she nodded. "Well, Michael, I think you ought to go and wipe your mouth. You've been dribbling all over your beard." And still smiling, she skipped off into the kitchen.

Feltman remembered to shut his mouth before he turned around. The restaurant was glowing with the reflected light from bared teeth – it's always nice to see another man go down.

Not that anybody was actually looking in his direction. Except for Ma, who was staring straight at him, all black teeth and wicked grin. Feltman managed a weak one in return and eased himself out the door.

26

Two

It took Feltman a hundred paces to lose the rigid walk of embarrassment. Then the sore weariness of his body forced him to relax. He found he had stomped back down Grant, past the intersection with Stonewall, and had stopped, of all places, right outside the Marshal's office.

He stood for a moment, contemplating. Not too far ahead on Grant, the street started to veer gently to the left and began, literally, to disintegrate.

Shanty Town.

He had found where the poor people lived. Where the homeless find a home among the cut-throats and ne'er-do-wells. Waiting for death, mostly.

Across the street was a newspaper office, the 'Limon Optic'; printing presses clanging and wheezing and voices hollering. On the roof, linemen were pulling wires along the timber shingles, connecting up the new telegraph message service.

Enough. Save it for later. He needed to be clean. He had passed a hotel on Stonewall on his way to Ma's and, if height equalled luxury, he would get a hot bath there. He turned and started back, letting his mind wander at the thought of it, drifting along.

"Mister Feltman."

From his right. It was not threatening. It was hesitant.

He looked down to the street. A well-dressed kid was keeping pace with him. Feltman stopped and the boy stopped also. Maybe not so much of a kid. Eighteen. Nineteen. But well turned out; hardly a speck of dust on his three piece – which was no mean achievement – a neat little necktie; a wide-brimmed, cream-coloured hat.

The boy opened his mouth to speak but closed it again when his view of Feltman was temporarily blocked by a passer-by. He tried again with the same result. Feltman moved over to the edge of the sidewalk to give the boy a clear view of him.

"My father would like to speak with you."

"Who's your father?"

"Mr Hartford."

Mr Hartford's son was not going to volunteer any further information so Feltman stepped off the boards and nodded. The boy pivoted on his heel and headed back up the street towards Stonewall, turning into the cross-street and continuing on, eyes straight ahead, staying right in the middle of the street.

Feltman glanced at him as he walked alongside. The boy was calm enough, but his quiet, purposeful walk did not seem natural. He made no allowance for the horses and wagons coming down the street, relying on the riders and teamsters to make way for him. Twice, Feltman nearly met his end under the wheels of a wagon as he moved to avoid the oncoming traffic, only to see them swerve in turn to avoid his guide.

Feltman had thought they were heading for one of the merchant houses, but the boy surprised him by turning right, going deeper down Lincoln which had already started to curve to the right in a mirror image of Grant. Much further and they would be in amongst the hovels. But the boy veered to his left across the street and disappeared into the noise and confusion of a building site.

Feltman followed, picking his way through the construction debris, keeping his eye on the cream-coloured hat as it dodged ahead.

The main building appeared complete; its frontage resplendent in brick and dressed stone as craftsmen applied the finishing touches. The bulk of the workforce was concentrating on an annex being built alongside; half as high but with walls two foot thick being built in random stone and lime mortar.

By the time Feltman worked his way around to the rear, the boy was at the other end of the yard passing through a gap in a whitewashed adobe wall. There was a guard on the opening, and he was looking at Feltman.

The journey across the yard was no less hazardous. It was being used as a lay-down area for materials and preparatory work. There were masons cutting stone and carpenters sizing timber and labourers mixing sand and lime.

The guard was unarmed, likely allocated from one of the work crews. A tough looking little sod, but he knew Feltman was coming and he nodded him through into a different world.

It was a proper garden. A hacienda garden, fully terraced in weathered flagstone; large ornate pots bursting with fragrant, vibrant blooms defining a subtle pathway through the taller trees which gifted coolness and dappled shade. A few yards in, the aggressive noise of the workmen faded. It was there, but not intrusive.

Feltman felt his body relax. It helped with the weariness, but he reminded himself to stay sharp. He could see the kid through the blooms and moved to join him.

The boy was standing beside an ornate table, a circle of stone set on cast iron legs. Must weigh a ton – and cost a fortune. He was staring intently into the shade offered by the arched veranda and on through the open casement doors of the hacienda, waiting for the shadowy figures inside to stop conversing and recognise his presence.

Feltman waited with him.

"Thank you, Michael."

Feltman gave a slight start at the use of his first name before realising that the authoritative voice dispatched from the shadows was addressing his guide. An impeccably suited gentleman followed the appreciative greeting into the sunlight. The father of the son.

"Mr Feltman," Hartford extended his hand. "I'm glad Michael found you so quickly. My name is Hartford. I manage the Western and Central bank here in Limon."

Feltman transferred the rifle and clasped the proffered hand in a brief, neutral shake. Where he would have given his own name there was a slightly awkward silence, since it was already known.

Hartford used the pause to dismiss his son. "Michael, would you head back to the house and tell your mother that I will be back in time for lunch?"

The boy gave a tight smile of acknowledgement and strode past his father to disappear into the shadowy interior, merging with the multitude of phantoms still inside.

Hartford looked at Feltman and smiled. "My son is a little slow," he apologised. And, as always, immediately regretted his compulsion to offer explanations for Michael.

Feltman kept his face neutral, not helping.

Inside, the low tones of conversation had ended and the remaining two silhouettes emerged on to the veranda.

"Feltman," already Hartford had dropped the 'Mr', "allow me to introduce Judge Perry, our host."

The man who approached Feltman moved with a practiced dignity. Over sixty, and not wearing it too well.

His flowing grey locks were thick at the sides but thinning fast on top; his eyes lacked sparkle, recessed under heavy brows and puffy bags; but the hand was firm.

Feltman chanced a little humour. "Did my invite stress I had to come in via the '*help*' entrance?"

The judge snorted. It could have been a laugh. "You can't possibly be offended?" He spread his hands. "You don't like the garden?"

"And this is Mr De Brecco," interceded Hartford, continuing with the introductions.

Feltman nodded at the pen-pusher, the one without the moustache. "We've met. How's the We ... the guy that got hit with the rifle?"

De Brecco grinned. "Lost a few teeth. He'll live."

"Yes, you made quite an impression on Brec here, Feltman." The Judge did not sound as if he altogether approved.

"But a more lasting one on Willy," De Brecco cut in, laughing.

"Shall we sit?" Hartford was keen to move on to the business in hand.

They moved over and seated themselves on the ornate wrought iron chairs around the stone table. As the trail dust rose from Feltman's pants, he supposed that maybe the garden entrance wasn't such a bad idea.

"Could I pour you a refreshment?" asked the Judge. And, at Feltman's raised eyebrow, added, "Chilled peach juice."

"Brec here, described you as efficient, Feltman," said Hartford. "And we happen to be in the market for your particular brand of efficiency."

Feltman was glad that De Brecco had missed the end of the show. He gulped down his peach Juice. It was delicious and he helped himself to a refill, waiting.

They weren't sure. They were waiting also.

"What brings you to Limon, Feltman?" enquired Hartford.

Feltman closed his eyes, making a point of his irritation. If it was background they were after; they didn't need to know. If it was politeness and small talk; he did not want to engage.

"Mr Hartford, I don't remember applying for a job. Can we get to the point?"

"You must be here for some reason?" Hartford looked to De Brecco and the Judge for guidance. When none was forthcoming he ploughed on. "Look, you must've seen how this town is; it's bursting at the seams, doubling in size over the last year; and it'll get bigger. And all down to the mine on the other side of that mountain." Hartford waved vaguely to the west. "There's a lot of money to be made; dreams to be realised." Hartford paused and looked directly at Feltman, "But, as I'm sure you're aware, a boom like we have here in Limon, attracts every lowlife, pimp and cut-throat who can get here; all swarming around, desperate to get a piece of the action."

Feltman smiled. Hartford was asking again why he was here. "You invite everyone to sample your chilled juice before you run them out of town?"

De Brecco waved the question away. "You know that's not why we asked you here."

Feltman knew. But he was starting to enjoy himself. "You can't seriously be asking me to clean up your town for you?"

"Well, yes an' no, but ...." De Brecco broke off at the sound of a polite rap on the door.

Feltman swung his head as she flowed into the sunlight. Good god almighty! It was following him around, teasing him.

"Good morning," her bright, cheery greeting embraced them all. "Papa, your other guests have arrived."

Only then did Feltman register the presence of the two men waiting patiently behind her. These men were not being subservient. They were simply being polite, and one of them was Chinese.

Feltman realised he was still sitting. He scrambled to his feet, pulling his hat from his head,

The Judge thought about it, quickly coming to the conclusion that it would be impolite not to. "Carrie, this is Mr Feltman. We hope to conduct some business together."

"Good morning, Mr Feltman."

A lot of men would pay good money to be nagged by a voice like that. Feltman reached out and touched the proffered, light-brown hand. But he did not trust the constriction in his throat. A nod and a friendly smile were all he could manage.

"Would any of you gentlemen like coffee?" offered Carrie.

The Judge lifted his head to enquire of the men behind her. Their answer would define the response of the group.

"No, thank you."

"I am fine also," confirmed the Chinese, declining courteously.

"Thank you, Carrie," said the Judge, in polite dismissal.

"I'd love some coffee," declared Feltman, finding his voice.

He was rewarded with a flashing smile, just for him. "I'll only be a minute." And she was gone.

Feltman had no time to dwell. He was being introduced to the new arrivals. "This is Peter Galbraith. Mr Galbraith represents the shareholders of the Limon Mining Corporation. And this is John Oh," The Judge continued. "John looks after the interests of the railway; their holdings and proposed acquisitions and such."

"Johnny, please, Mr Feltman." Mr Oh was smiling, sure Feltman recognised the lazy and derogatory term commonly used for a Chinese navvy working on the railroad. A confident man. As was his companion. Both dressed in the best cloth money could buy; but casual, open-neck shirts; and Johnny Oh's had to be silk.

"Gentlemen, please?" The Judge invited them to sit.

"Please, no," answered Galbraith. "We really can't stay that long. We simply came to offer our support to you gentlemen in your efforts to ... to bring back a modicum of civilisation, if I may put it like that, to your wonderful town. And to assure Mr Feltman that the promise of any reward or remuneration made to him will be discharged in full on completion of any assignment he agrees to undertake."

Galbraith had been looking steadily at Feltman as he spoke, searching for signs of insight and intelligence. Feltman sat back down. He was clearly being informed who was ultimately in charge – and it wasn't Judge Perry.

Feltman decided to play just a little ignorant. "How much 'civilising' does this town need? It doesn't show too many signs of 'gold fever'."

In response to Galbraith's quizzical eyebrow, Hartford opened his hands in a slight, depreciative wave, "We haven't got very far as yet."

"Ah," Galbraith nodded his understanding. "In that case, I wonder if we should perhaps ...?" He indicated the nearest chair and looked inquiringly at Mr Oh, who concurred with an inclination of his head.

Galbraith pulled the chair round and sat primly down.

De Brecco reclaimed his spot, but since there were only four chairs and Mr Oh made no move to take up the remaining place, etiquette forced Judge Perry and Hartford to remain standing.

"Not gold, Mr Feltman. Silver. Vast quantities of silver. Galena to be more exact," Galbraith explained. "A lead ore from which our very clever mining engineers are able to extract upwards of two percent pure, precious metal; and when the base metal we will be able to ship out is included – well, our shareholders are positively dribbling at the mouth.

But, to address your key point about the town; Investors, Mr Feltman, are inclined to be exceedingly nervous." Galbraith smiled to emphasise the light-heartedness of his next remark, "Probably in direct proportion to their greed.

Hustle and bustle are always good for commerce. Fear and death are not." Galbraith looked at De Brecco. "How many?"

"Two or three." De Brecco understood the question.

"Every day?"

"Every week, just about," De Brecco clarified.

"Still, it's too many, Mr Feltman. It interferes with profits. Because, while these departed souls may well have belonged to deserving miscreants, the perception is one of random death. And large commercial enterprises like ours need live, willing bodies to service it."

Galbraith paused and looked at Mr Oh, seeking guidance on whether he felt it necessary to spell out the reality of the situation in more detail.

Mr Oh did. "I think, Peter, that we owe it to all of these gentlemen to make our position absolutely clear."

Something else then. Feltman had been drifting, bored. But now he focused, instinctively knowing that Johnny Oh's clarification could be useful.

Galbraith sat with steepled hands as Oh took up the mantle. "The projected rewards are, of course, immense;

but the initial and continuing financial investments are quite unprecedented. Despite all assurances, and placating talk of calculated, manageable risk, our shareholders are extremely nervous. For the railway, this is nothing like the initial push west; no federal land grants and no sixteen thousand dollars a mile for laid track. Every foot up from Cheyenne had to be purchased, more often than not at extortionate rates."

"I didn't see any signs of a railway," queried Feltman.

"Still two miles out. Coming in from the south-east," supplied Hartford.

And now the question Feltman really wanted answered, "And silver? I thought silver mines were closin' down? Not worth workin' them any longer?"

"Ah," Galbraith nodded. "There's certainly been reduced returns over recent years; and no profit margins that would justify the level of investment John has just outlined – until now that is."

He looked at Feltman with renewed interest, continuing mainly for his benefit, and perhaps that of De Brecco. "Our friends in the East have just passed the Bland–Allison Act, essentially tying our monetary system to silver; that is, our government will buy silver to mint coins, Mr Feltman. And the really important part of the Act is that they must – enshrined in law – they must purchase a minimum of two million dollars' worth of silver a month, every month."

Galbraith was delighted with the reaction. Feltman was impressed and had no problem showing it; De Brecco also. Hartford had been coy about the scale of this thing. The Judge meanwhile was pawing the flagstones, plainly irritated that his role in the proceedings had been reduced to that of bystander; and possibly disturbed by the amount of information being made available to a complete stranger sat at his garden table.

"Of course, not all of that will be purchased from the Limon Mining Corporation," Mr Oh liked to be precise. "But enough to ensure a baseline margin which justifies the level of initial investment. Our Congressmen shareholders feel they can hold off any move to repeal for a decade or so – much to the chagrin of our beloved President Hayes, who apparently likes to keep his personal investments in gold."

Hartford smiled dutifully as the financial duo beamed appreciatively at each other.

"But, as I was saying," Mr Oh continued, "our masters in the East control substantial holdings in both our stocks, 'strategic speculation' I believe is the term, and some, as you know, Andrew," he was addressing Hartford, "have majority stakes in Western and Central. Now those particular gentlemen, would naturally like to see W&C as the premier, not to say only, bank in Limon. They consider it eminently reasonable that they should reap the ancillary benefits of the steady flow of financial transactions associated with a booming, commercial hub which, in their eyes, they have helped to create.

And they are," here Mr Oh paused, affecting to search for the current colloquialism, "... a tad miffed that Mr Benson's aggressively enterprising ways may well encroach on those profits."

Hartford could not prevent the colour rising in his cheeks. However, he remained composed and silent. Judge Perry cleared his throat on his friend's behalf.

"Therefore, our clear preference is that you gentlemen come out on top when this unfortunate squabble is settled. That is why we have dealt through you in investing so heavily in these public works projects. The courthouse," Mr Oh waved his hand at the bottom of the garden. "And bringing over those two remarkable young men to plan and oversee water and sewage provision for your growing population. Stability and permanence are what we seek."

Hartford cleared his own throat this time. But he was forestalled simultaneously by the sound of a light rap on the door and the placatory raising of Mr Oh's palm. Mr Oh gave way in turn as Carrie breezed back into the room.

She directed her smile at Feltman as she placed the tray of cups and a coffee pot on the table.

"Sorry I was a while. I decided to make a fresh pot. And extra cups, in case you gentlemen changed your minds."

Feltman leaned in close as he relieved her of the flowery, delicate cup. He caught her scent; and was immediately aware that his own might not be so alluring.

"Anyone else? " asked Carrie.

"I'll have a cup, Carrie, thanks," De Brecco accepted, sounding as if he needed something stronger.

"There's sugar there if you need it."

"I thought there was a shortage of sugar?" Feltman tried to make conversation.

"Is there?" Having satisfied her curiosity for the moment, Carrie encompassed them all in a final smile. "Well, I'll leave you undisturbed."

Please don't, thought Feltman. But she was gone.

Feltman could sense the Judge's eyes boring into him. Hartford was looking at Mr Oh. Feltman followed suit because Mr Oh hadn't finished.

"Firstly, we sense your irritation that every word we've said this morning has added to Mr Feltman's bargaining power but, really, that is a minor matter. Because, and here is the vital point, while we would much prefer that you prevail in your parochial battle with Mr Benson – ultimately, we don't care."

"What? The Judge was spluttering. Hartford and De Brecco looked shocked. Feltman was interested, waiting for more.

"Perhaps you might rephrase, John?" chided Galbraith.

"Ah, yes. I apologise. That was clumsy. But, in my defence, I was simply trying to convey the brutal reality of your situation."

Our situation? That did nothing to help slow down the heart rates or improve the facial expressions of his core audience.

"Peter and I have a mandate to steer our joint venture to financial success. We will achieve that; and we will also ensure that those board members who have an interest in the Western & Central gain a further margin by putting all our business through your bank, Andrew."

That elicited a small nod of appreciation from Hartford.

"But," Mr Oh continued," they will consider that to be their gift. Their judgement on your stewardship of the branch will be determined solely on the amount of ancillary business being done via the bank."

Hartford flinched; but remained silent. It was hard to dispute the logic of what had been said.

"And, with respect, Mr De Brecco, it can make no difference to our shareholders who owns any business in which they have no interest."

De Brecco bristled at that. "You think Benson will run a fair house?"

Mr Oh shook his head sadly. "Fair or not, only if it affected our enterprise would we feel it necessary to intervene."

It was too much. "Then why are you backing us?" Judge Perry could not contain his anger. "Why don't you throw your weight behind that reprobate over in the Limon Hotel? You know he had Vern Casgil murdered to get his hands on that hotel. And you say you don't care?"

Galbraith attempted a calming response but the Judge was in full flow. "Or maybe you are backing Benson?

Maybe that's why you are being so "frank" in front of Feltman, here? Hoping he'll run over to Benson to give him an edge?"

Galbraith stood up, resting his hands on the chairback, trying not to show his irritation at the Judge's failure to grasp some simple truths. "That's plainly ridiculous, George. Mr Feltman needs to understand the whole picture so that he can be of maximum help to you."

Galbraith could not prevent the 'I told you so' grimace he flashed at John Oh. He had argued they should let them get on with it; that they would deal with the consequences, whatever the outcome.

"As to informing Benson, well ... There is nothing that Mr Feltman could tell him that he will not already know."

"What do you mean?" demanded the Judge, whose outrage made him the spokesman.

"Before we leave this afternoon, we will be taking up Mr Benson's kind invitation to lunch," Galbraith announced, "during which we will reiterate to him everything we have told you. We will be taking great pains to emphasise our expectation that Limon will have lost most of its 'wildcat' image by the time we return in twenty days. And, candidly, we will be telling him that because we do not know who he is - and he's not telling us – we would much prefer to liaise with you gentlemen on issues with regard to our companies' role in maximising the expansion and wealth of Limon."

The judge was apoplectic, "We are a preference?"

Hartford touched the Judge's sleeve, stepping beyond him so that he was almost eyeballing Galbraith. "Are you trying to start a fucking war?" His voice was cold and the profanity slightly shocking. His anger had won the battle with caution, pushing any thoughts of an adverse report to head office out of his mind.

Feltman mentally cheered as he watched Hartford's balls drop. Galbraith took an instinctive step back as Oh answered for him. "This war has been going on for some considerable time. Cooperation is what we seek. Not war"

"Well, you are going a strange way about it," Hartford's contempt dripped from every word. "You are virtually inviting Benson to take over this town."

Galbraith appeared shaken and contrived to ignore the comment. "We should be going."

"Twenty days?" Feltman's query was concise.

"The rail bridge and the terminus at the smelter will be complete in twenty days. That's when we shall return," Mr Oh answered Feltman's question. "Hopefully to a town that is open for business." Mr Oh took a breath. "Gentlemen, I assure you that it will be made clear to Mr Benson, as we have made it clear to you, that while we will deal with whomever prevails in your upcoming struggle, he will simply not be allowed to gain a controlling interest in any of our enterprises. At least, not through violence."

"But you don't mind if he uses threats and murder to take over our businesses? That it?" sneered De Brecco.

Mr Oh swung his hands away from his sides and let them fall back. The talking was over. The judge delved deep for what courtesy he had left.

"I'll see you out," he said stiffly.

Galbraith paused on the veranda, his irritation ensuring he had the last word. "Twenty days, gentlemen."

There was silence while the Judge was out of the room. There was silence when he returned. Finally, it was De Brecco who broke first; the need to say something futile was simply overwhelming, "Chiselling bastards."

The others were grateful. Judge Perry and Hartford had been marshalling their thoughts; the Judge's perhaps less complex, so he went first.

"I don't give a damn what that pair of Machiavellian shits want or expect. I want this cesspit of a town cleaned up. I want Benson dead, in jail or run out of this town. And I don't care which."

As a statement of intent it was fairly unambiguous.

De Brecco felt the need to further declare his defiance, "He's not gettin' his hands on the Lady Anne."

They were talking to each other now. Feltman held off on asking the obvious question until Hartford had said his piece.

"I think they made it plain that the bank itself is not in jeopardy, but that obviously did not include me. And I did not uproot my family and travel all the way here simply to be thrown on the scrapheap at the whim of a couple of pragmatic, morally bankrupt ..." Hartford faltered as he sought to complete his invective.

"Snakes." De Brecco was happy to supply a descriptive insult.

Hartford looked at Feltman, regretting the lapse into his own personal issues in front of a stranger. He cleared his throat. "Nothing has changed. Let's not be coy. We need someone like you to front up our attempt to clean up this town. And those carpet-baggers just offered to underwrite your payday. So, can we get down to it?"

"Who's Benson?"

"Him an' his mouthpiece, Edgemount, arrived in town six weeks ago," answered De Brecco. "Waltzed into the Limon Hotel as the new owner. The very day after the old owner had his head blown off in a card game."

"Vern Casgil was a top class hotelier, Feltman," Hartford took up the tale. "And a recreational gambler. He would never have risked his hotel on a hand of poker."

"But you heard the judge, he was murdered all right," De Brecco continued. "Some of Benson's men had been in town for weeks. They set him up in the Purple Pit; concocted some story about Vern losing the Hotel an' getting' caught cheating trying to win it back. Guy called Joe McCabe shot him in the face."

"That's not a crime in Limon?"

"His cronies swore Vern had pulled a gun. McCabe and his brother now openly work for Benson; he has over thirty thugs on his payroll; all of them drawin' the same kind of money as the miners – without sweatin' ten, twelve hours a day for it."

"Since then, Edgemount moves in after Benson's thugs have softened up the targets. Whether it's shares in the mine he's after or their business for his bank, he's mopping up the rest of the town."

Feltman managed a quizzical look, so Hartford added, "Yes, he's opened a bank."

"You can do that? Just open a bank?"

"The groundwork had undoubtedly been prepared months before. But all it takes is a little legal advice, sound financial backing, and the unswerving loyalty of your clients. The First National Bank of Limon, founded by Mr Charles Benson. He had been in town exactly three days."

"But it's not illegal?"

"Providing the cash reserve out of your own pocket – if, indeed, that's what he did - is not illegal. Using McCabe and his gunmen to harvest clients most certainly is."

"He's a devious, dangerous bastard, Feltman," De Brecco added. "The word spread fast. Apparently, if you didn't want to be the poor, hapless sod who had his store window smashed in during some random midnight brawl, transfer your account to the First National. A sort of magic perk of banking with Benson."

"So, you worried he intends to empty the vault an' hightail it."

"No. I'm not." Hartford shook his head. "It may be his fallback plan, of course. But I think he intends to legitimise once he has a strong base. Why be illegal when you can make a fortune being legit?"

"You mean like any other bank?'

Feltman's lack of sympathy was beginning to upset Hartford. The Judge seemed to sense they were being less than persuasive, so he pitched back in. "Look, Feltman, your cynicism is duly noted. If the business side holds no sway for you then I suppose it would be naive of us to think that talking about the innocent people dying out there in the street would make any difference."

The Judge was in full flow. He came to the table and planted his fists on the stone table; glaring down at Feltman.

"So what would make a difference, Feltman? Money? Is that what sways you? Well, let me repeat. I want this town cleaned up. From those degenerate half breeds over in the Oglala to that Mexican pimp and his filthy whores squatting in their slums, right up to that ruthless bastard Benson himself. I want them flushed out. And we're prepared to pay. We don't need your approval. We just need your help."

Judge Perry was finished. Maybe because he had run out of breath.

"Why don't you call in the army?"

Neither Hartford nor De Brecco could help the quick, apprehensive glance they gave each other. Judge Perry pushed himself from the table and stared blankly at a mountain azalea in a pot.

"We tried that. It didn't work." Hartford sought out the correct words. "Galbraith and Oh used their connections to get a troop sent down from Fort Laramie, and, for a while, it went well. The first weeks or so were quiet. The soldiers went round in pairs. It was a form of martial law I

44

suppose, but nobody was going to bring down a trooper. But, as the days wore on, things changed. The troopers got bored, and that combined with…" here Hartford paused, "… a certain lack of leadership, made them almost as much of a problem as the one they were supposed to be solving. They took to hanging out at McGarvey's; getting drunk; causing fights." Hartford shrugged. "In the end, we asked them to leave."

De Brecco started to breath normally again. He made a mental note to be more appreciative of Hartford's oratory skills in the future.

Hartford looked steadily at Feltman. "One thousand."

Feltman laughed. "So, on the basis that Mr De Brecco witnessed me defend my breakfast, you're goin' to give me a thousand dollars an' the marshal's badge; an' I'm supposed to go out there with my guns blazin' an' make this a town fit for you to live in? Just how desperate are you people?"

This time, all three men exchanged anxious glances. How to handle this one. Again it was Hartford.

"Pretty desperate," he admitted. " But no."

"What?"

"Despite the impression we appear to have given you, Mr Feltman, we're not fools. We don't expect one man to stand alone against Benson. No matter how proficient he is in the art of thuggery." Hartford sounded a little irked. "And neither can we offer you the marshal's badge."

Hartford scraped a chair across the flagstones until it was directly opposite Feltman. He sat back down.

"But there is one man who Benson certainly fears. And that's a rancher called Brian Cairns. He runs a huge spread to the northwest. We intend to ask Brian to come in with his men and help us run Benson out of town."

"So why am I here?"

"We can only do that once. Brian would have to be

convinced that we wouldn't come running to him again when the next thug waltzes into town." Hartford did his best to ignore the look of amused wonder on Feltman's face. "You would represent us, the town. You would be a visible sign of our intent. Hopefully, our competence."

"But not behind a badge?"

"Eventually, after we've dealt with Benson. That's what Brian would expect. Our peace officer in waiting."

"Why not now?"

"Harry Judd was elected some weeks back. He's Benson's man; on a retainer. He gets the drunks off the streets; those that are too far gone to object. Other than that, he adds an illusion of legality to Benson's activities. What he most definitely doesn't do, is arrest any of Benson's men – no matter what barbarism they engage in."

"Then vote him out"

"That," Hartford nodded towards the house, "was a collection of Limon's finest, gathered to discuss that very issue. Most, for one reason or another, would rather not go against Benson in so open a manner."

"The reason is fear,' cut in De Brecco, "for themselves and their families. Besides, we don't have any candidates. Not even you, apparently."

"There a county sheriff?

Hartford nodded 'yes'.

"Well?" But Feltman knew the answer.

"He operates out of Red Rock Springs. He doesn't appear here. Paid not to."

"Which makes him a wise man," said De Brecco. "His predecessor dropped in for a visit and never left. Has a nice plot in the bone orchard, right alongside our old town marshal. That brave man got his tryin' to drag a woman and her young daughter out of the crossfire when Benson's gunslingers were baiting a couple of Cairns' cowboys."

46

Feltman leaned back and massaged his temples. He was weary and he got the picture. Just get on with it.

"Benson had Judd drag those cowboys off to jail. Claimed they shot the marshal. Wanted them hanged to send a message to Cairns."

"Of course, Brian wasn't about to let that happen. He flooded the town with his hands. Most of them battle-hardened veterans. I think even the McCabe boys were beginning to piss their pants." Hartford surprised himself at how easily he dropped into the colloquialism. It might serve him well if he got posted to yet another frontier town.

"Judd couldn't get those boys out of their cells fast enough. Cairns is a good man. He doesn't think he is above the law, but he sure wasn't goin' to let his boys hang while Benson and his crew laughed up their sleeves. He's loyal to his hands and he's a friend to us."

Worried that Feltman's demeanour was indicative of an outright dismissal of their proposal, De Brecco ploughed back in. "Look, Feltman. The way we figure it is this. Brian Cairns has a big stake in this town. The man practically founded it. An' he detests Benson. With his men an' you representin' us, we can box Benson in. With Benson finished, the rest would fall into line."

"A month is all we're asking.," Hartford tried to finish the pitch persuasively. "Take the badge for a month after we get rid of Judd. Brian needs to be convinced the town can stand on its own two feet once Benson's finished."

"Just the Month?" Feltman asked, sweetly. "You wouldn't want me as your permanent lawman?"

"Not at a thousand a month." Hartford dismissed the ridiculous notion. "Fifty and found, if you were really interested."

Feltman rubbed his hand over his head and down to his neck. He looked up. "Gentlemen, you are out of your

47

collective minds." Feltman made 'collective' sound like the worse kind of profanity.

There was silence as each of the other three men considered a different area of the garden. Apparently, that was another idea lost in the swamp of its own desperation. There seemed to be no way round Benson.

"Two thousand." Feltman broke into their reverie.

There was no immediate response.

Then, "What?"

"Two thousand," repeated Feltman.

Hartford leaned forward. "A second ago, you were scornful of what we proposed. How does it suddenly become any more feasible for another thousand dollars?"

"Because it would be my plan, not yours. A plan that has some chance of working." Feltman needed to stretch. He got to his feet. "Look, your dog just won't hunt. You'd have cowhands goin' against gunmen out there. Mayhem. And what about the rest of the town's hardcases? Who'd you think they would back up?"

"Us. They'd back up us," said De Brecco. "There's no love lost, believe me. Benson is as much a threat to them as he is to anybody else."

"They wouldn't have to love him to back him up. They'd know that if he went down, they'd be next. An' what about those shopkeepers you like to sneer at? You really think none of them have any sand in their bellies? They kowtow to Benson because they're fearful for their families. That's what matters to them.

Feltman paused and looked directly at Hartford. "You just accused Galbraith of tryin' to start a war. That's exactly what you'd get if you call in Cairns. An' what about those innocents caught in the crossfire? There would be bodies all over the place. The town would never forgive you."

"But you have a thousand dollar suggestion?" The Judge

48

made no attempt to hide his cynicism.

Feltman nodded. "Get Benson on your side. Calm the town down. Take away anything, anyone, he might lean on. And then, take him."

"I don't think we understand you"

"Benson can't go on rulin' by terror forever. He's opened a bank, for christ's sake. He's lookin' for respectability. Offer it to him. Tell him you've accepted what inroads he's made; he can keep what he's got but you want his help in cleanin' up the rest of the town. So you can all live happily ever after."

Feltman ignored the identical looks of blank amazement that spread over their faces. He went on, "When you've taken all the other shitheads out of the game, and when the town's been without its daily dose of violence for a while, Benson will find it that much harder to reintroduce it. That's when you get Cairns help to take him."

They were dubious. Struggling to think it through.

"Your proposal's absurd," argued Hartford. "It will never work."

"It'll work. You have to look at what Benson wants. An' it's not to have thirty gunmen on his payroll for the rest of his life. It's got a much better chance of workin' than your plan. And," Feltman added, "it's the only way I'm comin" in."

"Benson will never go for it."

"The first measure you take is to ban Cairns' cowboys from town. He'll go for it."

"What? Yes, he'll go for that. But Cairns won't." Hartford was incredulous. "You're going to antagonise Cairns? Then ask him for his help in taking out Benson?"

"We have to lull Benson. Your Mr Cairns will understand that. We need to get Benson's help in calming the town down first. Get him to feel he's in charge. And

Cairns will appreciate his men being out of the firing line while that happens. Then he helps us to move in on Benson."

"I don't see it. Brian won't see it. It sounds too devious."

"What's he got to lose? All he has to do is agree to keep his boys out of town for a couple of weeks. If it doesn't work out with Benson then he's no worse off. But if it does, then he can help to rid the town of Benson once and for all."

"He'll still take some persuading"

"That'll be the only part you'll have to do. I'll do the rest."

There was a long moment of contemplation, while the three men came to terms with their options. Or lack of them. Finally, the Judge nodded, sensing consent from Hartford and De Brecco. "Very well, Mr Feltman. You seem to have something of the politician about you. Your proposal might have some merit. Maybe we will even be able to convince ourselves it has a slim chance of success. At any rate, it seems to be the only one on offer."

"But two thousand dollars?" De Brecco queried.

"Yeah, well, I'll be the one out there on the street, dodgin' bullets an' lookin' out for back shooters. Besides," added Feltman, "I thought the Celestial and his pompous friend were bankrolling you? And I'll need every cent. This is a very expensive town to live in."

"You plan on puttin' down roots?" De Brecco inquired?

"Maybe. In your bone orchard if this goes bad."

"All right," said Hartford. He was brusque, wanting to bring this to a conclusion, "two thousand but ...."

"Half now. The rest when the job is done."

"Don't you trust us?" the Judge asked, dryly.

"Should I have to?"

50

"It's not a problem in any case," interceded Hartford. "The cash will be ready for you in the morning. But how do we go about this?"

"Well, we start off with me havin' a bath. Then one of you introduces me to Benson an' we put it to him."

"As simple as that?"

"You want to make it more complicated?"

There did not seem to be anything left to say. So everybody said something.

"Very well."

"All right, then."

"You can have that bath over at the Lady Anne."

The last one was welcome. Feltman jammed his hat back on. "Do I get to leave by the front door this time?"

"We were being circumspect, Mr Feltman, not rude." Judge Perry waved his hand magnanimously towards the interior of his house. "Please."

"Ah, Feltman." De Brecco said, wryly. "It's actually quicker this way."

Feltman nodded adios to the Judge and Hartford, his tight smile acknowledging the humour of the situation as he followed de Brecco back along the flagstone path.

He was halted by the Judge calling after him.

"Mr Feltman. You've forgotten your rifle."

Christ. Again. One of these days his memory would be the death of him. De Brecco wisely walked on while Feltman waited for the Springfield. The Judge did not exactly beat around it.

"I'm a proud man, Mr Feltman. I'm proud of my daughter. She's not for you. I hope you understand me."

It would have been hard to misunderstand that.

"Yeah. Would you like to try and understand me?"

The Judge did not flinch either.

"I don't like people talkin' down to me. I don't like

bein' told what to do an' what not to do. But I won't go near your daughter. An', that way, you won't have to tell me again, will you?"

There were a few replies that the Judge could have made but Feltman turned and strode away before he had a chance to form them.

De Brecco was waiting for him at the gap in the adobe wall. "Warning you off?"

"Yeah. He make a habit of it?"

"Since his wife died. I suppose I better fill you in."

"As long as you lead me to that bath while you're doin' it."

Three

Feltman came down the wide, curving staircase of the Lady Anne feeling clean and refreshed. It was amazing what a hot bath and a shave could do for a man.

His gear had been safely delivered to his room while he bathed, all intact. But his wardrobe didn't consist of much. He had dumped his trail jacket; got out of his stinking blue shirt and changed into his only spare, a grubby, washed-out grey piece of cotton, dusted down his pants and scraped most of the congealed shit off his boots. He would pass.

There was no sign of De Brecco in the foyer. Feltman approached the desk clerk who was struggling through the one page tabloid of the Limon Optic.

"You seen De Brecco?"

The clerk glanced up. "He's waitin' on you through there." He jerked his head towards the saloon and went back to his battle with the printed news-sheet.

The saloon was not much full. A couple of girls were in, but they were relaxing rather than working. He supposed the rest still had their heads down. It was an impressive place, with two separate staircases leading up from the main floor area. The whole place had to take up more room than the adjoining hotel. De Brecco was at the bar.

"Feel better?" he asked Feltman.

"Yeah. I can't smell myself."

"Drink?" De Brecco signalled the barman to bring another glass.

"No. Let's get over an' see Benson."

De Brecco nodded and knocked back his own shot of whisky. He caught Feltman's look. "It's not Benson," he explained. "It's the crowd he has around him. Those McCabe brothers scare the shit out of me."

Business was brisk as they emerged out onto Stonewall. De Brecco's Lady Anne sat central on the east side of the cross-street, occupying about a third of the block. They turned left towards Lincoln and left again, continuing on up towards Main.

Old Roving Eyes latched on to them as they started to cross the diagonal at the intersection. He had shifted across the street as the sun had climbed and had become too harsh for his sensitive eyes. Now he was lounging outside the main entrance to the Limon hotel, contemplating the stranger and Brec as they weaved their way through the early afternoon traffic.

The old man tossed the possibilities about as he saw their line would take them straight into Benson's hotel. This boy sure didn't have no love for cowhands; an' here he was sidin' Brec, headin' for a friendly chat with Benson. The old gossip felt his rumour juices stir, waiting for the feast he suspected was to come.

De Brecco indicated a window on the second story, above and to the left of the hotel entrance. "That's Benson's office."

Feltman nodded at the old man sitting under Benson's window. "That one of the McCabe boys?"

Old Roving Eyes caught the nod and nodded back. Polite young fella.

De Brecco made a grimace he thought was a grin. "Wish to hell he was."

The Limon Hotel was opulent. To their right, a formally dressed receptionist stood behind a magnificent oak desk. He was attending to an affluent looking couple, exchanging pleasantries as he helped them check in. Beyond their stacked luggage, a fully carpeted staircase rose from the highly polished wood floor. The foyer was dotted with expensive sofas and high-backed armchairs. Through an etched glass door, Feltman caught a glimpse of white shirted waiters flitting about amongst their privileged clientele.

It irked him. It shouldn't have but it did. Dressed as he was, Feltman had a sense of being out of place.

"Vern knew how to run a hotel," said De Brecco, as he moved to their left, leading them through a set of double doors under a crafted sign that informed them that they were now entering the 'Gentlemen's Bar'. "And Benson has delusions of grandeur."

This was not a saloon. The bartender was in waistcoat and apron, serving over a bar whose brass rails gleamed against the dark polished wood, his few customers conversing quietly in hushed, civilised tones.

There was a separate entrance to the street, but no batwings here. A set of half glazed doors lay open, allowing a welcome breeze to circulate. If the staircase leading up from the near side of the bar was not quite as lavish as its neighbour next door, it was not far behind.

Feltman let his eyes drift upwards, following the switch-back of the double landing and the final flight of stairs leading to the suite of rooms which fronted on to Main.

And back down again, pausing at the landing, returning the stare of the guard who was perched on a chair with a shotgun laid across his knees; and down again to the bright young man sat comfortably on the third step, a human sign post: 'Private, No Entry'.

The young guard stood up when they approached. He looked even younger when you saw the big forty-five strapped too low on his thigh. Feltman wondered idly if he would be able to lift it high enough to point it.

The kid did not say anything. Just waited. Very sure.

De Brecco craned his neck and came in for openers. "If Benson's in, we'd like to see him."

"He's in." A shake of the head; up and down.

"Tell him it's Brecco."

"He's busy." A shake of the head; from side to side.

"It's important."

A shake of the head. No.

No one could say the boy suffered from a lack of confidence. De Brecco looked over at Feltman and shrugged. Feltman smiled at the kid and said, "You know, if you shake that head much more, it's goin' to fall off."

And then he drove his clenched fist deep into the boy's groin. As the kid pitched forward, Feltman stopped his head with his left hand, grabbing at his mop of hair to haul and pull and send the cocky young gunman over the balustrade.

He was vaguely aware of the kid's body slamming into the curve of the bar top, but he was more interested in the gunman on the landing, who had sprung to his feet, the shotgun hovering as he took in Feltman's forty-four.

Feltman was not surprised. A shotgun against a handgun pointing uphill at that range, and Feltman would bet on the shotgun every time. But no one likes to go against a drawn gun.

"Sit back down an' lay the scatter gun against the wall," Feltman ordered.

The man did as he was told.

"Did you have to do that?" De Brecco looked a little pale. "We'd have got to see him eventually."

"We don't have the time." Feltman led the way up the

stairs, pausing at the landing to pick up the shotgun, motioning to the guard to remain still.

De Brecco had overtaken him and now stood outside a door at the very end of the gallery. "It's this one," he said, then knocked twice and stood back waiting patiently for an answer. It did not come. De Brecco raised his hand to knock again but Feltman stopped him with a look, laid the shotgun against the wall, opened the door, holstered his forty-four, and walked straight in.

The reaction of those inside was the same as that of most men used to being interrupted by flunkies.

They ignored them.

The big, bull-like man at the window was the first to realise that these were uninvited guests. He was puzzled, but, since there did not seem to be any immediate threat, he just looked. Benson felt the tension in the room and broke off from poring over the contents of a leather folder on his desk. The guy who had been perched on the edge of the desk swung to his feet when he saw Benson's focus had shifted. He was not fazed either; calmly assessing them. And Feltman and De Brecco now had the attention of everybody in the room.

"We're here on business, Benson. And it's important." De Brecco was behind and partly hidden by Feltman. he spoke quickly, cutting off whatever it was Benson was about to say.

Benson tilted his head to see round Feltman. "If you plan on stayin', Brec, you might shut the door."

He waited until his guest complied with this reasonable request then said, "And, if you introduce me, I might even ask you to sit down."

"This is Mr Feltman." De Brecco waved his hand. "Feltman, this is Charles Benson, one of Limon's leading citizens."

Benson smiled at that and indicated the two hard-backed chairs in front of his desk. "You know McCabe, Brec," he said, as a way of introducing his man to Feltman. "An' this is Ethan Colby, the latest addition to my staff."

"Did those boys just let you walk in here?" This from McCabe at the window.

Feltman said nothing and De Brecco didn't feel the question was directed at him.

McCabe pushed himself off the wall, walked behind them and went quietly out.

Feltman watched as Benson reached into a drawer with a chubby hand which reappeared clutching a long cigar. Chubby now, but they had seen some work. The same went for the face. Running a little to seed but it had been rubbed in the dirt a few times. Benson stuck the cigar in his mouth and set fire to it. He did not offer them around.

"Well?"

"We've got a proposition to put to you," said De Brecco, suddenly wishing it was Hartford who was here.

"You an' Feltman'?"

"The town," explained De Brecco, immediately regretting the implication.

"The town?"

De Brecco was about to hone it done further but Benson laughed. "Just havin' a little fun Brec." He flicked some ash away. "Less than an hour ago, I had a very interestin' lunch with a couple of big buddies of yours. You here to talk about that?"

"Yeah. Yeah, we are," De Brecco admitted. "Look, Benson, you know what this town's like. It's been a hellhole ever since the mine opened." (He almost said, 'since you got here'.) "Too many people dyin' in the street; women and kids getting' hurt. That doesn't benefit anybody, nobody profits from that. We have to come together an' bring some civilisation back to Limon."

Benson held up a hand to stem the flow of De Brecco's words while he tried to relight his cigar. "I hope you're not about to suggest that I might be, in some way, ah ... detrimental to the civilisin' of Limon?"

"Charlie, straight talkin'. You've come a fair way in this town. And now we're askin' you to be satisfied with what you've got. Hold off on any expansion plans you have for now, an' give us all a chance to bring some order back to Limon." De Brecco sat back. "Before our mutual friends bring it all down about our ears," he added. "You know they can, and they will. They must have made that plain to you at your interestin' lunch. They made it plain enough to us."

The meaning of 'expansion' was not lost on Benson but he let it slide for the moment. "I don't follow your line of thought. I agree the town's a little on the wild side, an' I don't like that more'n anybody else, but we've got a marshal. If he's not doin' his job, let's get rid of him." Benson paused for a puff. "Maybe Mr Feltman would like the job? Or maybe you're ahead of me?" he asked, innocently.

"He said straight talkin', Benson"

"Ah, it speaks."

"Yeah. So why don't we cut out the crap an' talk business?"

The door opened and McCabe came back into the room. Benson followed his movements as he regained his post at the window. Except it was not the same McCabe. It was a replica McCabe. And this one was carrying the shotgun.

"Why don't we? Okay, Feltman, I'm listenin'."

"What De Brecco here was sayin', in his own diplomatic way, is that you're a crook."

McCabe stiffened at that. Funny how even obvious truths can cause offense. Benson just smiled.

"But you're an intelligent crook. You must know that you can't go on like this forever. If you don't drive Limon's law-abidin' citizens to desperate measures, then one of your fellow villains will do for you eventually."

"I'm glad Edgemount isn't here. He's a very sensitive person."

"Either way, it won't make any difference to you. You'll be finished. Your best bet is to go respectable ..... straight respectable, while you still can."

"That's good o' you. Warnin' me, I mean. When all you had to do was wait until I met my dastardly end. So why the charity?"

"Because it would take too long. An' because you'd likely be replaced by somebody else."

Benson laughed outright at this. "Better the devil .. you don't mince your words, Feltman. You'd never make a politician," he advised, contradicting Judge Perry's earlier assessment.

"An' because we need your help to enforce the law on the street," Feltman finished.

"You askin' me to pay for more deputies?" Benson inquired, like he would give the matter some serious thought.

"We both know this town doesn't need any more paper lawmen.

Benson put on his quizzical face.

" You have to get a message out there, Benson. It seems our town marshal has had an epiphany ..."

"A what?"

Feltman smiled at Benson's pretend ignorance. "Judd is about to start acting like a real lawman ... you know, impartial, upholding the law, serve an' protect, jailin' hellraisers – that kind o' thing."

Benson laughed. "Is he?

"That's the word you need to get out on the street. Judd's the law an' your boys will be backin' him up."

"Now that could be a mite awkward. I've heard some of my men are prone to let of a little steam; have some harmless fun after a hard day." Benson smiled, "They might forget they're supposed to be on Judd's side"

Feltman nodded. "They might. But that's when I'll be backin' Judd. But then, it'll only be the stupid that die. The ones too drunk to remember that their boss is backin' me."

"Ah ... no. I don't buy this. It's horseshit." Benson leaned back and regarded Feltman thoughtfully. "What you want, is for me to send my men out there to battle with those crazy cowboys, an' then you move in to pick up the respectable pieces, showin' me the exit at the same time. Uh ... uh."

"Benson, you got a choice. Either we go to Cairns for help, an' those crazy cowboys of his wipe you out, or ..."

"An' you wouldn't leave this room alive."

"Neither would you."

You could see Benson conceded that.

"Or," Feltman continued, "you help us, an' we tell Cairns that his men aren't welcome in town until it's been cleaned up a tad. You'd be the town hero. A grateful populace might even vote you mayor."

That eased the tension a little.

"You serious?" Benson was addressing De Brecco now, and he was not talking about being mayor.

De Brecco nodded.

"Old man Cairns will love you for that."

"Consolidate what you've got," said De Brecco, " an' when the town settles down, you'll be sittin' pretty. Any deals you need doin' can be done legit."

"You sayin' they haven't been?"

De Brecco didn't feel the need to answer.

"I'm not convinced you'll get Cairns to go along with you. That old man hates my guts. But ...you pull that off, an' you got a deal."

De Brecco was surprised, and could not help the sigh of relief.

"It's important you get the word out to your boys, Benson," Feltman emphasised. "Startin' now. An' remind Judd he's supposed to be a marshal. Anybody does anything against the law out there an' Judd pulls them in. An' your boys back him up, whether it's against one of their own or not."

McCabe came away from the window and stood behind Feltman. "You're clever, Feltman. But you're not very polite."

Feltman's snappy reply died somewhere in his throat. It is not easy to utter sharp rejoinders when you are flying through the air. Instead, he yelled in pain as his head and left shoulder slammed into the wall beside the window.

McCabe kicked the fallen chair out of the way and took the two paces up to Feltman, the shotgun swinging carelessly from his right hand.

"The men do what I tell them."

De Brecco had backed to the door, looking paler than ever. Colby was waiting for a lead from Benson, who had sprung to his feet. "Joe. Leave it."

"Leave it? You know this hero busted two of Andy's ribs? Didn't you, hero? Mashed his cojones up as well. Couldn't ask him, could you. Had to show him, didn't you?"

The last 'didn't you' was accompanied by the shotgun punching into Feltman' belly. McCabe's big hand stopped Feltman's head from coming forward and slammed it back into the wall.

"Cal ….hi …off ….Bensss." Feltman's voice was so hoarse and breathless he couldn't even make himself out.

But McCabe could. "Call me off? I ain't no dog, Feltman." And the shotgun moved again.

This time, the pain was so bad it stopped. Feltman could feel his stomach at his throat. He could not see. And through that haze just this side of consciousness, he could hear them debating the merits of hitting him again.

" …st one more. Just so he gets the message."

Feltman let his body slid over in front of the window. He could not take another one. He suddenly experienced a little belated sympathy for Jimmy. The pain came back. But it brought some awareness with it. As the shotgun came stabbing forward, Feltman slid a little more, and the twin barrels made a neat hole in the window behind him.

Desperately, he grabbed at the wrist behind the stock and heaved. Off balance, McCabe jerked forward and his massive head followed the shotgun barrels through the glass. Feltman's boot was under McCabe's knee. All the way. And he heaved again. The window completely shattered and McCabe disappeared through it.

Below, Old Roving Eyes had looked up at the sound of the gun barrels breaking the glass. Half the street looked up when McCabe's bloody head came through after them. But Old Roving Eyes missed the best part when he raised his arm and dropped his head to protect his face from the shards of glass as McCabe's body scribed a graceful arc though the air surrounded by the glinting particles of fragmented window pane. He heard the thud though. When he took his arm away, McCabe was lying crumpled, half on, half off the glass-strewn sidewalk His neck looked kinda funny.

Up in Benson's office, Feltman was struggling to get his gun out to cover Colby. But he was taking too long. He was going to be too late.

However, when he finally managed it, Colby was simply standing alongside him, staring down at the scene below. De Brecco had not moved but Benson had a gun out and was covering Feltman.

"You stupid bastard. I should kill you myself."

"Can I help it if you can't control your own men?"

"You didn't have to throw him through the fuckin' window."

"One more, an' I'd have been dead." Feltman had one hand across his middle and the other holding the gun loosely, trying to make his mind up where to point it.

That dilemma was resolved when the door burst open and the guard from the landing burst in to the room, this time holding a rifle.

"Easy," commanded Benson.

The guard complied; confused, trying to work out what was going on.

"We still got a deal?" Feltman asked.

The anger in Benson's eyes held for a moment, then subsided. He nodded briefly and lowered his gun.

"Dave's down there with his brother," announced Colby. He pulled himself back from the window. "I reckon he'll be burstin' through that door any second," he observed mildly.

"You'd better rein him in," Feltman warned, "or you'll lose your left hand as well."

"Shut the door,' Benson issued the order to the guard, "an' back up against the wall. When Dave comes in, cold deck him with that rifle butt."

The guard did as he was bid but the second half of the instruction obviously had him baffled.

"You got that?"

The guard nodded but Benson wasn't convinced. He

looked at Colby who moved away from the window and positioned himself against the other wall beside De Brecco.

They waited.

The bellowing came first. Followed by the sound of Dave coming up the stairs at a thumping run. Then the door crashed open, flung to the wall. McCabe's eyes were blazing, filled with hatred. "He's dead. You broke his neck." It was a flat, unbelieving statement.

"Dave, Feltman didn't have a choice." Benson had his gun up again. But now it was levelled at the surviving McCabe. Dave took no notice. He raised his arm and extended his index finger. "Feltman, I'm goin' to kill you."

"But not now." Feltman waved his gun hand to remind Dave that he had it. "Now you're goin' to move away from that door an' we're going to leave."

Dave McCabe smiled a manic smile. He didn't seem to think that was likely.

The guard was ignoring the eyeballing he was getting from Benson, who was seriously swithering between shooting him, McCabe or Feltman.

McCabe took a step towards Feltman. The gun was simply not enough of a deterrent. He pulled a wide-bladed hunting knife from his belt, letting Feltman see his fate; a single bullet would not stop Feltman's chest from being ripped open.

"You … are .. goin' to diiiiiiieee."

The butt of Colby's revolver smacked into the side of McCabe's head as he began to launch himself at Feltman. His trajectory changed from forward to down, his elbows taking the brunt of the collision with the floor, the big knife bouncing away across the room. He rallied for an instant, then his forehead slowly came to rest in supplication at Feltman's feet.

"Jesus christ," exclaimed Benson. "Is he dead?"

"Doubt it," Colby seemed unperturbed, "he has a skull like a buffalo."

Faces began to appear at the open door.

"Back off," Benson waved them away. "And somebody tell Walker to get his ass in here." Benson stepped over Dave and looked down from the window at the crowd gathered below. "And let the doc know he's fussin' over the wrong McCabe. We have one up here he can help."

De Brecco was still plastered to the wall. Feltman was rubbing his gut. Benson shook his head at both of them. "You came here offering solutions. An' all you've done is leave me with two big problems."

"One big problem," corrected Feltman. "Deal with it."

"You think I'm goin' to put a bullet in his head? You know that's the only way he won't come after you. No, I said we still have a deal, but you'll just have to tread carefully, Feltman."

Benson glanced at De Brecco. "An' that goes for you too, Brec. Don't cross me on this. I've suffered a lot of damage and I'm takin' a hell of a risk. So you let me know what old man Cairns says. If it's a 'yes', I'll hold off Dave as long as I can, if it's a "no", well, then you're on your own. Either way, you two should watch your backs."

Benson peered out from the door, and shouted "Okay. Brec an' Feltman walk out of here. Let them go."

Feltman, still nursing his gut, went through the door without a backward glance. De Brecco peeled himself off the wall and followed him out.

"You asked for me, Mr Benson?"

Benson turned to nod at his clerk who had appeared in the doorway of the anti-room.. "Come in, Walker. Shut the door." He turned his attention to the young guard who had hardly moved a muscle.

"What's your name?"

"Morris"

"Okay. Well, Morris, Mr Walker here is gonna draw thirty dollars from petty cash an' hand it to you. You are then gonna get on your horse an' ride out of town, never to come back."

Morris had been baffled since he stepped into the room and this was not helping. "I'm sorry, Mr Benson, I didn't know …. I mean I wasn't sure that's what you wanted. Mr McCabe bein' your man an' all."

"Yeah, I know, son. But we're tryin' to help you. When Dave wakes up an' finds out you decked him, well, he's gonna rip you limb from limb."

"What? Me? But I di …."

Benson held up a cautionary hand. "Mr Colby, who was it suckered Mr McCabe from behind?"

"That would be Morris, there."

"No … I .."

"Mr Walker, what is your understanding of who brought down Mr McCabe with the butt of his rifle?"

Mr Walker was a little confused as well, but savvy enough to lift his finger and point at Morris.

"You see, Mr Morris. For your own safety, your best course of action would be to go with Mr Walker now, gratefully accept the thirty dollars and hightail it out of town."

Benson jerked his head at Walker who immediately disappeared back into the anti-room. Morris trailed after him but paused in the doorway. " Uh, Mr Benson."

Benson tried to be patient, encouraging.

The young man was nervous but felt he should say something. "Eh, I don't have a horse."

"Jesus fucking christ. Walker!" Benson managed a reassuring smile as Walker's head appeared back in the doorway. "Mr Walker, will you see that Mr Morris is supplied with a horse."

"Yes, sir."

Colby laid a reassuring hand on Morris's shoulder as he ushered him out behind Walker. "It'll be fine. As long as you keep your mouth shut and don't come back," he smiled.

When they were alone with the door shut, Benson and Colby stood contemplating the prone form of McCabe.

"You know he'll not let this go," said Colby.

"Yeah, I know.

"So?"

"So, we'll just have to persuade Dave that revenge is best served cold. Let Feltman work for us, make us all rich. When this is over, Dave can slice him up any way he likes, eat his rotten heart if he wants. Feltman can die when he's served his purpose."

"An' if he can't be persuaded?"

"Well," Benson leaned forward to check. "He definitely out?" He picked up his cigar and tried to get it going again. "If Dave can't be selfless an' act in everybody's interest, then," Benson shrugged, "maybe we'll have to bring forward that reorganisation we talked about."

Old Roving Eyes watched as Brecco and Feltman skirted the crowd and made their way back down Lincoln. Hell, that boy did not look too well. But he was alive, and that was surprising. He hung around and took in every detail until they hauled Joe's carcass away. Then he headed off for McGarvey's. He'd earn a few beers tonight.

Four

Feltman came down the wide, curving stairway of the Lady Anne feeling like hell. It was amazing what a shotgun barrel in the gut could do for a man. At the bottom, both Hartford and De Brecco were waiting.

"You look like you need some rest, Feltman," greeted Hartford.

Feltman had tried that. It had made it worse. His lungs felt as if somebody had been using the linings for a barber's strop. He took a breath deep enough to talk with. "Where're the horses?" he wheezed.

"Right outside," answered De Brecco. "We borrowed a nice big grey mare for you. That buckskin looked more knackered than you." He threw out a 'good luck', more at Hartford than Feltman, and disappeared gratefully into his saloon to look over the increasing trade.

"You sure this can't wait until tomorrow?" asked Hartford. "It'll be near dark by the time we get back."

"Let's get it done now, before Benson changes his mind."

Outside, Feltman patted the flank of the beautiful grey and heaved himself gingerly into the saddle. He glanced back at the two riflemen stationed either side of the hotel door. "De Brecco gettin' nervous?"

"We all are. And as yet, you're not helping."

They rode down Stonewall and turned up Grant onto Main. The traffic was still heavy as they followed the curve round, running back parallel with Grant. As they swung past the Sawmill, heading north west out of town, Feltman could not help wrinkling his nose at the foul odour.

"Fresh air alley," Hartford laughed. "That's the slaughter house. Those pens and coops you see beyond are the piggery and chicken ranch."

Feltman felt sick. The rancid smell and jostling of his tender ribs was a bad combination. His nausea eased a bit when they cleared town, the road fading to a gently rising track through the fertile grasses of a high valley.

It eased still further at the distraction of the gorgeous woman coming towards them in the buckboard. Good christ almighty. What was it about the women in this town? Perched up in the driver's seat, the shape of her was just a sensual, I-can't-take-my-eyes-off-you delight.

She laughed at Hartford tipping his hat as she passed, head back, eyes and teeth flashing, piling it on, knowing what effect she had on men; even a straight-laced banker.

In deference to his troubled gut, Feltman raised an inquiring eyebrow at Hartford.

"That's Angie," Hartford smiled, "The town squaw."

He could sense Feltman's puzzlement, anyone would be. So he continued, "She belongs to those two crazy breeds. You'll get to them. They run a saloon, the Oglala, on Lincoln."

"Belongs?" Feltman eased out the question.

"Yes, I think that's the right word. They're 'shacked up together' as Brec puts it, over at the old Harmony ranch. They sort of share her … you know?"

There was a lot Feltman would like to know, but he would leave it until his breathing returned to something resembling normal.

Angie reined the two horse buckboard to an expertly controlled halt exactly outside the Oglala. As she jumped down from the wagon, most of the passing manhood of Limon fixed their admiring gazes on the juggling going on within the confines of her light, cotton blouse. When that settled down, their hungry eyes came up to catch the soft, shaggy mane, taking in her bright, confident smile, before drifting briefly down, over her tight-panted limbs; then back up, to rest. And if she was wearing anything under that blouse, it had to be made of raw silk.

Red was at the bar, talking to Clancy as Angie forced her way in between two miners on their way out. She did not take offence. She was used to it. Despite risking the wrath of the breeds, not many men made way for Angie. Branded shithead or not, there was always the chance that some delicious part of her would make contact as she squeezed by.

Andrew Hartford must have been the only man in Limon who imagined that Angie could belong to anybody. And describing the Oglala as a saloon was letting his prejudices get in the way of reality. It was a decent Hotel, with a saloon attached. And Angie owned it.

Angie came up behind Red, wrapping her arms around his strong, lithe body and thumping her forehead lightly against his back. Red's own arms reached back quickly, seeking her ass.

"Yeiiih." Whooping, he pulled her round and they laughingly embraced.

Clancy did not bother hiding his reaction to Angie and Red leaned over and punched him on the shoulder, none too softly. "Yei! You got as much chance makin' it with this wiwasteka as I got bein' elected to congress."

Clancy grinned back at the big Indian. He always thought of Red as an Indian. He had total Indian looks;

hardly a hair on his body, strong, brown face surrounded by lank black hair. But Horse ... now Horse was a breed. He looked like an Indian with a beard. Horse ... Clancy's smile widened at the thought of it. It never got any less funny, no matter how often it came to mind. Red Cloud and Crazy Horse. Those two breeds callin' themselves after Sioux Chiefs; hitchin' up with Angie an' buyin' this place; changin' the name ... the 'Oglala'. Sweet jesus. Thumbin' their noses at the whites. Clancy's grin grew even wider.

"You speakin' for me, Red?" asked Angie, faking some irritation.

"Ang, girl, I know better." Red did know better.

"Clancy, when's your birthday?"

"What? Ain't for a time yet." Clancy knew the joke was coming, but asked anyway. "Why?"

Angie glanced at Red and winked at Clancy. "Well, you know, ...woman needs a change. I thought, maybe, I might give you a treat."

They all burst into renewed laughter at this, Red maybe forcing it just a little. Finally, when the merriment had died down, Angie gestured towards a painted, pinewood screen that sealed off an area at the back of the saloon.

"Horse behind there?"

"Yeah, they ran into some dumb dude," Red explained. "They're skinnin' him now."

"Well, what are you doin'? You gonin' to come back with me?"

"How long you gonna be?"

"Coupla hours, maybe."

"Take a turn past on the way out. We'll probably jump the wagon if Horse's finished in there."

Angie nodded, giving them a cheery backward wave and an enticing sway of the hips as she left.

Red's version of the poker game was not strictly accurate. At least, not then. Mallinor may have dressed like a dude, but he was far from being a dummy, though, admittedly, right now he was not feeling any too clever.

Because, right now he had a hell of a pile of money in front of him; and he had been trying to lose it for the last half hour.

It had been right about then that he had realised it was not going to be enough not to cheat. He would have to play badly as well.

When he had first met in with this guy Horse and his cronies at the bar, he had thought the gambling gods were smiling favourably on him; that he was about to make a killing. But something in the atmosphere when they were all sitting down at the table warned him off.

So; no cheating.

But he had not had to. Professionally speaking, none of the other five men at the table could play cards. In a little over an hour, he had amassed a small fortune in front of him. Mistake. If he had not been so pleased with himself, he would have seen the signs earlier. But they finally made it through his euphoria.

The one they called Horse was mad. When he packed a losing hand, he packed it; his eyes never leaving Mallinor's face. But it was not that. Bad losers were common enough. It was the others who tipped him. They should have been ignoring their surly friend …because bad losers were common enough. But they were not. Instead, they were becoming more and more restless, actually fidgeting. They seemed to be expecting Horse to explode. And if they were expecting it, it had happened before. And if it had happened before, then it was damn well going to happen again. Because Horse was mad; crazy mad.

So; no winning.

But the gods of chance were not finished with him. They were toying with him. Because, now he wanted to lose, he could not. Every time he discarded to break up a possible winning hand, he drew three queens; or made a flush; or drew two fives to the one he had retained.

And he couldn't even pack into the pile unseen. Horse deliberately turned over any of his packed hands, daring him to complain at the blatant lack of etiquette.

In the last half hour, he had lost seven dollars. Seven miserly dollars. My god, he would have to play into next week to give them their money back. And Horse was not going to wait that long.

So; Cheat to lose.

And Mallinor sweated it.

Feltman looked over at the figure of Hartford, mounted on a sturdy little paint, more like an Indian pony, which was almost cantering to keep up with the grey's ambling gait. "You don't seem too upset about this meetin' with Cairns?"

"Recovering?"

Feltman gave a slight nod. The jarring of the ride seemed to be cancelling out the searing pain in his gut.

"I'm trying not to think about it," answered Hartford. "I'm not relishing the thought, believe me. I only hope we're going about this the right way."

Feltman could understand how the banker must be feeling, trying to convince himself that this roundabout route would get them there in the end but half his brain crying out for direct action. Like dragging Benson to the nearest tree.

"Well, if we get bust on this, you'll still have the railroad coming through with the telegraph," Feltman said, consolingly. "You can always scream for help"

"But who'd listen?" asked Hartford. "And the telegraph is already working, right up to the office at the new railway station. Even the bank will be connected soon."

They were approaching a small creek and Feltman followed Hartford's lead, so that both riders changed direction slightly, bringing them into line with a shallow basin that gave onto a stony crossing.

"You know," said Hartford, searching for bits of idle conversation, "I can remember when they crossed this country for the first time with the telegraph, back in sixty-one. A whole damn continent; ocean to ocean; and you could get a message across it in less time than it took a rider to change horses. I remember trying to picture it in my mind; the genius who had thought it all out." Hartford shook his head in wonder at the memory. "And you know what I hear now? You can scream down that line for help. And whoever's on the other end will hear you, plain as day."

Feltman looked at him.

"I'm telling you straight." Hartford's tone emphasised that he knew it was hard to believe but that he would be offended if it was thought he was just repeating casual saloon gossip. "No keys, no code. You talk to him and he talks to you."

"Over how far a distance?"

"Doesn't matter. Miles. Same as the telegraph."

Now it was Feltman's turn to shake his head. That was a new one on him.

They went down into and through the creek, which was shallow and fast-running over the fording area of gravel and flat stones. When they came up and out of the cottonwoods on the far side, Hartford said, "We turn more north here. Less than an hour."

This was true cattle country now, hardly a tree showing

in the long grasses. They were cutting across what seemed to be an endless valley, stretching away to the north west, their mounts straining, wanting to run.

They let them. Both riders and horses enjoying the thrill of power and movement, the tall prairie grass whipping at them as they surged on, carelessly scattering a small heard of grazing cattle in the process.

After a mile or so they slowed. There were a group of dismounted cowhands ahead and Hartford changed course to bring them closer in passing. There were three hands and they were bent over two dead cows. As they approached, one of the cowboys raised an arm, either in greeting or instruction, and they pulled up.

The same cowboy walked over, sizing them up as he came. He tilted his head up at them, a gloved hand shielding his eyes; the sweat beads running gently down his bare chest. And yet he was wearing a greatcoat; a long, loose, ex-army version, which once must have been either blue or grey, but was now threadbare and filthy after years of living rough with the owner.

"Ya headin' fur the house?"

"Yes, we have some business with Mr Cairns." Hartford answered for them both.

The dirty cowboy looked from Hartford to Feltman, continuing his assessment. "Mr Cairns know yur comin'?"

"No."

"Well, ya head on in. A'll let Coleman know." And with that he walked back to his horse.

As Feltman and Hartford urged their mounts on, they could hear the sound of the rider crossing to their rear, and turning, they saw him in full gallop, to their left now, heading north-west into the heart of the valley, his greatcoat billowing out behind him.

"Coleman the foreman?" asked Feltman.

76

"Yes. The old man doesn't like surprises."

Twenty minutes later, Hartford came up level and pointed silently across the ears of Feltman's grey.

"I see them."

Two horsemen. Just specks at that point, but getting bigger as they closed on a collision course. Then one of them broke away, riding hard to get ahead. Greatcoat.

"How can he wear that thing?" Hartford mused.

Coleman was what you would call a competent looking fellow. Not much of anything. Not tall, not short; not big, not skinny. He looked tough, and filthy. But then, he was a working foreman.

The range boss shouted out a 'Howdy' as he joined them. Hartford returned the greeting with a 'Hello, Matt' and introduced Feltman. The three of them followed the flying cowboy at a steadier pace, Coleman obviously holding back the spirited bay he was riding.

The first sight of the Cairn's holding was impressive. They came to a depression in the plain leading down to a creek basin and, on the far side, the ranch-house and outbuildings were laid out. Neat; gleaming. All imported wood and white paint.

Downstream, and set some distance apart there were three, separate, small corrals straddling the creek. In each of the outer two stomped a massive, round-bellied, white-faced bull. In the centre, standing imperiously between his rivals was a beast of a different origin; blacker than the ace of spades.

"Herefords an' a Black Angus," Coleman explained, when he saw Feltman's interest. "Cost over a thousand dollars apiece to get those big boys up here."

They made way for a covered wagon as it splashed across the stream, greatcoat perched up front, a fresh horse tied behind.

Mallinor stared at Horse in stark disbelief. He could not be serious. Nobody was that crazy. Horse was leaning forward on the table, his big, ugly face grinning into Mallinor's, enjoying himself now. Crazy Horse was happy.

Mallinor looked around the table, but there were no allies to be found there. Three of the other card players looked as happy as Horse, and, if the forth had any reservations, it was certainly not going to run to contradiction.

"Look," Mallinor pleaded. "Look at my hand. That's a bust hand. Why the hell would I slip a four to make a bust hand?"

For god's sake, surely they could see that. Sure they could. He was wasting his time.

"Don't matter," Horse made the flat, terrible statement. He sounded happier than ever.

"Whaaa," Desperately, Mallinor tried to stop his voice from shrieking. "What do you mean it doesn't matter?" Panic forced him to keep trying. Even though he knew he may as well sit back and let it happen.

"All o' us saw that four o' clubs at the bottom o' the deck when you wis dealin'. An' now it's in your hand. An' that makes you a cheatin' son o' a bitch." Horse sat back, pleased with the logic.

And, aside from the parentage, that last part was no lie. Mallinor had been cheating for the whole of the previous hour. And he had lost one hundred and seventy two dollars doing it. But he was a professional. He would not slip any stupid black four from the bottom of the deck. Not that they would be able to see, anyway.

Mallinor got shakily to his feet. "What are you talking about? What are you trying to do?" He had had enough. His voice was shrill with anger. And fear.

Horse made a gesture with his hand and they came at him. They grabbed his arms and his head and forced him back into his chair.

"Leave me. Let go of me." Mallinor screeched, struggling in terror.

Horse just laughed and walked over to look out beyond the pine screen. "Red! Luta, come on back here. We've caught ourselves a cheatin' white easterner."

Mallinor lost all control at that point. Kicking and spitting, he raged at them. "Animals. You're just animals. You're not usin' me for bait."

And then a heavy fist took him out of it.

Brian Cairns had settled on the great plains the second time around. He had come west in the mid-forties to hunt the buffalo everyone was talking about. And, if he had not exactly made his fortune, he had, at least, enjoyed the experience. Fighting off the Crow had proved to be easier than fighting off his creditors back east.

But making fortunes was what it was all about. Or so he had thought then. So he had joined the forty-niners in their rush to the California gold fields. And, at times, he had made it. He had claimed it and lost it. He had stolen it and lost it. And the next twenty years had found him starving to death in one stinking mining camp or another. Always hoping. Always losing.

He had been at Pike's Peak, at the head of the South Platte, in fifty-nine. Then the mad rush up to Florence in sixty-two; all along the Salmon river; Salmon City; Bonanza; Pierce City; you name it and he had starved in it.

And finally there had come a time in sixty-eight when he had to admit he was not going to make it. He wanted to eat more than one decent meal a week. He was sick of feeling constantly damp and of waking up in his own vomit after blowing what little he had on a drunken orgy, because his paltry profits did not merit any other fate.

So he got himself a job with the Central Pacific, on a grading crew, heading east through Utah, desperate for miles, because the Union Pacific was doing exactly the same in the opposite direction, battling its way westwards.

And the competition was fierce, since the federal government was giving the land adjacent to the laid tracks to the respective railroad company. Not to mention the huge grants, there for the taking.

The vermin and scavengers that made up the bulk of the camp followers were every bit as bad as anything he had seen in the mining camps. But he was drawing a steady wage and what 'fun' he had was tempered by the need to make his shift the next morning – and all the more enjoyable for it. He only really let loose when they met up with those Union boys at Ogden. Both grading crews had kept right on going, overlapping their rivals only a few feet away, until common sense had prevailed and the high-ups had degreed that the twin tracks must join up on the summit at Promontory.

And then another beat of his life was over. Paid off with hundreds of others, shuffling around while the dignitaries patted themselves on the back as they waited impatiently for their ceremony to be set up, desperate to quaff champagne and fine wine and rush off back to Washington and San Francisco to invest their profits in the next big official scam.

So he had watched while they had lined up that last, fancy silver tie and had stood in sanctimonious prayer for a full ten minutes. Then that fellow Standish had pretended to bash in a golden spike, and the band played and that was that.

Afterwards, with his payoff wad strapped around his

waist, he had jumped a free ride east, intending to go back to New York. But, for some reason, he had got off at Cheyenne. Maybe because, as he had sat there in the depot, watching out the window at the bustling populace going about their business, he had realised that there was nothing for him in New York. Nothing for him anywhere, so he may as well start here.

For days he had just walked around doing nothing, no gambling, not much drinking, nothing, and enjoying it. He had seen the cattle being driven up from Colorado. They were Texas cattle, and, at first, he could not understand why they were being driven so far. The Chisolm trail out of Texas and the railheads at Abilene were famous. Why would anyone drive their cattle all the way up here? But they were not looking for railheads. They were searching for better grazing.

So he had had a look himself, and had thought, 'what the hell', it was no crazier than chasing imaginary gold. So he had bought twenty-three head of the scrawniest longhorns anybody had ever seen, and he had headed north, going further than any of them, driving his tiny herd into the lands where he had once hunted the buffalo. Only there were not so many buffalo now and the Sioux had all but replaced the crow.

Alternatively, he had fought and made friends with the Sioux, though he supposed they were only playing with him. Or maybe they had thought it was a good idea to have some cattle to hunt in place of the disappearing buffalo. Because, then, they could have wiped him out if they really wanted to. But not now.

Now, he must have something like twenty thousand prime beef cattle grazing over more square miles than he could count. But for how long? Not too long, probably. Not with people like Glidden churning out his silver thread for the farmers. And Hayes; encouraging them to come west in droves with promises of land. His land. He doubted whether these would be sod-busters would recognise a plough if they saw one, far less the difference between a steer and a heifer.

But it really did not matter. It had been a long time since he had got excited over anything. Not his land, not his friends, not the mess they were making of the town, not a woman. He was weary. And if all this was going to get chopped up, well, let them carry on. They were welcome to it.

So when Reb had told him that Hartford was on his way in to see him with some gunslinger in tow, he had put aside, for the minute, the complex problem of how to avoid beating himself at chess and turned his attention solely on to the question which he knew Hartford was going to ask.

Brian Cairns knew also, exactly what his answer was going to be. No.

It was not his answer that needed some thought. It was how he phrased it. Brian Cairns had developed a core of kindness in his later years, was more diplomatic, maybe. Andrew would likely be upset. His expectations crushed.

But no, he was not going to back up any new play against Benson. What if the town was driving itself to hell? So what? He was not going to ask his boys to go in and fight for something they would never have. Not so Hartford and Perry and a few others could sit back and become 'civilised' rich.

And that was a laugh, anyway. That mine. He had travelled thousands of miles in search of a big strike only to come back and find that he had been sitting on top of one from the very first.

So, no. If they wanted to make any gains down in Limon, they would have to do it themselves. They could count him out.

But now, looking across at Hartford and Feltman, seated together on the heavily stuffed couch opposite, Cairns' easily prepared answer melted away in the silence that had held in the room for something approaching a minute. He was stunned.

Hartford noisily cleared his throat and said tentatively, "If you think about it, Brian, it makes sense."

Slowly, Cairns got to his feet, favouring his right leg, and limped over to the drink-laden side table. "Can I offer you something stronger?"

Both men shook their heads. Neither of them had touched the wine which had been pressed upon them on arrival. Cairns did not allow their refusal to influence the size of the whisky he poured for himself.

"You sure you know what you're doin', Andrew?"

"Nothing else has worked. The town won't survive if things continue the way they are." Hartford's use of 'town' when he meant 'privileged elite' did not go unnoticed by their host but he refrained from comment.

Hartford shrugged, "We have to try something."

"I'll be honest with you," said Cairns. "I thought you were going to ask me the opposite. To bring my men into town."

"Well, we will," said Feltman, "once we have Benson isolated." These were the first words he had spoken since their polite greeting had been exchanged.

"Or if it doesn't work at all," Cairns countered.

"That," replied Feltman, "won't happen."

Cairns downed his drink and placed the glass carefully on the table. "Benson might have reined in Dave for the moment, but that can't last. He'll come for you, no matter what deal his boss agreed."

"I know."

"You'll have to kill him too."

Feltman nodded. "I know."

Cairns held his gaze for a moment longer but he had already decided. "I'm going to give you what you want. There'll be none of my men loosen off in your town for the rest of the month. They'll just have to travel further afield for their fun."

" That'll be more ….."

Cairns interrupted with a wave of his arm. "No. I'll give you to next payday. But you have to understand, even with threats, some of them will still head in – whisky an' women, a combination hard to resist. And there'll be men in for supplies an' whatever."

"They won't be a problem," assured Hartford.

"They'd better not be, Andrew. Because if they boys don't come out the same way they went in, I won't come lookin' for Benson, or Feltman here. I'll be lookin' for you. You an' Perry."

Hartford thought that over for a moment. But there was not really very much he could say. Their interview had been short. And it was over.

Clancy reluctantly held out the coil of hemp and cautioned, "Take it easy, Red. Don't wipe the dummy out."

"You kiddin'?" Red demanded, snatching the rope out of Clancy's hand. "You heard Horse. That's a cheatin', white easterner we got in there."

Clancy shook his head sadly as Red stormed off behind the painted screen. They were all easterners for christ's sake. Just depended how far back you went. He allowed, though, that it was their attitude that marked some men out. Misplaced arrogance and sense of entitlement; often faked. And deflated when their pomposity was pricked.

Cheatin', white and easterner. Any one would have been bad enough, but all three together? To hell with it. He wasn't paid to get upset. Let's hope they kept the screams down.

"Open his eyes."

They opened his eyes.

"Slap his head."

They did that too. And Mallinor began to come round. Slowly at first, then faster in confusion and panic as he felt the constrictions of the rope on his legs and body and the rough hands which forced his arms out in front of him, flat on the card table.

He would remember those grinning faces for the rest of his life. He was as sure of that as he was unsure of how long a period that was going to be. They were smiling happily at him, like they were cooing over a new-born. And it was frightening. He choked as he tried to speak.

"Please. I haven't done anything. Let me go." He was almost crying as he spoke. He knew that they were not going to let him go. "All the money's there. Take it. Take all of it."

Horse was delighted with his pleadings. It always made it better. "You're stupid, you know? We've already done that." There was laughter all round, except for Mallinor, of course. "Naw, you've spoiled our gamblin' with your cheating, that's what you've done."

Horse slipped his hunting knife from his belt and drove it into the table, inches from Mallinor's manicured fingers. Mallinor screamed. He could not help it.

"Ain't that right, boys?" Horse asked, just on the off-chance that one of the boys might disagree with him. But the boys all nodded. They looked really upset about losing out on their gambling.

"I reckon it's only fair he feels the mee-lah, Red?"

"Yei!" Red pulled out his own blade and Mallinor's whole body shook as that too was plunged into the table. Sportingly, Horse began to explain the rules. "You got a choice, bright boy. Either you keep your fingers closed, in which case we'll cut them all off, or you can keep 'em as wide spread as you can. That way you'll only get cut up a little."

That seemed simple enough. Mallinor screamed.

"Gag him."

Mallinor twisted his head away from the filthy rag, but they pulled him back by the hair; fingers grabbed at his lower lip, pulling his jaw down until they could ram it in, holding it there with a bandana tied behind his head. Degradation momentarily turned his terror into anger and hate. They were using him like a … like ….

"Place them bets, boys. Whose gonna draw first blood?"

"Ten on Red. He always was a little clumsy."

The add-on utterance was immediately regretted. The crony winced, pretending not to see a dark look from Red.

"Fifteen says Horse. Nothin' makes a man angrier than a cheater."

"Ah'll match that." And they laughed excitedly. Now they were having fun.

"Hold him steady," commanded Horse.

With two men bearing down on each of Mallinor's arms, and with a hand on top of each of his wrists, holding his palms flat on the table, the game began.

Red took the left hand, Horse the right. Both Breeds pulled their knives from the table and, concentrating now, held the hovering blades over their victim's spread fingers.

Mallinor's eyes bulged. He would not have moved if they had let him go. He was rigid with fear.

The Breeds' cronies began a steady chant.

One … and both blades flashed down into the table

between Mallinor's thumbs and forefingers. And out.

Two … and down again between the fore and middle fingers. And out.

Three … down again between the middle and third fingers. And out.

Four … between the third and little fingers. And out. Hovering.

"Clean run. No blood."

"Go it."

Quicker now. One …thud; two …thud; three …thud; four …thud. And out. Hovering.

"Shit, 'nother clean."

"These boys be too 'curate. Give 'em a drink."

Even quicker. One ..thud; two ..thud; three ..thud; four ..thud!

Mallinor screamed as Red's blade was deflected off the bone of his third finger and sliced into the flesh. But only his brain heard him. God, don't let me be sick. I'll die if I'm sick.

"First blood's on Red."

"Slide them greenbacks right over here."

"Damn." Red leaned over and cuffed Mallinor on the side of the head. "Boy, you keep them fingers spread."

"Leave 'm, he's neutral."

"C'mon, pick up those bets. Let's go."

Fast. Onethud; Twothud; Threethud; Fourthud!

"Yeiii!"

Mallinor closed his eyes to try and close out the nightmare. But that only made it worse. He stared at his bloodied hands. There wasn't any physical pain. Only terror.

"Cancel those bets."

"Blood cut both sides."

"Twenty says Red for first o' them pretty digits."

87

Faster: Onud! Twud! Thrud! Foud!

"Yaoooh. Told ya Red was clumsy." The joy of being right outweighed the danger of being reckless.

Mallinor strained through the mist. His little finger was lying, completely on its own, at the far edge of the table. They had cut off his little finger.

"God damn!" Angrily, Red swept Mallinor's butchered pinkie from the table. "I swear," he complained, bitterly, "this son o' a bitch is tryin' to clean me out."

Mallinor had the strange thought: my finger's on the floor. What if somebody stands on it? And then he screamed. And he screamed. And screamed. Only, this time, not even his brain heard him.

Five

"We've got a reception committee."

Feltman looked up from his steady gaze between the Grey's ears. "Where?"

"Up ahead, by the jailhouse," Hartford pointed.

Feltman could pick out the Judge and De Brecco amongst the small knot of figures standing on the sidewalk underneath the dilapidated and tilted sign that read 'Marsh.'

As they dismounted, the younger of the two other men stepped forward, keen to be efficient. "I'll get these horses over to Duggan's."

The other one had to be Judd, if only because of the star pinned to his chest.

"What's up?" asked Hartford.

"I'll tell you inside," replied the Judge.

So they all trooped into the dank, gloomy jailhouse. Feltman immediately caught his breath. They all did, except for Judd.

"Jesus. You'd've been better tellin' us outside."

It was a squarish room of bare stone, with a desk and chair arranged in the middle of the damp floor and an unmade bunk in the far corner. There was a blackened, decrepit looking, cordwood stove against the front wall, while the wall on the right supported a ledge and chain which served as a gun rack. Two ancient shotguns and a

Henry. The shutters over the only window were closed.

Feltman crossed over to the rear door and yanked it open. He shut it again, double-quick, as the sickening stench of stale urine caught him full in the face. The air in the main office was sweet by comparison. Deep breath. Open door. Stick head in. Two bigger cells squeezing a smaller one in the middle. No back door. No windows. Head out. Close door. Breathe.

"Jesus christ. You live here?" Feltman asked Judd, pointing to the bunk.

"Yeah, I live here." Judd sounded offended. "That stink ain't mine. It's the drunks. They don't know enough to ask for a bucket half the time."

The Judge was impatient for news, despite promising to share his own. He turned to Hartford. "How did it go with Brian?"

"He agreed," answered Hartford shortly. "Huffed and puffed a bit but gave us until next payday. Gives us three weeks or so. And, we better hope to god none of his men get themselves hurt in the meanwhile. So what happened here?"

"Just the latest piece of evil from those half-breeds," explained De Brecco. "They got hold of some poor shit of a gambler, just arrived in town to try his luck. It was all bad. They cut his fingers off for him."

"They what?"

"Not all of them. Two on his right hand. One on his left. The rest were bare to the bone. Then the callous bastards threw him in the back of a buckboard an' kicked him off outside of Brady's surgery. Christ, the way people are around here, the guy could have bled to death."

"It's that woman I can't understand," complained the Judge. "She doesn't bat an eyelid at anything those two degenerates get up to. She accepts it all. Why?"

Even Judd could have offered an answer to that one but nobody felt inclined to reply.

"In any case," the Judge continued, " that's why we're here. They must be held to account for this."

"Well? Where are they?" Feltman summoned up enough energy to look accusingly at Judd. "Hasn't Benson had a word with you yet?"

"Sure he has," the Marshal bristled. "But none of his boys were involved. The only witnesses were them that done it. An' they ain't likely to tell us about it. I can't beat it out o' them."

The prospect of this little runt of a man beating anything out of anybody was so remote that Feltman had to agree with him.

"That gambler fella wasn't havin' any either," said De Brecco. "He just wanted out of here. So we gave him a few dollars and put him on the stage."

Feltman shrugged, "So we missed them this time. We'll get them again."

Just then, the guy who had taken care of the horses appeared in the open doorway. A little taller than Feltman, and a hell of a lot younger.

"Feltman, this here is Josh Cohen," De Brecco introduced. "Josh's one of my firewatchers. We thought you might like a little help getting acquainted with the town."

Feltman nodded, agreeing while he thought it over. Might be best. If it didn't complicate matters any. "Fair enough." He turned to Judd. "I want you out on the streets tonight. Get over to your boss an' tell him you need a posse of his men with you. Then get to haulin' in the rollers an' cut-throats. I want a full courthouse for the judge in the morning. An' no old drunks," he warned.

"That courthouse ready?" Feltman asked the Judge.

"Ready, but not as yet used," confirmed the Judge, who seemed happy that something, anything, appeared to be happening at last. "We'll leave you to it then."

Hartford and De Brecco accepted their cue and all three men trooped outside, glad to be back into the fresh air.

"I suppose I'd better deputise you two." Judd rummaged in a drawer and pulled out a couple of grimy badges.

"You can stick those badges up your ass, Marshal." Feltman' smile and tone were dismissive. "Just do what Benson told you an' make sure you have a supply of hardcases for the Judge tomorrow. An' pay somebody to have this pig-pen cleaned up."

The younger man preceded Feltman outside, leaving Judd to suffer at the insults.

"What is it they call you? Josh"

"Yeah, Josh. You hungry?"

"I'd rather have a drink," replied Feltman. "What's this Mex place that gets up the Judge's nose?"

"Ramon's?"

"Yeah. Well, we'll start there."

With Josh leading the way, they followed Grant as it curved round to the left, finally merging with Lincoln to form a flattened apex at the most westerly part of town.

This segment of Limon consisted of a ramshackle arrangement of rough and ready shacks, thrown up in a flurry of enthusiasm and hope by repeated waves of new arrivals, telling themselves it was only temporary, just until they managed to secure a piece of the action. Most had never left, and those that did were quickly replaced by the scavenger element.

Josh pointed to a large, flat-roofed building of mudbrick and timber, submerged in a maze of shanty dwellings.

"That's Ramon's cathouse."

As they picked their way across the street, Feltman's nose twitched and he had the feeling that Judd would be at home here. Inside, though, the place had a better feel than he had expected and the smell deadened as the door closed behind them.

The bodega was near empty. For most people, sex was a night time activity. Even illicit sex. One drunk trying to hold himself up at the bar. Two girls, pretty enough to warrant a second look, sitting and chatting quietly at a table in the corner, engrossed in their gossip but sparing a professional assessing glance as the two men walked to the counter. Back against the outside wall, another gaggle of ladies were shaking the last of the sleep from their bodies, helped by a mixture of strong coffee and cheap booze.

An enormously fleshy woman waddled up the bar to serve them. Her eyes were clear, her face still beautiful, but it was impossible for either man not to be overawed by her size.

"They say they go to seed after they're past it," whispered Josh."

The woman's head came up quickly, combining a suspicious look at Josh with an inquiring, "Si?"

Josh pretended not to notice. "Tequila?" he asked Feltman.

"I'd rather have rotgut whisky than tequila," answered Feltman.

"And I'm sure you would rather have a good whisky than a bad one."

They both swivelled at the sound of the smooth voice behind them. He had a smooth smile as well. Ramon spoke quick Spanish to la moza behind the bar and turned back to his guests. With his charmingly solicitous attitude, you were made to feel that you were a guest rather than a customer. And that impression would probably hold until you got his bill.

"You are Senor Feltman. But you," he smiled at Josh, "I do not know"

"That's just great," complained Josh. "He's been in town less than a day. An' it's me you don't know."

Ramon made an apologetic gesture and said, "Come, let us sit and discuss the honour your presence brings me.'

They picked up their drinks and waded their way through the heavy sarcasm to one of the roughly hewn bench tables in the almost empty whorehouse. Josh's fresh-faced cuteness elicited genuine, friendly smiles from the two pretties and Feltman thought that his beaming grin was as wistful as it was embarrassed.. He sympathised. But maybe the youngster was just being polite. He took a sip of the generous whisky. It was good.

He said to Ramon, "If you were expecting us to call, then you know what about."

"The whole town knows what about," Ramon replied easily. "The word is out that you are Judge Perry's latest answer to evil and debauchery." The Mexican's eyes were mocking him now. "And everyone knows that all the evil in this town is contained within these walls."

"We're more interested in the deaths and beatings which take place just outside your walls."

Ramon shook his swarthy head. "Believe me, Senor Feltman, my influence stops at that door." He pointed at the door, just in case they got confused over which door he meant. "I have no control over what happens outside. This is a very tough neighbourhood, with a lot of desperate people. Anyway," he finished convincingly, "It wouldn't be good for business."

"Maybe that's true," Feltman acknowledged. "Maybe not. And maybe a change of ownership might help."

"Ha. Maybe. But we are not likely to find out," Ramon

met the unsubtle threat, "are we, Senor Feltman?"

"Well, we'll give it a week or so." Feltman kept his voice friendly. He tossed back his whisky and stood up. "It may have settled down by then."

"I will try and keep an eye on it for you," said Ramon, helpfully.

Feltman nodded his thanks and walked out.

Josh was caught out by the shortness of the conversation and Feltman's abrupt exit. But Ramon's raised eyebrow and amused smile brought him to his feet. Still he hesitated. Because he thought Feltman had been a little careless. But backing out on his own would have been ridiculous, so, with the hairs on the back of his neck rigid and avoiding any eye contact with the girls, he followed Feltman out the door.

As Josh disappeared outside, the heavy curtains at the far end of the bar were pushed aside and two of Ramon's men emerged, holstering their weapons as they made their way back to the girls.

Ramon had followed his guests to the doorway where he stood, watching as the boy hurried to catch up with Perry's regulator. He remained there until Feltman and his young friend had vanished into the fading light before moving aside to usher in the first customers of the evening, the bonhomie of his business smile broad and welcoming.

His hosting duties over, Ramon left the bar by its third exit. A beaded curtain which opened on to a tight corridor with a door to the left giving access to his private quarters. If you progressed around the narrow passage it led you deep into the entrails of the bodega, passing the girls cribs, each small, functional and lockable, ideal for entertaining those of the customers that were interested. Most were, there were better places to drink.

Christina was kneeling up on the bed, waiting for him.

"What did they want?"

"What we thought they would want."

"What are you going to do," she asked, anxious.

Ramon looked down at her, luxuriating in her dark, sensual beauty. "I thought, perhaps, that we might continue with our late afternoon siesta?"

"You checkin' out the whores, deputy?" Feltman asked when Josh caught up.

"Naw, you took me by surprise is all." The young man was vehement. "Leavin' the way you did."

"Sure? Some pretty ladies in there."

"Yeah, I guess." Josh agreed. " Just ... anyways, you hungry yet?"

Feltman decided to leave it alone. "Yeah, I could do with somethin'. An' then bed. I need to sleep."

"There's a place back down on Main. Ma's. Cheapest in town. Good food."

"Hmmm. Why don't we try Brecco's restaurant?"

"Aw, c'mon. There's a nice little waitress in there." Josh mimed her shape with his hands. "She's some looker."

"You know her?" It was out before he could stop it.

"Sure I know her. Bedded her more than once."

That almost stopped Feltman. He missed half a stride but kept going. Was this shithead romancing or what? Jesus, hell and damn. He could feel the green bile rising to form angry words at his throat.

"Horrible experience, sleepin' with that bitch," Josh continued.

What?

"Too skinny to keep a man warm. Her feet were always freezin'."

Is this bold boy serious?

"Still," Josh went on, "when you're four years old, you

gotta sleep where your mama tells you."

Feltman stopped this time. "You craphead."

Josh laughed. "She's my sister."

Feltman laughed with him. Relief tinged with an element of anticipation.

"She reckons she was a little rude to you this mornin', an' that you might be cryin' your heart out in some dark corner. So she asked me to dry your eyes an' drag you along for some supper to make up for it."

"She didn't say that, asshole." Although, thinking back, she might have.

Feltman was relaxed, infused with a sense of well-being. They were sitting in a small, intimate room, out back above the restaurant, where the residual heat from the kitchen kept the place warm and cosy. Rachel and her brother had turned what was really the roof space into clean, comfortable accommodation for themselves.

"You should have seen this guy," Josh was saying, "he almost crapped his pants, Rach, when I said I was makin' it with you."

"Joshua! That's not funny."

"Then why are you laughing?"

"And don't call me Rach. I don't like it."

"Customers call you Rach. What's wrong with Rach?" Josh looked to Feltman to support his tease. "Rach has a nice sound to it, huh, Mike?"

"Yeah, I like it," said Feltman, giving it.

"Oh, do you Micky?"

Feltman held up a placating hand. He was not going to get on the wrong side of this argument. "What do you like being called?"

"How about my name. Family, and friends, should be respectful. My name is Rachel."

And so it went on. An evening that had begun with friendly, slightly reserved politeness developed via good food, coffee and sexual expectation into pleasant, unforced small talk until, eventually the question of how Rachel and Michael would get together again was resolved.

As a matter of fact, she knew a delightful spot upriver a little; she'd make up a basket, tomorrow, after the breakfast trade was over, and they'd make a picnic out of it. And no, Josh couldn't come.

It was after ten, when Feltman and Josh got back out on the street. It was jumping, but not too violently. Every place at every bar, faro table and poker game was taken, and every girl was rationed.

The meal and Rachel's company had revived Feltman. He was still dog-tired, but in a pleasant, fuzzy kind of way. He thought it well worth the effort to let Josh guide him round town. A good report could make all the difference.

As they moved through town, drifting in and out of the numerous watering-holes and gambling joints, their path twice crossed that of Judd's. The marshal seemed to be enjoying his renewed standing in Limon society. The fact that any obedience on the part of the town's citizens to his lawful commands was entirely due to the back-up presence of half a dozen of Benson's gunmen did not seem to diminish his delight in any way.

Coming out of the '*Coyote*', Josh pointed across Lincoln at the Oglala hotel. "Want to check it out?"

Feltman shook his head. "No point. They're not there."

"Clancy's there. The breeds head for home most nights. Cant' say I blame them," Josh added, wistfully.

"We'll leave it. Let's drop in on McGarvey's"

"You know what that is?" asked Josh, pointing again to the hotel, meaning the name.

"Yeah," Feltman said. "I know."

Done out of the lecture, they went the rest of the way to McGarvey's in silence.

You could not have heard an anvil drop as Feltman and Josh fought their way inside the saloon. McGarvey's was tiny and it was packed out. They shouldered their way to the bar and tried to shout up some drinks. After five minutes, three different barmen and much abuse, their valiant battle, against overwhelming odds, to hold on to a tiny, sacred patch of counter was rewarded when two shots of liberally watered-down whisky were dumped down in front of them.

At least, they could have safely assumed their shots were watered down. As it happened, they never got the chance to find out as one of McGarvey' big hands dropped casually down to cover both of the glasses and draw them back out of reach.

"What'd you want, Feltman?" It was a shout but it sounded like a whisper, drowned in the general clamour for alcohol.

"Those drinks'll do for a start, McGarvey." Feltman hollered back.

McGarvey shook his head and tried to inform Feltman that he had his reputation to think of.

"McGarv …" Feltman gave it up. It was hard to remain calm and shout at the same time. He had lost this one.

McGarvey dismissed them with a superior smile and moved off down the bar with their confiscated drinks. Josh turned to Feltman with a look that said 'Well?'

In answer, Feltman began to force his none too gentle way for the door. Outside, Josh repeated the question. "Well? What do we do now?"

We go and get some sleep. We wouldn't have won any battles in there tonight."

"Shouldn't we keep an eye on Judd?"

"All night? Let him earn some of that money Benson's paying him. I'll see you in the morning."

"I'm kinda used to nights since I've been workin' for Brec. Mind if I take this shift."

"No. You do that. It makes better sense anyway. But don't get involved. Just watch."

They parted on the corner of Stonewall and Feltman trudged up to his room in the Lady Anne. He managed to get his clothes off before he fell asleep.

Six

"Thinking of running out on us?"

Feltman grinned as he stuffed the neatly banded bills into the canvas money sacks which were being held open in turn by a very helpful teller. "I'll be around to pick up the rest."

Hartford signalled to the cashier that he was no longer required and the man moved away to supervise the dispensing of the more mundane services which Western & Central had to offer.

Hartford had a point to make. "You realise, Feltman, that Galbraith and Oh were only guaranteeing any shortfall in available funds? Most of those men gathered at Judge Perry's have contributed to your fee."

"So?"

"So, you work for us, Mr Feltman."

The 'Mr' was back.

"I know who I work for."

Hartford nodded, not entirely satisfied. "And you're sure I can't open a checking account for you?"

Feltman threw the last of the small sacks into his saddlebags and swung them over his left shoulder. "Take it easy, Hartford," he admonished. "I just don't like banks. No offence."

Feltman went outside and tied the bags securely on to

his waiting buckskin. Actually, Feltman was fairly comfortable in dealing with most banks, and it made him feel slightly foolish, knowing what he was about to do with his down payment.

As Hartford watched him ride off down the street, he contemplated having him followed, but thought better of it. You had to trust somebody. And, if the battle lines were a little obscure in this latest campaign, at least it appeared they had engaged the enemy in serious combat.

Logic outweighed trust in any case. Because, while having Feltman followed might tell them if he was running out on them, it would not stop him if he was. And, if he was not, well, there was no point in aggravating the situation.

Made sense. It didn't stop him worrying.

Rachel was standing in the street outside Ma's, waiting for him, stroking and talking softly to a cute little golden brown and white pony who was nuzzling in close.

"Words of love?"

Rachel turned her head at the sound of his voice. "Morning. Yes, they'd have to be, wouldn't they? Isn't he gorgeous?" she asked, not needing an answer.

So was she. Rachel had dressed for practical horse riding; a pair of brown corded pants, long leather boots and what looked like her brother's best shirt. Her short, black hair was shining and free, no hat. All of it subtly enhancing the fact that she was a very lovely young woman.

Feltman was glad he had taken the time to buy a new shirt, a pale blue that he fondly imagined matched his eyes.

Rachel gave her pony a last affectionate slap and jumped up behind the two wicker baskets tied in front of the saddle.

"We've got plenty of goodies here, Micky. Lead on, we head south out of town."

"Yes, Rach."

Feltman's buckskin, rested and frisky, towered above the little pinto as they rode side by side down Limon's main street. He felt, literally, ten feet tall; the hustle and bustle of the busy street flowing either side of them was separate, not intruding. He leaned over and down, to stroke the pony's short neck, bringing him closer to the scent of her. "Where'd you get him?"

"Oh," Rachel considered, "an admirer."

At Feltman's smile she continued, her gentle laugh delicious, "The wranglers come up from the Bar-L occasionally; bring in a bunch of horses for auction. I was making a fuss over him; couldn't believe anyone would sell such a beautiful animal. Anyway, my admirer, a very nice man, insisted on buying him for me. Such a beautiful present to give anyone."

Rachel stood in the stirrups and leaned forward to brush her nose gently between her pony's ears. Feltman took a breath at the shape of her. The effect she was having on Feltman was not lost on Rachel. Still with her ass in the air, she twisted her head and smiled innocently up at him. "His name's Lennie."

"The pony? Or the admirer?"

Rachel laughed.

"He must have been in love with you"

"He is."

They veered right as the main street narrowed into a slow curve beyond Maple, swinging round to split at the staging post at the edge of Limon. There had to be more than a couple of dozen horses in the corral out back, six of them being coaxed out to switch with the team that had just pulled in. A line of buggies waited to take the stage's passengers on to their final destination in town – those that could afford not to walk.

"Three coaches run all the time between here and Red

Rock Springs. If it's daylight, they're hauling." Rachel was proud of her town.

"Railway'll kill that, won't it?"

"Some, but there'll still be a stage."

They took the south-east fork out of town. When they had come right around the base of the eastern slopes, Feltman just had to pull up the buckskin, stopping to take in the panoramic scene laid out before him.

"Impressive, isn't it?"

Feltman nodded, drinking it all in. The trail stretched out in front of them for a half mile or so, more or less holding a line, until it reached and forded a meandering river. On the far side it changed direction, swinging away through the bottom lands to skirt a huge purple-black spur of the Rocky Mountains which cut deep into the southern horizon.

The view alone gave cause to pause. But it was the tents, hundreds of them, which had forced Feltman to rein in. On and on they stretched, either side of the trail, spreading their regimented lines of uniform shape and size, supplemented here and there by a covered wagon or a timber shack, showing grey against the brown and green of the trampled prairie grasses, until they petered out against the barrier of the tree-lined river bank.

Beyond the tents, to the south, carpenters and labourers could be seen working on Limon's new railhead, roofing over the associated buildings and fencing off the cattle stockyards. The sharp sound of their hammerings carried clearly over the faint but deeper and more powerful throb of the steam pumps at the mine, coming from some invisible location behind them, lost in the slopes of the western peak.

Striking out from the railhead, grading crews were busy paving the way for the laying of the final section of timber ties, their route already marked by the telegraph poles which disappeared round the far side of the butte heading for the terminus at the smelter.

"And there's more," said Rachel, pointing south. "They're putting in sewer pipes, taking it to the river, about two miles beyond the railway. There's hundreds of men down there."

"That'll be sweet for the next town down river."

Rachel laughed at the thought. "Not actually the river. What's another word for swamp?" Rachel thought and then answered her own question. "Reed beds. It comes out at the reed beds this side of the river. Supposed to filter out the worst of it."

"How'd you come to know so much?"

"I'll get you an apron." Rachel was pleased with the compliment. "Then you'll know as much as me."

She nudged her pony forward and presently turned off the trail, leading the way diagonally through the camp, which was now showing signs of being half alive, making its gentle way through the morning.

The odd card game was in lazy progress outside the open flaps of some tents and, here and there, a bit of dubious cooking was being attempted, but mostly those on the night rota were relaxing, resting their weary bones in the sun, harnessing energy for another shift.

And some were trying to get their ration of serious sleep, as attested by the reaction elicited when Lennie and the Buckskin engaged in some loud, competitive, and frankly strange, whinnying in the direction of what must have been a particularly alluring, hobbled mare.

A plea to 'keep that damn horse quiet' was the politest of the requests emanating from a canvass dormitory still faintly emblazoned with the battle flag of the republic.

Rachel laughed. "Must be the night shift."

"Where the hell did they get all these tents?"

"Mine supplied them, mostly. They're ex-confederate army," she added, needlessly. "There was an army sergeant here a few weeks back, McVey. I heard him joshing with some of the miners over breakfast. He was threatening to lead a cavalry charge on their 'Reb' camp and wipe it out."

Rachel's laughter was infectious and Feltman had no trouble joining in, despite disputing whether the sergeant's sense of humour actually merited their appreciation.

Now they were passing out of the bachelor's quarters and into the section set aside for families. Here the tents were much larger, though there were a lot less of them. Up ahead, one of the wives was tending her cooking over an open fire, her three small children dangling around her as if attached by invisible strings.

The woman was calculating their approach with care. For the subtle complexities of the camp women's relationship with the townsfolk meant that her 'good morning' would have to be just right.

There could be no escaping the plain fact that she was bringing up her family in a tent. Neither the temporary nature of the situation nor the fact that they had left perfectly respectable accommodation back in St. Joseph would do anything to alter her present lowly position on Limon's social register.

But this tent was her home. And she would allow no lack of pride in it to show in any contact with the townsfolk. She must not appear to be waiting on them. Just a quick, friendly 'Good morning' as they passed by.

She fussed over her cooking, then turned abruptly, reaching into the tent on some imaginary chore. Her children, clinging to her skirts were swung in an arc and dragged along behind. Inside the tent, the woman finally selected a thick, wooden spoon and turned back quickly to a stew that needed no tending as it simmered enticingly in the pot above the fire.

This time, the smallest of her children lost her fragile grip of the hanging skirts and was bowled over, crying.

The mother bent down to gather up her child, hugging her, soothing her, quietening her, all thoughts of impressing the passing townspeople immediately forgotten, so that when the morning greetings were exchanged, they were as pleasant and natural as she could have wished.

As Feltman and Rachel left the encampment, they came to an area criss-crossed with wheel markings and dotted with the remains of burnt out fires.

"Wagon trains? They still coming?"

Rachel nodded. "It's a handy stop if they're making for the Sweetwater valley; gets them a head start for Oregon. They don't stay long. Well, they don't stay long if they're not staying."

Rachel giggled at her own verbal clumsiness. Only it didn't quite come out like a little girl giggle and Feltman suddenly found it necessary to shift in the saddle. This girl would have him demented. It had been a while since he had felt like this. Not just randy. Overwhelming desire. And not for just any woman. This woman.

"And that," Rachel continued with the guided tour, pointing to some newly dug foundations forming the outline of what was going to be a moderately large building. "Will be a church soon. Some of the camp wives have sent for a priest. He's supposed to arrive with the first train."

"Didn't see signs of a church back in town. No pastors in Limon?" Feltman knew enough to know that the Catholics would not be allowed to dominate the path to God. No matter how superior their numbers were. Even then, he had no real interest in the response. But he liked to hear her talk.

"Uh-uh. There's a couple of lay preachers, but they're usually too drunk to say much. I heard the high-ups are arguing over the location of their church, something grand and central. Oh, and there is …."

"What?"

"I was going to say… someone like you. I don't mean he looks like you. Or is even like you. I just meant he's, you know …" Rachel let her glance skim over the .44 in his holster. Limon was not the place to wander about unarmed, not even, or perhaps especially, on a picnic with a beautiful woman.

Feltman was amused. "A gunman?"

"Ooooh, sorry. I didn't mean to compare you. I was just trying to describe him." Rachel was contrite. "He's a righteous gunman with a dog collar. And he's nasty. And he has a bodyguard; who is definitely a gunslinger. And they claim to be pious. You know, spreading the word of the lord. And happy to shoot anyone who challenges them."

"A pair of chisellers? Playing the lord's cards?"

"Something like that."

"C'mon," Feltman smiled, anxious to show he took no offence, "Let's see what Lennie can do." He let the reins slacken another inch and eased himself back in the saddle, which was all the encouragement his mount needed to launch himself at the open range.

"Can't!"

The buckskin reared up at the sudden change of instructions as Feltman pulled him to a dead halt. "Why?"

"Because, Michael, I've got beer in one of these baskets."

"Beer?"

"Yes, beer," Rachel answered patiently," allowing her

voice to hold that 'I'm talking to an idiot tone.'

"You do like beer, don't you, Michael?"

"Rachel," Feltman said with feeling, "you organise a great picnic."

With their horses at a walk, they followed the meanderings of the river upstream until the treeline on the banks expanded and merged with the forested slopes.

Presently, after another few minutes of Feltman dodging branches which his oblivious guide could happily ride under, Rachel signalled that they had arrived.

"Like it?" she asked, softly.

It was an idyllic spot. They had emerged into a sun-drenched glade adjacent to a series of rock pools. Through time, the rushing waters had cut avenues out of the layered rock and now the clear, sparkling liquid gushed and tumbled over and down through these deep, narrow passages until they exploded into an even deeper and wider pool.

There, the cascade was calmed; before picking up momentum again on the other side of the dark, steadied water, to spurt on, gouging further into the weird etchings of the weathered rock.

They relieved Lennie of his baskets and while Rachel carefully screwed the small clay urns which contained the beer into the gravel at the edge of the pool, Feltman lead their mounts back into the trees to tether them.

When he had loosely tied both sets of reins to a handy branch, he looked back. Rachel was out of sight, still lying flat at the pool edge. Quickly, he flipped open his saddlebags and lifted out the four canvas money sacks. He moved on past the horses, through a leafy thicket and up a small slope to get behind a large rock. Here, he pulled up what grass roots there were and scrabbled away at the sandy soil until he had enough depth to take all four of the sacks.

He dumped them in and swiftly covered them up, confident that no animal would bother to dig them out; they only smelled of money.

And with a bit of luck, they wouldn't be there long.

When he emerged again from the small clump of trees, Rachel was already standing up and looking over at him, puzzled. He let his hands drop to fumble with the buttons on his pants and planted what he hoped was an embarrassed smile on his face.

She laughed and dropped back out of sight. Feltman stayed long enough to unsaddle the horses and make sure they were able to graze before joining her at the pool.

"Feel better?"

Feltman smiled. "Must have been the sound of all that running water."

Rachel fished around one of the baskets and produced a couple of thick sandwiches, "Try one of these."

He flopped down beside her. Steak. Butter dripping from the freshly baked bread. It was delicious. "Hmm," so good he had to ask, in wonder, "you cook this?"

"God, I'll like to learn. I watch her but I still don't know how. That's Martha. Ma's cook."

"No wonder her ass is so big. I made food like this I'd pig out too."

"Rude. I'll have you know that woman used to be the most sought after courtesan in the whole of New Orleans. Men apparently paid her a fortune to get their hands on that big ass." Rachel giggled, "Though I don't suppose it was anything like as big then."

"You storytellin'?"

"No. Made so much money she didn't have to bother. Went travelling. Now, here's Ma's story." Rachel made it clear she couldn't vouch for every part of what was coming next. "Seems she made a rest stop in Limon when the town was just getting' going. Dropped into his restaurant, but the food was so bad she went straight into the kitchen and cooked herself something edible. An' she's never left."

Feltman laughed. "Now you are kiddin'. That's a campfire tale."

"I swear. She doesn't need the work. She says she does it because she's sorry for the old fool. She has one of those houses in the Oval, with a servant."

Rachel was laughing at Feltman's expression. "I know, but it's true. She does what she wants. Ma convinced himself she was in love with him, but she soon put him straight. Says she'd had enough men to last her another lifetime. And said if she ever did feel the need it certainly wouldn't be him."

"Jesus," was all Feltman could say.

"And there's more. Ma and Mr De Brecco almost came to blows over her."

"De Brecco? De Brecco's in love with her?

"Noo. Well, I don't think so. He's been trying to get her to come and cook for him in his hotel restaurant. Ma's says if he approaches her again, he'll skewer him with a pork belly iron."

Feltman wanted to stop laughing because he wanted to eat the rest of his sandwich. He wiped his mouth, feeling good, wanting to feel even better. "That beer be cool yet?"

"Give it a chance. There's cheese there as well."

When he had finished the last delicious morsel of bread and steak, Feltman asked. "So, how'd you come to be in Limon?" Mundane, but he liked to hear her talk; and he was interested.

Rachel did not answer immediately. The question seemed to cause her to withdraw into herself, pulling memories.

Eventually, as if there had been no pause, she said, "Oh,

111

the usual tale of heartache," trying to keep it light but unable to match it with her tone. "We lost our parents coming out here. Not here. We were very young, part of a wagon train heading through New Mexico." She turned to him, her smile was not sad exactly, just not happy. "I've no idea why we were there. In search of a better life, I guess. But we got hit, Apaches, Comancheros, never really did find out. Anyway, our parents were both killed. Just them. Our parents and a horse. Don't know why I remember the horse. Everyone else was fine."

The warmth of the morning sun could not compete with the chill that had enveloped them. Feltman silently cursed himself for not having the sense to avoid innocent sounding personal questions.

Rachel was still talking, almost to herself. "The wagon master was a very practical man. He auctioned off what was left of our belongings, gave it to the Franciscan friars in the next village and left us with them."

Even with the self-caution not to dig deeper, Feltman could not help himself. "Franciscan monks?"

Rachel laughed. A knowing laugh; coming out of it.

"I know. But they were very nice monks. And there was a convent attached. So I was homed there and Josh stayed at the Priory. But we saw each other every day, we were schooled with the village children."

Feltman risked it. "So, you're a nun?"

The laugh was fully natural now. "Well, I wouldn't have minded," she lied. "The nuns were very nice too."

"But now you're a very good catholic girl?"

"You know, they didn't even try. They told us we were Jewish – well, they told me, Josh was too young – but they didn't try to convert and they didn't treat us any different from the rest of the children."

"So, what, they kicked you out when you started givin'

them some sass?"

"I was a very good girl. The sass came later." Rachel laughed. " No, they must have thought about it a lot. I think the nuns would have been happy for me to stay and help, but I guess the Prior was genuinely worried about what was right for us. And, I was being eyed-up by some of the villagers as potential bride material. Respectfully, nothing nasty, but I really didn't want to go down that road."

"You ready now?"

Rachel was full of pretend shock. "Michael, you can't be proposing?"

Feltman was glad he had finished his sandwich. "I meant, if you found the right man." At least, that's what he thought he meant.

Rachel gave him a big, big smile. "Well, I'm always on the look-out." She was just loving this. "Anyway, the Prior gave us what the wagon master gave him. More, I think, and got us a berth with two families who were heading north. Tearful goodbyes, us, not them, too dignified for that; and, that was it. We left."

Another change, some of the pain was back.

"I'm sure they cried later."

"I hope so. Buckets. Alone in their little cells. Because I did. For days and days. I miss them."

Feltman wanted to touch her. Stroke her hair. Instead he stood. "I'll go get the beer."

They spent the next hour or so talking, and, much to Feltman's relief, laughing softly, allowing Rachel's memories to fade and dissipate into the warmly relaxed atmosphere as they munched their sandwiches and drank down the cool beer, until, presently, it was enough to lie back on the grass and soak up the sun.

But Rachel felt confident enough to tease. She rolled

and laid her head on Feltman's chest, allowing the tips of her fingers to slide between the buttons on his shirt, feeling the warmth of his skin.

"Mike," softly.

"Hmmm?"

"I'm going to walk round the pool. There's some gorgeous wild flowers I want to pick."

"Hmmm. Fine" He felt her leave him, but he was enjoying the drowsy luxury of the sun seeping through his eyelids too much to sit up and watch her go. He had forgotten it was possible to feel so relaxed.

It didn't show. And it had not shown throughout the whole of the morning session. Not even the tiniest facial muscle had deviated a fraction from the judicial solemnity of its frozen setting. And yet, everybody knew.

Judge Perry was enjoying himself.

For with each authoritative pounding of his gavel, with every sternly imposed fine, after each separate but totally similar expression of shock and disbelief from the confused souls who were led before him, his heart lifted.

So much so, that if this inaugural session of the Limon courthouse went on much longer, there was a very real danger that this rather important part of the Judge's anatomy would float away altogether and end up contemplating the proceedings from a higher plane, leaving an empty shell dispensing relative justice from the bench. No one would have noticed the difference.

Perhaps, if anyone had been close enough to penetrate the grey, twiggy brows of the Judge and had been able to discern the gleam of pleasure emitting from his eyes, even that would have been interpreted as a reprimanding glare, which, under the circumstances, was understandable.

This one was going to argue. The Judge was so sure of

his man that he raised the ornate gavel in symbolic anticipation. His heart lost another pound.

"Thirty!" It was not a question. "Ya can't fine a man that for takin' a drink, ya crazy, old man." The voice was one which was trying to surface from a drowning in alcoholic liquor. "Ah'll blow your ass out o' that high-backed chair if'n ya keep throwin' your shit at me."

The threat was well mouthed but lacked menace since the miscreant had had his weapon removed as a basic precaution.

Beside him, but carefully out of reach, Marshal Judd frowned his official disapproval at this resentful outburst and pondered whether he should make his feelings clear in a verbal manner. He decided against it.

The Judge merely dropped his gavel. "Fifty dollars."

The lunge at the bench was thwarted by the combined efforts of one of Benson's henchmen and Josh, who were both stationed there solely for that purpose.

Judd allowed his frown to deepen.

"And seven days."

At the back of the courtroom, behind the heads of that amazed and semi-stunned section of the populace who had managed to squeeze into the confines of the pristine brick building, Charles Benson unclamped his almost perfect teeth from the very fine unlit cigar which was jammed into the left hand side of his mouth and asked, "Is that one of ours?"

Both of the men who flanked him, nodded.

Since this communicated nothing to Benson who was staring straight ahead, totally absorbed in the continuing verbal battle which had already reached one hundred and twenty dollars and from which there could emerge only one winner and two losers, McCabe added, "Yeah."

"I thought you were going to make it clear to them that

115

all they were to do, was button up, look contrite and let Edgemount pay their fines?"

Benson kept his tone even, but his displeasure at the unnecessary scene being played out in front of them was plain, the reprimand obvious.

"You made it clear to me. I made it clear to Colby. And Colby made it clear to them." McCabe neatly deflected the censure. If Colby was going to replace Joe, he would damn well earn his keep.

The other man waited for the minute movement of Benson's head that would indicate that his employer was ready for his explanation. "They were told. Most of them were still drunk. None of them understood contrite. They were told again by Edgemount before they went up before the Judge. That one's a hothead. He doesn't work for you, as of now."

Benson nodded briefly, satisfied. Colby had not been in his camp for very long but he was already shaping up well. Joe's unfortunate demise had been a bit of a blow at the time but there was always some good to be found in any situation. Colby was cool and concise; he gave no sign of wilting under criticism; he would be a greater asset than Joe had ever been.

Benson watched as his former employer was hustled, still protesting out the side door. The one-sided negotiations had stopped at one hundred and fifty dollars and fourteen days. He caught Edgemount's eyes in the well of the courtroom. The lawyer signified his helplessness with an apologetic gesture.

Benson turned again to Colby. "What's the tally so far?"

"Includin' damages? About eight thirty, maybe forty."

The strong teeth penetrated a little deeper into the rapidly deteriorating cigar. "Emphasise to them that this was the one and only time. No more. Tell Edgemount not to waste my money on that idiot's fine. No. Screw that. Pay it. In fact, see if another twenty and an apology will get Perry to waive the jail sentence. I don't want that bum hangin' around; I don't want people reminded that I used to employ cretins. And get it through to him that if he ever wanders through here again, he'll end up as a permanent resident."

Benson left that transparent threat in his wake as he exited the courtroom, closely followed by Dave McCabe, whose job definition of a right hand man was to be confident that the left hand man would do the needful.

His confidence was not misplaced.

Feltman heard the splash. Rachel was in the water. He sat up, blinking his eyes open, waiting for her to surface.

He scrambled to his feet to watch her distorted form rise slowly from the sun-stabbed depths until she broke the surface, dead centre in the pool, laughing and shaking the water from her eyes.

Five seconds later he was shuddering as the coolness of the mountain water hit his own body. He twisted in the water, getting his bearings, then came up beyond her.

"That woke you up." Rachel was smiling at him, her eyes dancing.

He nodded his agreement, which is a stupid thing to do when your nose is only three inches above a hundred tons of water.

He choked a little and asked, "You see that hole in the rock down there? Leads through to the next pool."

Rachel yelled that she knew and indicated to Feltman that he should follow her down. He choked again as she raised herself in preparation for the dive. Then she was going down, beneath him and through the smooth-walled opening.

Feltman spluttered, gulped a deep breath and followed.

He was right behind her as she rose to the surface of the neighbouring pool, the sun glancing off her body in a thousand different ways, making her lithe contours shimmer in the refracted light.

Feltman reached out and touched her ankles. She allowed his hands to gently trace the delightful curves of her body as he rose up behind her, letting them linger on her waist while he fitted his body into her enticing shape. She leant back, resting lightly on his chest. They lay like that for a little time, treading water together.

Sensual or not, synchronised treading is not easy and Rachel decided to make a move before it got awkward.

"Mike."

"Yeah?"

"This is lovely." Rachel twisted round to try and kiss him and they both went under. They rose again, gagging and spluttering.

"Idiot!"

She made a face at him in answer, and then she was gone again, back through the hole. He followed her, lost sight of her and came up in the middle of the pool. Rachel was not there. He spun in the water. She was already scrambling out.

"Cheat!"

Feltman hauled himself out and ran naked round the edge. He dived at her as she was hopping around with one leg in her pants, spinning her round by the waist to bring her down in a cushioned fall as he rolled to get on top. Rachel shrieked and tried to squirm away and then they were kissing.

Their whole bodies were in that kiss; hers soft and sensual, his hard and urgent. They broke slowly, the wetness of their skin charged, prolonging the contact. He felt his body take over, his hand moving down to slide across her belly. But her hand was in the wrong place, stiffened against his shoulder, her eyes seeking out his.

"It's been a lovely day, Mike."

Reluctantly, he raised his eyes to meet her gaze. "Been a lovely day? Dismissal?" He tried to keep the frustration out of his voice. He liked this girl.

"Rachel shook her head, a little desperately, willing him to understand. "No, it's not like that, Mike. I'm not dismissing you. It's just that I don't think we should. I mean, I don't really want to. Not right now."

Feltman took his weight on his hands. "I'd better go and get some clothes on."

Rachel was waiting, fully clothed and not a little embarrassed, when he returned with the horses. They picked up a basket each and began to tie them on either side of Lennie's saddle. She looked across at Feltman. "You mad at me?"

"Let's say I'm sulking in disappointment."

Rachel ducked under her pony's neck. "I wasn't teasing. I'm afraid I was brought up to be a good little girl." And that was no lie. But she had definitely strayed off the path over the last year or so. And that was part of the problem. She did not want to be a stray.

She laid a gentle hand on his shirt front. "So what are you going to do about me?" She forced a smile to lighten the mood, worried that she had lost him altogether.

Feltman did not have to force his smile. He wanted her. And not just because he was randy. He reached out and swivelled her round, helping her on to her pony, though it was hardly necessary. "Good little girls shouldn't swim around naked in the river. Not even in front of a gentleman like me."

"And gentleman," Rachel stated with a certain amount

of dignity, "should not grope ladies' rear ends while pretending to help them mount their horses."

"I know who I'd like to mount."

"Mr Feltman! Really." Rachel glanced back as she reached the edge of the clearing. Slight regret gave her the confidence to tease. "Anyway, you had your chance. Maybe I was waiting for you to be a man."

"What? Why you little ...."

"Last one back to town's a ..." Whatever vile concoction Rachel had dreamed up was lost to distance and the pounding of Lennie's chunky hoofs.

Feltman smiled as he watched her duck low to miss the last of the branches, urging Lennie into a rarely attained gallop. He wasn't sure why, but he felt good. His horn wasn't even bothering him. And he'd beat her back to town. She'd be too polite to gallop through the camp.

Seven

Josh and Feltman were sitting a couple of doors down from the barber's shop on Grant, their feet up on empty packing cases, partly blocking the sidewalk as they relaxed and took in the comings and goings of the town. And watching Old Roving Eyes, parked in a similar position across the street, watching them.

"No point in getting' mad at him," Josh advised. "You're just his main bet for startin' any action'd be worth the re-tellin.'"

"Well, I'd rather he sneaked about an' peered round corners," answered Feltman. "It's the way the old bastard just sits there, waiting. Anyway, you were sayin'?"

"The looks on their faces? Yeah, it was funny. Judge Perry wasn't exactly laughin', but you could tell he was enjoyin' himself."

Josh paused, adjusting his crossed legs to bring back the circulation and to ease the cramp starting in his left foot. "Never seen Judd look so respectable; think he enjoyed it the most. Especially haullin' up Benson's men. Some o' them boys must have given him all shades o' shit over the months. An' the looks? Hell, their own partners givin' up the goods against'm."

Feltman was only half listening, concentrating on the main street intersection.

"It was Benson's cash that was payin' the fines though," continued Josh. "I wasn't countin', but it musta been near as damnit a grand."

Feltman smiled, appreciating that. "McCabe there?"

"Yeah, he was there. But it was a gunman called Colby who was callin' the shots. Seems Benson made him up to replace Joe."

Feltman was just about to ask Josh what the hell he was doing in the courthouse anyway, after putting in a night stint, when the sight of Angie and her buckboard crossing the intersection drove the thought from his mind. The breeds were right behind her, messing around, each trying to force the other's horse to give ground.

Josh nudged him. "There go those lucky breeds. Imagine goin' home to that every night."

Imagine. Feltman stood up, wondering how they managed to play house together without anybody dying. A man could not live under the same roof as Angie and not try for it. And jealous men don't mess around together like kids.

"Josh, start at the Mex's an' tour round the saloons an' halls. Don't worry about handlin' any trouble. Just have a beer an' keep your eyes an' ears open. I"ll be doin' the same comin' the other way."

Josh got slowly to his feet, easing the last of the cramped feeling out of his legs. "I may not be too welcome at Garve's."

The abruptness of Feltman's orders had changed the relaxed atmosphere between them, and there was a certain element of resentment in the younger man's statement.

"Then don't go in."

Feltman was prepared to leave it like that but Josh caught hold of his arm as he made to move down the sidewalk. "Hey," he protested, "why're you proddin' at me? I was just sayin'. I ain't afraid to go in. I just reckoned you maybe had somethin' planned, didn't want to louse it up."

Feltman had been spun round to face the full force of the rebuke and now he held up his hands. "All right. I know why you said it. But you maybe need to grow some thicker hide."

He eased his arm out of Josh's slackening grip, watching the anger die in the young deputy's face. "You're right. I do have somethin' in the pot for him. And if I'm careful about how I talk to you, I might just live long enough to cook it."

Josh could not stop the crimson flush from spreading over his face at the heavy sarcasm, but he bit back. "Now who's got thin skin?"

This could get serious. For god's sake, don't get into a brawl with her brother. "Call it a draw?"

"I guess."

Feltman looked pointedly at the badge on the young man's chest. "You know that makes you a target?"

"It just felt wrong, walkin' into places like I was a deputy but not havin' the badge."

"Yeah, well, your choice." Feltman held back on the advice to learn to walk into a place like he wasn't a deputy. "But be careful. You meet trouble, get a hold of Judd and that Benson crew he's got trailin' around with him."

They walked together down to Stonewall and parted there, the atmosphere between them still a little brittle. Josh continued on down Grant, while Feltman headed for Lincoln, glancing back at Old Roving Eyes, who had struggled to his feet and was stomping along behind.

By the time Feltman had crossed over Lincoln and disappeared into Johnston's stables, the old man had barely turned the corner into Stonewall, his failing eyesight ensuring that he lost his prey in the crowded street.

Feltman's buckskin was already rested and rigged up; his Springfield, minus its protective cover, comfortable and secure in its scabbard, waiting on him.

One thing about that mean little shit Johnston, he kept a good eye out. Nobody was stealing anything from his customers.

Feltman exited Johnston's via Maple, swinging back round on to Main, just in case Old Roving Eyes was taking his vigil a mite too seriously.

The traffic going north out of town was light, and by the time Feltman had come across the place where Angie habitually swung the buckboard off the main trail, heading north east, he was reasonably sure that there was no one between him and his quarry.

He kept a good quarter mile behind them and, rough though the terrain was, trailing was not necessary, the impressions of the buckboard's many journeys over this route plainly visible. In any case, he could hear them.

They went steadily on, getting deeper and deeper into the rugged White River country, the laughing cries of Horse and Red drifting back on the light breeze to Feltman, the half-breed brothers vying with one another in their attempts to make Angie laugh, oblivious of the pursuit.

The wide meanderings of the trail were so slow and lazy that only the gradual change in the attitude of the sun indicated that it was happening at all.

Presently, Feltman realised their shouts were getting louder and that he could hear them more frequently. They had stopped. He closed the distance between them carefully, not wanting to stumble in on top of them, until he could hear the breeds charging about on their mounts, still out of sight around the next bend in the trail.

Feltman looked about him. The ground on both sides

swept up and away from him, rocky and treacherously loose. Too noisy and steep to take the horse up and he could not risk going forward to the clump of bur oak on the bend to take a look.

Reluctantly, he pulled the buckskin tight to the side of the trail behind a clump of stunted juniper and dismounted. He tethered the reins loosely and made his way carefully up the rise to his left, making some noise but not enough to be heard.

He reached a line of sharp-edged boulders balanced on the ridge and used them for cover as he toiled up the incline, going for the height he needed to see over the tall stand of oak. He was suddenly exposed when he stepped into a gap left by one of the weathered rocks when gravity had taken it to join its ancestors at the bottom of the scree pile. He stepped carefully back, and hunkered down. He needn't have worried.

The laughing trio were completely engrossed in the brothers' shenanigans. The boys were having themselves a time. They were chasing a lively, stray longhorn while Angie offered laughing applause from her perch on the buckboard. Those breeds weren't no cowboys, that was for sure. They stood more chance of roping each other than of catching hold of that old bull. He was a wild one. He was matted, shaggy and mean, and even the obvious fact that he was winning the game had failed to improve his disposition any.

He avoided Red's latest attempt with contemptuous ease, turning on nothing to face the wild charge of the horseman, then swerving, propelling himself forward to have a lunge at Red's terrified mount as he thundered by, leaving the breed floundering, vainly trying to change his grip on his lariat to lasso something that was no longer there.

The old bull skidded to a halt, executed another perfect turn, and stood, front legs braced rigid into the dirt, nostrils flaring, staring evilly at the buckboard team, waiting for the next round.

Angie was knotting herself, and this spurred the boys into a final, joint effort. They came forward steadily, until they were both less than twenty feet from the imperious old bull. Simultaneously, they urged their reluctant mounts into charging runs, lariats held open and wide, and then flashing out over their cornered prey.

It was pathetic.

The old bull simply went straight at the buckboard team, reared them up, cut around them and headed off into the trees, tired of the game and its lack of competition.

It was too much for Angie. She collapsed full length across the buckboard seat, squealing and holding her side in helpless agony. Red had actually managed to lasso Horse's horse and was now doubled up in his saddle, still holding the end of the rope, creasing himself.

Feltman had to laugh. Softly.

"Shit." Horse was laughing too, even as he brought his boot up and sent Red crashing to the ground. "I'm gonna see the hide off that old cow if it takes me all night." He threw the rope off his mount and wheeled the animal into the brush, screaming threats.

Feltman watched as Red slowly got back into the saddle, coiling his rope and gradually allowing the last of the merriment to drain away as he discussed with Angie the odds on them sitting down to a platter of tough old bull that night.

Feltman gave them a full five minutes before he slithered back down to his buckskin. It was another ten before he came to the low lying hill that seemed to squat across the trail. He stopped instinctively. This had to be home.

The trail moved along the base of the hill to the north east and he could vaguely hear the buckboard still. He waited until the faint, oil-starved squealing ceased, then he moved off the trail to the north west, then north, following the broken L-shape of the hill until he came to a small stream which was now barely more than a dampness that the spring rains had gouged out of the slope.

He stopped there and dismounted. He removed the rifle and laid it gently against the stump of a long dead and withered tree. Then he stood and contemplated his horse for a moment. The buckskin had been saddled up and waiting for most of the afternoon. Yet he could not allow him to graze free. He compromised by unsaddling the big, wise looking animal, giving him a brisk rub down with the saddle blanket and allowing him almost ten minutes without the weighty feeling of the leather on his back.

Then, re-saddled and waiting once more, he left the buckskin tethered securely to a patch of scrub brush and slowly, and as quietly as he could, began to make his way up the steep slope, using the stock of his Springfield as an old man might use a cane.

It was tough going, but it did not take him long. It was not much of a hill. There was virtually no plateau at the top, just a rounding. So he took his rest on his side of the slope, waiting until his legs had lost their slight tremble before crawling forward and looking down.

The hill was slightly steeper on this side. He let his gaze wander down over the brush and sparse wild grasses and the occasional stunted tree desperately clinging to the rocky soil. Something over eighty yards down to the base and from there, another fifty yards back, bathed in the late afternoon sunshine, sat the Breeds' ranch house.

Whitewashed, neat enough, but, with the exception of an open-sided barn used for stabling, the outhouses looked disused. The buckboard team and Red's horse had been left outside, tied to the porch rail, and he could hear the chatter coming from the house. He let his eyes drift away to the right, back along the trail to where they had skirted their side of the hill.

Clear line of sight. He shifted his gaze back to the small ranch-house. Something over one hundred and twenty yards as a bullet would fly. Too far. Well, too far to be sure. Besides, he had to get off the skyline. Feltman eased himself forward and, headfirst, began to crawl very carefully down the hard, uneven slope.

He almost missed it. He was already beyond it before he caught sight of it out of the corner of his eye. A dark, weathered depression underneath a foot thick overhang of rock. It would be ideal.

Crab-like, he moved across into the cover of a huge flowering bush and got into a crouch. Holding this stooped position, he made the yard or so back up the slope to the overhang.

The small indent in the hillside was only five feet wide and less than three deep. Even so, it was all that he needed and he gratefully stretched out on the moist black earth, rubbing and flexing his elbows until they came back to normal.

His view was clear over the hundreds of tiny yellow petals which seemed to explode out of the grey deadness of the gorse. Something under a hundred yards to the porch. In bright, clear sunlight. Not too difficult.

Feltman lay along the length of the hollow on his belly, jamming his splayed feet into the far face. This put his shoulders tight against the rooted soil of the other side wall. Still on his belly, he twisted round until he was facing outward and began to move his hips into the soft earth, searching for a comfortable position. He settled for one he could tolerate.

He reached down with his left hand and managed, with a struggle, to undo his gunbelt which he dropped in the dirt beside him. He adjusted his body slightly and then he was satisfied. It was as good as he would get.

He took his hat off, threw it on top of the colt and picked up the Springfield, easing it into his left shoulder. Feltman was not left-handed. Just left-eyed. Left-eyed and slightly short sighted. And his Springfield wasn't a Springfield. Not anymore. The rifle had been bastardised and rebuilt by a genius German armourer. With the addition of the very latest Mauser bolt action, it was tooled to perfection to suit his shooting style. But it looked like a carbine. Not out of place in any cowboy's scabbard. Until you pulled it out.

Good for five hundred yards, even with the short barrel, Emmett had insisted. 'Well,' with a smile, he had clarified, 'in the right hands.'

Anything over two hundred and Feltman didn't bother.

He put the rifle down again as the door of the porch opened and Red emerged, minus his shirt, to tend to the horses. Angie followed him out into the sun, squinting back along the trail, her hand over her eyes.

Feltman reached into his shirt pocket and pulled out a small, soft leather case which contained a pair of metal-rimmed eye-glasses. He slipped them on, bringing Angie and the porch into sharp, lovely focus.

He reached again for the rifle and settled it back into his shoulder. With his right eye closed, he lined up the sights, the curves of the buckhorn cupping Angie's breasts; the pinhead resting between them. He opened both eyes wide and took a firmer grip of the rifle, easing the safety off and dropping the pinhead lower, well down and central between her legs.

Again he closed his right eye and began to gather in the slack on the trigger. And gently now.

And gently.

And squeeze and …….click.

Angie moved out of the sights and he relaxed, letting the tension drain away. He was happy enough with that. He had accommodated her slight movements and the sight had barely wavered. The recoil would have brought the bullet up and into the chest area.

Feltman watched as she said something to Red before they both disappeared back into the house.

"Yeah, Angie," he muttered his agreement, "where the hell is he?"

Almost an hour. Feltman rolled off his back and peered for the umpteenth time at the ranch-house. The sun had swung well round to the west and was going down fast. Night might still be a fair way off but his position had already been overrun by cool, pointed shadows which, in places, reached out to touch the base of the hill.

He should have stuck to a recce. But he was here now. How long had he got? Quarter of an hour? Certainly less than half an hour before the lengthening shadows finally engulfed the whole ranch area, making his task impossible.

Resigned, Feltman put his eyeglasses back on and picking up the first of the five .45-70 shells which he had laid out neatly on their small square of canvas, he fed it into the Springfield. Next, he checked out the soft soil of the wall behind him, prodding for stones or anything that might cause a ricochet. Nothing.

So he moved his hat and took his .44 from his holster with his left hand, holding the muzzle about an inch from the back wall. Then he turned away, burying his head in his free arm, covering his ears as best he could.

Even so, the loud, reverberating clap of the handgun

going off in that confined space made his head shake for two or three seconds. When he looked up, Red was already out, almost minus his pants this time, but with a gun in his right hand, peering suspiciously into the bushes at the foot of the hill and occasionally glancing along the trail.

It had been the right choice. To Red, the gunshot had been muffled. Loud enough to warrant investigation but not so loud as to keep him in the house while he was doing it.

Feltman sighted in on the doorway, dead centre on the opening, released the safety catch, and waited.

Slowly, Red made his way back, pausing occasionally for another careful look, until finally he stepped backwards up on to the porch. Feltman adjusted his sights on to the smooth, hairless belly while Red had a last look round.

And squeeze.

Red disappeared from the rifle sights as the bullet took him in the chest, slightly to the right of the breastbone, crashing him back and down against the wall under the small window to the right of the door.

Feltman did not waste a glance. Quickly he worked the action and fed in another shell.

Angie came out. He should have taken her then as she was framed in the doorway. But he hesitated, held by the sight of her. She was wearing Red's discarded shirt. That was all. He simply had to pause and let her drift through the sights as she knelt to examine Red. There would be nothing she could do for him.

Angie must have realised the position in which she had instinctively put herself, for she suddenly jerked upright, her front already smudged and dripping with Red's blood.

Feltman fired.

Too fast this time. He imagined, rather than saw, her surprise as the bullet took her in the shoulder, slamming her back against the open door.

Feltman cursed as he hurriedly slapped another shell into the Springfield and lined up again, forcing himself to take the extra second, gambling on the shock to hold her transfixed to the door. And easy. She was beginning to move. And gently this time.

And squeeze.

This one bounced her off the open door and into the house on her back. Her knees up, her lower legs protruding beyond the doorway. Angie would be quite dead. He was sure of that.

In the heavy silence that followed the fading echoes of the rifle shots, Feltman watched the shadows sneaking towards the ranch-house.

So where are you, Horse? Why aren't you galloping round that bend to the rescue?

Because he's behind you. That's why.

Feltman did not know when he knew or how. Or if the sweat that was lashing off his forehead and into his eyes and out again like tears had started before or after he knew. But he knew.

That crazy breed was behind him.

He felt the bile in his throat and he knew that he should do something but his brain would not work. So he lay there, motionless; for minutes that seemed like years, fighting the panic that was rising from the tangle in his stomach.

Until, finally, staying motionless was not enough to combat the wild, screaming urge to flee. If he did not do something soon, he would roll out of the hollow blasting away and he would die.

So he reached out and gently pulled the barrel of the rifle back under the overhang. A useless gesture. But now his mind was beginning to work, frantic for something that would give him hope.

He pushed the rifle out again. But this time almost in the middle of the hollow and settled it in as if he was taking up a new firing position. Then, gently, he turned over and slowly moved until his back was tight against the sidewall and the stock of the Springfield at right angles to his boots.

That was it. All he could do. If the breed came round the far side, he would get him. If he came over the top of the rifle, he would get him. Pointless to worry about the other ways.

A surge of panic flushed through him as he took in the empty holster but receded as he retrieved the colt from his hat. Not enough to completely steady his hand though. So he rested the barrel of the gun on his groin and waited.

He had a long wait. Crazy Horse was not in any hurry.

The futile chase after the old steer had taken Horse quite a way west of the ranch-house. When it became obvious, even to Horse, that the only way he was going to get a rope round that bull was to shoot it first, he gave up. But not before he gave that course of action due consideration.

However, at that point, perhaps sensing that the rules of the game were about to change, the wily old longhorn disappeared from sight altogether by charging down a draw and crashing into the dense woodland at the bottom.

So Horse had headed home without even having had the satisfaction of blowing his adversary's brains out.

The discovery of the buckskin had been a surprise but its significance immediately obvious. Leaving his own mount tethered out of sight, Horse had started, with some agility, up the slope, only to freeze at the muffled reverberations of the gunshot. Impossible to pinpoint the exact direction but definitely on the other side of the hill. He judged the ranch-house to be almost directly over the hill from where he was standing. He went straight on up.

The second shot, this time almost certainly a rifle, had come before he reached half-way. It did not interfere with his stride.

The third booming echo had come simultaneously with his headlong dive that had flattened his body on the brow of the hill. His assessment was immediate and cold. His brother was dead. Angie was about to die.

He tore his white man's eyes from his woman and scanned the shadows below, intent on the flash that would give him a focus for revenge. He did not see Angie die.

About twenty yards down, a little to the right. Not a flash so much as a change in the air. He had to fight off half his body, beating down the rising hate that would make him charge down the slope to cut and rip and stab at whoever had taken his brother and Angie from him.

Patience, stealth; and revenge would be his.

Feltman's movement of the Springfield was lost on Horse since the angle of his crawl down the slope prevented him from seeing the protruding rifle barrel, even if the fading light had allowed. However, with the bushwhacker's position indelibly etched in his mind, he moved unerringly on.

When he reached the beginning of the jutting slab of cold rock, Horse sat back on his haunches and cleared his mind. Carefully, he removed his handgun from his belt and laid it down to the side. It was an unnecessary hindrance and it was not the tool for the job.

Slowly, ever so slowly, he inched out, a foot of solid granite separating him from his quarry, removing any small stones from his path, meticulously pulling them to the side until his knees were less than six inches from the edge of the overhang.

Silently he withdrew his wickedly bladed hunting knife. Crazy Horse raised the knife until it was just under his chin and felt for the rock edge with his left hand. He steadied himself for a moment then eased back and gathered the battle yell in his throat.

Committed now, he launched himself forward, screaming out his hatred as he whipped out and down.

Unbelievably, Feltman missed.

The roar of the .44 merged with Crazy Horse's wild yell as the breed's body jack-knifed in, his blade slicing through the air where Feltman's throat should have been, ripping out a groove across the leather of his boots and embedding itself in the black soil of the back wall.

The breed's body filled the hollow, yet, somehow, Feltman's bullet had found a space. With a sickening feeling of defeat, he watched Horse's hate-filled face twist towards him and even as he fired again he felt the simultaneous blow under his ribs.

And then he was being sick, bringing up all sorts of gunge over the breed's hair while he watched the blood spread thickly between them.

It was through a haze that Feltman saw the bound handle of the knife sticking out of the dirt wall. Only Horse's fist had come. He had left the knife in the wall.

Feltman would have laughed. But he would have choked. He was still not entirely sure whether he was alive or dead and it took him another minute to summon up the strength to heave the mess off his chest.

Finally, he made it and crawled out over what was left of Crazy Horse. His bladder screamed for relief but as he pushed himself upright and tried to undo his pants, he stumbled, going down on his face with his legs slewing round beneath him on the slope. He continued to fumble at his pants and urinated where he was, letting the surge of piss flow in a river between his legs while he puked feebly into the dirt.

He lay in that same position for a full five minutes. He doubted if he had an ounce of moisture left in his body. A light wind swirled along the shadows of the slope. Both refreshing and chilling, it raked his body into spasm, giving him the impetus to get up.

There was not much point in attempting to brush himself off so he headed back up the slope and got a hold of the breed's bloody carcase and began to drag it down the hill towards the ranch.

He only got ten yards down before he stopped and heaved the body off to the side where it slid another few feet.

Fuck it.

He made his way back up the slope again to retrieve his guns. His eye-glasses were in pieces, covered in blood and vomit. He scooped them up amid handfuls of dirt and threw them viciously at the flowering bush.

And that.

He did not know anyone that clever anyway.

Eight

The light-green one caught his eye. But there were also a couple of quiet blues which were subtle enough not to offend his dress sense. Feltman was down to his last shirt. Again. The one his back, the washed-out, murky grey.

The previous night he had been very cautious on re-entering town, anxious that neither his dishevelled appearance nor the stinking mixture of disgorged vomit and blood which still clung to his shirt would arouse any unwelcome comment.

He had made Johnston's without incident, apparently fitting right in with Limon's night-time revelry, and if the boy who had taken charge of his horse had noticed anything untoward in his appearance, he had kept it to himself.

The brightly lit reception area of the Lady Anne should have been his biggest test but on the way there he had passed more than one bloodied and battered face and so, in the end, he had just walked through the crowded lobby and on up to his room. The distasteful aftermath of a drunken brawl was not exactly an uncommon sight in Limon, though, hopefully, all that was about to change under Marshal Judd's revitalised regime.

So now he stood outside the garment store window on Stonewall with the early morning sun warming his back, contemplating his rather flattering reflection in the glass whilst luxuriating in the simple pleasure of choosing a shirt. He supposed he could have all three.

"Good morning, Mr Feltman."

He recognised the soft voice at once and was ready for the vision that presented itself when he turned around.

"Miss Perry," he greeted her. "And it's all the more beautiful for your presence."

Carrie was delighted. "Why, Mr Feltman. And to think there are people in this town who don't consider you to be a gentleman." She reached out and touched his sleeve. "You do need a new one."

"I know. I'm trying to find a colour to match my eyes."

Carrie laughed, then suddenly, mischievously, "I hear you like picnics?"

Christ. Straight out. "It's a nice way to relax."

"Yes. It's a while since I relaxed." Carrie let that hang for a moment. "Maybe you could escort me on my picnic? I'm sure my father would be glad to know that the town saviour was protecting me."

Feltman thought that perhaps his handsome image in the store window was more accurate than he had supposed. Now they were fighting over him. "I'm flattered, Miss Perry, but I'm afraid I'll have to earn some of that money the town's paying me. Another time, perhaps?"

Carrie took the refusal without flinching, deliberately holding her smile. "Please, don't be flattered. Rachel is a friend. I was teasing." She made to go but paused, "Though I have to say, if my father can scare you off, Mr Feltman, I really don't hold out much hope for the town." Carrie nodded politely as if the stinging barb she had just delivered was a mundane pleasantry and moved past him.

Regretfully, Feltman watched her go. Her body scent still lingered, filling his senses, enticing him to run and catch and apologise. Never mind he had nothing to apologise for. It had been an open, direct invitation. If accepted there would have been no disappointment. Now it was very unlikely there would be another time.

He considered that depressing thought while he watched her attractive behind bobbing smaller down the sidewalk. He had heard it said that when a woman suffered the experience she had, it either sent her cold as ice or as hot as hell.

He was on the verge of changing his mind and seeing just how hot hell could get when another 'Good morning' broke into his indecision. He knew that voice too.

"Mornin'." Feltman returned the greeting as he looked up at the young deputy who was sitting astride a big roan and was in the process of coaxing Feltman's buckskin in closer to the sidewalk. "We goin' somewhere, Josh?"

"You cheatin' on sis already?"

Feltman summoned up a patient expression and waited.

"A wagon train got in this morning."

"So?"

"So, one o' the Judge's pet theories is that half the trouble in this town is caused by the human garbage that falls off those trains an' which the rest of the settlers conveniently forget to pick back up."

"So we check them out?"

"Yup."

"I'm trying to buy a shirt," Feltman complained.

"Which one you tryin' to impress?"

"You're right. Let's go."

Feltman mounted up and they set a steady pace out of town, letting their horses pick their own way through the ruts as they negotiated the traffic.

"Any problems last night," Feltman asked?

Josh shook his head. "The Judge was in Brecco's place

139

when I got there. Bought me a drink. He's happy as hell at the change in town. Reckons you can feel it. Says everything seems more controlled."

He waited on a comment from Feltman, and, when none came, continued, "Well, he was praisin' you up anyway. But Mr Hartford didn't seem so happy."

He got something back this time. "How come?"

"Dunno. Might be worried about Benson still havin' the bulk of the bankin' business when things settle." Josh had been paying attention to the loose talk in the saloon.

"Maybe," was all that Feltman offered.

"I never saw much of you last night," Josh probed.

"I never saw any of you."

Both horses broke into an easy canter as they cleared the bustle of town and within minutes they were approaching the lead wagon of the sizeable train which had stopped in line on the far side of the miners' camp.

Most of the teams had been released to graze on the lush grasses by the river and the settlers were busy reorganising their loads to make room for fresh supplies.

Feltman scanned the teamsters for an intelligent face and settled on a thin, wiry guy who was lashing a water barrel on to the side of the third wagon down.

"We're lookin' for the wagon-master. He around?"

The man pulled the last knot tight and took his weight off the barrel. "Kindle? Na, he's in town, arguin' with the traders."

"About what?"

"About prices. What else?" The settler eyed Josh's badge. "What you boys want."

"How long does Kindle plan on stayin'?"?"

"Coupla days."

"Any of the families stayin' on?"

"Here?" The man shook his head. 'None o' the regular

train. Well, sayin' that, some pilgrim's lost his fiancée."

"Lost?"

"Run off. Guess she's in town somewhere."

"You ain't lookin' for her?" Josh was surprised.

"Well, folks reckon she's done herself a favour, you know?" He didn't seem fussed whether they knew or not. "An' we got a tagger we picked up a day past. Don't know what they're doin'."

"Which wagon's that," asked Josh.

"Cleery's. Right down the end. A four mule team."

They nodded their thanks and moved off down the line, Josh flashing the odd speculative smile at any female between the ages of fifteen and forty who looked like they might smile back.

"You on the make, deputy?"

"It's if any of them are, that's the point, Mike. You should see those stop-over dances they have. Some of these women have been known to stray, know what I mean?"

Feltman knew. But doubted it. He was kind. Let the young man have his fantasy.

Cleery's wagon was not anything like a settler's wagon. More like a medicine shop. Anywhere you looked – in the wagon, on the wagon, on the ground beside the wagon – there were bottles. All shapes, colours and sizes of bottles. Filled with green liquids, red liquids, any colour you liked liquids, even clear liquids.

The middle-aged man working amongst them looked the part of the drug peddler. From his grey suit which had once been respectable, to the dazzling, knotted cravat which supported a heavy grey-black stubble, to his quickly appraising salesman's eyes as he registered their interest.

"You Cleery?"

"I am, Sir. And you are the law. Or, at least, half of you is." A bright, well-pitched voice, accompanied by an

141

inquiring look that requested their half of the introductions.

"We hear you plan to stay." Feltman lied, indicating the profusion of bottles. "To peddle that?"

"Well, I certainly did not intend to pour it into the river." The modulated voice dropped easily into the sarcasm but came back repentant. "Forgive me, gentlemen. Yes, I did plan to stay for a few days to see if I could persuade any of your good people to invest in my medicines."

"You alone?"

"No. My daughter travels with me. And also, at the moment, young Mr Henderson."

"And what does he do?" All the questions were coming from Feltman.

"Well," Cleery shrugged his shoulders, "nothing, exactly."

"So why is he travelling with you?' asked Josh.

"He has come to rely on us, I suppose. He is a rather dependant type of person." Cleery waved his hands vaguely in an attempt to get his meaning across.

"You mean he's simple?"

"Now that's rather a harsh description ……" Cleery broke off and pointed beyond them. "You'll be able to judge for yourselves shortly."

They followed the line of his extended digit and fixed on the stocky little mule which was holding a determined trot as it closed the distance to the wagon, completely dwarfed by the long trailing legs of its rider. Only the girl's limbs were visible as she rode astride, her skirt hitched up to her waist, her arms wrapped around the young Mr Henderson.

"He got the job, Papa," the girl shouted, as she slid from the mule's back, all skirt and hair. "Starts tomorrow."

Feltman took in the big fellow as he dropped his left foot

the necessary two inches and stepped off the grateful mule. At least six-four, build to match. Only the vacant look on the face of the young giant as he smiled around him detracted from the magnificence of the specimen.

"Gentlemen, this is my daughter, Sammy, and Mr Henderson."

Not so much a girl. Definitely a woman. Samantha gave them a polite smile while Henderson gave them each a slow, almost formal, nod.

"These gentlemen have come to look us over, Sammy. To see if we are fit enough to mingle with their good people."

"And are we?"

"Naw, it's not like that," protested Josh, smiling at Cleery's daughter. "It's more like a courtesy call. My name's Josh," he added, hopefully.

"Where have you found work, Henderson?" Feltman broke into the deputy's flirt.

"At Mr. Van's," Samantha answered for him.

"The gunsmith," Josh filled in for Feltman's benefit.

"Yes. Cleaning and moving the heavier stuff. General help .... That sort of thing." Samantha was still talking for Henderson. Now she turned to her father. "There's a pitch just this side of town, Papa. It would be ideal for catching the trade."

"Fine, Sammy, fine. We'll move on up there directly." Cleery turned and looked up inquiringly at Feltman. "Would that be all right, gentlemen?"

"I would have thought you would have been better staying here, amongst the miners, especially if you've got anything in that lot that cures hangovers?"

"Your point is well made ..." again, the inquiring look which finally managed to convey to Feltman that Cleery would really prefer to know who he was talking to.

"Feltman."

"Mr Feltman, but, in fact, I have always found that remedies of this nature always seem more effective when a little effort has to be made to obtain them. Then, of course, there is also the added advantage of the respectability which a town site brings."

"You seem to know your business, Cleery." Feltman indicated to Josh that they had wasted enough of the morning and both men wheeled their mounts to head back to town. But not before Josh had flashed a final smile at Samantha.

"You were tryin' a bit hard, weren't you?" Feltman prodded Josh as soon as they were out of earshot.

Josh just shrugged.

"I mean, she's not exactly beautiful, is she?" Feltman pushed.

"No," Josh conceded.

"A little bit on the plump side, if a man had to be truthful."

"Maybe."

"In fact, old enough to ..."

"All right, all right," Josh surrendered.

Samantha flicked the long strand of light brown hair away from her face, removing the irritation from her contemplation of the backs of the departing riders.

In his digging at Josh, Feltman had been less than kind. Samantha was not slim, not a raving beauty, but her features were far from plain, her body curves were not uninteresting and it would be a very discerning man who passed her over if the offer came.

Now she turned to her father, her eyes sparkling. "*You seem to know your business, Mr Cleery,*" she mimicked, playfully picking up a bottle containing a vivid green liquid which the label proclaimed would surely cure your gout.

"Well, I hope you know it better than you know how to sell this stuff."

Cleery made a face and Samantha yelped as the young Mr Henderson slapped her ass. "Show more respect for your father."

Nine

The funeral parlour was a mess. There was not a coffin in the front display room which was not now trampled matchwood on the glass-strewn floor, while the rich linings from the more expensive offerings lay rumpled, damp and stinking of urine.

"If you think this is bad, you should see the back shop."

The broken glass crunched under Feltman's feet as he turned to face the weary-sounding, flabby bulk which he presumed belonged to Wilson, the undertaker. "You here when it happened?"

The fat man reached out a pudgy hand and picked up a fold of fouled cloth which he held at arm's length for a moment, making much out of regarding the wretched item with evident distaste before dropping it back in the corner.

He shook his head. Both in sorrow and in answer. "No. And I'm glad I wasn't."

The practised sadness of the undertaker's voice was a definite boon in these circumstances. Wilson appeared to be implying that actually watching the destruction of the craftsmanship of his employees would have been too much for the sensitivities of his soul.

"But if you're asking who did this, I can tell you that. It was a crowd out of McGarvey's. Five of them. Drunk as hell according to Russell."

"Russell?"

"The fellow I've just left at Doc Pardoe's," replied Wilson, glaring balefully through the shattered windows at the gathered faces of curious onlookers. "He's a mess too. Not that he didn't bring it on himself. It seems he stumbled into them in front of the shop here, and cleverly complained that they were making enough noise to wake the dead."

The undertaker shook his head once more, this time at Russell's stupidity. "So they put him through the window and then followed him in, just to see if he was right. They didn't stop until they had both the bodies laid out in the back room out of their coffins – well, they stopped short at the girl, probably what sobered them up - but they left the old man in some state. Let's hope we can get him tidied up before his relatives get here."

Wilson did a bereavement shuffle past Feltman and made his way through to the back parlour, anxious to help, confident that the quiet sincerity of his verbal encouragement would spur his assistants to even greater efforts.

Feltman had a last, depressing look round before pushing his way outside through what was left of the gawking crowd. He met Josh coming across the street, trying to dig the last of the sleep from his eyes. "I just heard. Anyone hurt?"

"They were already dead."

Feltman motioned the young deputy to follow him as he cut through the alley between Johnston's and the Oglala. Josh thought that Feltman could be a pain in the ass at times but went after him anyway and both men made a fast silence down Stonewall to the marshal's office on Grant where Feltman headed straight for the rife rack.

"At least the stink isn't so bad," he commented while he

examined what the rack had to offer. "You got a key for this?"

"Yeah." Josh pulled open one of the drawers in Judd's battered old desk, and after fishing around for a while, threw a small, black key to Feltman who released the padlock on the security chain and threaded off the Henry repeating rifle.

"So what's happening?"

"It was a squad out of McGarvey's," Feltman answered, thinking that was explanation enough. "Shells?"

Josh nodded and produced a box of .44 ammunition from another drawer. He reached over for the rifle and began to slide the shells into the loading gate.

Just then, the door opened and Judd came in. "You boys look as if you're about to start something. Need a hand?"

"No," was the short answer.

Feltman turned back to Josh. "Let me go in first. Wait until I reach him, or, if he's behind the bar, until I reach the bar. Then come in, go to your left and put your back against the wall. Loose off one shot, into the rafters, work the action and cover the room. If anyone is crazy enough to start anything, blast off in their direction until they stop."

"You goin' for Garve?" Josh paused in his calm, over-deliberate loading of the rifle. "We can't put this down to Garve."

"Can't we? He made his buck fillin' them with liquor. It's time McGarvey appreciated the responsibility that goes with earning that buck. We'll point it out to him and, hopefully, he'll point it out to them."

Josh was dubious, but he went back to the loading of the Henry. Feltman waited until he was finished then asked. "You ready?' And, at the deputy's nod, "Let's go."

Judd closed the door quietly behind them and mouthed 'bastard.'

149

As he walked stiffly along the sidewalk, mixed emotions swirled inside Josh's head, drawing momentum from the confused tumbling in his stomach. There would be people he could call friends drinking in McGarvey's right now and he might find himself shooting at them. But he wanted to be a lawman; could do a better job than Judd for sure. And this could be Rach's man he was siding with. Time to choose.

The ache in his wrists forced Josh to slacken his vice-like grip on the Henry. He glanced across at Feltman and was envious because the older man showed no signs of tension while he could feel his own breath coming faster and faster, competing with his heart. He took bigger breaths and held them for longer in an effort to calm himself down. But he could do nothing about the churning in his stomach. All too soon, they were there.

Feltman did not pause. It was early yet and while later there would be an impervious human barrier between the door and the bar, at the moment the assembled customers were no more than a mild hindrance to Feltman's progress towards McGarvey who was half-heartedly cleaning the ornate gantry underneath the cracked and dusty bar mirror which clung desperately to the back wall.

There was something wrong with Josh's eyes and his image of Feltman shoving his way to the bar was blurred. Nonetheless, he found himself moving through the batwings. The wall felt good.

But it did nothing to dispel the dream-like quality of the whole affair as he watched Feltman use the conveniently placed shoulders of two of McGarvey's clientele to hoist himself onto and over the bar-top, his handgun coming out as he caught the astonished saloon-keeper by the hair and hauled him round for his first lesson in community responsibility.

Josh fired. He must have. Because everybody was looking at him. Including the two guys who had moved quickly to help McGarvey and who now found themselves in the vulnerable position of half on, half off the bar-top. They could only gape as they slid back down to the floor.

There were plenty of handguns in evidence but all remained holstered since none could have been drawn with anything resembling speed and precision. But time enough to die. The place was full of thugs and hardcases but there was not a gunslinger amongst them.

Josh remembered to lower the rifle but forgot to work the action. It was dead quiet.

"You fucking crazy, Feltman?" At least, that is what McGarvey tried to say, but with two inches of gun barrel rammed into his mouth and the blood from a broken tooth running down the other four, the words came out as a slurred, angry mumble.

"Just listen," Feltman hissed, grinding his knee further into McGarvey's pelvis and forcing his left forearm into the hapless man's throat. "You're damn particular who you serve in this stinkin' pig-pen." The venom in Feltman's voice cut through the uneasy silence in the saloon. The words were not solely for McGarvey's benefit. This was for them all, and they knew it. "Well, you'll put five names to the top of your blacklist. The same five who turned an old man out his coffin."

Feltman waited, letting that sink in. "You hear me."

McGarvey spluttered something.

"Don't try an' talk, you stupid bastard. Nod your head if you understand."

McGarvey was not that stupid. He was not about to choke on another two inches of gun barrel. His eyes showed he understood everything. His eyes asked if Feltman understood.

151

Feltman stepped back and roughly extracted the gun-barrel from McGarvey's bloodied mouth. But, wisely, he still held it up threateningly to the saloon-keeper's quivering face. A face that was shaking in anger, not fear.

"You keep the bums that come in here under control, McGarvey, or you an' me are goin' to fall out." Feltman slid over the bar-top and put his gun away.

The atmosphere in the room relaxed as McGarvey's customers realised that the pointless fury could end without anybody dying.

But McGarvey had other ideas. He was over the counter, yelling and screaming obscenities as his big, grasping hands strained after Feltman's retreating back, but was grabbed and held by those regulars who were more mindful of the rifle in Josh's hands than of their host's need to smash Feltman to a pulp.

"You arrogant bastard, Feltman." McGarvey's voice screamed hate and frustration. "You're not fuckin' invincible. I'll have your balls for this."

Feltman paused at the door. "You keep your boys in line, McGarvey, an' you might get to kiss them."

Josh's heart almost stopped as every eye in the place bar two again turned in his direction after Feltman disappeared through the batwings. He wanted to be out and away from them but found he was loath to break contact with the wall. With an effort, he heaved himself off it and stumbled out backwards, almost falling down the two steps of the raised sidewalk as he hurried to catch up with Feltman.

Feeling the various grips on his body slackening, McGarvey angrily shook off the last of the restraining hands and spat blood in the general direction of the doorway.

He tensed again, ready to shake off the new paw on his shoulder, but relaxed when he recognised old Don's raspy voice. "Seems that boy don't take too kindly to bein' refused a drink, Garve."

The saloon-keeper nodded his agreement, all the while holding his eyes rigid on the swinging bats, as if trying to conjure Feltman back into his presence. But by the time he had turned to look down at the craggy old face beside him, the beginnings of a smile were working at the corners of his blood-drenched lips. "You think he might be holdin' a grudge, Don?"

"I reckon it's possible, Garve."

McGarvey's smile became more grotesque as it widened. "You want a drink?"

"That ain't a bad idear, Garve."

Josh thought it was a good idea as well.

"Where the hell do you think we were headin'?" Feltman's voice was tight and Josh was surprised at the grey pallor of his face. Christ! He hadn't been the only one shittin' himself. Josh didn't know if that made him feel better or worse. But since they had already reached the entrance to the Silver Hat, he didn't waste any more time thinking about it. He skirted around the table at which Hartford was already ensconced and headed straight for the bar, leaving Feltman to flop down beside the banker.

The Silver Hat was Hartford's slum den of choice. It was the most salubrious of the saloons at the scum end of Maple and the habitual venue for chats with De Brecco away from the Lady Anne.

Josh had just got back from the bar with the bottle and glasses when De Brecco strode in the door. He called over his shoulder for an extra glass and another beer.

De Brecco assumed Hartford had summoned Feltman and the young deputy. He pulled out a chair. "So, what do you make of it?" he asked of the table in general. "Steady, Josh," he added as he watched the young man slosh whisky into the tumblers and quickly down his own. "I didn't think it would affect you that badly?"

"What'd you think? I got nerves of steel?" Josh demanded.

De Brecco looked puzzled. "So, It's a bit unsettling but …. what are we talking about?"

"What are you talking about?" asked Feltman.

"The Breeds. What else?"

"They haven't heard," said Hartford, happy to contribute the obvious.

"What about the Breeds?" demanded Josh as he reached over for one of the beers the bartender was sliding onto the table.

"They were bushwhacked. Out at their place. Red got it cold. Seems Horse put up more of a fight. At any rate, he died a lot less tidy than Red did from what Clancy was saying."

"Bushwhacked. Christ …" Josh shook his head, much like an old man despairing of the world he now lived in. "Jesus, you just wouldn't reckon on that pair of scary bastards getting' it."

"How's their woman taking it?" asked Feltman.

De Brecco shifted in his chair. " Well … that's the sad part. Angie got it as well."

"What?" This was Hartford. "Dead?" The banker sat back in his chair at De Brecco's nod. "I've got to admit that I wasn't exactly upset when I heard those two degenerates were on their way to hell. But Angie? You sure, Brec?"

"Clancy himself brought the bodies in. I just finished talkin' to him."

There was silence as each man contemplated his drink and thought about Angie.

"I suppose she would have seen who did it," reasoned Hartford, "That's maybe why."

"I suppose," Feltman agreed quietly.

"Was she touched?" The adrenalin was still running through Josh and he spoke as the thought came, aided by alcoholic bravado. But that wasn't enough to counter the flush of embarrassment when the question escaped. Still, he wanted to know.

"Doesn't seem like it." If De Brecco thought anything of the macabre nature of the inquiry, he gave no sign of it. Maybe he had asked it himself. "Clancy reckons she was shot from a fair distance. Both her and Red."

Hartford turned to Feltman. "Do you plan to follow this up?"

Feltman took a slow sip of his beer and replaced the heavy glass on the table. "How?"

"I just wondered. You wouldn't be short of suspects."

"What about that gambler, Mallinor," ventured De Brecco. "Maybe it festered; got brave an' angry when he had time to mull it over."

"Thought you put him on the stage?"

"Yeah, just musin'. Didn't seem the type to discover his balls. Tell the truth, don't know anyone who would have the sand for it. An' Angie? Who would do that?"

"Could be Benson," suggested Feltman, "Tryin' to make some gains outta town."

"Nothin' to be gained. Cairns rented out that old Harmony place to Angie. Benson ain't getting that. Why would he want it?"

"Maybe he wants the Oglala?" said Hartford.

"Of course he wants the Oglala," De Brecco answered, scathingly. "He wants them all."

"If it wasn't for the woman," said Feltman, "I'd forget about it all together. As it is, there's not much we can do. We'll keep our ears open. Somebody might get around to boastin' how they fixed those Breeds."

"I hate to add to your troubles," De Brecco cut in, "but

..." He suddenly remembered the earlier confusion. "What were you talkin' about, Josh?"

"Just a little disturbance over at Wilson's, the undertakers," Feltman answered for him. "You were sayin'? Troubles?"

"Oh, that. Yeah, I saw the mess as I passed. Well, that's nothin' to what's goin' to happen later on tonight."

He had everyone's attention. "The miners are on the warpath. They're aimin' to march on Ramon's cathouse an' burn it out."

"You're joking?" Hartford really was not sure.

"Why?" asked Feltman, more to the point.

"Well, they reckon that it's a disgrace the way a place like that is tolerated in a decent town." Thee sets of eyebrows shot up as De Brecco continued deadpan. "So they intend to make Limon a community fit for their womenfolk to live in."

Hartford spluttered.

Josh was incredulous. "But most of those guys ain't even married," he said, stupidly.

"What's the real reason?" asked Feltman.

"I'm tellin' you," De Brecco protested, "that's their official storyline."

The three men waited patiently for the unofficial version.

"C'mon, Brec," Hartford maybe wasn't as patient as the other two.

"Well, the guy that's doin' all the proddin' an' makin' all the real noise is a miner called O'Sullivan. He ...."

"O'Sullivan?" interrupted Hartford. " That Irish son of a ... the same one?"

"Yeah, definitely the same."

"What's he been up to?" inquired Feltman.

"Everything. That cunning bastard ..." Hartford paused,

as surprised as anyone else at the curse, momentarily worried it seemed to be becoming a habit. "He's a supervisor. Had those miners so well organised they wouldn't go for a shit without his say-so. But more to the point, they wouldn't work either. Gave the investors a hell of a time when the mines first opened. Total disruption. Set right into everyone's profits. In the end it was cheaper to pay him off."

"Yeah, well now he's lookin' for somewhere to invest all that hard earned cash and Ramon's will do nicely."

"The miners ain't that stupid. They'll never go along with that."

"Listen, half the damn payroll from the mines ends up passin' through Ramon's greasy fingers," claimed De Brecco, jealousy and enthusiasm combining to make the exaggeration. "There's been more Irishmen worked over an' rolled outside that whorehouse than there are green flags deckin' out New York on Saint Patricks day. So there's a lot of scores to settle. And those that are wise to O'Sullivan don't care. They're not goin' to object if those Mexes an' their whores are replaced with a nice affable Irishman and his lovely colleens brought in fresh from the emerald isle. That's the kind of soft-hearted, gentile ladies these boys want out here. They think."

"Well, Hartford?" Feltman looked across at the banker, genuinely interested in how the man would view the situation. "Do we stop them? Or do we let them clean up the town a little?"

"No. No, we can't allow them to set fire to the place. The drunken bums might set the whole town alight. And I'm not so sure I like the idea of O'Sullivan getting his hands on that kind of action."

"Yeah, you're right," agreed Feltman. "And it'll give Benson a chance to show his good faith." He turned to De

Brecco, ignoring the puzzled frowns. "What time's this shindig set to start, Brec?"

"Christ, how should I know?" De Brecco shrugged. "Any time after dark." He glanced over his shoulder, peering out at the flimsy shadows of twilight. "An' it's getting' on for that now."

"You going to ask Benson to deal with O'Sullivan," Hartford just beat Josh to it.

"Well, Judd ain't goin' to deal with it. And I'm not going to face down a crowd of drunken miners on my own, am I? Benson will have to supply the men."

It seemed that every time Feltman came down the stairs of the Lady Anne there was a reception committee waiting for him. But, disturbing though the sight of three of Benson's henchmen undoubtedly was, they had been expected. His escort. And they were being monitored in turn by De Brecco's fire-watchers.

He was just organising himself to be polite when he caught a glimpse of Benson off to his left in the main bar. That was surprising. He had not expected the man to come to him.

One of the three peeled off and followed him through to the bar, the casual swinging of a sawn-off shotgun eliciting painful memories in Feltman's gut.

"Your boys seem nervous," greeted Feltman.

"They're paid to be."

Feltman looked round the saloon, taking in De Brecco and his worried expression at the far end of the bar. His bouncers were dotted around the place, on edge and all cradling scatterguns. If anyone was foolish enough to set things off, they'd all die.

There as a fair crowd in already but, significantly, there was an inordinate amount of elbow room on either side of

Benson's stance at the counter.

"It's not much of a place for a conversation."

"It's noisy enough to be private. Get on with it."

"I need at least ten of your boys tonight. Fifteen for choice."

"You plan on rustlin' some cattle?"

"I plan on preventing Ramon's place from bein' burned out."

Benson took the time for a swallow at his drink while he thought about that. "Who?"

"A bunch of miners. O'Sullivan."

"That little shit."

"You don't like him either? You an' Hartford have something in common."

"He cost me a lot of money. Yeah, and Hartford."

"So there's no love lost. It's too good an opportunity to miss. And it'll let the town see where you stand." Feltman looked pointedly at the empty space on the bar-top in front of him. "It also wouldn't do any harm to be seen buyin' a drink for the appointed defender of the righteous."

"Where I stand. Christ, if they don't know that by now." Benson made a gesture to the barman and called out to Feltman's escort who was standing five feet off, watching his charge intently. "Harvey, go an' get McCabe an' Colby."

The man hesitated just long enough for his employer to see how concerned he was about his safety before trotting off obediently.

"I practically picked up the town's tab on you, Feltman, at that court sitting yesterday, without buying you a drink as well."

Feltman laughed but he wasn't feeling joyful. McCabe would be a powder keg and he would be walking through that door any minute. He knew Benson was thinking he

159

could use the tension to his own advantage, but they'd all have to be careful McCabe's lust for vengeance didn't fuck everything up."

Feltman took another sip of his beer. He had time to get half way down it before the two men answered the summons. McCabe was in control of himself but the hate he had for Feltman was plain and he wasn't wasting any energy trying to hide it.

Benson gave them a quick rehash while Feltman finished his beer and sized up Colby. Joe McCabe's replacement according to the wind of rumour blowing through the town. He was half a head smaller than Feltman, slightly older, tanned, tough and competent. At least, that's how he looked; and Feltman didn't think he'd be wrong.

"We'll call it a dozen," Benson was saying. "Should be enough."

"Have them meet me outside Judd's office," Feltman intruded. "An' you better be quick."

"They'll meet you nowhere, Feltman." McCabe spat the words out, individually wrapped in ice. "They're our men. We'll handle it."

Yeah, thought Feltman, you'd like to handle me right out that upstairs window.

"C'mon, hero. You still ain't told us when all this action is supposed to start." McCabe was pushing, happy for it to start right there and then.

"Well, O'Sullivan did make a point of tellin' me, but It slipped my mind." Feltman also conveniently forgot that he had asked De Brecco the very same question.

Benson moved a fraction, just enough to put his shoulder between McCabe and a direct line to Feltman. "You goin' senile, Feltman? Get out of here."

Feltman was chagrined, since he'd been about to take his leave anyway, in search of better company. But, as he squeezed past the barely contained hulk of McCabe, he thought that maybe he shouldn't say anything.

Feltman moved down the length of the bar to join De Brecco who was looking past him, keeping a nervous eye on McCabe.

"You need to relax. He's not going to start anything here," Feltman reassured him.

"Yeah? You relax. I reckon if he manages to kill you, I'm next in line."

Feltman's smile was genuine. He picked up the whisky the barman had pushed to his elbow. "Here's to us not dyin'."

De Brecco's 'Amen' was accompanied by a stretching lean so he could see past Feltman. "They're leavin'."

They watched as Benson and his entourage left by the hotel exit. McCabe deliberately lingering over his drink to ensure he was last out, pushing himself off the bar to include them in a final sweep of the room. His version of subtlety.

"Thank christ." De Brecco offered his glass and Feltman met it with his own to produce a satisfying clink.

"Another?" De Brecco offered.

"No, I'll .." Feltman curtailed his polite refusal because Josh had stepped into the saloon and was walking across towards them. And he looked like he had something on his mind.

"Mike, there's somebody outside'd like to talk to you."

"Somebody?"

"Who?" asked De Brecco.

"It's Mr Barnes."

"Aaron?

"Yeah, he doesn't want to come in."

Feltman was wary. Josh wasn't nervous, more like troubled. "You know what he wants?"

"Yeah, but," Josh glanced across at the poker tables, "I

161

reckon it'd be best you see him outside."

Both Feltman and De Brecco followed the young man's fleeting look across the room and were none the wiser.

"I know Aaron some," said De Brecco. "He delivers sowbelly to the restaurant. Seems straight enough."

Feltman nodded, both to De Brecco for the reference and to Josh to lead the way. The young deputy turned left on the other side of the batwings and moved to the edge of the sidewalk.

"Mr Barnes, this is Mike Feltman."

Aaron Barnes was a short man, but lean and muscular due to thirty odd years of working as long as it took to get the job done. His eyes were clear, shining out of an open, honest face. He got right to it.

"I came to see you, because I'm not a criminal."

"All right."

"But tonight, when I return home, I'm going to get my rifle and kill two men."

That gave Feltman pause. He looked at Josh who had heard this tale. No guidance was offered.

"You want to tell me about it?" Feltman asked Mr Barnes.

"About two weeks ago, that fake preacher and his bodyguard got their claws into my neighbour's wife. They've moved into the house. They've taken everything; stripped them bare. And when those evil sons of bitches come back tonight I'm going to put a bullet in each of their black hearts."

They were blocking the sidewalk. Feltman touched Mr Barnes on the arm and they both moved close into the walls of the saloon between its two large front windows.

"I'll need a little more, Mr Barnes."

"He ain't no preacher. But he waves the good book about and calls on the lord. Sylvie went along to one of them so called prayer meetings. That pair had already been bumming their way through this town in in the lord's name for a couple weeks, taking collections, but people weren't turning out in the same numbers. Those vultures recognised the need in Sylvie right off. So she was a true godsend."

The pent up anger was evident in every sentence of the tale. This was a man who had taken all he was going to take on behalf of his friend and neighbour.

Feltman did not interrupt.

"They had the gall to tell her that, the heartless bastards. She had been sent by god to help the good preacher and his angel guardian root out all the evil in this town. Can you imagine that? An' Sylvie cryin' Hallelujah because she ain't right in the head. Never has been since they lost their boy."

"But your neighbour, the husband?"

"Frank can't do nothin'. He worshiped the ground she walked on. But that woman ain't there anymore. She's long gone. Man can't bear it. He works fourteen hours a day to keep them bastards in vittles an' drinkin' money. Sylvie gave over all their savings day one. Even gave that false prophet the married bed. If Sylvie still had anything of the woman about her, I reckon they'd be pirootin' with her in god's name. Probably convince her she was the virgin Mary. If Frank tries to throw them out Sylvie gets hysterical. Calls on the lord to help get the devil out of her husband because he knows not what he does. Man's at breakin' point. I think he might end Sylvie an' then himself."

Aaron stopped. Because if Feltman hadn't got the picture by now he was wastin' his breath.

"Mr Barnes," Feltman's tone was respectful, "I appreciate you comin' to us on behalf of your neighbour.

An' I'll deal with it. No need for you to pick up that rifle."

"You've misunderstood me, son." Barnes' tone was flat. "I'm sure grateful for that offer but I didn't come out here to get you to handle it. I came out here in case that gunfighter managed to put one in me an' I was in no condition to explain; so Frank wouldn't get the blame laid at his door when that gospel sharp an' his angel are lyin' dead in his yard come mornin'."

Barnes nodded at Feltman and moved past him to step off the sidewalk.

Feltman was loath to grab at the man so he pleaded, "Mr Barnes?"

Barnes stopped and waited for Feltman to say something relevant.

"Mr Barnes, I promise I'll deal with this. Right now. You have my word. You know where they're at?"

"Sure, right behind you at Brec's poker table. That agent o' the lord calls himself Jeremiah Caine. Don't know what name his angel shootist goes by."

"Then leave it with me. I'll get it done."

"No offense, son. That gospel muncher may be pretend but his gunslinger friend ain't just a showman. I'll still be picking up that rifle supposin' they get past you." Barnes looked straight into Feltman's eyes. "Pity none of our exalted leaders saw fit to take some action before now. But I swear this to you. One way t'other, those two evil shits are goin' to meet their devil this night."

Feltman let out a long slow breath as he and Josh watched Aaron Barnes walk off down the street. They turned when De Brecco pushed at the batwings to join them. All three stood a moment in a silence no one felt inclined to break. Finally, De Brecco said, "I guess Aaron's question was fair."

Feltman nodded his agreement. "Yeah. So how come

our pompous friend doesn't get all het up about this?"

De Brecco took a second. Josh was looking down, shuffling his feet, as if he was solely to blame for the town's lack of cojones.

"Don't rightly know, is the straight answer," De Brecco said. "Guess most folks get fearful when the lord's name is invoked by some fire an' brimstoner claimin' to be spreadin' the word. An' those who knew it was a crock o' shit, wouldn't likely say so; might get a visit from the angel o' death."

It was a fair answer. "You want to point this phony preacher out to me?"

All three men returned to the bar where De Brecco ordered them a round of beers. "You look over my shoulder at the table in the far corner, you can pick out this preacher. He's to the right of my dealer with a sizeable pile of winnings in front of him."

Feltman looked. All in black, including the hat. About forty, relaxed and confident. "No dog collar?"

"He removes it when he comes into this den of iniquity. Puts it back on when he leaves; after he's done showin' these sad souls the error of their ways by takin their hard earned dinero off them an' leavin' them dirt poor."

"Ain't that what you do?"

De Brecco laughed. "Yeah, I'm jealous."

Josh looked from one man to the other. He wasn't sure what he was learning here.

"An' that'd be his protector, leanin' against the piano?"

"Tall, light grey suit an' hat? Matching shooters under his coat? Yep. That's Felix Harbin, built himself a bit of a rep."

"You only take their guns if they're playin'?"

"Did I take yours?" De Brecco smiled. "If they sit down at a table, they have to peg their hardware, yeah."

165

"So, a lone player could get intimidated."

"Could do. But we can't go much further. If we banned all weapons on the premises, our trade would diminish considerable."

"How much is he up?" asked Feltman.

De Brecco called over the barman. "Chuck, send Pete over to relieve Rosco. An' ask Rosco to give me a minute."

They sipped their beers and watched as the dealers switched. Rosco wandered over. "You wanted a word?"

"Yeah, Rosco. That preacher, how much's he up?"

"Not as much as it looks. He started with a fair pile. Maybe coupla hundred. I guess he's about doubled his stake."

"He cheatin'?"

Rosco smiled. "Naw, I'd have spotted it. He's a decent player havin' a decent run is all." The dealer moved off, grateful for his early break.

De Brecco asked Feltman, "So what you got planned?"

"Hold off if he's still winning. Then maybe point out to Preacher Man and his chaperone that the good lord would surely appreciate some o' that cash goin' back to Frank and Sylvie for bed an' board."

So they waited. De Brecco wandered off occasionally to tend to business as the saloon filled up but always drifting back, curious, not wanting to miss out.

Eventually, when it became clear the Preacher's luck was static, his pile neither gaining nor losing much, he decided to call it a day.

He stood up, thanking his fellow players for their donations and retrieved his gunbelt from its peg behind the dealer. His guardian angel stretched himself off the piano, leaving a friendly pat for the enthusiastic musician, but no tip. Preacher and Protector exchanged satisfied grins and headed for the door.

Josh was out ahead of them, moving straight across the street to take up station on the opposite sidewalk.

Just look. Don't interfere.

Feltman followed them out.

"Gentlemen."

They stopped. And turned around slowly. Preacher Man was unruffled. "It's Mr Feltman, isn't it? What can we do for you, sir?"

Angel was more wary, confidant but scanning, looking for the danger, picking up Josh across the street.

"You forgot to put your collar on"

Momentarily disconcerted, Preacher Man recovered quick. He laughed a friendly laugh. "I only wear it when I'm serving the faithful. I find it makes those I wish to convert a little nervous."

"What about you, Mr Harbin? Them fancy pistols of yours make people nervous?"

Harbin wasn't nervous. He had assessed quickly. There was no other danger. Just Feltman. And now his eyes never left him. He didn't reply.

Preacher Man continued with the sermon. "You mustn't get the wrong idea, Mr Feltman." he said, producing a soft covered bible from his coat pocket. "Spreading this word can be a very dangerous business. Felix ensures the safety of the lord's messenger, so that I can walk the land without fear or favour to bring the joy of god to those wretched souls that chose to see the light."

"You a believer, Felix?"

No answer.

Now Preacher Man was getting a little ruffled. He had to fill the gap. "A convert, Mr Feltman. One who saw the light and now does god's good work."

"That right, Felix? You do god's work? He must be pleased with you. He gave you a few extra days."

Still no response. Still Preacher Man prattling. "I'm not sure we follow you Mr Feltman. We'd all like a few more days. Life is so short. That is why, with the good lord's help we can ....."

Feltman was hardly listening. And he certainly wasn't looking. His eyes were on Harbin. "That how it works, Felix? Jeremiah here distracts them with his righteous babbling while you gun them down?"

Harbin smiled. "Man likes an edge, Feltman."

He flipped back his coat to reveal the pearl handles in all their shining glory. His smile got colder. "Doesn't mean I need it."

Feltman was impressed. "Those pearls sure are pretty. A sight to behold. So, do you ..." he drew and shot Harbin in the chest, driving the shootist back against the saloon wall and turned and put a bullet in Preacher Man's gut. He didn't want him dead. Not just yet.

Feltman stepped over the fallen angel and put a second bullet in his head. He turned to Jeremiah, who was sprawled on his back across the step boards to the sidewalk. His hands were pressing the bible into his stomach, trying to stem the flow of blood pulsing from his body.

Feltman pushed the hand that held the bible higher up to cover Jeremiah's black heart. "This is a message from Frank."

Preacher Man's eyes were desperate in their pleading. But now he was lost for words. Feltman put the muzzle of the .44 against the good book and emptied the chambers.

Josh walked slowly across the street and just stood, staring. He didn't know what to say. De Brecco appeared from the batwings and said, "Fuck me."

Feltman reloaded his .44 and put it away.

"Do me a favour, Josh?"

"Yeah," Josh agreed quietly, "Sure."

"Strip all the cash off them an' see that Aaron gets it. He should be the one who gives it back to his neighbour. You should get a decent price from Van for the pearls. An' make sure that fat fuck of an undertaker gives these parasites the cheapest ticket to hell in his catalogue."

"What'll you be doin'?"

"I aim to see how McCabe handles O'Sullivan. See if I can learn something about diplomacy."

As it turned out, it was Colby who handled it. Feltman watched the whole of the proceedings from under the awning of a stinking one-roomed shack, while the occupants, an old whore and her pimp, wondered who the hell was camping out on what they called their porch.

But since there was no way they were going outside to ask and since business had been a bit slack of late, they decided to go to bed together. Which was something they had been meaning to do for a while but had never found the motivation.

None of Benson's men were visible. Feltman had watched them arrive in twos and threes and disappear into the shadows on both sides of the street and around Ramon's. So it was certain that none of the noisy rabble which were now weaving their way up the middle of the street knew of their existence.

About thirty of them. Feltman listened to the rich Irish brogue as he counted them off by the light of the two torches blazing at their head. Two torches amongst them; and they were only there to light the way. You couldn't fault O'Sullivan's business sense.

It was nice the way Colby did it. When the miners were just stomping into the area where his men were set and waiting, Colby stepped out into the light of their torches, hands hanging loose at his sides, and stopped right in their path.

His timing was dead right. The lack of aggression in his walk and stance and the fact that he was alone brought the mob to a halt, their chatter dying as they sized him up.

And then Colby did a strange thing. He took off his hat.

The miners, who had just about decided to move forward and trample all over him, settled back again, trying to work it out.

Colby held his hat in his hands, like he was being respectful. One of the men at the front of the mob moved forward to within a few feet of the solitary figure. Broader, shorter, squatter than Colby, his features blank due to the torches at his back.

"Well, bhoyo, is it a talk that yer wantin', or what?"

"Some would say it's always better talkin' than fightin', Mr O'Sullivan." The tone was respectful as well.

"Now there, I wid agree with ye. But, ye see, we've bin drinkin' up all night for this very fight, an' here ye are, standin' between us an' our little bit o' enjoyment. So, me boy, if ye wouldn't mind getting' yersel out o' the way…"

O'Sullivan's words slowed as he looked fixedly over Colby's left shoulder. Colby turned to follow his gaze, as did Feltman. Ramon had stepped outside the cantina on to the sidewalk and was now standing stock still, framed in the light slanting from the open doorway at his back.

It was not the noise which had brought him out; it was the sudden lack of it. But what also showed up in the shaft of smoky light coming from the bodega was the barrel of a rifle, extending out from some hidden hand in the darkness and which ended buried in Ramon's throat.

Soft, indistinct words were spoken and Ramon stepped carefully backwards away from the rifle, closing the door in front of him to shut out the light.

There were three or four seconds of nothing. No

movement, no talk.

Finally, O'Sullivan leaned his upper body confidentially towards Colby and asked, "Is there maybe somethin' yer not tellin' me, bhoyo, besides yer name I mean?"

"There is something, Mr O'Sullivan." On cue, the sound of the actions of a dozen rifles being worked chorused out of the darkness. "We really wouldn't like you to burn down Ramon's."

O'Sullivan straightened up. "Ye tell me that?"

Now the large round head was shaking in disbelief. "An' here wis us thinkin' we had the backin' o' the whole town. Ah well, we'll jist have to go back an' have another drink an' a think tae oursels." O'Sullivan gave Colby a friendly pat on the shoulder. "I'm obliged te ye, for puttin' me right."

And that was it. Off they went, back to their drinking as if all they had been doing was having a stroll around the block to get their second wind. But O'Sullivan would be doing more thinking than drinking. Of that, Feltman was sure.

He hung back until he had seen the last of Colby's men filter away. Benson's new left hand had managed the situation with aplomb. Efficient, very impressive. Mr Colby would stand a little watching.

It had been full dark when Feltman had taken up his discrete position under the awning. Now, as he stood and stretched, he realised that it had got darker still. Between the few remaining visible stars dense, swirling clouds were massing, having come in heavy-laden from the east. It looked like rain.

Ten

It was raining. The strangely comforting noise of the heavy drops of pure water smattering against the canvas mingled abrasively with the shrill sounds of argument coming from within the confines of the tent. Of the four shadows that the tilley lamp cast against the tent wall, two were large and moved constantly, two were small and kept very still.

The rain was getting heavier. But the argument raged even more heated and the lashings of the rains were relegated into background noise as the voices rose to screaming pitch in hurt and frustrated anger.

Abruptly, the verbal hammerings ceased and, for a moment, all that could be heard were the soft defeated sobs of a woman crying. Then the tent flap was thrown violently aside and a man emerged, stumbled, and ploughed away through the rapidly softening earth, churning it to mud behind him.

The woman followed. Bareheaded and wearing only a light summer dress, she was drenched in an instant. But, oblivious, she stood outside the tent, her bare feet sinking into the wet earth as she peered after the vague shape in the darkness that was her husband. And the mixture of love, anger and despair welled up inside her to make her cry out. "Con! Con, don't leave me. Not alone. Not now, Con."

The last shout of her husband's name was barely a whisper that left her lips. Her head came down and the tears fell freely as despair won the emotional battle.

In the next tent along, Mrs O'Neill resolutely closed the flap the scant inch she had had it open and went back to her knitting. It had been more than a struggle not to rush outside and throw her arms around the weeping woman. But Mrs O'Neill had seen a lot of suffering and misery in her time and it had made her wise. Or, if not wise, had given her an attitude towards life that was both sensible and caring. There was simply no point in interfering in other peoples' lives uninvited. But if they came knocking on your door, well, then you helped in any way you could.

Mrs O'Malley knocked on Mrs O'Neill's door some twenty minutes later.

"Why, Deary, come away in. Don't be standing out there getting a soaking."

"No. I won't Mrs O'Neill. I just …"

"Now in ye come," Mrs O'Neill commanded, taking Mrs O'Malley firmly by the arm and pulling her into the warmth of the dry, cosy tent. "I won't be holding a talk with someone who has the water dripping off her back."

But now Mrs O'Neill looked at Kate O'Malley with fond approval. Ye wouldn't think that the lass had been standing out in that rain, soaked to the skin and weeping fit to burst, not half an hour before.

Kate had changed her dress and her hair looked dry under her bonny headscarf and her wide waterproofed hat. With her heavy coat and stout shoes, she was a match for anything the skies would throw at her that night.

"I'll be glad to watch the little ones for ye."

"Oh, …" Kate O'Malley reached out a grateful hand to the older woman. "Mrs O'Neill, it's good o' ye. If you would just look in on them now and then and …"

"Hush now. Ye know I'll enjoy lookin' after the little darlin's. Will ye have a cup o' tea before ye go back out into that terrible rain?"

"No, I won't. Ye've done enough already and I have to go."

Mrs O'Neill did not press Mrs O'Malley to stay; not when the woman was going after her man.

"Mrs O'Neill, yer a dear, dear woman." And before Mrs O'Neill had time to recover from the affectionate embrace and the kiss on her cheek, her young neighbour was gone.

Contentedly, the old woman went back to her chair and her knitting. Give it five minutes and she'd go and have a look in on young Connor and Bridgit. Aye, it was fine the way things could work themselves out.

But her contentment would have changed to puzzlement had she seen the direction Mrs O'Malley took after leaving the tent. Mrs O'Neill had not spared a thought as to how Mrs O'Malley was going to get into town. For the rain would be nothing to a woman intent on fetching her husband.

But Kate O'Malley was not heading into town. Instead, she was making her way in the completely opposite direction, moving steadily back through the lines of dripping tents, carefully avoiding their stay ropes and skirting round the wide puddles, made deeper by the shedding water.

With the encampment behind her, she pressed doggedly on, squelching across the quarter mile of open grassland to find herself standing on the tree-lined bank, contemplating the fast flowing river, which was now running in spate, feeding on the heavy rains.

The riverbank overhung where Kate stood and she looked up and down for an easier route to the water's edge. But for the short distance she could see, the bank was unchanging. So she put out a tentative foot, slipped and half fell down the four foot embankment. She landed in a crumpled heap at the bottom, her left hand splashing into the muddy shallows.

Shaken, Kate got to her feet, brushing the leaves and small, sandy stones from her heavy coat. The coat had saved her from suffering any more than superficial damage. Only the fall itself had been disconcerting. Her breathing quickly eased and came back to normal. She was calm again. Once more she looked up and down the riverbank. Decided, she made off downstream, her outstretched right hand feeling for the sloping bank as she groped and pulled her way down the river's edge.

Occasionally, Kate would lose her footing and her left leg would plunge into varying depths of swirling water, but she pushed on resolutely, keeping going until she reached a rock strewn widening of the river bed with virtually no bank at all.

Here, she sat on a large, smooth-polished stone which rose from the river shallows and composed herself. The rain which ran down her face found no tears to mingle with. Her face was quiet and very sad.

Kate undid the strings on her hat and reached up to pull it off, letting it fall into the current, to be carried quickly away. Immediately, her headscarf became sodden and she had a little trouble with the knot under her chin but it came loose after some persistent tugging and it too was carried away, this time by the wind, into the darkness.

He hair, soaked by the driving rain, flapped in damp straggles around her face as she bent to undo the big buttons on her coat. One by one they came free until finally she was able to shrug the garment off and it fell from her shoulders to lie draped across the rock beneath her.

The sturdy, sensible shoes came next, loosened and

kicked off to float against the rock, held there for a brief moment by the rushing water before being sucked into the torrent. Her legs were bare under the flimsy protection of her thin cotton dress. Kate sat there like that, crouched above the angry river for timeless minutes.

Eventually, she slipped off her rock and walked into the water. It was not even cold.

Matt Coleman gratefully pulled the door closed behind him and shook the water from his hat. He gave the bunkhouse one last, useless scrutiny and asked, "No?"

The shaking of heads was unanimous. "He ain't been back. He's skedaddled to town. Must have. Nowhere else he'd go."

Matt nodded, accepting the logic. He'd only been putting off the inevitable. "I'll go an' tell the Old Man."

He stuck his hat back on and made his way up to the ranch house through the pouring rain. Stupid little runt. Matt hated to give the Old Man bad news at any time, but he particularly disliked to disturb him now when he had a visitor.

The boss didn't get visitors often. In fact, he couldn't remember the last time somebody had made a social call at the ranch, and this guy had apparently been greeted like a long lost brother. Still, he had to be told.

Reluctantly, Matt thumped the door, waited for the shouted acknowledgement, and went on in. He stood dripping just over the threshold while Cairns rose from his comfortable chair opposite his guest and came to meet him at the doorway. "Something wrong, Matt?"

"Sorry to disturb you, Mr Cairns. I can't find Bobby Willis. He ain't on the spread."

"You covered everywhere?' Cairns knew the answer.

"Yeah, but on a night like this he'd be in the bunkhouse,

payin' for lessons in poker."

"He's in town then?"

"Looks that way." Matt glanced over the room at his boss's guest. Or rather at the back of the chair that he occupied. Matt's gaze took in the brandy bottle placed strategically next to the chess board on the small, mahogany games table. Buddies from way back. Fairly shifting that expensive liquor anyway.

"Take two, no. Better make it four of the boys an' go get the stupid little fart back. But don't look for trouble, Matt," Cairns warned. "Just straight in an' straight out. We'll call it twenty for the four volunteers."

Matt nodded. But don't let on until the end of the month.

"But don't let on until the end of the month," Cairns finished.

One of these days, Matt wasn't going to be able to help himself and he'd finish off that sentence for the Old Man. He didn't like to think about how that would go down.

"Right. I'll take care of it. Sorry again about disturbing you."

"No, no. Don't give it a thought. I'm sorry about havin' to send you out on a night like this. But we need him back in one piece."

"Yeah, I should've made sure he was bedded down. The little sod's got too much spunk in him."

Cairns laughed. "It was always goin' to happen, Matt, unless you cut his balls off. And I guess it's a bit late for that. But you let him know that he'll feel it in his pay at the end of the month."

"I'll do that. Goodnight."

"Goodnight, Matt." Cairns closed the door behind his foreman and limped back to his visitor. "A real good man that."

"Appears so." His guest nodded as he reached once more for the brandy bottle. "I think you've got troubles."

"How's that?"

"It's your move."

The heads in the bunkhouse swivelled expectantly as Matt came back in, water droplets flying from his slicker as he spun to slam the door. He didn't keep them in suspense for long. "First four on the bonus list," he announced.

"Hey!" shouted a cowboy from his top bunk. "I must just be about there."

"Your ass is just about there," was the reply as one of the players leaned back from the poker table and pulled a board-backed sheet of paper down from the wall. "Chico, Dez, Bull An' Mitch."

As he reeled off the names grunts of appreciation went up; three bodies rolled from their bunks and began to pull on their boots while Mitch took a last look at his poker hand before reaching for his slicker. "Just as well. How much, Matt?"

"Twenty."

"Twenty! Hey, don't be too hard on that randy little sod. He's keepin' me healthy."

Matt opened the door and looked up at the solid sheets of rain being driven down from the black sky. "You'll earn it."

Feltman had been walking around for a while, thinking about Colby's efficiency and McCabe's temper and trying to decide which was the most dangerous when the rain started. Soft at first, it quickly became a heavy torrent, pounding on his shoulders.

Sitting under that awning, watching Colby at work had allowed the hot blood to dissipate and cool in his veins. He always got high afterwards. Not during. After.

And he always needed a woman. His thoughts drifted to Rachel. He liked the girl. The look of her. The feel of her. The smell of her. But she wasn't here. He smiled ruefully to himself, wondering if he had been too much the gentleman.

But he recognised it simply hadn't been right. She wasn't ready. Not for him. He could still see it in her eyes. Not wanting to be used. He wanted her, but he needed her to want him.

He was getting wet. And if he didn't do something about his horn soon, he was going to trip and do himself an injury. He looked across the street at De Brecco's and thought, 'Why fight it?'

The first sight that greeted him on the dry side of the door was a pair of well supported breasts trying to entice a poker player away from a winning hand. The place was packed. It was amazing she had found room to bend over.

He shoved his way to the bar, pausing frequently to have a good look down a plunging neckline or to rest his hand inadvertently on an inviting behind.

One of the bar dogs recognised him and he was speedily served up a blond brew that was nine-tenths froth while the bartender cheerfully ignored the pleas and screaming threats of those already waiting.

He waited until the froth had settled sufficiently to give him half a glass of beer then had a long pull which almost drained it and had a good look round.

Christ, De Brecco must be worth a fortune. He could understand why Benson was so keen to get his hands on the place. There was not a game of any kind that was not packed more than four deep. They were fighting each other to throw their money at him. Even the poker tables had a compulsory house dealer, taking a straight fee from anyone wanting in on the game.

For a while, Feltman amused himself by eyeballing and comparing the girls. Which one did he want? Did it matter? Did he just need a body? Someone not too ugly; someone to hold while he came down from his high.

Stupid questions; so his musing evolved into trying to figure out what happened after the trollops trapped their willing prey. There was some sort of system working but he couldn't put his finger on it. Happy, randy drunks were going up, and down, both staircases in steady streams, but not necessarily with the harlot who hooked them.

Whatever the system, it was being orchestrated by an obese woman who had squeezed herself into a dark-green satin dress, folds of fat straining for release, huge breasts barely contained, and topped off by a mass of bogus blonde curls which cascaded down to coyly frame the many layers of slap and rouge that made up her face.

"How'd it go with O'Sullivan?" De Brecco was at his shoulder.

"Yeah, it went. Colby dealt with it."

Feltman could sense the reappraisal. He turned to see the look in De Brecco's eyes. He'd seen that look before. "Worried about what you've bought, Brec?"

"Put it this way," De Brecco said, "I thought McCabe scared me."

Feltman needed to change the subject. He nodded at the box herder. "She doesn't seem your type, Brec. I'd thought you'd have gone for something younger; long an' elegant."

De Brecco was not insulted. "I don't go to bed with her, Feltman. Just do business. Besides, I don't know of anything young, long an' elegant that'd be able to control a bunch o' whores."

Feltman reached behind him to put away his empty glass and pick up the full one which had appeared at his elbow. Always helps to know the boss.

181

"So how'd you cut the action in here?"

"How'd you mean?"

"The girls get to keep any? Or just the tips."

De Brecco looked at him. A little puzzled by the line their conversation was taking. "They do all right. Some o' them do a lot better than all right. There's a lot of money floatin' arou.... aw, hell!" Feltman almost lost his beer as De Brecco gave him an apologetic slap on the shoulder. "I'm sorry, Feltman. I wasn't thinking ...hang on a minute. Bel! Bel, come on over here."

A big smile was switched on beneath the blonde wig and it waddled over.

"Bel, this is Mr Feltman," De Brecco introduced, "an' I get the feelin' he would like a try-out with one of your girls."

"I know who he is, Brec."

Feltman held up a hand in what even he would have admitted was a half-hearted protest. Of the two previous occasions when Feltman had experienced the delights of paying for sex, both had ended abysmally in embarrassing failure. That had always been his trouble with the professional lady. He wanted to, but he didn't want to. He could feel another disaster brewing.

De Brecco breezed on, happy in his hospitality. " And this is Miss Bel Grade. The best madame this side of Paris."

"Any side of Paris. An' that's Paris, France." Lest there be any doubt. "But what's all this Miss and Mr stuff, Brec? I'm Bel to guys an' girls alike." She turned to Feltman whose head was half way down his beer glass. "What do your friends call you, Mr Feltman?"

He was half-tempted to say 'Feltman', but he found himself staring right into Bel's smiling, red-blotched face which even her liberal application of slap had failed to tone down, and he couldn't. Christ. It was the falseness of the whole thing which caved him in. He capitulated and croaked out, "Michael."

"Michael." Bel breathed his name out slowly. She seemed to like it. "Now, Michael, just you look around. What we have here is a collection of the finest pieces of calico ever seen in the west. An', sure, you might see the odd soiled dove shakin' her tootsie in some old sourdough's face but that's because no matter how old, how ugly an' how shallow your pockets are, none o' that is a barrier to havin' a good time in this establishment."

She gave her business partner a light slap on the arm. "We'll skin anybody, right?"

De Brecco joined her in a bout of conspiratorial laughter. Feltman thought De Brecco actually liked this woman. Maybe they were sleeping together.

"Them girls, Michael," Bel breathed his name again, "are mostly catalogue brides who believed that washing the shit off their spouse an' bein' fucked when the mood took wasn't what they'd signed up for. If you're gonna get fucked you may as well get paid decent for it."

Bel, you're just a saint.

"So, Michael," Bel spread her fat arm and swung it to encompass the whole saloon, "choose your pleasure and be delighted."

Bel would have been great at selling horses. But with every word she spoke Feltman could feel his ardour shrivel. The trouble with you, Feltman, is that you've never entered the spirit of this thing. Start talking their language.

He looked around briefly and pointed "Her there. The slim one with the big tits."

The fat old cow never batted an eyelid. "That's Marie-Louise. She's only just arrived. Run off from that wagon train just in. She's practically a virgin. You pick good."

De Brecco gave Feltman a final, friendly clap on the

shoulder and moved off into the throng to look after his money which had been struggling along on its own for the last ten minutes.

Bel grabbed a passing girl and whispered the summons in her ear. Feltman only had to wait the time it took Marie-Louise to diplomatically disengage from her negotiations with a potential customer before the girl was standing in front of him, ready for inspection.

She stood a fair look. This girl was actually pretty. Deep blue eyes staring, straight forward, into his. A light smile on her lips; just one layer of delicately applied make-up. She even smelt nice. And you could lose yourself down that cleavage. Not a bad pick at all.

Bel took one arm each in hers and guided them to the bottom of the right-hand stairway. "Room five, Marie-Louise." Bel slipped her the key. "As long as you like."

Marie-Louise gave Feltman a friendly, inviting smile and went off ahead up the stairs while Bel gave his ass a pat and informed him he was about to get the best tumble of his life.

Feltman knew the state of the thing dangling between his legs and had to disagree. But watching Marie-Louise's professional sway as she climbed the stairs, he felt the first awakening. By the time they were installed in the locked room he was willing to be convinced.

Marie-Louise knew how to undress. Feltman only got as far as his gunbelt before he gave up fumbling and sat himself down on the bed to enjoy the show.

Expertly, teasingly, Marie-Louise removed everything except her dress. It would have been easier then to slip off her shoulder straps, allowing the pleats of dark red to slither to the floor.

Instead, with a last, tantalising smile she went up on her toes and bent forward, reaching down to lightly grip the hem of her dress. Head up, she held the pose for an erotic second before slowly bringing the dress up over her head.

Feltman's horn continued to rise with the dress. All his anxiety and doubts had vanished. By the time those lovely breasts had bounced down he was on his feet, smothering his face in her flesh before the dress had hit the floor.

Clamped together, they fell back on the bed, Marie-Louise twisting round and down to bring Feltman on top of her. "If a girl asked you nice, would you take off your clothes?"

He was willing. While Marie-Louise took care of his shirt buttons, Feltman got his pants loosened. But he had some trouble getting them down over his bulge so he planted a fist deep into the mattress beside Marie-Louise's sun-kissed thigh and stuck his ass provocatively in the air, using his free hand to push determinedly at his pants, forcing them down over his gleaming, white backside.

Feltman did actually hear the wild, raucous yell which somebody let loose in the corridor. He also heard the loud reverberations of the gun being fired in that same confined space. But, in his precarious position, balanced above the lovely Marie-Louise and gazing down lustfully on the prize which awaited him on completion of his difficult manoeuvre, he decided, understandably, to ignore them both.

Unfortunately, the bullet from the afore-mentioned shot had the gross ill-nature to splinter its way through the meagre door panelling of room number five, whizz across the sexual bed and exit, with a musical tinkle, via the bedroom window.

Feltman almost experienced his first instantaneous climax as he sprung a good three and a half feet in the air above his screaming partner and came down, awkward and heavy, on the far side of the bed, his exposed flesh ripped and sliced by the shattered glass.

The way Feltman left that girl, you'd have thought his ass had been scorched with a bullet; which it had.

The total effect was one for which countless owners of indiscriminate dogs had been searching in vain for years. It had the old bucket of water routine beaten by a country mile. Without doubt, the bullet across the rectum technique had been proven, under test conditions, to be a first class, one hundred percent, grade A passion killer.

Feltman was lying on the floor, grinding glass beneath his buttocks, trying to be philosophical, but finding that he did not really believe this, when Marie-Louise decided to stop screaming and join him behind the bed.

She had always been a trifle awkward, had Marie-Louise, in matters other than sexual, and her left knee made squelchy, unerring contact with Feltman's groin.

"Ooogaagh! Get off me you stupid fucking trollop," screamed Feltman, with remarkable restraint.

Angrily, he brushed the wide-eyed girl from him and scrambled for his gunbelt at the bottom of the bed, muttering his earlier musings out loud, "I don't believe this."

Another yell of unbounded joy from the hallway and Feltman's instinctive duck at the boom of the accompanying gunshot sent his head thudding into the solid oak bed leg. Sadly, this impressive evasive action was entirely unnecessary since this particular bullet had decided to annoy someone else.

Feltman pushed himself to his knees, threw his head back and screamed, "*I don't fucking believe this.*"

He shuffled for the door, buckling on the belt as he went, the curses coming thick and strong. "I'll kill this drunken fuck."

With the colt in his left hand he flattened his back against the wall beside the door and sought out the key with his right.

No key.

"Where's the key?" he shouted across at the girl.

Only the top of Marie-Louise's head and eyes were visible, peering over the rumpled bed at him. "In the door."

"Shit!" Feltman bent down to grope on the floor for the key just as another bullet battered its way through the panelling. "Sweet fuckin' jesus!" He pushed off with both feet and went careering over the bed to end up piled on top of the squealing girl again.

"What are you doing? Can't you just be still?" Marie-Louise pounded at him with her tiny fists, anger and suspicion combining dramatically on her face. She wasn't quite sure whether Feltman was getting his own back. She let out a yelp as her beautifully sculpted belly was used, without ceremony, as a springboard.

"Where are you going?"

Feltman was tugging at the window sash, gave it up and put his boot through what was left of the glass. "To sort that bastard out."

"Come back here. You just can't ... Oh, my god!" Marie-Louise lay back down on the floor and waited for the world to get sane again.

Feltman went down the wet, greasy overhang feet first and too fast. He hoped the guttering would hold. It didn't, but it checked his momentum for a second and he was able to grab at it as he went by, ripping it away, but slowing him still further so that at less than full stretch he feet found the hitchrail.

He grabbed at the upright and swung himself neatly on to the sidewalk, only to be confronted with an unlucky, aggressive drunk. Surprised, the guy made a grab at him.

Feltman didn't hesitate. He head-butted him full in the face and the wretched man went down like a stone. Wrong time, wrong place. Feltman reached down and relieved him of his pistol, just in case.

It had stopped raining. He hurried along the slippery boards, buttoning up what was left of this shirt as he went, the filched pistol in his left hand, his own .44 still holstered.

He heard the gun boom out again just as he reached the saloon entrance. A nagging doubt scratched at his brain, but his dander was up; no time to pause. Through the batwings.

He got about three feet.

Three feet before his progress was stifled by the throng of revellers. That and the fact there was no one to fight.

That's what had been grating at him. The combined volume of the individual carousing, which left the saloon in a single, load noise, had not wavered a fraction after that last shot. No one gave a bison's burp. The goddamned piano had not even stopped playing.

He was attracting attention. Mostly because of the pistol dangling from his left hand as he stood, braced, just inside the doorway. That and possibly the spreading news of the preacher man's demise.

No doubt about it. Sexual frustration went for the brain. He took a breath and began shoving his way to the bar, ignoring the puzzled looks and unasked questions.

He was consoling himself with the thought that it could have been a lot worse when he spotted De Brecco shouldering his way towards him. Oh, christ.

"What happened to you? You look like shit."

"Nuthin'."

"What?"

"Nuthin'."

He made the bar and slid the pistol over the counter without comment. The bartender considered the weapon for a moment, then shrugged and deposited it in some cubby hole behind the bar. He must have decided it was legal tender for he immediately set Feltman up a beer. It was gratefully received.

"Hey! What've you done with Marie-Louise?" Bel's dulcet tones rang in his left ear while his right was busy ignoring another 'What the hell's been goin' on' from De Brecco.

Feltman took a deeper gulp of his beer and was saved from muttering 'nuthin' by the sound of two closely spaced gunshots which were accompanied by a now very familiar, wildly joyous yell.

His beer glass dropped unheeded on the bar. As he spun his gun hand was already moving, bringing up the colt. Only Bel's quivering blubber and De Brecco's restraining hand kept him from firing.

"Take it easy."

"Hey! No need to be like that, he's only a kid."

A kid who now held the laughing attention of the crowded saloon. He looked about twelve, could not have been more than fifteen. He stood, legs apart in bravado, on the staircase landing, his left arm wrapped around one giggling girl, his gun hand held harmlessly aloft by another. And goddamn if that piano had not stopped playing.

"I'll swing for him."

"Oh, don't. He's just happy. One of the girls felt sorry for him. Comin' around all the time with those big, pleading eyes."

It was too much.

"You tellin' me he's shootin' off that gun just cos he got rid of his first horn?"

"Well," asked Bel defensively, "weren't you happy?"

"I don't remember."

"Uh..oh. Here comes the cavalry." Both De Brecco and

Feltman followed Bel's glance to the street entrance where Matt Coleman was fighting his way in at the head of a posse of black-slickered cowboys.

They veered right as they saw the kid. He saw them too. "Them's my buddies."

And, before either of his lovely escorts could stop him, he had leaped up onto the balustrade, presumably to give his buddies a better view of a virile young man. "Hey, Matt. Matt, I sure did some ramroddin' tonight."

And then he was on his way down.

The whole room winced as he hit the front edge of the poker table feet first. The players scattered as it whipped up and skelped young Bobby's ass a hell of a blow, sending him flying into the waiting arms of Bull and Chico.

It's amazing how things take a serious turn when money's involved. The poker players were not happy. There was not one of them who was still laughing.

"Fuckin' asshole. Do you know how much was in that pot?"

"You ought to geld that little fuck."

More than one of them instinctively reached for their weapon. Only the House Rule: *'If 'n you're packing, you ain't playin'.'* prevented the bloodbath as angry hands slapped against empty thighs.

De Brecco was already moving to calm the situation. Feltman took the opportunity to head for the door. He'd just about made it when Marie-Louise's shrieking voice assailed him from the landing. "Michael, where are you going? You've forgot your hat. Michael! I've got your hat."

Feltman kept going. If he managed not to kill anybody before he got to his room, he'd find sanctuary in his bed.

It had stopped raining. But the fresh wind that had gotten up fairly compensated for the drunken walk of Con

190

O'Malley as it breezed him along between the orderly lines of sodden, dripping tents.

There was not any doubt in the world about it. Kevin Kilhooley was getting on for being a saint; a good friend and a wise man.

"Wid ye care te tell me wit's troublin' ye, Con?"

Con O'Malley had stared back at his friend through drunken eyes. "An' what is it that ye'd be wantin' me te tell ye?"

"Sure, man, it's only the sorrow in ye that's keepin' ye standin'. Ye've put away mair o' the hard stuff tonight than … well, Ah'll tell ye this, if ye stop, it's buckets at me feet ye'll be weepin'. It's no drunken mists I see in yer eyes."

"Aye, I'll not say yer wrong, Kevin."

The two of them had been leaning against McGarvey's bar for hours. Con's first beer stood in front of him still, with barely a sip out of it. But the best part of a bottle of whisky had disappeared between them, and of that only a drop had passed Kevin's lips.

Con looked at his friend. "It's Kate. Me an' Kate have had a terrible fight."

"Is that it? Mother o' god, man. No wonder yer crying. Here's me offerin' ye a shoulder when it's yer lovely wife yer needin'."

Kilhooley thumped his glass down emphatically, adding another score to the bar top. "It's time I wis at the mine. Ye'll be needin' a lift." It was not a question.

So Kilhooley had bundled him unprotestingly into the buckboard and they had set off for the camp, with Con being lectured all the way in a harsh but friendly manner.

Finally, with his backside being threatened with a hefty miner's boot if he didn't start treating that lovely wife of his the way everybody and the good lord knew she deserved, Con was deposited at the camp edge while Kilhooley made for the mine and an understandably late start to his shift.

"Katie, darlin', I'm back." Con did not repeat his announcement since it was obvious his wife was not in the tent. A sharp pain of anxiety cut through his semi-drunken state as he switched his gaze from the empty marital bed to the cot occupied by his sleeping children.

He knelt down at their double cot and softly spoke their names. "Conor, Bridgit, are ye awake."

Young Conor kept his eyes firmly shut but Bridgit could not deny her Da.

"Darlin', where's yer Ma?"

Bridgit shook her small head as much as her pillow and the tight blankets would allow. "I don't know, Da. Ma went out."

"Aye, darlin', but ..." Hearing the tent flap open behind him, Con cut his next enquiry short and sprung to his feet.

"Katie, darlin', thank god, I ..." Con passed both his big hands behind Mrs O'Neill's back and drew her to him, into the light.

Her small fists came up to rest lightly on his chest, but she kept her head down, unable to look at him. Slowly Con dropped his arms from her, anxiety flooding back to rack through his body, shutting his mind down for an instant as he fought the despair that came with accepting something was dreadfully wrong.

"I'm sorry, Con. I shouldn't have barged in like that." Mrs O'Neill lifted her head up to look at the big, broken-hearted man. "I thought it was Kate returning."

"Aye, so did I. Where is she, Mrs O'Neill?"

"Didn't ye see her at all? She went into town to look for you."

Again, Con experienced the surge and flow of relief and apprehension. "Are ye sure that's where she was goin'?" Con walked over to the tent flap and had a speculative look out. "I didn't see her."

Conor could not keep his eyes closed any longer. "Da. Da, Ma didn't go that way."

In an instant, Con was back at his children's bedside, his hands clasped on his young son's shoulders. "Where did she go, son? Where, Conor? Where?"

"I don't know, Da. She didn't go the town way," Conor cried. "Ma was walking the other way." Vaguely, his small hand indicated the direction through the tent wall, his young heart filled as full as his father's with fear and foreboding.

Con released the sobbing child and looked questioningly at Mrs O'Neill, pleading with her to contradict his son.

"Oh, Con, she …" The old woman was distraught. "I only thought …she didn't really say."

Con stared at her for a long moment. Mother of god, Katie. Oh, please, no. Con was running. Running and shouting and falling and calling. He tripped and fell at every stay rope his wife had stepped over and went splashing through every puddle she had carefully avoided. Nevertheless, he covered the five hundred yards to the river in minutes, slithering to a halt not yards from where his wife had stumbled down the steep bank.

"Katie! Katie! For god's sake please answer me."

Frantic, he twisted his head to search, up and down the riverbank. Which way? Any way.

Running again, he stumbled off upriver, calling her name continuously. Twenty yards. Nothing.

Fifty yards. He stopped. The wrong way. If she had gone in, she would … He cut off the cold reasoning and started to run back downriver.

"Katie!"

Not even an echo came back at him. The howling wind carried his hopeless shouts away, shredding them into the night to make them nothing at ten yards

Something. There, swirling in the river. Con charged down the bank into three feet of turbulent water. "Katie!"

Nothing. Something. A reflection. He stumbled out of the water, the despair in his voice absolute. "Please, please god, Kaaaaaaaaaa ...."his wife's name became a drawn-out, screaming cry. She can't be gone. Katie, you can't be gone.

And on. Until he had to stop, unable to see for tears of desperation and sorrow and guilt. His whole body sagging, he reached out for support and his hand closed on the soggy lining of his wife's coat.

And that pitifully tiny, hopeful spark that even then was burning, died.

Con drew the coat to his face. There were no more tears. Gently he put the coat back on the rock.

"Katie." But softly now. With love.

He walked into the water to look for her. Unhurriedly, he circled the rocks in the turbulent shallows, and finding nothing waded deeper, allowing the current to take him where she would have gone.

Seven times he crossed the deep central channel before he found her, drawn by the skirt of her dress, floating in the shallows on the far side of the river.

"Katie."

She was barely a foot under the surface. The strong current had dragged her down and jammed her upper body into a cleft in the rocks. Her right arm floated free. Gently, Con took her hand and sliding his body under hers, he grasped her waist in an attempt at making the river give up its cruel hold.

Her faced brushed against the ragged rock and he stopped. He went under the water, then, and tried to turn her head. He was gentle. He did not want to be rough. But her head would not move.

Con surfaced and adjusted his position under Kate's lower body. He took her hand again and drew her close to him as he squatted in the rain-swollen river, his head barely above the rushing waters.

He stayed there with her, exactly like that, motionless, except for the pull and release of the current.

He was still holding her some two hours later when the search party alerted by Mrs O'Neill found them in the flickering light of their firebrands.

Eleven

J. Sylvester Johns was a very busy man. Anyone who had ever been even remotely acquainted with him could have told you that. And, if you had had the privilege of sharing Mr Johns' private coach on its torturous overnight journey from Red Rock to Limon, you would have undoubtedly arrived, very quickly, at the same conclusion.

Because, if Mr J. Sylvester Johns' constant scribblings on, and poring over of, the very important looking, quality papers which he extracted periodically from his monogramed notecase throughout the night was not enough to impress that fact upon you, then J. Sylvester himself would have been only too happy to tell you, as often as you liked, that he was, in fact, an extremely busy man.

Besides the very real danger of the swaying tilley lamp becoming detached from its precarious hook above the industrious head and being sent crashing to the floor to engulf both the coach and J. Sylvester in the ensuing flames, the only other minor irritation on the journey came when the stage driver reined his team to a halt and informed his important passenger that this was as far as they were going that night, since the ever-increasing number of heavy, black clouds had finally blotted out the starlight by which he had been negotiating the road.

It had taken the promise of another fifty, a commitment to meet any damages and, more importantly, a full five minutes to persuade the fellow to proceed on the basis of as fast as was safe. This gave rise, on occasion, to the wheels of the coach turning through their own circumference only once per minute. But it was progress.

Now, the last quarter of the shimmering sun had nudged its way over the horizon when the sudden jarring of the coach announced its arrival on the heavily rutted streets of Limon. The sole occupant of the carriage grimaced distastefully as the remaining transparent sections of the coach windows went a mud-stained opaque as the wheels churned up the softened crust on the bone hard road.

Above him, the hired shotgun man dug his elbow none too softly into the ribs of the driver and motioned with his head.

"Yeah, I see it."

Momentarily, the shuddering of the coach increased as the driver cut his team across the ruts, then the vibrations ceased altogether as he pulled them up with an expert flourish outside the Oglala hotel.

Inside, J. Sylvester rearranged the papers in his notecase, putting one particular set to the top, checked that he had his card readily available in his wallet and sat back to wait for the coach door to be opened.

Thankfully, he was not a patient man, otherwise he could have been waiting all day. With a shake of the head, one which conveyed a very definite opinion on the standard of the help he had engaged, he thrust the door open and stepped regally down. Or as regal as you can get when one expensively shod foot lands damp in a pothole and the other on a bumpy crest between two ruts.

Idly, his two hirlings surveyed him from the sidewalk. The driver threw his thumb over his shoulder and asked,

"This where ya want to be?"

J. Sylvester glanced up at the battered sign. This was indeed where he wanted to be. "Thirty minutes, gentlemen. No more," was the curt command as he sailed past them and through the double doors.

The teamster looked at the shotgun man, looked at the horses, shook his head sorrowfully and led the way in after his passenger.

J. Sylvester was surprised. There was a knot of people, all male, gathered at the reception desk with an assortment of luggage scattered on the floor around them. Salesmen, peddlers, chancers. Some checking out; but other in animated conversation as they tried to set up their business day. He made to move forward to negotiate the various pieces of baggage but was restrained by a far from dainty hand which clamped around his immaculately-suited right elbow.

The look that J. Sylvester gave his driver should have shrivelled the man to a grubby puddle on the floor. But his tried and tested means of controlling underlings seemed strangely ineffective, because J. Sylvester was drawn inexorably towards the door.

"See them horses?"

"I do."

"Them horses need feed an' waterin' an rest. An' ya see us?"

J. Sylvester saw, but did not bother to give the affirmative, which, in his opinion, was superfluous. He believed he had the trend of this particular conversation.

"How long?"

That was more like it. "Four, five hours maybees."

"Two hours, Gentlemen. No more." He held up his hand to forestall any further protest. "I'm sure a change of horses can be obtained. Add the extra to my bill." And J.

199

Sylvester was away, stepping high to clear the luggage.

Of course, he did not join the queue, which, by now, had shortened to three. He went straight to the reception desk and waited for recognition.

He got it when the desk-clerk had attended to the last of the check-outs.

"Mornin'. How long?"

"I will not be staying."

That brought the head up.

"I wish to speak with Mr James Clancy."

"Yeah? Well, speak."

"My card, Sir. J. Sylvester Johns of the law firm Bradbury and Davis, Chicago." That last was in case Clancy could not read.

"That's what it says here." You would not have thought that Clancy was capable of such subtle wit. Maybe he wasn't. Before the conversation could develop further, they were interrupted by a shout from the saloon door.

"Hey, ain't your bar dog out of his sack yet?"

With a resigned shrug, Clancy excused himself and made for the adjoining saloon, shouting "Seth!" at the top of his voice.

J. Sylvester was sorely tempted to advise his driver that peak efficiency would be obtained if he first arranged for the horses to be changed before he and his companion took their version of rest. Wisely, however, he held his peace, rightly interpreting the toothy grin that was thrown at him from the doorway as a mischievous challenge. Calmly, he waited for Clancy to return.

"Yeah, so you're a John from Chicago. What can I do for you?"

J. Sylvester let the observation pass without comment. He had the distinct impression that his temporary help had not been singing his praises. However, years of experience had dampened any need for futile recriminations and he focused solely on the inquiry.

Opening his notecase, he smoothly extracted the relevant document. "Firstly, you can glance at the figure in the sixth paragraph of this contract and inform me whether that would be an acceptable sum for the purchase of this hotel. If so, I will then briefly run through the pertinent details of the rest of the document, and, if they are also agreeable, I would then ask that you sign both copies, retaining one for your records."

Clancy's eyes glazed over and he bent his head down to search out the figure. His head remained bent for quite some time, although he had no difficulty at all in picking out the printed sum. It leapt at him.

When he did raise his head, he had a false start at talking, cleared his throat and started again. "That's a very nice number, but we have a problem."

"Which is?"

"I don't own the hotel. I only manage it."

J. Sylvester was not in the least perturbed. "I believe that you will find that you do. Sometime today, a Mr Davenport will call on you. He is a local lawyer, as I assume you know." That was conversational. J. Sylvester never assumed anything. "I am reliably informed that the purpose of his visit will be to inform you that his office in Cheyenne holds the last will and testament of your former employer, Miss Angela Miller, in whose name the ownership of this hotel was registered. She has nominated yourself as sole beneficiary. This legacy will not be contestable."

There was a short silence while Clancy digested what had been so eloquently thrown at him.

"Angie never went near no lawyer. Not that she told me. You sure them pilgrims down at the Legislature can't get their claws into this place?"

"I assure you, Mr Clancy, that will not be the case. In any event, it would not affect our transaction. My client is prepared to pay the agreed sum for your signature transferring ownership to his company. Any problem arising from whether your signature is legally binding will be entirely his. Or ours on his behalf."

"I sign, you'll pay the cash?"

"With certain conditions. The first, and main, is that you continue to run this establishment in a managerial capacity for a period of one month, drawing the salary as noted in paragraph nine." Again, Clancy bent his head. "The proceedings during this period to be banked at Western and Central in the name of the company mentioned in paragraph seventeen."

J. Sylvester waited until Clancy's eyes were raised once again to meet his own and, seeing no hint of inquiry there, continued, "The second is that you remove the name 'Oglala', immediately, from the signboard."

"I what?"

J. Sylvester did not bother to repeat the second condition. "Do we have a deal, Mr Clancy?"

"Yeah, I guess we do." Clancy hesitated in reaching for the proffered pen.

"What about payment?"

"Half the amount has already been lodged with the Cheyenne branch of Western and Central. You will be able to draw on that sum after the Limon branch opens today; contingent on you signing this document. The rest, one month from now, or sooner at my client's discretion. I may say that any irregularities in the deposits from the hotel during that period will result in a similar amount being withheld from your final payment."

"Who is your client?" The company name had meant nothing to Clancy.

J. Sylvester's expression did not change but he somehow managed to convey the impression that Clancy's question was naïve in the extreme.

But Clancy had been fond of Angie, and he felt duty bound to ask. "So how'd you get here so fast? Ah mean, how'd your … client know Angie had bought it?"

"My client has been interested in purchasing this hotel for some time. An acquaintance informed him by telegraph of Miss Miller's unfortunate demise. While some may feel that he has proceeded with undue haste, business is, as they say, business."

J. Sylvester proffered the pen again. Clancy looked at him.

"Mr Clancy. I leave Limon in two hours. With or without your signature."

"Yeah, so give me the pen."

One copy of the signed contract disappeared efficiently into the tidy notecase. "That would seem to conclude our business, Mr Clancy, but since I am obliged to spend a further two hours in Limon, I wonder whether it would be possible to furnish me with a room for that period, with some hot water, perhaps?"

"All the rooms are furnished." Again, one could not be quite sure whether Mr Clancy was having an attempt at humour. "You want a bath?"

"No. No, a small basin of hot water and a towel will do."

"Sure? What about some food?" Clancy pressed, and noting J. Sylvester's hesitation, added, "It's fine. I eat here myself."

Good manners precluded J Sylvester giving any hint that that fact might not, necessarily, be grounds for recommendation. "Well, then yes. Thank you."

"Room nine." Clancy handed over a wooden square

with two keys dangling. "The big key is for the necessary at the end of the hall"

J. Sylvester paused on the stairway. "Would you be good enough to attend to one other thing for me?"

Clancy nodded, his soul still glowing from finding his own personal pot of gold.

"Would you please keep track of my driver and have me informed the minute my coach is ready. I cannot afford to remain here a moment longer than necessary. I am an extremely busy man."

Needless to say, Feltman's horn was bothering him. Well, it had to be, hadn't it, after the unfruitful frolics of the previous night. And now, this morning, bright and fresh after the rains – it made a man feel good. Yeah, his dander was well and truly up and he would need to find a pleasant and non-frustrating method of getting it down, fast, to clear his mind to concentrate on the more important matters to hand. Either that or one of those more important matters was going to put a bullet in him.

So, it was to that end that he was standing on the sidewalk on Main, the back of his newly-purchased light green shirt solidly planted against the thin clapboard walls of Midler's general store, his reclaimed hat (left hanging on the doorknob of his hotel room) pushed back from his forehead, contemplating a group of kids who were playing a balancing game on the ruts in the street outside Sammy's.

He had a plan formulated, but they looked a little young to be trusted with a message. His problem seemed solved when a slightly older kid emerged from the bit house carrying a large pitcher of beer.

The other kids stopped playing and gathered around the boy as he proudly showed off his purchase. Their leader had returned.

Feltman pulled out his old timepiece and glanced at the cracked face. The breakfast trade would be well past by now. He pushed himself off the wall, "Hey, Kid."

They knew what kid he was after.

Doubtfully, with much looking around, the leader of the pack advanced, his herd around him, tactically halting with the two young girls in the gang still between him and Feltman, the three remaining boys ranged at his back.

"Like to earn a quarter?"

The kid decided to be non-committal.

"Know Miss Rachel? Pretty lady, works over at Ma's."

A cautious nod.

"Run over and tell her that Mr Duggan wants to see her urgent, down at the livery."

The kid thought that over.

"Her pony's taken bad." Feltman compounded the lie.

Decision. "A quarter ain't much."

Feltman looked into the hard business eyes. Ten years of experience shone back at him. "Fifty cents then."

"You ain't Mr Duggan."

Hartford and Benson had better watch out. "We'll call it a dollar." To prevent further argument, Feltman fished in his money belt and produced the hard cash.

Sensing that the bargaining was over, the kid dodged round the girls and closed his fist over the proffered coin.

"She ain't there."

The big kid stopped, unsure whether he was about to lose the dollar. Feltman looked down at the pretty little thing that had made such a forthright declaration.

She was standing steadfast, a slight purse to her lips, slightly scared to have interrupted but knowing she was right.

"Where is she, Honey?"

"Over at Miss Rosalin's."

"You saw her?"

"Uh-huh. She said good morning to me. She's nice."

Feltman looked at the big kid. "You know where that is?"

"Yeah, I know. Right next to where I got to drop this off for the Smith. Over at Johnstone's livery."

Feltman released his hold on the coin. "Then get gone."

The kid shuffled off, moving as quickly as the sloshing of the beer would allow, while the rest of his gang settled down on the edge of the sidewalk. Their demeanour subdued; the excitement over.

Feltman fished again in his money belt. Why not spread a little joy. "Hey!"

The children's expressions changed from surprise, through amazement to glee as Feltman sent the bright coins spinning through the air. While the boys compared their catches, Feltman leaned between the two young girls and allowed them to pick the last of the dollar pieces from his palm.

It's hard to say what gave the pretty little things more pleasure. Their sudden increase in wealth? Or the way Feltman politely tipped his hat and murmured "Ladies," before strolling off to complete his selfish quest.

Rachel felt absolutely wonderful. A hectic breakfast shift; a quick bath and change, and here she was, relaxed and happy, sprawled on Rosalin's sofa with a glass of luscious red wine in her hand.

Red wine. Deep, deep red wine. What debauchery. She giggled, leaning forward so she did not spill her drink. Rosalin and Megan exchanged a deliberate look and then laughed with her.

"I'm sorry," Rachel took another significant sip of the delicious liquid and put the glass down safely on the table.

Rosalin was smiling at her, indulgent and fond. Megan was smiling at them both, enjoying the interplay. Rachel giggled again. "I just feel so … fine."

"And so you should." Rosalin reached over and patted her knee. "We should all feel fine. All the time."

Megan laughed now. A young girl laugh. Very young, barely seventeen; a lithe, wisp of a girl, curled on the rug, but her eyes knowing and content.

Rachel sat back and watched as their strikingly handsome host refilled their glasses from a bottle of her husband's favourite wine. She supressed another giggle. Wine before noon and not an ounce of guilt between them.

And, despite the joking, continued reference, it was not Richie's favourite wine any more than root beer was his favourite tipple. Richie was very definitely a bourbon and brandy man. The wine was Rosalin's, imported by the case by her husband for propriety's sake.

Rachel had felt sorry for Richie when she had first been introduced to the Dressmaking Society. But she had quickly learned to admire him almost as much as she liked and admired Rosalin. He was simply one of the most kind, considerate, straightforward men she had ever come across.

Rachel had been dubious at first, when the invite had come from Carrie. Her friend had never quite seemed the same since that evil shit of a lieutenant had taken advantage of her. She had been the opposite of withdrawn; uncommonly outgoing and independent. But dress-making? There were several in Limon already, with the townswomen keen to take advantage of the skills of the professional seamstress. But it was not something that appealed to Rachel.

"Give it a try. You'll be surprised. It'll be fun," Carrie had coaxed. So, she'd humoured her. And it was. Fun.

Rachel had been naïve in the extreme. But the veil had

lifted soon enough. The first few evenings had been pleasant; light friendly chatter aided by a small glass of the delicious wine, and some very professional fittings carried out in a downstairs bedroom converted for that very purpose. The resulting creations were sold directly for the price of the cloth or put up for sale in Richie's mercantile and haberdashery shops.

And Rosalin was simply a wonderful host, charming, chatty and tactile. On the few occasions when Ritchie returned before the ladies had dispersed, he was welcomed with enthusiasm and delight; the love and respect between them was palpable, Rosalin dropping everything to ensure his needs were met; hot, fresh coffee to accompany the bourbon and cigars as he disappeared into his study.

But the morning sessions were altogether different, much more select. "Come in the day, just when you can," came the whispered invite. "You'll find the wine flows a bit more freely."

Rachel was a little disconcerted to find that Carrie had been attending the morning sessions for some weeks. Her friend had laughed, "I only went in the evening to keep you company. If I want a dress, I'll buy it. Rosalin likes you, but she had to be sure you weren't too straitlaced."

Now curious, she went. And it was even more fun. The wine flowed copiously as Carrie and Rachel joined Rosalin and Megan and three other very friendly and outgoing young women, Sally, Jess and Molly (collectively referred to by Rosalin as the Tryst) in chat and laughter and no dressmaking whatsoever. And Rosalin everywhere, lissom, alluring, filling glasses, hugging and waxing lyrical about her heroes. All women, of course.

Rachel was enthralled. This wonderful woman had views and was not afraid to air them. It was actually a physical pleasure listening to her eulogising on the pioneering women of the west. Not totting guns and seeing off the savage natives whose land they were stealing, but those who had fought for equality and suffrage.

Rosalin had actually known Esther Morris, who had scaled the heights to sit as a justice of the piece. And while Rachel had never heard of Louisa Swain, she had drunk many a toast to her since, after learning how she had grabbed her chance to vote over in Laramie back in seventy. Case in point, 'To Louisa Ann Swain'; another bottle opened and glasses re-charged.

But there was one man to whom Rosalin allocated hero status. Her husband, Richie. He had been the campaign manager for Bill Bright who had introduced the bill into the Territorial Legislature. And without that Act being passed, women in Wyoming would still be in the same position as all other women in America were now; no rights and no voice.

Rachel had absorbed it all. Things happening all around her; things to which she had never given a thought or of which she had even been remotely aware. She had felt a sense of excitement that had not left her since.

And then Jess, one of the ladies of the Tryst, had abruptly got to her feet and announced, "I need to straighten my stitching out." She had extended her hand in invitation to Molly, who accepted it gracefully and rose to her feet. The two of them had then wandered hand in hand into the dressmaking bedroom, quietly closing the door behind them.

There had been silence. Then Rachel had become aware that the four other women left in the room were looking at her. Expectantly.

"Oh." Rachel had expressed her realisation. "Oh, my goodness."

"No need to look so shocked," Rosalin had

admonished, mildly, smiling and leaning over to take Rachel's hand in both of hers. "Or worried. It's not compulsory."

That had broken the tension, bringing some light laughter. In truth, Rachel had been neither shocked nor worried. Hadn't she been schooled by nuns? She just felt slightly stupid. Another thought had struck her then and she had looked directly over at Carrie.

Her friend had seemed to have anticipated the inquiry. "No. Not me. I'm with you," Carrie had then made a thoughtful face, "I think." Before adding, "I'm only here for the wine and fabulous company."

Rachel felt she had to say something. Practically anything. She looked at Rosalin. "I mean, doesn't Richie mind?"

"No more than I mind him emptying his balls into one of those trashy whores over at De Brecco's. We all have needs my dear. Happiness is having them fulfilled without rancour." Rosalin switched her gaze between Rachel and Carrie. "And now I've divulged the sexual secrets of my marriage, how's your love life going? What are those handsome young men called? Nice Water and Bad Water?"

Rosalin knew very well what they were called. But Carrie raised her eyes to the ceiling and corrected her anyway. "Clean Water and Dirty Water."

That let out a little more tension.

"Well?"

"Well," Carrie complied, "I had Mr Clean," she paused and looked across at Rachel. "Actually, I had both of them," this pause deliberate, "chasing me at one point."

Rachel giggled, allowing the others to join in; and any remaining tension dissipated, allowing the return of the warm and convivial atmosphere.

"But I wasn't ready for their charm," Carrie continued.

"Still not. Anyway, they were a bit too cocky for me. And I think I might mean that literally."

That brought another round of the giggles and all eyes turned to Rachel.

"Yes," she admitted, "I had Mr Dirty."

"Literally?"

To howls of laughter, and a rueful smile from Rachel. Oh, for goodness sake. If candour is the name of the game.

"Oh, yes, quite definitely literally." Rachel stole a description from Martha about a man she hadn't been sure she liked. *"That dirty man stroked me until I begged him to fuck me and then he poked me until my fire went out."*

The ladies were screaming now, their hilarity unconstrained. "He was quite nice actually. Smelled wonderful; better than me."

"Oh, god," tears of laughter hindered young Megan forming the question, "Why aren't you married?"

"Because she's found a new beau," ventured Sally.

"Oh. I suspect Tomas wasn't after a wife. At least, not this one." Rachel went a bit pensive.

That brought them down a bit but not much.

Sally tilted her head at Rachel and asked, in a kindly fashion, "What are you thinking?"

"That …," here Rachel made an apologetic grimace, "… that tryst doesn't mean three?"

That set them off again. And so it went on in waves of brazen chatter and rueful merriment, until eventually Jess and Molly emerged, glowing, happy, and curious.

"What was going on out here?" demanded Jess. "We were almost jealous."

"Almost," emphasised Molly.

Jess and Molly got the truncated version of Rachel's reaction, including the slaughtering of the Water Boys, as the Tryst walked Megan back to her rooms at the rear of the larger of Richie's stores on Grant. Megan was a runaway, a scruffy vagrant shown mercy by Richie - much to Rosalin's delight – who now split her gentile working life between helping the town's ladies in their choice of curtain and dressmaking cloth in the store and 'light' housekeeping duties at the Richie family home.

Carrie had accompanied Rachel back to her place above Ma's for tea and calmness before returning home to smile sweetly at her father. Rachel had had an early night, refusing to rise to the quizzical looks and comments from her younger sibling.

And that had set the pattern for the last few weeks.

Now here she was, the pattern broken. No Carrie and no Tryst. But wine, good company and contentment. Even if the good company had taken itself off meanwhile. And of course she didn't mind. Not at all. She was quite happy in her own company, luxuriating in it, in fact. It allowed her to dream.

Dream about Tomas. Dream about Mike.

What she had told the society about Tomas wasn't strictly true. Carrie knew that, and sort of understood.

Tomas had thought he had wanted to marry her. But Rachel could only imagine the regret when he got back to New York or London, surrounded by sophisticated women of society.

So she had done his thinking for him. Carrie thought she was crazy. They'd made love. More than once. And she really liked him. She really did. But she had backed off, leaving him puzzled and slightly heartbroken.

And now Mike. He did light a fire in her. But maybe she was just randy and should have stuck with Tomas.

She just didn't know what she wanted. Well, she knew she had wanted Mike down at the pool. Wanted him badly.

But those nuns had saved her from herself more than

once. Teaching her all about rhythm and nothing about dancing. She had not been ready. Not in a 'I'm not sure I want to' not ready but in a 'It's the wrong time of the month' not ready. She was ready now.

Or had she been using that as an excuse. Regretting her decision over Tomas. Wanting him back. Safer.

Her mind was drifting, stretched out on the sofa, her wine glass balanced on her bosom when the thumping on the door broke into her reverie.

Rachel swung her feet to the floor, a coordinated hand conveying the wine glass safely to the table. That was odd, simply because it did not happen often. It couldn't be Richie. He would have come straight in.

The thumping came again. Rachel skirted the sofa and rapped on the dressmaking door in the agreed fashion. She waited for the 'just a minute' before heading for the outside door, getting there just in time to forestall another round of thumping.

She smiled down at the embarrassed young boy. "Hello, what can I do for you?"

"You're Miss Rachel?"

"Mmm, you're looking for me?"

"Mr Duggan says you're to come urgent." The boy hoped he wasn't going straight to hell. "Your horse has taken bad."

"Lennie? Lennie's sick? What's happened? I'll come." Rachel stepped out over the threshold before catching herself. "Wait, I'll be right back."

The little liar didn't wait. He skedaddled.

Rosalin was already opening the bedroom door, her dress back on, composed. Behind her, Megan, dressed only in her chemise, was sticking pins purposely into the mannequin. "Yes, my dear, what is it?"

"Oh, no, Rosalin. It was for me. I'm so sorry."

213

All pretence was dropped. "What is it, Rachel? What's happened?"

"Lennie's sick, or injured. I don't know. Mr Duggan's sent for me. I'm sorry, Rosalin, I have to go."

"Of course you do." Rosalin's concern was genuine. "Go, go." Rachel was ushered to the door. "Don't give it a second's thought."

As they reached the door Rosalin gave Rachel a brief, consoling hug. "I'm sure he'll be fine. Now hurry."

Rosalin gave a sigh as she watched Rachel scamper through the picket gate. She closed the door and turned and leaned her back on it. Megan was at the bedroom door. They gave each other a sympathetic smile on Rachel's behalf.

"Shall I …?" asked Megan.

"No you shall not." Rosalin turned again and slammed home the top bolt on the door. "You get right back in that bed, young lady."

Megan squealed and complied.

The stables used by Duggan's long term clients were adjoined but separate from the main livery barn. There were just a dozen or so stalls and two larger pens for fresh hay and straw. The lean-to was compact, quiet and cool.

Feltman walked over to Lennie and allowed the friendly animal to nuzzle into his shoulder. The rangy beast in the stall opposite had her long neck over the dividing slats, checking to see if Josh's roan had left any of his breakfast. Neither paid Feltman any attention.

He heard what he hoped was Rachel's light footsteps coming quickly across the yard and he stepped smartly back behind the open stable door.

She came bounding between the stalls, a trifle breathless and made straight for Lennie. "Darling, what is it? Mmm?

Are you all right? Are you okay, boy?"

The obvious concern in her voice made Feltman feel a bit guilty. But only a little. He remained still, allowing himself the luxury of watching Rachel fusing over her beautiful brown and white pony; checking he was breathing okay; running her hands down his short, stocky legs; examining his fetlocks. "You look all right to me, Lennie."

"He is all right," Feltman confirmed. He walked in a slow arc, closing the stable door before his filly could bolt, and dropped the heavy wooden bar into the single, metal bracket.

"Oh!" Both of Rachel's hands grabbed nervously at thin air as she spun round. "Oh, Mike. It's you." She sighed in relief and pulled her arms back to her breast. "What a scare you gave me. Is Mr Duggan there? He sent a boy round with – a – message – for - me."

Something in the way he was walking towards her. "Why did you bar the door, Mike?"

She did not care for the look on his face either. "Mike, will you talk to me? Will you say something? Mike, please, you're frightening me."

Rachel did not sound very frightened. Curious maybe, and then a rueful, almost dismissive, smile as understanding dawned. "Oh, no."

"I've decided to take your advice."

"My advice? About what? Rachel was backing away from him, but there was really not a lot of room in which to manoeuvre.

"About being a man."

"About b.... What?" Rachel laughed. A little high-pitched, perhaps, but it was a laugh. "Oh, c'mon, Mike." She stopped moving backwards and stood braced with her hands on her hips. She could play this game. "Stop acting the fool. You've had your fun."

"Not yet. But I will."

Rachel stared at him. He was serious.

"Mike? Michael! We're not doing this."

Feltman dropped his hands to his gunbelt.

"What? You're going to shoot me?"

Feltman was still smiling. "Save you shootin' me" He hung the belt over the nearest stall and kept on coming.

Rachel felt the adrenalin and went on the attack. "What kind of man does that? You know how much Lennie means to me. You're despicable." She lunged forward and swung an open hand at his face.

Feltman made no attempt at avoidance and her palm made noisy, slapping contact with his left cheek. When his face settled down he was still smiling. It wasn't even a weird smile. It was a friendly, anticipatory smile. It was a 'I'm going to enjoy this and I know you will too' smile.' The arrogant bastard.

Rachel retreated, instinctively backing into the feed stall. Well, if you are about to be thrown violently to the ground, it's as well to have a soft landing. No need to make things worse by getting stomped to death by a frenzied horse.

"Now, Michael, I don't believe you're serious about this," Rachel lied, adopting a schoolmarm tone in the use of his formal christian name. "Michael! ...oh, you pig!"

Rachel was on her back, her arms outstretched, held there by Feltman, his rough hands clamped on her wrists, his body pinning hers down, almost submerging her in the soft hay.

"What are you doing?" Now that it was absolutely certain he was going to do it; Rachel's quasi terror was replaced with doubt. And he was heavy. "Get off me."

He tried to kiss her. Furiously, Rachel flung her head from side to side, desperately avoiding his lips. "I don't want you. Do you hear? I don't even like you. I hate you."

Somehow, Feltman did not look like a man with a rejection complex. When Rachel stopped shaking her head she found that he was smiling at her. A very friendly smile.

"What are you smiling at? Stop smiling at me. Stop it."

Easily, he moved both her hands above her head, holding them securely in one of his. With the other he took hold of the neckline of her dress.

"No, not my dre ... Oh, my god. Did you have to?"

Feltman was lost in his own world of desire. He ripped the thin material of her camisole down to her waist and looked down on her exposed breasts like he was staring deeply into her soul.

Even knowing what was coming, Rachel was shocked at how much he wanted her. He was ignoring her and savouring her at the same time. He raised his eyes to look into hers, then dropped his face joyously into her bosom.

Rachel got back in the game. "You filthy swine." Viciously, she tried to whip her knee up into Feltman's groin, but it was a futile gesture, out of which he easily took the sting by deftly shifting his own body weight.

Calmly, his right hand continued its work, pushing up her skirts and deliberately tearing at her frilly drawers, rather than waste time and temper trying to get them off.

Rachel was totally helpless in his coldly efficient hands. All the racking and twisting of her body achieved nothing as he relentlessly tore their delicate protection away from her writhing frame.

"Oh, my god. Look at you, you smiling bastard, you've done this before."

Rachel felt her legs being pushed wider, and, as Feltman began to unbutton his pants, she changed tact, although she wasn't quite sure that she wanted to win this game. "Please don't, Mike," she sobbed. "Please, I'm scared. I want to.

217

Honestly, I do. But not here. Please, not here."

Rachel shuddered.

Her body only wanted to play one game. Her head went back as he entered her, fully, easily. But she resisted the urge to wrap her legs up around his back.

And she rallied. "Bastard."

As Feltman began to move with a slow rhythm inside her, Rachel brought her head up to butt him; bite him; but his was tucked safely out of harm's way, buried in her breasts. She fell back in frustration. "All right, pig. But you won't enjoy it. I'm not going to move. Not a muscle." Her words came out slowly, spat out viciously through clenched teeth. "You'll have to do it all yourself. You'd be as well putting a fist round your stalk, you filthy degenerate."

Her body immediately lost its arched rigidity and became dead weight under his own. It's doubtful if he consciously noticed but his hand eased its grip on her wrists, losing it completely to slide inside her ripped garments, caressing the velvet softness of her back. Rachel brought her freed arms down to rest, splayed out, her head flopping to the side as she waited silently for him to finish.

It did not take long.

Rachel winced as the passion exploded then seeped out of Feltman's body and his full weight came crushing down on her. He lay there contentedly, exhausted but happy.

Rachel raised her head to squint awkwardly down at him. Her delicate hand made a small fist and she knuckle-punched him on the head. "Are you quite finished?"

Feltman shifted his weight slightly. "Mmmm."

Taking that as the affirmative, Rachel lay back. She dragged a few irritating strands of hay from her hair and wiped her rapists sweat from her neck.

"Well, would you mind doing it again? I didn't enjoy it the first time."

Rachel and Feltman were leaning against the back wall of the feed stall, knees up, the gap between their calves and thighs jammed with hay. They were practically submerged.

Rachel gave him a shoulder bump. "You been savin' that up, Cowboy?"

"Not for want of tryin'," was the pointed reply.

"That sure was a lot of rude juice."

They laughed together at the teasing compliment. They must have been sat here for the best part of an hour, luxuriating in the afterglow. Only once had they been disturbed when the side door had opened and one of Duggan's regulars had come in to fetch his horse.

They had stayed still, part buried in the hay, and he had led out his mount without even glancing their way.

Now, when their laughter had subsided, they settled back, content. But it was time to talk. Or go.

So Rachel laughed.

"What are you gigglin' at?"

"Oooh, that I'm such a bad girl. That I've just been ravished by lucifer, a man who smites down the emissaries of the lord."

"Yep. Those nuns'll be gettin' their rosaries in a twist."

"Maybe. Or maybe they'll be cheering. They never had much trouble pickin' up the stench of hypocrisy."

Rachel took a breath and asked, because she had to, "So what are you, Mike? A gun for hire? Is that what you'll always be?"

Feltman thought about it. "I guess I am." He said evenly. "But not forever. Man needs to do what he can, to survive. Survive the way he wants."

"I want you to survive." She smiled and added, "Especially if you plan on there being an us?"

Feltman searched for words in the silence.

Quickly, Rachel filled it. "And I don't want Josh hurt. Or worse."

"He won't be. I'll keep him out of the firing line. He just patrols an' reports." Feltman was relieved to be able to reassure her, and mean it.

Rachel looked up at him. "You still want me, Mike? Now that you've had me?" The question was straightforward, her eyes steady.

"Yeah. I've always wanted you. From first sight."

"Ah, c'mon. That was lust." Rachel felt confident, at ease with him. "An' have you any idea how much you reeked? You were foul."

"Take your word on it. Guess I was pretty high."

"High? You were rancid. Mind you, I wasn't far behind. I was honking. I'd been in that kitchen all morning; steam an' grease don't do a lot for a girl."

"Probably fresh as prairie flowers to me."

"I believe you. Nothing puts a randy cowboy off."

He laughed and struggled to his feet. He took her hand and hauled her out of the stall. She stumbled to his side, her breasts swinging, unbound by her tattered dress and camisole.

Rachel looked up at him quizzically. "Any suggestions?"

Feltman looked around and held a finger in the air. He went over to the rig room and emerged triumphant.

Rachel wasn't impressed. "What do you expect me to do with that?" Feltman made a sweeping flourish with the blanket and draped it around her shoulders.

"I'm going to walk down the street wearing a horse blanket?"

"Why not? You look pretty; a sexy senorita."

"Well, you're coming with me. If anybody says anything, shoot them."

"Now's the time for it, definitely."

It was a coaxing statement and yet a question. A question directed, not for the first time, at Stevenson. So the big man leaned dangerously back in the impossibly small chair into which his broad hind-quarters were crammed and brought his glass of somewhat dubious whisky up under his nose for closer inspection.

Stevenson had been trying to avoid giving a direct answer to that question for the last half hour. In turn, he had side-stepped it, ignored it, went under it, went over it and went round it. Now, he realised, he would have to answer it.

The alternative was to say nothing, get up from the table and walk out the door. And he was not about to do that. No, you could never tell exactly which way things were going to come down.

But even as he made up his mind, he hesitated, jealous of the man sitting to his right. Clem Bono had answered their question immediately. Straight up, straight out. No.

And he had smiled while he was doing it.

Stevenson had trouble with that. He knew he overthought things. Made them more complicated. It was just the way he was. He always wheedled and prevaricated, desperate to end up on the right side of the fence.

Clem's business was less complicated as well. He was jealous of that. Harvest ice from the river in winter. Store it at the mine; sell it in summer.

Even his expansion plans seemed simple; running water and piped sewage; doing nothing except holding on to a majority share in his own company, allowing the mine and the railroad to take the risk.

To hell with it. He wasn't Clem.

So Stevenson finished his contemplation of the dark amber liquid and drank it down. He placed the empty shot glass on the centre of the table, which action, combined with his grimace at the lack of quality of the beverage, indicated that he would not be requiring another.

The two debonair young gentlemen seated opposite recognised that they were mere amused spectators in this verbal affray and were not offended when he ignored them, switching his gaze continually between Hartford and De Brecco while he contrived to form his answer.

The truth was simple. He was comfortable being careful.

Carefully he had built up a very modest construction company on a Cheyenne back street into a multi-trade design and build company employing hundreds. His share of the dripping roast that was Millionaires Row in Cheyenne had been the making of him. But only as a sub-contractor. The big boys were not about to let him near the high-end profits afforded by the egos of the gentlemen ranchers, who insisted on bringing out architects from New York and Washington.

So Limon had been an expansion godsend. His architects had designed the Oval on Maple, building it around the Judge's old hacienda; he had the contract for the courthouse and jail and he supplied a steady stream of material and men to the mine and the railroad. Not to mention his input into Clem's sewer and fresh water projects overseen by these two bright young dandies opposite. He had a lot to protect.

His business needed a huge and steady income to cover overheads and outlays, mostly to the large number of independent sub-contractors he engaged. Those stone masons cost a fortune. So cash flow was a constant problem.

Added to which, there were his own personal needs to consider; life, after all, had to be worth the living. And the stipend that he was consequently able to extract from those flowing dollars afforded him the luxury of living life just exactly as he pleased.

Not least the pleasure of releasing his infrequent sexual urges in a manner which gave him immense satisfaction, but which cost him dearly in the monies needed to maintain discretion.

There was also the not inconsiderable amount he poured into the bottomless pit that was his loving, spendthrift daughter and her wastrel fob of a husband, mostly to keep their particular brand of mischief respectable.

It was of these things he thought as he made up his mind to follow Clem's lead and give a very definite 'no' – that and the more minor issue of keeping himself in malt whisky and fine cigars, the ash of one of which he now flicked off his tastefully pin-striped lap.

Decision taken.

He leaned forward. "Look, boys, I understand your position and I agree with most of what you've said but I just don't get your hurry. Now ...." He went to go on but Hartford interrupted.

"Ron," the banker's irritation came spinning off the long drawn out sound of Stevenson's given name, "somebody's got to make the first move."

"Sure," Stevenson nodded in belligerent agreement, "But not me." He held up his hand to ward off any further interruptions and continued, "The guy that's brave enough to make the first move could well get wiped out. Benson don't take no prisoners. Maybe the second guy too, and maybe the flood of the brave and the righteous comes after that and everything is just dandy. You're fine, Andrew. Brec here is fine. The whole damn town is fine. But what about guy one an' guy two? You gonna cover their loses? Assuming there're the kind of loses that can be covered?"

"Oh, c'mon, Ron, that's ...."

"Sure, c'mon, Ron! This is business we're talkin' here.

223

Benson's payin' out the same interest rates you are. His charges are lower. Nobody's losin' by bankin' with him. And they ain't goin' to gain nuthin by transferrin' back to you just yet."

Stevenson paused and took a steadying puff of his cigar. "An' with respect to these two fine young gentlemen, usin' them as an example doesn't quite cut it, does it?"

The two young gentlemen in question smiled appreciatively, enjoying Hartford's discomfort.

"I don't doubt their salary would make your eyes water, but it is a salary, not turnover. You can't compare."

"And if he goes bust? Or, more likely, steals your money?"

"If he wins, he ain't likely to go bust. An' if he loses, he'll likely be dead."

"For god's sake, Ron. If he comes out on top, Benson 'won't leave it at that. You're damn near the richest man in Limon. He'll want his cut."

"Yeah, an' I have no problem with that. It's called business."

"With a gun pointing at your head? That's crime, Ron, not business."

"And what do you do, Andrew? How is that any different from Benson. A homesteader has a bad year an' can't afford to pay off the mortgage. So big hearted Western an' Central offers to give him a new loan. Of course it's only fair you double the interest rates. How is that any less of a gun? Givin' a man with no money a loan at robber rates is extortion, pure and simple."

Stevenson shook his head at himself. Start out all considered and careful and then ramble on, making enemies. Never fails.

Hartford didn't look pleased but he had no counter argument to offer.

Stevenson tried to end in a conciliatory note. "Look, I don't like the man either. I'm rootin' for you. I am. An' I'll move the accounts back when you see him off."

Clem Bono scraped his chair back and stood up. "Seems you're pressin' too early, Andy." He smiled round the table. "You've made a play, let it pan out," he advised.

Hartford was ready to come back on that but Clem wasn't looking at him. His attention had switched to a very relaxed looking Feltman who had approached unnoticed while they were all focused on the outcome of Stevenson's dithering.

"Mr Feltman," Clem smiled his bonhomie smile and extended his hand in greeting. Only the sourest of men could have spurned such an effusive welcome. And Feltman was a happy man. They shook hands warmly.

"I've no idea what you're doin' out there, preacher men excepted, but it certainly seems to be working." Clem indicated the chair he had just vacated. "Please, I've got things to do." He tipped his hat at the table. "Gentlemen."

Stevenson pursed his lips. That was Clem all over. Disagreeing with everyone and on everyone's side. He had a lot to learn still – and he was pretty damn sure not enough time or inclination to learn it."

"What's this about seeing Benson off?" Feltman was relaxed maybe, but still looking pointedly at Hartford.

"No need to get at them, Feltman," said Stevenson, "They weren't lettin' me into any deep, dark secrets."

Feltman turned his gaze on Stevenson, waiting.

"Hell, this devil's alliance you got can't last."

"We've been trying to get Clem an' Ron to set the ball rollin'," explained De Brecco, "by transferrin' their accounts back to the Western. You met Ron? Ron Stevenson, Mike Feltman."

"What was your answer?" asked Feltman.

225

The reply was lost in an explosion of outraged denials which appeared to be responding to a single accusatory voice cutting through the clamouring coming from a large booth on the far side of the saloon. A booth that was overflowing with miners in mourning.

"I said no," repeated Stevenson.

"Wise man."

"And these young geniuses are bringing us water and takin' away our shit," De Brecco continued with the introductions.

"Tomas Hawksley," the first of the confident young men nodded across the table at Feltman. He pointed at his colleague. "Freddy Bateman."

De Brecco, who had been scanning the room in a failed attempt to gain the attention of one of his staff, stood up. "Whisky?" he inquired of Feltman.

"No, thanks. Just a beer."

"I hear you are having some notable success where others have failed?" A smiling Freddy was addressing Feltman.

"Yeah, well. A fair way to go yet."

Freddy's laconic smile was transformed into a patronising chortle. "Ah, no. I was referring to a certain young lady." The laconic smile was back. "Unless, of course, that is also to whom you were referring?"

Feltman stared at Freddy with cold, calm eyes.

"If I may apologise on my friend's behalf, Mr Feltman?" Tomas Hawksley intervened. "His impetuous attempt at humour was ill-advised." He shot his friend a warning look. "I'm afraid he has to be constantly reminded that the rules for polite conversation are different out here in the west."

Feltman had not taken his eyes off Freddy. "She turn you down?"

"Me? No, not I. But she did turn the head of Tomas

here. Completely besotted he was." Tomas Hawksley's cheeks flushed above his impeccably groomed whiskers as Feltman transferred his gaze. "Flowers and sonnets," Freddy piled it on. "Picnics organised, even a pony gifted."

"There were no sonnets," Tomas Hawksley muttered his denial.

"Alas," continued Freddy, "all in vain, if my good friend is to be believed."

Feltman could see the attraction. Rachel could have succumbed to the charms of this young man. He turned back to Freddy. But not this one. This arrogant shit had been nowhere near her. He might kill the ponce anyway.

Freddy's demeanour changed as even he realised he might have gone too far. "Mr Feltman, please don't shoot me." His tone was still jocular.

"No, Mr Feltman," pleaded Tomas Hawksley, "please shoot him."

Freddy gave his friend a look that combined an apology with feigned hurt.

"Gentlemen, gentlemen," Hartford was genuinely concerned that Freddy might be heading the same way as the preacher and his cohort.

Feltman was still staring at Freddy.

Freddy opened his jacket. "I am armed, Mr Feltman," and put his hands on the table, "But I assure you, only for purposes of machismo. If I have overstepped the mark, then I sincerely apologise."

"I promise not to shoot you, Mr Bateman."

De Brecco arrived back at the table and slid into his chair. He glanced between the protagonists. "You boys havin' fun?"

Freddy smiled a tight smile. "I appreciate your gracious assurance, Mr Feltman," he was simply unable to keep the facetious note out of his voice, "but I wonder if you might clarify that that would include all means of ending my life?"

"Enough, Freddy." Tomas was losing patience. "For god's sake."

Feltman laughed. "You're safe enough Freddy. I don't kill children." Maybe he would let him live.

Another burst of agitation emanated from the miners' booth. "What goes on over there?" asked Feltman.

Hartford swivelled his neck around. "An Irish wake, I think. For that miner and his wife who drowned. Doc Brady is in amongst them somewhere."

"Damnedest thing, that," mused Stevenson. "He didn't drown from what I heard. She did. Bur seems he died just holdin' her."

"Where'd you get that from?"

"Gossip on the site. It's usually accurate enough. There weren't no water in him. Just died holdin' her."

"How'd you mean, holding her? asked De Brecco, "You mean holdin' her under? He done her in?"

"Naw, it weren't like that. He tried to stop her. She done herself in," Stevenson explained. "He was sort of huggin' her, poor guy."

Bel herself brought the tray of drinks. She placed Feltman's beer in front of him and flashed him a big smile. "There you go, Michael. Drink it all down. It'll help keep your strength up."

Feltman's expression did not change. "Didn't think you'd be up an' about this early, Bel? Girl like you needs her beauty sleep.'

De Brecco laughed at the thinly-veiled insult. "Better leave off, Bel. I think he's a little prickly this morning."

"Yeah? Well he was a little prickly last night an' that didn't come to nuthin'.''

That drew a round of delighted guffaws of appreciation at the quick rejoinder; even Feltman couldn't disguise a rueful smile. He was definitely happy today.

As Bel swished away, Hartford said, "Another strange thing happened this morning." He had their attention. "Some lawyer turned up at first light and bought out Clancy."

"Clancy? But he don't own nuthin'."

"That's what was strange." Hartford was pleased with this predicable reaction. "But this lawyer was of the opinion that the hotel had passed to Clancy on Angie's death."

"How would he know that?" asked De Brecco, sceptically. "Angie make a will? Where'd he come from, this lawyer?"

"Chicago, Clancy thought. But actually up from Cheyenne. Travelled overnight from Red Rock Springs," Hartford answered the second question first. "And no, he wasn't Angie's lawyer; but he was right. Because just after this Johns fellow left town, Lester Davenport comes across to the Oglala and confirms that Angie did make a will. Everything to the Breeds. And in the event, everything to Clancy. I got all this from Clancy himself," the banker added, less anyone should think he was repeating unsubstantiated rumour. "He was at the door when the bank opened up this morning, wanted me to check out a pending transfer he had for part payment on the hotel."

"Decent price?" inquired Stevenson.

"I'm sure Clancy thought so."

"What do you think?"

"A steal, considering the potential of the place."

"But, hell, Clancy's the manager," De Brecco cut in. "He must've known what the place was worth."

"The manager, yes, but he was offered ready cash for something he wasn't even sure was his to sell."

"What about this will?" asked Stevenson. "It legit?"

"Perfectly, according to Lester. I paid him a visit as soon

229

as I was done with Clancy. Seems Angie had made a trip down to their Cheyenne office soon after she bought the place. All signed and witnessed."

"But how would this other lawyer know that?" De Brecco reasoned. " He would have to be on his way almost before Angie got hit. Somebody set this up," he ended with the obvious.

"Well, even lawyers talk," conceded Hartford.

"Isn't Davenport your lawyer, Andrew?" Freddy was smiling across the table.

"I don't think anyone imagines saloon-keeping is my forte." Hartford dismissed the mischievous remark.

Stevenson turned to Feltman and gave him a sly look. "Kinda puts a different light on them breeds bein' bushwhacked, don't it."

Feltman considered. "Maybe. Could be a combination of grudge an' profit. Or somebody just steppin' in to take advantage."

"Couldn't be that," De Brecco was adamant. "That mouthpiece was way too quick."

"Could be Benson," suggested Feltman, "lookin' for ways to gain ground."

"Well, we've all been thinking that," said Hartford. "But why a high priced lawyer like Johns? That wouldn't fool anybody. He'd been as well getting Edgemount to handle it direct."

"That could be just to throw you," Feltman reasoned. "I guess it could be anybody."

"Hey," De Brecco protested. "don't look at me. I got enough problems holdin' on to one hotel."

Another loud chorus broke out in the far corner, but this time it was mostly respectful shouts of farewell to Doc Brady who had managed to extricate himself from the midst of the boisterous group of grieving miners and who was now weaving, a trifle unsteadily, towards the door.

Stevenson struggled out of his chair and caught the doctors arm as he went past. "You okay, Doc? If I didn't know better, I'd say you was sloshed."

"Would ye?" Violently, the doctor wrenched his arm from Stevenson's grasp. "Well, ye don't know any better than me."

"Take it easy, Doc. Here, grab a seat." It was with curiosity rather than kindness that Stevenson pulled a chair from an adjoining table and offered it to the still belligerent Brady.

De Brecco pushed the whisky bottle and his own glass across the table. "Have a settler, Doc."

The Doctor did as he was bid, throwing the small glass of burning liquid down his throat, barely pausing before pouring a refill. He looked aggressively around the faces of his new audience and thumped the whiskey bottle down challengingly in the centre of the table.

"Are yer noses botherin' ye?" The drunken perception was keen but lacked subtlety.

The men at the table glanced uneasily at each other. Stevenson got the first hint that perhaps his invitation to the Doctor had been less than wise.

"Sure, we're curious, Doc," De Brecco took the responsibility. "An' with cause. We've never seen you in this state before."

"Have ye not? Well, I'm in a damn sight better condition than that young couple we pulled out the river this morning." There was a film forming over the lenses of the Doctor's spectacles and when he snatched them off and stuffed them into his vest pocket, the mist was still there, in his eyes.

Without raising his head from his deep contemplation of his beer, Hartford said, "Yes, we heard. That must have been pretty bad."

"Bad," Doc Brady repeated slowly. "Bad." Suddenly his hand came crashing down flat on the table, making bottles and glasses jump and heads snap up. Droplets of whisky and beer arced through the air and splattered his startled audience.

"Bad!" Doc Brady's voiced roared out, choking and hoarse. "A stupid, useless, senseless tragedy. That's what it was."

The three men who best knew the doctor were stunned. His anger sprayed at them in a cloud of spittle. "That – ," Brady half turned and pointed behind him. "That bunch of demented bog-sods there. I've bin tryin' to tell them."

Whatever message the Doctor had been attempting to convey to the miners, it had struck home. Whilst they had obviously heard the collective insult, they kept their heads down, muttering amongst themselves.

"Tell them?" Brady repeated in disgust. "Sure, that's right, Doctor. Ye never said a truer word, Doctor. I'll tell ye, there's no wiser bunch o' men in the whole world right now than that pack o' donkey's shite over there in that corner."

Hartford glanced over at the crowd of miners, trying to gauge their reaction to this latest insult. They had heard this one too, but did not seem inclined to dispute it.

"What's this all about, Joe?"

"About?" The Doctor looked up and re-focussed on Hartford. "About?" he repeated in drunken emphasis. "It's about a stupid, hard-workin' son of a starvin' Irishman; comin' to a bright new land, an' havin' a loyal wife an' a lovely young family, an' work, an' money in his silly pocket. And being too dim of the brain to realise the worth of what he had."

They waited in silence while the Doctor paused to

collect another spray of drunken words.

"Not enough for him." The words were heavy in condemnation. "Too damn thick to take pleasure in his wife an' family. Ah, no. He has to go an spend his money, their money, on the other delights this world has to offer."

Again Brady turned around, this time pointing an accusing finger. "With that shower o' sods leadin' the way."

He poured himself another drink into a glass that was already full and watched as the liquid overflowed to form a murky puddle on the surface from where it sent out streams of alcoholic ash, each seeking the edge of the table.

"An' not even the sense to keep himself clean while he was doin' it."

All the heads came up at that. It was De Brecco who leaned forwarded and asked, "You sayin' … What are you sayin', Doc?"

"That the stupid shite went with one dirty, filthy woman too many. Good christ, do I have to draw you a picture, Brecco?"

De Brecco sat back, perplexed. "But people don't go around killin' themselves because they've picked up a dose, for fuck's sake. Half the miners would be hangin' from trees."

"Is that right? Course it is. I wis forgettin' you were the expert in these matters." De Brecco went red-faced under the onslaught. "You'd know all about a young, Irish girl who had an unhealthy respect for her own body drummed into her since the very first day the good father poured the water over her? Who wasn't even sure she wasn't committin' a sin when she felt desire for her own husband. You'd know everything about how that religiously repressed young woman would feel, eh? Hundreds of miles from the nearest priest. In constant sin because she couldn't attend mass; an' the only thing holdin' her together in her little tent with her children was the indisputable sanctity of her marriage. Aye, you'd know. You'd know how a fine young fella would react when he realised what he'd done to the lovely girl he'd cherished? Why, he'd head right back to your gin palace an' dance a jig with those lovely colleens. You'd know?" Doc Brady had swayed to his feet and was directing his angry, bitter words solely at an ashen-faced De Brecco. "You know nothing."

The whole room was silent now. Doc Brady took a step backwards and knocked over his chair. His face registered alarm at the noise it created in the quietened bar. "Well, gentlemen, I believe I have said my piece for the night."

He carefully lifted his over-filled glass from the table and just as carefully put it back down again, untouched.

"I'll apologise to you in the morning, Brec. Right now I have to go and sleep this off. You never know when somebody might need a doctor in this god damned town."

The silence held while the Doctor negotiated ten unsteady steps to the door. Then, gradually, all eyes came up to look at De Brecco who was staring fixedly at nothing.

There was not even a semblance of colour in his rigid features. At the bar, Bel, who knew the sensitivities of her business partner better than most, was glancing anxiously across at their table, trying to decide whether she should come over.

Finally, Stevenson said, "Hell, Brec, don't take it so bad. The old butcher had no call to lay it at your door."

Without replying, De Brecco got up abruptly from the table and walked stiffly to his office under the main staircase. He wrenched the door open and disappeared inside. Bel followed, closing the door quietly behind them.

Stevenson shook his head. "I should never have got the drunken old bastard to sit down. Why pick on De Brecco, for christ's sake. Bel's girls are the cleanest in town. I know that for a fact." In trying to make amends for his lack of judgement, Stevenson was becoming a little indiscreet.

Hartford had a try at a wry smile. "Yes, we know"

"But, hell, the Doc should know that better'n anybody. He checks them out often enough. So why the sermon?"

When this last contribution did not even generate the expected polite nods of agreement Stevenson decided that it was time to head home. He consoled himself with an accusatory glare at the remains of the bottle of cheap whisky and pushed himself out of his chair. Other than refusing Hartford's overtures, he had made an ass of himself every time he had opened his mouth. Resolving not to open that particular orifice again that day, he gave a curt nod to the table and left.

Hartford sat for a few moments, contemplating whether he should attempt to heal the rift which had sprung up between himself and Ron. Ignorant of the silent promise Stevenson had made to himself, Hartford drank down the few remaining drops of his beer and, with a friendly enough nod at Feltman and the Water Boys hurried out after his former customer.

Freddy spread his hands, "Dominos?" the laconic smile was back in place, not a shred of empathy for the trials and tribulations of others. "It was, after all, the ruse Andrew employed to give him an opportunity to cajole Mr Bono and berate dear Ronald."

"Another time," Feltman smiled a polite refusal. "I'll leave you boys to play with yourselves."

As he watched Feltman take up a position at the bar close to the miners' booth, Freddy tilted his head back towards Tomas and said, confidentially, "I do believe our Mr Feltman regards himself as something of a wit."

"As opposed to my half-wit of a friend," said Tomas.

Feltman scanned the bereavement huddle until he picked out the bull-like features of O'Sullivan whose cunning eyes were constantly darting between the faces of his companions, judging their reactions to his own quietly spoken words.

He was winding them up nicely.

Out of the corner of his eye, O'Sullivan had seen Feltman stand up and had realised immediately that the gunman intended to come over. O'Sullivan recognised the professional mercenary. This one was more than a hirling with a gun.

Well, he had dealt with plenty of that kind before. You could always handle them one way or another. Deliberately keeping his head turned away from where he sensed Feltman was standing, O'Sullivan continued to survey the faces of the men who were tightly packed around him in the large booth; hunched over and animated, all were eager to reach agreement on the appropriate course of action drink and their righteous souls demand they take.

Eventually, as it became obvious the heat in the conversation was about to die altogether as man after man became aware of Feltman's hoovering presence, O'Sullivan stood and squeezed himself out of the booth. He went past Feltman without a word as he moved further down the bar. Feltman followed.

Behind them, the conversation picked up again, though on a new tact.

O'Sullivan indicated to the barman who put up a bottle of rye and two shot glasses. O'Sullivan shoved one of the glasses back at him. "Safer not to feed firewater to a man wi your temper," he said to Feltman. "An' I'm not religious in case ye were wonderin'."

Feltman smiled. It was hard not to. "You think they didn't deserve it?"

"Ah, they did that. As sure as the blessed balls o' Saint Brendan." O'Sullivan threw back his rye. "But we don't all get what we deserve now, do we?"

"You think you deserve to own a nice little bodega?"

"I wis wonderin' when ye wid be getting' around te me." And at Feltman's pretend puzzlement, "Ye've bin round everyone else."

"You been feeling left out? I'm only tryin' to stop trouble brewin', O'Sullivan. It's easier than meeting it head on."

"Well, now, doesn't that have a familiar ring to it?" The Irishman gave him a big smile and said, " Ye know, I insist on all me friends callin' me Sean." He downed the small shot of rye with obvious relish and helped himself to a refill. "You can call me, Mr O'Sullivan."

"I might be callin' you Sean yet."

"Ye might be after havin' no teeth."

"You might be thinkin' your boys are wound up enough over this suicide to have another go at Ramon's?"

O'Sullivan was disdainful. "Me bhoys?" he queried. "They're not my bhoys, Mr Feltman. They're not even all Irish. Did ye not hear the Polish mixin' wi the brogue? What they are, is a group o' hard-workin', independently-minded individuals who, after due consideration o' the facts o' the matter and a certain amount of friendly argument, will arrive at their own decision."

"And prompted by you, there's a good chance they'll decide to take care of Ramon. After all, he does run the dirtiest whorehouse in town. Not to mention bein' a lyin' cheatin' robber of drunken Irishmen."

O'Sullivan gave Feltman a curious look. "Now, that bein' the case, why are ye tryin' so hard te keep him in business? I take it that smart young fella, Colby, was doin' your bidding?"

"Yeah, he was. An' he'll do my biddin' tonight as well. He should get there just after you've taken care of Ramon. Just in time to make sure the bodega is left undamaged."

For once, there was just the hint of hesitation in the single, flowing motion O'Sullivan used when downing his drink. "Barman, there's two men drinkin' here, an' only the one glass between us."

Turning to Feltman, he said, "The judge an' his friends wouldn't be getting' ye cheap, would they?"

"No," Feltman admitted.

"Good, because the barman needs payin'."

When O'Sullivan had finished his third drink and Feltman his first, the squat Irishman said, "Ye've surely not bin here long enough to work out the way things are. Who wis tellin' ye that I had me eye on Ramon's?"

"You have to do something with the pay-off you got from the mine owners," Feltman repeated De Brecco's reasoning, refraining from adding, 'unless you've already pissed it all away?'

"So that's the way it is? Rather a troublesome Irish lad than a greasy Mexican. Gawd, but Ramon must be a terrible stink under Perry's nose. An' the man himself approves o' what yer doin'?"

"He won't know for sure what I was doin' and nobody is goin' to object to the outcome. Especially if the girls are kept in check, and clean," Feltman assured him. "What I don't get is how you'll keep the miners on side, after they figure out your motives were less than pure?"

"Well, I won't be sittin' on me throne surrounded by harlots, will I?" O'Sullivan asked with theatrical sarcasm. "Financial backing only, me bhoy, with a good return an' the odd fiery red-head thrown in."

Feltman was genuinely intrigued. "Bel got a twin sister?"

O'Sullivan touched his nose. "A lovely little woman from New York, jist dyin' to get out west an' do some pioneerin'."

They both laughed at that.

"But I'm right in thinkin' ye'll be wantin' a little something for yourself?" O'Sullivan was watching Feltman closely. "I mean, the place will have to be shut down for a while; a week or so, memories are short. But I wouldn't want anyone thinking they could maybe queer me pitch."

"It's yours, that's the deal. You can bunk in there if you like. Take possession," Feltman shrugged, "Who's gonna argue?"

"I wis thinkin' more along the lines o' a temporary hostel for wayward women. Sure, it would be a harsh man who wid throw those poor whores out on the street."

This time they shared their merriment with a smile. But O'Sullivan was wary, still sizing it up. He was a bit suspicious that Feltman hadn't asked for a cut. But maybe the gunman simply couldn't see the bigger picture. The cantina was just the start, a toehold. O'Sullivan intended to own all of the west end apex. Because that slum would not be standing for long. Perry and the rest simply would not allow it. It would be demolished to make way for the civilised expansion of the town – and they would pay top dollar.

"So, me bhoy, how were ye planin' te go about this?"

"As before. Except Colby will get there too late, thinkin' you'll make your move at full dark. But you go in early, real early ….."

"In daylight?"

"So much the better; no one will expect you. Only, this time, don't make a parade out of it. Gather in the back streets an' come in like you're customers, get the drop on them and get it over quick."

Feltman paused to pour himself a drink. "I expect you to deal with Ramon yourself."

"Well, that's kind o' ye. There's nothin' like mixin' business wi pleasure. But tell me now, what happens when that efficient Mr Colby comes runnin' with all them dangerous lookin' rifles?"

"You've said it. He's efficient, an' he'll do exactly as he's told. No miners get hurt. The town wouldn't like it. By the time Colby gets there he'll only be tidying up. Course, if any of your crew is unlucky enough to catch a bullet from Ramon's boys …"

"Aye. An' you get another bit o' the town cleaned up at no risk to your good self? 'Tis a bright lad ye are."

"Do we have a deal, Mr O'Sullivan?"

"Wis I no tellin' ye me name's Sean?"

Setting up Colby was simpler but required more patience. It took the best part of an hour's careful watching and waiting before he finally caught the man on his own. There was no way Feltman wanted another run-in with McCabe and to have approached Benson direct would have been to invite just that.

He eventually managed to get hold of Colby when Judd called him out to deal with a couple of Benson's boys who, despite all previous warnings, and liberally aided by copious alcoholic intake, were amusing themselves with a little excessive baiting of the gunsmith's new help.

By the time Colby got there − closely followed by Feltman − this happy pair had already altered Henderson's hairstyle with the discerning use of a can of grease; coated his shirt with a blue-black slick of gun oil and, intent on lubricating the big man's pecker, were engaged in a feeble attempt at removing his pants.

Feeble, because the sight of this six foot plus giant

covered in gun oil had reduced them to near helpless laughter.

To be fair, they had started off good-naturedly enough with some light-hearted banter about the guy's size. But, between old Van telling them to lay off and Henderson's infuriatingly vacant stare, they had probed deeper and more viciously, looking for a reaction. When it still did not come they had got mad and sought retribution in physical abuse.

Colby got there just in time. Because Mr Van had had enough and was coming round his counter with a very serious looking peacemaker in his left hand.

Colby hit them once each - behind the ear with his forty-four - and ordered, "Get them out of here."

Judd, with a growing efficiency for which he was becoming renowned, duly obliged.

Mr Van was scowling at Colby and Feltman, the big peacemaker swinging competently in his hand. "This shit happens again, Colby, an' I'll blow them fuckers away."

"Alfred!" This warning on the inappropriate use of language came from Mrs Van who was now administering aid and comfort to the young Mr Henderson.

Colby simply nodded his agreement. Mr Van turned to Feltman. "Ain't we payin' you to put a stop to this kind of nonsense?"

"It got stopped."

"After it happened." Mr Van believed he had made his point and so left the gunmen chastised, contemplating their shortcomings.

"So what do you want?" asked Colby as they walked off along the sidewalk.

"O'Sullivan intends to hit Ramon's again tonight."

Colby stopped. An invitation to Feltman to explain what the hell O'Sullivan thought he was doing.

"Yeah, I know. But things have changed."

Colby said nothing, waiting for more.

"He thinks that suicide last night gives him the edge, that the town's on his side."

"And are they?"

"Yeah. They are."

"So what do you need me for?"

"Tonight you side with the miners. Make sure none of the crazy bastards get themselves killed."

"Yesterday we stopped them. Tonight we help them?"

"Yeah. Only let them get on with it. But your guys step in if any of O'Sullivan's boys look to be in trouble."

"Hard to guarantee. Those pistoleros who hang around Ramon ain't exactly a bunch o' Marys. Easier if we just take them out."

"No. Has to be the miners. You're just there as back-up. An' don't mention this to McCabe."

Colby smiled a sad smile. "You think I can muster a dozen men an' Dave won't notice?"

"Tell Benson then. Let it come from him. McCabe's got the red mist. He's not reliable. Benson knows that."

Colby nodded. Made sense. "What time you need us there?"

"Don't know for sure. O'Sullivan will probably want to be certain they're well liquored up before he lets them loose." Feltman thought about it. " An' they're half way there already. Best you round up your guys an' have them ready an' waiting as early as you can. I'll send Josh to fetch you when we know. Come runnin'."

Colby acquiesced without further query; but he had another question, "You know he's goin' to kill you, don't you Feltman?"

"I know one of us is going to die."

Josh and Feltman were slouched on a couple of chairs

on the sidewalk at the very tip of Grant, just before it disintegrated into the tenderloin district. The multitude of faint shadows which the fading twilight cast on the street in front of the bodega had the effect of making what light remained very deceptive. But only for detail. Anything the size of a man would be clearly seen.

Feltman was getting a little twitchy. He had expected O'Sullivan long before now.

"I still can't believe he's havin' another shot at this," said Josh, in a slight variation of what he had been mumbling since they'd sat down.

Feltman did not bother to reply. Josh had helped to drag the couple out of the river last night. He knew why.

So they waited, one silently fretting; one idly speculating. And what they saw just five minutes later was a pair of apparently merry Irishmen (who, no doubt, had gone to a great deal of trouble to make the illusion seem as real as possible) weave their way across the street and disappear noisily into the cathouse.

Feltman was impressed. A man who could take advice was no fool. It would be easier for O'Sullivan if he already had some of his boys inside. His opinion waned a little when another four of his brave bhoyos repeated the process less than a minute later; and he positively winced when yet another group of miners staggered up to the whorehouse.

"Balls!"

The one word invective neatly summed up Feltman's reassessed opinion of commander O'Sullivan's tactical abilities. Ramon wouldn't be, couldn't be, that stupid. O'Sullivan was going to make a pig's ear out of this.

Josh nudged him, but there was no need. The lines of crouching miners now approaching the whorehouse from both sides were plainly visible. Feltman would have hated to get into a street fight with O'Sullivan but god help his

243

troops if the burly Irishman was ever called upon to wage a guerrilla campaign.

Urgently, Feltman grabbed Josh's arm. "Get over to the hotel fast an' tell Colby to get his ass over here."

Josh's fleeing footsteps had barely faded when a single, high-pitched shriek indicated that one of Ramon's whores had spotted O'Sullivan's intrepid fusiliers. Or maybe somebody had just squeezed her too hard. Either way, all hell broke loose.

There were flying miners everywhere. Smashing and leaping headlong through windows; hurling themselves through doorway (there was only the one, so a certain lack of timing led to a bit of bickering); jumping up and scrambling on to the roof. The roof? What the fuck where they doing on the roof? Feltman went in at the run, doing a passible imitation of a miner himself as he dived through the front door, gun drawn.

For all his doubts, the fight was definitely a little one-sided. If you ignored the biting, kicking and scratching of the women, most of Ramon's vaqueros had been jumped before they had a chance to draw their hardware and, with two exceptions, were sprawled about in various stages of unconsciousness, completely helpless.

In the far right hand corner, near one of the curtained exits from the saloon, a hand to hand knife fight was in progress. There could be no doubt about the outcome. For even if the more skilful looking Mexican was to gain the upper hand, the ring of pick handles and spike hammers surrounding the combatants would rain ruthlessly down, ending the contest.

And directly in front of Feltman, a dark, wiry vaquero was struggling desperately under the weight of his two assailants; wriggling and sliding frantically along the timber floor, he managed to get half his body clear and clawed in a frenzied motion for his still holstered pistol.

Feltman stepped forward and placed the chilling coldness of his gun barrel against his throbbing temple. The man froze, turning his frightened eyes as far as they would go without moving his head, instinctively trying to see who stood behind the gun.

"Up."

The command was directed at Ramon's man but the miners made it easier for him by also obeying and removing their combined weight from his legs.

"Where's Ramon?" Feltman asked as he relieved his captive of temptation.

No answer.

"What's your name?"

The man was subdued, not stupid. No point in suffering unnecessary pain. "Miguel."

"Where's Ramon, Miguel?"

Miguel pointed and Feltman pushed him through the other curtained exit, leaving the miners to get on with whatever rape and pillage they could handle.

They emerged in a narrow painted hallway. Feltman was again about to inquire 'where?' when the sounds of battle, liberally interspersed with O'Sullivan's rich and inventive cursing, made the question superfluous.

Nudging the smaller man forward, Feltman holstered his own gun and followed, stopping outside the open door where Miguel was peering inside with some trepidation.

Feltman clipped him softly behind the ear. Not too hard. Not hard enough to put him out completely but hard enough to make his knees buckle and send him crashing to the floor inside the bedroom.

The master's bedroom. For this was no crib. But the lavish décor was being systematically destroyed by the two separate battles being waged under the glow of the surviving oil lamp.

On the far side of the bed, O'Sullivan was battering hell and features out of Ramon's head while at this end Ramon's woman was clawing great chunks of skin from what used to be a miner's face.

Feltman waited patiently while the woman's arms and legs were finally quelled in a huge bear hug then waved his captured gun from the doorway. "Get her out of here. Take her back to the saloon."

The miner nodded his bloodied face in acknowledgement. He released his hold and pushed Christina towards the door. Which was a mistake. She whirled and her viciously long blood-red nails slashed out and gouged yet another strip of flesh from his hideously pulpy face.

"Suka!" The polish curse was spat out in flecks of blood and the mistake was rectified by a hard left to Christina's chin which sent her head snapping back, knocking her cold. The gallant miner caught her neatly over his shoulder as she bounced back off the wall. He brushed past Feltman, reaching down with his free hand to grab Miguel by the belt as he went.

"Leave him," Feltman ordered. "I'll bring him."

"It is no trouble."

"I said I'll get him."

He turned his attention back into the room where the fight seemed to be between rounds. Both men were still on the far side of the bed, but O'Sullivan's hands now hung loosely at his sides, his breathing heavy, recovering from the punishing toll of trying to beat the holy shite out of his opponent. Ramon himself was half-collapsed over a mirrored dressing table, his two mutilated heads trying to hold each other up as he summoned reserves of strength to continue the fray.

"You plan to club him to death?" Feltman asked O'Sullivan.

"God, but you're an impatient man. He'll go in his own good time."

"We haven't got the time," Feltman reminded him. "The cavalry will be here any second."

Ramon turned then, and pushed himself off the dresser. In his left hand, a long, slim blade gleamed wickedly in the wavering, artificial light. The man's black eyes blazed hatred across the room. His words were muffled behind lacerated, puffed up lips; but the meaning was clear.

O'Sullivan appeared unconcerned. But Feltman was not. Anxiously, he glanced down at Miguel who was beginning to show signs of coming round. He could not afford to hit him again. He might not recover from the second one.

O'Sullivan was calling out encouragement to Ramon. "C'mon then, ye black heathen. Let's be havin' ye."

Feltman shifted his focus back just as Ramon took a vicious, arcing swipe at O'Sullivan's face. The broad, bulky Irishman sprang back with commendable alacrity, then quickly forward again, trying to get in close while Ramon's knife hand was across his own body.

But the Mexican was just as fast. As O'Sullivan rushed in the knife was flashing to meet him, stopped only by the big, sure hands that clamped down on Ramon's wrist.

For a second, Feltman considered putting a bullet through Ramon but, as he hesitated, O'Sullivan gave a tremendous heave on his opponent's arm which threw both men off balance, sending them crashing to the floor out of sight behind the bed.

"For christ's sake," wailed Feltman, "finish him, O'Sullivan."

Feltman jerked around when he heard the sound of the

heavy curtain parting. He stepped over Miguel, pulling the door over behind him. The cavalry had finally arrived. There were three of them, all carrying rifles.

"One of you get back in there," ordered Feltman, "an' make sure nobody else comes through that curtain."

Colby must have briefed them well. They didn't argue. One gunhand stepped back through the curtain on guard duty while Feltman turned to the others. " You two check out these rooms for stragglers. Herd them round and hold them in the bar."

The men nodded and moved on, kicking open the doors of the whores' cribs as they went, working their way out of sight round the corner.

Feltman could feel the sweat running damp on his spine as he pushed the door open again.

The sounds of the savage struggle were still coming from beyond the bed. Suddenly, a heavy, gasping grunt signalled the end of the conflict.

Everything went quiet.

"O'Sullivan?" Feltman asked of the bed. "O'Sullivan, that you?"

Cautiously, he extended Miguel's gun, sighting along the barrel about a foot above the bed.

The hand came up first, clutching at the cover. Slowly, inch by inch, the Irishman's bull head appeared until his chin was level with the top of the bed.

"An' jist who the hell else wis ye expectin'?"

"O'Sullivan." Feltman breathed out the name in a sigh of relief. "O'Sullivan, thank christ it's you."

And then he shot him. Just the one bullet. In the face. And if O'Sullivan had time to register surprise it was quickly wiped off.

Miguel was already on his feet, shaking his head groggily in an attempt to clear it. Feltman prodded him in the back of the neck with the hot muzzle of his own gun.

"Move."

They took the long way round, Feltman checking as he went for any stragglers Benson's boys might have missed. A worried Miguel led the way around the rectangle of cribs until they arrived at the other exit behind the bar.

"Miguel, wait." It was a soft command. But Miguel had no wish to antagonise his captor further and stopped immediately. Ahead, the babble of sullen and angry protest could be heard mixing with the harsh, disinterested commands from Colby's men, together providing a further barrier of sound beyond the heavy fabric.

"Turn around."

Nervously, Miguel did as he was told, looking uneasily at the wrong end of his own gun. He jerked uncontrollably, and then stood, gaping in astonishment as he realised that this maldito gringo had leaned forward and deftly replaced the weapon in its rightful holster.

"That belongs to you." Feltman was smiling at Miguel, still talking quietly.

But the first inkling of relief which had begun to spread though the little man's body vanished when he saw Feltman's hand drop to hoover over the butt of his own gun.

"I like to give a man a chance."

Then, Miguel had a choice. He could have gone for his own gun. Or he could have taken a dive through that handy curtain. After pondering it for no time at all, he went through the curtain.

The reception on the other side almost stopped him dead. Literally. Wildly, he half-spun round, away from the circle of rifles, caught sight of Feltman's .44 cleaving its way through the heavy-beaded curtain, and flung himself, headlong and desperate, through what was left of a busted window frame.

He landed badly. Going over on his shoulder, his left knee crashed sickeningly into a hitching rail upright, which was probably the only solidly constructed article in the whole district, causing spasms of excruciating pain to shoot along the entire length of his leg.

But he was badly spooked and he went off at a hopping run across the street, moving almost as fast as he had ever done on two good legs.

Three strides had taken Feltman to the shattered window. "Stop him," he roared at those of Colby's men who were covering the street, his own gun tracking the erratic run of the pathetic fugitive. "He killed O'Sullivan."

Miguel would never have made it up the wide-spaced timbers to the dilapidated boards that served as a sidewalk in this part of town had it not been for the helpful impact of the six or seven heavy-calibre rifle bullets which sent him upwards, twisting his decimated body round and dumping what was left of it in a ghastly sitting position at the top of the steps.

It stayed there, staring sightlessly back at Feltman for a few seconds before the head slid sideways, overbalancing the grotesque remains to send them tumbling back down the steps. Feltman eased down the hammer of his colt and tucked it away.

Three men were running up the street, using that universal gait which indicates a certain lack of fitness. As they neared the whorehouse, one of them broke off, heading for the decimated corpse, crumpled at the bottom of the steps. Doc Brady.

But two of Colby's men were already there, and, at a deterring wave of a rifle, he changed course again, back to the bodega. Feltman turned to find Colby giving him a cold, flat stare. He ignored it, as Colby was ignoring the hacked off punter whose interrupted sexual release had made him very irate indeed. "Can't a man have a roll with a bed fagot without havin' a rifle barrel jammed up his ass?"

Finally, Colby turned, "Go home."

The instruction was embraced by all of the bodega's early clientele and a stream of men made for the door, including those of the miners who had decided that now was a good time to leave.

Doc Pardoe brushed past them on his way in, closely followed by Perry. Colby motioned Pardoe through the curtains. The Judge, not quite certain what his role was under these chaotic circumstances, strode into the centre of the room, the better to survey the shambles.

There was a lot to look at.

With the exception of Christina, who had been laid out on a table especially re-erected to hold her inert form, all of the girls were now huddled behind the bar, and, with the loss of excitement that comes with the cessation of hostilities, most of them had taken refuge in what they fondly imagined was a show of womanly emotion. They were weeping.

Ramon's men were bunched together in the middle of the saloon, subdued and sullen, surrounded by Colby's riflemen. Those miners that had stayed were dispersed around the room in that variety of stunned and crestfallen poses adopted by men who are painfully aware that they have just taken part in a monumental fuck-up.

Brady entered from the street. He was ashen-faced but got himself together when he saw Christina and headed over to see what he could do.

The Judge became aware that his stroll into the middle of the room seemed to align him with Ramon's rabble and he took a few careful steps backwards, into the circle of rifles. "What in god's name has happened now, Feltman?"

Feltman thought it was fairly obvious but he gave him the hidden details anyway.

"O'Sullivan? Dead?" Judge Perry shook his head in a show of remorse that could only have been for the benefit of the miners. "Is there no end to this?"

Originality of oration is not a requirement for a county court judge.

Feltman told the miners to go home.

Pardoe came back into the room just as Doctor Brady finished administering to Christina. Pardoe was decidedly the brisker of the two. "Nothing I can do in there. Let's see if we can patch these people up."

"Do it down at the jailhouse, will you Doc?" Feltman commanded. He turned to address Colby and for the first time realised Judd was in the room. "Judd. You're gettin' around. Get the Mexes down to the cells. In the morning, let them have their horses. They're all leavin' town."

Judd, learning more every day, just stopped himself from inquiring where the hell their horses might be and began to herd his morose-looking charges out the door.

"Judge, you get a notice posted? Closing this place down?"

Perry nodded, and left immediately, happy to abandon his conspicuously useless position in the middle of the saloon.

Colby was at Feltman's side. There was no knowing look but his tone was flat. "What about them?" he asked, indicating the tearful whores.

"O'Sullivan had a good idea."

"His last one?"

Feltman smiled. He liked Colby. "He thought maybe this should be turned into a refuge for wayward woman."

Colby couldn't help the eyebrow.

"They can stay here. Where they eventually go is up to

252

them. But not her," Feltman clarified. He pointed at Christina. "She's got the fire in her. When she comes to, she'll be lookin' to stab somebody."

"So where?"

"Jail." Feltman was expecting a protest from Brady but none came. The doctor simply walked outside.

Colby leaned over the bar and pulled up a large tin box with a layer of coins in the bottom. He gave it a shake. "Not much there to keep them going."

"Ramon must have a stash. Try his boudoir."

Doc Brady was still on the sidewalk with Josh when Feltman came out. It was hard to distinguish any definite expression on his face in the rapidly deteriorating light but his voice was choking when he spoke.

"I set this off," he confessed. His troubled eyes searched Feltman's for understanding. "God help me, this isn't what I meant. I didn't mean for them to do this."

Feltman put a consoling hand on Brady's shoulder. "Take it easy, Doc. It's not your fault. It couldn't be helped."

Twelve

In the old days, back in Holland, Joep ten Dam had been cheerful and gregarious – and poor. Here, in the new lands, he was happy enough as a rule, but quiet – and a fair bit richer.

It was the language that had quietened him down. Or the lack of it. For even now, after all these years, he still had to think in Dutch before forming the words in English. And the same in reverse when someone was conversing with him. He found he still had to go through this tedious process in order to gain a full understanding of what was being said.

He supposed it had not helped that Annemieke had not taken to English at all. She understood most of the essentials of it but, aside from everyday store purchases and the quick phrases of salutation and farewell, shyness or some other inherent reticence had held her back from immersing herself in the new tongue; and now, he knew, she never would.

Now, as he looked across at his beautiful wife, her head bowed over the checker board in deep concentration, Joep gave himself a mental slap. He could never blame his lovely wife for any of his many failings.

And this was a failing. He could not be sure he had understood properly. And yet he was sure he had. The doubt gnawed at his stomach; his distraction obvious.

Annemieke glanced up from her study of the board having failed to work out how her normally ruthless opponent was going to achieve her annihilation. Her smile showed her concern for his mood as she gently admonished him for taking so long between moves.

He smiled at her. "Het is niets."

He stopped scratching his bushy beard for a moment and leaned forward to give the board a cursory inspection before moving one of his few remaining dark-grained pieces. Annemieke studied the board in detail. It was not unknown for her devious husband to lead her on until with only one of his crowns remaining, he was able to clear the board of all her pieces.

Joep sat back and lapsed once again into private thought. Earlier that evening, as another hectic day at the sawmill was winding down, he had gone to give his answer. The offers had come in over a week ago and his deliberations had been long and careful.

Joep liked to work; he liked being his own man. But he had to face reality. He was getting old. And they had no son, nor a daughter, to inherit what they had built. He gazed down fondly on Annemieke's bent head, resisting the urge to caress the silver strands and golden flecks of her hair. His heart burst for her.

Both of his suiters had been patient, willing to keep him on. More than willing; preferring. But he could not take orders from men he did not respect. He was done with that. Done a long time ago.

So he would sell. But not now. And not to Mr Benson. Maybe to Mr Stevenson, perhaps even next year, if his old bones told him it was time to stop.

It had been time to give an answer. Mr Benson first. It was only polite since this would be a firm refusal. Mr

Stevenson would not mind waiting a little longer for a more hopeful 'No.'

At the Limon Hotel, Joep had been received politely by Mr Walker and asked if he would not mind waiting since Mr Benson was rather busy at the moment. Mr Walker would let him know Mr ten Dam was here.

So he had sat himself down on a comfortable couch in the hallway outside the secretary's anteroom and waited.

He used the time to get his thoughts in place for the polite refusal. And when he had that clear he passed the time in idle speculation on the many comings and goings from Mr Benson's office further down the hall.

And still he waited. Until he could wait no longer. He had rapped politely on Mr Walker's door and entered only to find the room surprisingly empty. He crossed the room behind the secretary's desk to the adjoining door and was about to repeat his rap and enter procedure when his brain started to relay the full meaning of the words being voiced behind the door. His clenched fist had frozen in the air, only inches from the door panel, while his confused mind tried to work out a course of action.

Perhaps he had misheard? No, he had not misheard. And, in any case, standing outside the office door with his hand poised foolishly in mid-air was not the best place to debate the issue. So he had left. As quickly and as quietly as possible, hoping all the while that he had indeed been forgotten.

The number of armed men gathered at the bottom of the stairway had spooked him a little, but he shouldered past them, able to breathe again as he hit the night air.

The walk back to his house on Maple had seemed unfamiliar, the town streets cold and depressing. He knew he had understood. But who to speak to? Who would listen.

Annemieke spoke softly to him, without triumph. Joep looked sharply down at the board on which they were only light-grained pieces. He shrugged, accepting his defeat gracefully. He reached out a big hand, pulling her head close enough to kiss.

"I am going out. I will not be long."

Annemieke was concerned now. She spoke quickly in Dutch. Joep shook his head, attempting to reassure her. "Ik ben zo terug. Just a little business."

He had decided. The doctors were his best bet. Doctor Pardoe lived just across the Oval and Joep was knocking on his door in less than a minute. Only to be disappointed.

The Doctor had been called out. Would he like to wait? No, thank you. Having come to a decision, Joep did not want to wait. He trudged down the less salubrious end of Maple to Doctor Brady's office and bachelor's residence on the corner of Main.

But no joy there either. Doctor Brady was apparently also out on call. 'He might be down at the jailhouse. Some o' those Mexes took a hell o' a whuppin'.' Whilst not fully grasping the story behind this information, volunteered by a helpful passer-by, Joep understood that he was likely to find the good Doctor down at the jailhouse. So he lumbered on. Resolute.

Feltman was relaxed. Not even the chill creeping through the bathwater dented his serenity. He had achieved a lot, much more than he'd thought possible. And in so short a time. At times like this, he wished he smoked. A big, fat cigar would round off the image he had of himself luxuriating in his bath.

He should slow down. Take a breath. No mistakes now. Not when he had found something he had not even been looking for.

The finale had always been the tricky part. Still was. Fraught with danger for everybody; and not least for him. He was comfortable with improvising. Even without the complication of Rachel, he had been reviewing his options. And now, with her? There was only one option. And he knew he was going to take it.

There was a rap on the door and Marie-Louise's magnificent cleavage preceded her smile into the room. "You ready for some more hot water, honey?"

Feltman smiled. He was sorely tempted. But no. "Marie-Louise, you know you're too good for this place?"

"I know." She did know.

"You should flash those bamboozlers at Freddy an' ... What's the other one?"

"Tomas."

"Tomas. They'd most probably fight a duel over you."

"An' the winner whisk me away to old London town?" Marie-Louise laughed as she came swaying into the room. "Don't be silly, they both had me already." She gave him an enticing, lingering view as she reached down for the empty bucket. "You sure?"

"Yeah, thanks."

She swayed away, not offended. "You're welcome."

The door clicked softly shut and Feltman eased back in the bath. But the water was getting cold. Time to get out. And sleep. Sleep would be good.

As Joep reached the jailhouse, he realised he could not go in. Judd was Benson's man. Even if the Doctor was in there he could not speak in front of Judd. He would have to wait. Where? Where would he wait? He was beginning to feel slightly ridiculous, and afraid.

He was tempted to head home. Deal with it in the morning. But he would fret. Worry Annemieke. And he would not sleep. He had to deal with it now.

The shutters were closed on the jailhouse windows. He could not even look in. He started to retrace his steps back up Grant towards Main. He stepped down into the gap in the sidewalk and peered into the alley at the edge of the jail. Darker; more discreet but too close.

He regained the sidewalk and kept going for a block until he was beyond the intersection at Stonewall. The next alley was even darker, but felt safer. He eased himself into the shadows and waited, watching; hoping for either of the doctors to come out of the jailhouse.

But each second was an eternity, feeding his anxiety. He was beginning to fall apart, realising now how foolish he had been. He should have stayed. These men were not stupid. They would be puzzled he had simply gone and wondering why. He thought maybe he should go back to Doctor Pardoe's and just wait.

The jailhouse door creaked open, but it was neither Doctor Brady nor Doctor Pardoe who emerged. It took Joep a second or two before he recognised young Josh.

He knew Josh. He had given the young man work when he had first arrived in town with his sister. A pleasant young man but not cut out for the heavy toil of working with timber. Josh. He would tell Josh. Josh would listen and convince others; and relieve him of this terrible burden. Joep went further back into the shadows and waited for Josh to draw level.

Josh was tired. He wanted to crawl into his cot above Ma's and sleep 'til Sunday.' Last night had been bad. Helping to get that young wife out of the river wasn't something he ever wanted to do again.

And tonight. Jesus. Three dead, including O'Sullivan. This town was just plain crazy. He just wanted to pull the covers over his head and sleep.

The clipping of his footsteps missed a beat then ceased altogether as he reached the break in the boards at the saddlers side alley. There wasn't much light here. His right boot had left the sidewalk and was poised briefly in mid-air as a prelude to a careful placing when the harsh urgent whispering of his name assailed him from the darkness.

His boot to come down much faster than intended and sent him forward in a stumbling run which he nimbly converted into a hopping turn as he whirled round, checking his rear; his hand sweeping down in an un-practised clutch at his gun.

Nobody.

A faint recognition stirred in his head as the croaking whisper came again.

"Joshua."

From the alley? Nothing. Just a great black hole relieved by neither moon nor starlight. But he knew that somebody was in there somewhere. Just as he was certain he knew the voice.

"Joshua. It is Joep."

And it was Joep. He was sure of that now. "You okay, Joep? Something wrong?"

Christ. What a damn fool question. Of course something was wrong. Normal folks don't go around whisperin' at each other from dark alleys by choice.

"Nothing is wrong." That made Joep as daft as he was. "I have to speak with you. Come, please, out of the light."

Josh put his gun away and, his nerves jangling with a mixture of trepidation and foolishness, he started to make his way down the track using careful, exploring steps. He could see nothing. Nothing at all. "Joep?"

"I can see you. Just another few steps."

Josh shuddered violently as he felt the contact made by the hand that reached out to touch his chest, stopping him.

"For christ's sake, Joep. Did you have to do that?" he took a couple of gulping breaths to steady himself and asked, "Okay, what's so damn important we can't talk over at your place?"

The bravado in the tone was an outlet for his nerves. Josh was concerned, not angry.

Joep did not answer.

"Or at my place?"

Joep, whom Josh still could not see, mouthed something intelligible at him out of the darkness.

"C'mon, Joep," Josh burst out in exasperation, "this is no time to lose the English."

When Joep still did not answer, Josh thought that maybe he was going to die.

You don't have to die.

Move.

You have a choice.

Step backwards. Pull out your gun and shoot.

Just move.

Jump. Dive. Roll. Pull out your gun and blast away.

If you have to die take your killer with you.

I'm going to die.

Run then. Nothing else. Just run.

Run.

It took Josh's brain the merest fraction of a second to issue this constant stream of suggested action and consequence in a kindly attempt at dulling the reality of his situation; the conflicting responses which flashed back to his nerves and senses acting as a self-inflicted anaesthetic.

When Josh did move, it was with his left hand only, reaching out his fisted fingers slowly until his arm was locked in full extension. He touched nothing. A foolish second passed before he forced his palm open and explored the extra four inches. At the straining extremity of their reach, his fingers came into flinching contact with Joep's bushy beard but then held rigid as the tough bristles scraped along their tips and were rigid still when Joep's body gave out a soft, crumpling sound as it hit the dirt.

Even then, he could still have saved himself.

Even now, you could still save yourself.

All you have to do is move.

Just move.

The hand was coming vaguely out of the darkness, parallel and a little above his own.

Swing your arm.

Knock the hand away.

Do it.

The hand was reaching behind his head. Clutching fingers took chilling hold of his neck.

You still have your gun.

Your feet then. Kick out.

I'm going to die.

Yes.

Slowly, under strong, even pressure, Josh found himself compelled to move forward and it was with an emotion imitating relief that he felt the warm blade puncture his skin, then drive up beneath his ribs, seeking his heart. There was no pain. The darkness got a little blacker.

Hatless, and without the hindrance of a gunbelt, Feltman was running, pounding along the sidewalk, the vibrating boards marking his path for De Brecco, who was toiling but not far behind.

The first of the vultures had already gathered, forming a solid line over the entrance to the saddler's alley. Feltman barely checked his speed as he roughly forced his way into the arena of garish light that illuminated the death scene. No one complained.

Doctor Pardoe was already standing, his brief examination completed. He did not bother to pronounce them dead. Feltman stepped closer.

Josh and Joep were lying almost head to head, on their backs near the corral fence. The heavy handle of a hunting knife was protruding at an obscene angle from Josh's blood-soaked belly. On the other side of the fence, behind the bodies, wearing only his pants and holding aloft a lamp, stood Walcot, the saddler, staring morosely down at the corpses.

Judge Perry, his attire less than immaculate was using his left hand to support his stout frame against the saddler's wall while his features portrayed everything of his raging fury, leaving nothing for an expression of sympathy for the actual victims.

"Who found them?" asked Feltman, keeping his voice steady.

The Judge turned and stared, his eyes accusing. "Where were you?"

"Some would be, drunken horse thief fell over the top of them," Walcot answered Feltman. "Must've scared the shit out o' him. Spooked the horses an' woke me up."

"How long?"

"They have been dead for about two hours," Doctor Pardoe replied in his even medical tone.

Feltman skirted the bodies and put his hands on the top spar of the fence. He could feel the deadness spread in his stomach. He could also feel the Judge at his back.

"I asked you where you were?"

Feltman did not reply.

Incensed, the Judge grabbed his shoulder and hauled him round. "Damn you, Feltman. That boy died doing your job."

The bitter accusation slammed into Feltman's face and,

in reflex, his hand swung in a vicious stinging blow across the Judge's cheek. This would have been followed by the rhythmic backhand across the other cheek had he not been immediately restrained by De Brecco and Doctor Pardoe, who stepped smartly between them.

"You think I killed him?" Feltman shouted, his resolve at staying calm shattered, replaced by a sudden explosive hatred for this pompous old man in front of him.

Judge Perry had stepped back, stunned. It had been a long, long time since anyone had struck him in any fashion- friendly, playful- far less in anger.

De Brecco held Feltman tight. "Calm down, for christ's sake. We're all upset here. He was a good kid. An' Joep? Who would want to stick old Joep?"

Feltman knew. He didn't know why. But he knew who. He had seen that blade before.

The fury in the atmosphere faded as one by one the men at the centre of the fray became aware that the fickle attention of the gawpers had shifted to Rachel, who had emerged silently from the fringe of the ghouls and was walking slowly, trance-like, towards her brother's body.

She called his name softly and broke into a short, stunted run. Hypnotised by her grief, no one tried to stop her and, weeping now, Rachel draped her body over that of Josh's.

Perhaps it was because her body made contact with the instrument of her brother's death or maybe the horror of what had happened got through to her.

Rachel drew her body back and screamed. A terrible wailing scream that went on and on.

Still, no one went to her.

Eventually, it was Feltman who came forward. There would be no consoling her. He grabbed a hysterical Rachel roughly around her waist and dragged her to her feet. He practically threw her at Judge Perry.

"Get her out of here."

Astounded, Judge Perry gathered Rachel in his arms but it was Doctor Pardoe's incredulous voice that was heard. "But, good god, man, it's you whom she needs now."

Feltman spared Pardoe a quick, searching glance before dismissing it from his mind. "Take her home. Get your daughter to look after her."

The gruffness of the command could not disguise its pleading nature and Judge Perry, recognising that his first priority was to help the girl, nodded assent and began to usher Rachel, clinging and weeping, through the crowd.

A thought struck him then and he turned his head to ask Pardoe about Mrs ten Dam. "It's being attended to, Judge. Doctor Brady should be with her now."

Judge Perry silently thanked the lord for the efficient, responsible behaviour of the town's medical men and continued to guide Rachel through the crowd.

One of the onlookers, more hardened than most, sidled up to the corpses and placed his tilley lamp beside Josh's body. He took a hold of the knife's decorative wooden handle and pulled. The blade came out about half an inch.

"Useless," the man stated, disappointed. "Won't budge."

"Leave it for the undertaker's," instructed Pardoe. I will attend to it there."

As the man stood up, Feltman came across and planted his left foot on Josh's stomach. He grabbed the knife, gritted his teeth, and heaved. A further two inches of blade emerged slowly but the last four and a half inches offered little resistance, slurping out with gruesome bits of Josh's insides and sending Feltman staggering.

"That was quite unnecessary." Pardoe's tone was scathing. He had had enough theatrics for one night.

Feltman sat down on an empty packing case, driving the

wide blade into the soft wood of another and tried to think.

De Brecco came over. He had recognised the knife.

"Why would he do that? An' why Joep? What the hell was he doin' here?"

Feltman didn't respond.

After two attempts at trying to coax him out of it, De Brecco gave up and left him alone.

With the removal of the bodies, the crowd quickly broke up and Feltman had the alley to himself, accompanied only by Walcot's lamp -and the knife.

There was no point in it that Feltman could see. The sawmill owner, old ten Dam, he did not understand at all. But Josh? Maybe just to get at him. But Benson would not have sanctioned that. Could only be McCabe. A warning of what was to come.

But it really did not matter now what the motives had been. Only the consequences. He had promised her. And he had failed. That thought deadened his stomach again. He had lost her. She would never forgive him.

He tried to clear his head. If he couldn't have her he'd have to accept it. Put it out of his mind and concentrate on what had to be done. There was no option. The town would be in uproar over these latest murders. These were innocents and society knew the difference. His clash with Benson would have to be brought forward. He would have to do it in the morning.

Benson himself was no problem. Colby? Dangerous, but not insurmountable. But McCabe. There was no way to cater for McCabe, except the one way. Even Benson wasn't able to rein in McCabe, a man whose sole ambition in life was to see Feltman dead.

McCabe was the risk he couldn't afford. The other risks were manageable. So, that was the way it had to be. He would play out the rest. Decide on the ending when he had to. But he would give McCabe his own special role.

There was less than two hours till dawn when Feltman finally got back to his room in the Lady Anne. He stayed only long enough to strap on his gunbelt and put on his hat. He gathered up the rest of his belongings, together with his rifle, and headed down the stairs, leaving the door open and the key in the lock.

He got a puzzled look from the night clerk as he veered past him into the bar. It was devoid of life. No stragglers allowed; only the presence of one of De Brecco's night guards who gazed at him with insulting curiosity.

He dumped everything on the counter and stepped behind the bar. Ignoring the rotgut, he found himself a decent bottle of scotch and stuffed it into his saddle bag. The guard watched in silence, then, when Feltman made for the saloon exit to the street, said. "It's bolted."

"You want to unbolt it?"

The guard thought about it. Then he put down the shotgun and walked over and slid back the bolts. He pulled the heavy doors back, exposing the batwings, and stood aside, inviting Feltman to exit.

The guard watched from the door as Feltman cut diagonally across Stonewall, heading towards Grant. His compadre from reception appeared at his side.

"He runnin' out?"

The saloon guard shrugged.

"Think we should tell Brec?"

"In the mornin'. I ain't rousin' him now."

Feltman walked steadily, if a trifle awkwardly through the quiet dark streets until he reached the Marshal's office on Grant. He raised his boot and brought it crashing down on the barred door.

"Open up in there."

"Uh? What is that? Who's there?" The sleepiness in Judd's voice diminished with every question.

"It's Feltman. Open up." He kicked the door again.

"Gimme a minute. I'm comin'." Judd was a little apprehensive. He detested meeting with Feltman at any time. But at this hour? Trouble.

There was the sound of the bar being lifted and the solid door swung ponderously open to reveal Judd, resplendent in his bright red underclothes.

"About time," said Feltman, and marched inside.

Judd stared. "What is it? What's goin' on?"

"You're goin' out. That's what's goin' on," replied Feltman, dumping his gear on Judd's desk. "I'm in. You're out."

"Wha'd ya mean?" The bit of Judd that wasn't showing bright red took on a hue at the other end of the colour spectrum. "Ya mean now?"

"Yeah, I mean now." Feltman wrenched open the door which gave on to the cells. "An' take your friends with you."

There were seven men crammed into one cell; five of Ramon's vaqueros and the two morons Colby had laid out. In the tiny middle cell lay some old drunk who Judd hadn't bothered to rouse out.

And the magnificent Christina in the other.

"But what will I do with them?" Judd wailed, "They're supposed to be leavin' town tomorrow."

"What the hell do I care what you do with them? Just get them out. Here, give me those keys." Feltman opened all the cell doors. "All right, out."

Ramon's men stared at him dubiously, fearing some sadistic trap. "I said out," Feltman repeated, drawing his colt. "Or I'll start blowing a few ungrateful heads off."

269

They moved then, slowly at first, then faster as they realised there were no guns waiting on them outside. The drunk, a shrunken old man, gave Feltman a toothless grin and a friendly pat on the arm as he went by.

"God bless yer."

"That's all right."

"Tarnation! Wait a damn minute." Judd was trying to pull on his pants and reach for a rifle at the same time. "You men. Wait there." Judd stumbled out the door.

Feltman could actually feel her presence behind him. He turned slowly. Christina was still in the middle of her cell, standing erect, her hands by her sides.

Feltman waited. There was no point shouting at this woman. Christina walked out of the cell calmly. She stopped when she was abreast of him, turning her head only. The dark bruise and scabbing on her chin in no way detracted from her beauty. But her eyes. The hatred in her eyes.

"I will watch you die."

Feltman acknowledged to himself that there was every possibility. But said nothing. Christina completed her dignified exit; ignored Judd, who was hopping about on the boards, and disappeared into the night.

Feltman kicked the door shut and dropped the heavy bar back into its slot.

"Hey! Feltman. Fur chrissakes, hang on."

There was a lot more inventive cursing and door banging in the next few minutes but Feltman ignored it and eventually it went away.

He dug out the whisky bottle and pulled Judd's tin cup towards him. It was so blackened it was impossible to tell if it was clean or dirty. Betting on dirty, he used a measure of scotch to scour it out before pouring himself a decent measure.

He went over and examined Judd's cot. Maybe not. He took a sip of good whisky, reached for the bottle and wandered through into Christina's cell. She wouldn't have thought so, but it was passable. Judd had been a gentleman.

Feltman caught the enticing woman smell of her as he sat down on the cot. He placed the bottle carefully on the floor and sipped from the tin cup. Just this one and another. Just enough to send him off. He was confident that he wouldn't sleep through his wake up call.

Thirteen

The first shafts of brilliant red light had just begun to streak the eastern skyline when the half-drunken cowboy staggered out of Sammy's saloon bar into the hazy dawn and an eyeball to eyeball confrontation with his horse, who was still saddled and bridled and tied to the hitching rail.

"Aw, jesus." The cowboy gave the animal an apologetic pat between its big, reproachful eyes. "I shoulda seen to ya last night."

The trouble with Sammy's was that they were too damn hospitable. They never threw you out. It was a hovel, and cramped; but cheap and an all-round good place to slake the dry throat of a hard-working cowboy.

This morning, the cowboy had fought his way out from beneath a table under which he had slid several hours before and where he had subsequently been joined by two others seeking a similar handy refuge for their slumbers. Sammy was going to have to introduce bigger tables for the comfort and convenience of his faithful clientele.

But he was going to have to give up these one night, drunken binges. At dusk the previous evening, he had ridden a fast ten miles from a remote Bar-L line cabin just to get roaring drunk and ride back again. In future, he would make sure he spent all his cash on payday. It made life less complicated.

Wearily, he tried to get into the saddle but his horse shied away. Now that was unusual, neglected or not.

"What?" the cowboy asked his horse. "Is it water? C'mon, we'll get ya water."

Deciding that lack of water was the principal problem, he lead his horse off down Main in search of a trough. He spied one a little further on, just beyond the Limon Hotel, and he veered across, his faithful mount plodding along behind.

But with two feet to go, his horse again shied away, this time from the wooden trough.

"Aw, c'mon hoss, I gotta get back pronto or Joe'll be cursin' my mama t'hell."

The cowboy grabbed hold of the bridle and tried to pull his stubborn mount forward. "C'mon," he coaxed, "have a drink," while at the same time he reached behind his back with his free hand and began to splash his fingers about in the trough, making what he hoped was an appetisingly watery sound. "See, nice fresh water."

His horse was not too impressed.

The cowboy had to agree with him. Slowly he brought his hand forward again, bringing it up to his face to examine the brown, sticky gunge clinging to his fingers. Hoping his guess was wrong, he dropped his hand from the bridle and turned round, peering gingerly into the trough.

With a pained look, he closed his eyes and started to massage his lids. Then he looked again.

On the sidewalk, Seb Ramsay, the Curious Butcher, just happened to be passing, heading for work and his habitual early start. Seb's expertise in the slaughtering business was legendary in Limon; a skill honed from an early age on the family farm where his fascination with the inner workings of rodents and all types of vermin were actively encouraged. Even his unauthorised dissection of the odd chicken and the fact that Seb's curiosity killed generations of farmyard cats was tolerated to a certain degree.

Unfortunately, unable to contain himself, he had progressed to the family dog and his father, fearful of the wellbeing of their one and only milking cow, had insisted he put down the knife.

Seb left, needing to expand his boundaries, and was now fulfilling his destiny as head slaughterer at Limon's meathouse. But while the dissecting of cows and horses had initially satisfied his curiosity to a greater degree, there had been a distinct waning of satisfaction over the years due to the sheer numbers and repetitive nature of his butchering.

So Seb had turned his attention to Homo Sapiens. Luckily, some instinct told him that his fellow humans came under the heading of his father's milking cow, and he had wisely contented himself with listening to every private conversation he could, butting in whenever possible, which was often, and generally behaving in a friendly, not to say nosey, manner.

So, naturally, having noticed that the cowboy had found something of interest in the horse trough, Seb just had to step off the sidewalk and ask, "What do you see, friend?"

Seb had taken to calling everybody 'friend', a remembered expression of his father's. It sounded so pleasant and, well, friendly.

The cowboy combined a yawn with a shake of the head as he unbent his back. "Tell ya the truth, I ain't sure I'm seein' straight."

Seb peered enthusiastically into the trough. Then he looked at the cowboy, who was looking at him and they both had a look together.

"He don't look none too happy," ventured Seb.

Which was not Dave McCabe's fault; and neither did he care. His body had been crammed into the water trough, his shoulders floating up to jam against the caulk line between the top two hewn planks, holding the length of him under an inch-thick scum of sticky brown water.

His eyeballs and teeth danced under the surface, catching the refracted light of a new day dawning. Only the handle of the knife protruded out of the mire.

Seb leaned forward and took a firm hold of the hilt, ignoring the goo which gathered and clung to his hand. He changed the weight of his stance and levered McCabe's head up until it broke the surface.

"I gotta say," said the cowboy, entering into the spirit of the thing, "it couldn't have happened to a nicer fella."

Seb's professional eyes was assessing the gaping slit on McCabe's throat; a wound that made the blade to the belly superfluous. "A person must've had a hatful of hatred for this one." He eased the pressure on the knife and allowed the death mask to slip back under the surface.

The cowboy stretched. "Well, listen, I gotta get back to work." He put his shoulder to his horse's flank and turned him round. "I'll leave you to pick up the glory."

"That's right neighbourly of you."

The cowboy waved a depreciating hand and swung into the saddle. There was no protest now, both horse and rider having forgotten about water for the minute. He flopped his hand again, this time in a farewell salute.

"Bye, partner."

"So long, friend."

Brian Cairns felt happy. The lively black stallion he was riding obviously shared his mood; prancing when held to a trot; stretching his long legs joyously when allowed to canter; but never satisfied, always striving for the gallop.

With the pleasant warmth of the early morning sun seeping into his tired old body, Cairns seriously doubted if there could be a better way of spending a couple of hours of anyone's time than moving briskly over the Wyoming range with a vibrant, straining animal clamped between your thighs.

He laughed at the connotation. It had been a fair while since he had that kind of animal clamped between his thighs. He stole a glance over his shoulder. Nothing. But it was not possible to see very far due to the rolling landscape. That, and the fact that his neck did not seem so flexible these days.

Just ahead was a large outcrop of weathered sandstone, dotted about with trees and bushes. He slowed the stallion, who complied reluctantly, and pulled him round behind a sizeable chunk of the yellow rock, big enough to conceal his presence from any approaching riders.

He did not bother with anything fancy, like going on for half a mile and doubling back. If they were there, they would not be tracking him; they knew where he was going.

He only had to wait five minutes. He counted them off. Nineteen. Nineteen riders, all armed and dangerous. He let them go by, far enough so that his horse would get a good gallop out of it, then gave the stallion its head and tore after them.

The beast responded magnificently and soon Cairns was flushed with the thrill of being part of such effortless, graceful power. Before long, however, he was forced to check the animal when he sighted the rearmost rider of his would-be pursuers.

They could not hear him, of course. The steady pounding of their own mounts' hooves effectively drowned out the sound of his approach and there was no reason for them to check their back trail.

As he drew abreast of the tail ender, the rider was startled, perplexed and resigned in short order, his instinct to call out curtailed without uttering a sound.

Cairns moved sweetly up through the group, eliciting similar reactions from each of the men as he passed, all staying silent, with a few wry smiles thrown in. Matt knew he was coming before he saw him but he waited until his boss's stallion was matching his bay stride for stride before he gradually tightened his hold on the reins, bringing the whole party to a halt.

Cairns let the silence hang for a moment. The other hands were either grinning sheepishly or whistling soundlessly, but none looked at Matt, who had his hands resting on his pommel, staring fixedly between his horse's ears.

"I said alone, Matt," Cairns reminded him.

His foreman pushed back his hat and gathered himself for the argument. "You expect us to let you go in on your lonesome? Nobody coverin' your back?"

"No, I didn't expect you to," Cairns confirmed the now obvious. "But that's the way it's got to be."

"Why?"

His boss considered this reasonable question. "Look, Matt, I promise you. It's under control. I'm in no danger. If we go in mob-handed now, it'll get loused up an' some of these boys will die."

"What did it say? You know that rider almost killed his horse getting' it to you?

"We lookin' after it?" Cairns had no real fears over the animal's welfare. But he was buying a moment to marshal his thoughts

"Yeah, we gave him a fresh one. So, the message?" Matt pressed. "That what makes it safe?"

"Matt, you're just goin' to have to trust me. I'll tell you what, how about you give me a couple hours?" Cairns instructed. He waved his arm over the lush range, embracing the easy flow of the creek just ahead. "There are worse places for a man to take his ease an' bat the breeze."

The discussion was over and needed no acknowledgement. The stallion, sensitive and impatient, pranced forward.

"Boss."

Cairns showed full respect for his foreman by pulling his mount right round to face Matt head on.

"I reckon that you're the sweetest, most cantankerous old bastard this poor cowboy's ever known."

Cairns laughed; he absolutely loved this man.

"An' if you're not alive an' kickin' when we get there, I'll burn that fucking town to the ground."

Brian Cairns wanted to say something, but his throat would not let him. He wheeled the stallion and went.

The pounding in Feltman's head would not stop. No matter how tightly he screwed his eyes shut, it went relentlessly on, driving into his skull until it threatened to split it apart. In desperation, he opened his eyes.

A second of disorientation before he realised he wasn't drunk. "Feltman! Will you open the goddamn door?"

He blinked and raised himself up out of Christina's haze. His wake-up call. Again, the thunderous, demanding bellow came at him from beyond the jailhouse door.

"Will you shut off that noise?"

If anything, the pounding on the door increased. He swung his feet to the floor, narrowly missing the bottle of scotch. He picked it up. Still three quarters full. He slid it back to safety against the wall. Wearily, he dragged himself to his feet, stretching his muscles as he as he staggered over to the door. "Will you pack it in?"

The hammering ceased and he lifted the heavy oak beam from its iron brackets and threw it carelessly against the wall, letting it bounce to the floor. The door swung open of its own volition, following the cant of the badly placed hinges. It was a full turn out.

"Come in, gentlemen. Don't stand on ceremony."

That had not been their intention. They were in before Feltman had finished his sardonic invite. The Judge first, followed by De Brecco and Hartford. None were smiling but the Judge was grim. "All right, we struck a bargain with you, and we're here now to ask you what, in the name of god, you think you're playing at?"

Feltman moved over to the blackened stove and checked that there were the making of a fire in its small belly. He drew a match against the wall behind it and threw the ignited head inside, waiting to see the first licking flames before he shut the door. Then he looked around for the coffee cup. He badly needed a cup.

"Do you intend to ignore us altogether, Feltman? Or are you still drunk?"

He found the short-spouted pot lying on its side under the table. There was enough left of Judd's late night brew to squeeze a cup out of it. He stuck it on the stove.

"Feltman, they pulled Dave McCabe's body out of a horse trough this morning." Hartford fought to keep his rising anger under control. "He had that hunting knife stuck under his ribs."

Feltman waved an inquiring hand at the pot on the stove. "Coffee?"

"Fuck's sake, Feltman," now it was De Brecco. Well, why not? Give them all a shot at it. "The time for being calm was last night. Not now. Now's the time for answers."

"McCabe was a rabid dog that needed put down." Feltman sat down in Judd's seat and peeled off his shirt. "You three upset because McCabe was on the right end of a bit of fast justice? So what? You don't think he was due?"

"Yeah, he was due. The whole town knew he was due. Easy to pin it on McCabe and right back to Benson. But you just couldn't wait, could you?"

"Look, Feltman," Hartford tried to be reasonable, " We all know the kid was your girl's brother. He was a nice kid; we were all upset for him and Joep. But you've let the real killer off the hook."

"Just when we had the bastard by the balls." The Judge cut in, scathing. "Yet, for some insane reason, you decided to give him an escape route. For god's sake, man, his head honcho had just butchered one of Limon's most prominent citizens, not to mention a young officer of the law. The whole town was up in arms. Benson's head was in the block. He was finished here." The Judge ran his tongue around his gums, trying to lubricate his words so he could get them out faster. "So why? Why in the name of all that's holy did you have to go and hand him a lifeline?"

The Judge was apoplectic, so Hartford took over.

"All we had to do was send for Brian. His cowboys and a whole town screaming for vengeance? Together? Benson was done. Instead, you call him out. A direct showdown; a gunfight in the street? Are you crazy? Without Cairns men here as back-up? How the hell can you win that?"

"You've given him cause, Feltman," De Brecco piled back in. "You know what he's doin' right now?"

Feltman had an idea but he was sure De Brecco was going to tell him anyway. "He's getting' himself an' Colby deputised. That's right, deputised. By the legally appointed town Marshal, Harry Judd. He's coming to arrest you, Feltman."

"Look, Feltman," Hartford was pleading now. "If your plan was to provoke Benson, then fine. But why not wait on Cairns? You have another plan? So tell us. Please. Just what the hell is going on?"

The three men waited expectantly. Feltman used his shirt to wipe the sweat from his armpits.

"Well?" The Judge was a hairsbreadth away from grabbing Feltman by the throat.

"Well, I'm goin' to have a cup of coffee an' a shave, an' then I'm goin to walk down that street an' take care of Benson. At which point," Feltman pointed at Hartford, "I expect you to come out of somewhere handy an' slap a thousand dollars on me."

"Oh, c'mon, Feltman, you're dreaming. You won't be collecting anything. Listen ......"

"No, you listen. I'm sick of your sanctimonious fuckin' bullshit. Look at you, the three wise hypocrites. All that clucking an' self-righteous sympathy over the old Lumber Guy an' Josh when what you were really thinkin' was 'Hallelujah.' Opportunity can always be found in other people's misery, eh?" Feltman sneered at the look exchanged between Perry and Hartford. "That the creed you live by?"

Feltman was feeling a little high. And low. He needed that coffee. He turned his tirade specifically on Hartford.

"The banker. The salt of the earth, without whom there would be no civilised society. You think those poor shits out there actually like you? They see you as the very worst kind of bloodsucker, the kind who smile at you while they drain you away. They work their asses off an' shovel the profits your way. An' if there are no profits they have to get their noses brown so their families can eat."

The bitterness of Feltman's words eroded any reply that might have been forming on Hartford's lips.

"And that's the real irony of it. The odd time these poor sons of bitches break down an' need a drink or a woman, their hard earned cash ends up back at the bank, via some bastard, hoverin' vulture, just waitin' for them to break.

Yeah, I mean you Brecco."

Feltman threw his soiled shirt in the corner. "An' you ain't finished with the poor shits yet. Because here comes the Judge."

The change of focus forestalled any protests either Hartford or De Brecco felt inclined to make. Judge Perry braced himself for the onslaught, too angry to speak.

"El Primo, lordin' it over us all from his high-backed chair. Just sittin' there, baskin' in the respect of his lesser man, occasionally issuin' a stern warning from the bench as he jails some poor drunken bastard who's just been kicked off his spread by Hartford here. We might have abolished slavery, but the peasants have got to know their place, right Judge."

Feltman was smiling now, relaxing into his diatribe.

"Nice, cosy hierarchy. Must've been a worry when it looked like your two compliant underlings were in danger of being ousted by one ruthless bastard. A man who would not pander to you at all. Who would just see you as an irrelevance."

This was too much for the Judge. His jowls shook as he croaked out his response to Feltman's mocking tirade "Do you seriously imagine that your warped oratory entitles you to ignore us? Ruin everything we have been striving for? We will simply not allow it."

"I don't think you're going to allow me to do anything, Judge. Your permission is not required. Get out."

"For god's sake, man, if Benson guns you down now, we'll be ten times worse off than when we started. I warn you. You step out that door before Brian Cairns gets here, and there is no chance of you getting another red cent out of us."

"You don't think too good, do you Judge? If I go out an' take down Benson, then you'll pay me what I'm due.

If I don't, well, I'm not likely to care a helluva lot, am I?"

"Feltman, please listen to me." Hartford's tone was conciliatory. "I've already sent a rider out to bring in Cairns and his men. We're only asking that you wait till they get here."

Concern showed fleetingly in Feltman's eyes. But his voice had lost much of its fire when he answered. "You'll have to trust me, Hartford. It's under control. You think I don't know who sanctioned Josh's killing? Benson is a dead man."

"Okay, so you have another plan. But can't you slow down a little? Why not wait for Cairns anyway? It'll give us all some insurance."

Feltman gave a very definite shake of the head. "It's done. Just relax, it'll be over soon." Feltman's voice had dropped to a much more reasonable pitch.

It was not enough for the Judge.

"I very much doubt if we three are the only hypocrites standing in this room." He turned and strode furiously out the door, angrily slamming it closed behind him, in his temper, either forgetting or not caring that De Brecco and Hartford had still to follow him out.

The door rebounded violently, banging shut twice more before it slowly creaked back to lie fully open, only coming to a halt when its movement was arrested by the heavy oak bar which Feltman had left lying on the floor.

Hartford and De Brecco spared Feltman a last, forlorn glance before making their way out after the Judge.

The Judge had only stormed as far as the corner of Grant and Stonewall and now he stood waiting on them, outside Bartlett's grain store, fuming.

Feltman was tempted to leave the door open to allow some fresh air to circulate, but every head that passed turned for a curious look inside, the same head more than

284

once. So he kicked it closed and dropped the oak beam back into its slot.

He hunted out Judd's tin cup and poured himself some hot treacly coffee. It was vile, but just what his body needed, something to compete with the fluttering in his stomach. He went back to the cell and retrieved the scotch. He cut what was left in the tin cup with a good measure and poured it down his throat. Then he set about getting some hot water boiled up. He hated to shave in cold water.

For a while, the three men on the corner stood about, frustrated and silent, effectively blocking the sidewalk. Another morning, their selfish stance would have elicited a steady commentary from passers-by on the merits of idiots holding meetings in crazy places. But not today.

Today, they formed only one of the many tight clusters of people dotted along the sidewalks as Limon's residents turned out in force for the show. If their group was distinguished, it was not by its elite composition but by its contrasting lack of vociferous expectancy.

Finally, Judge Perry could stand the silence no longer. So he asked, "Well?"

Hartford was surveying the street. "Word gets around fast."

From where they were standing, all the way down to Main, people were moving livestock and wagons out of the expected firing line, hurriedly making morning deliveries at twice the normal speed before whipping their teams away to safety back round into Main or tucked away down Stonewall.

As they watched, the stretch of Grant between Stonewall and the T-junction at Main steadily emptied and was soon devoid of life, with the exception of a handsome chestnut mare which a careless owner had left tied to the hitching rail outside Hank Brown's chop shop. Which was handy enough if she wasn't moved soon.

In contrast, Stonewall itself was swarming with people, packing the street and the sidewalks for fear of missing the start of the action. It was the same behind them, back down Grant towards the Marshal's office; crowds of people and wagons and everywhere that heavy, hushed sound that can only be heard when hundreds of people are whispering at the top of their voices.

Judging the optimum distance for safety and clarity of view, the spectators had chosen the gladiators battleground for them, knowing there could be no protest.

Judge Perry tried again. "There must be something we can do."

De Brecco shrugged. "Maybe we don't have to do anything. You should have seen the way he took down that preacher an' his friend. Either way, It's too late to do anything about it now."

The judge was still bristling. "And what he said about us? Our motives?"

"I sleep easy at night. Or at least I would, if it wasn't for Benson."

The Judge was slightly taken aback at De Brecco's philosophical perspective on things. But it appeared to settle him down a little and his features returned to something resembling normal.

"What about the guards you have at the Lady Anne?" he asked, trying to keep his tone conversational. "Couldn't you get them out here to back up Feltman?"

"Think he'd thank us? Besides, there's a big difference between sitting on your butt with a scatter gun across your knees, waitin' for trouble that might never come, an' steppin' out into a certain gunfight with bullets flyin' at you." De Brecco shook his head. "They'd never do it."

"So what do we do?"

"We get off this damn corner for a start," said Hartford, and with the banker leading, all three descended from the sidewalk and started across Stonewall.

It was a lot quieter than normal in the 'Gentleman's Bar' of the Limon Hotel, even for that time in the morning. It was the absence of trivial conversation which was the main contributor to an atmosphere that was almost serene.

Benson stood with Colby at the centre of the long, highly-polished bar. There were three other handy looking men with them; a select group, carefully chosen by Colby that morning. And Judd.

There were no customers. One other gunman sat at a table close to the street exit, retained as a presence in the hotel. All of Benson's other employees were out spreading the word. Your saviour is coming.

Unarmed and carefully briefed, his men would be mingling with the crowds and making their views known at every opportunity. No matter how crudely put, their mutterings would register just enough to raise doubt. Especially after Feltman went down.

'He murdered McCabe in cold blood. Wouldn't surprise a person if'n he'd sliced up old Joep an' young Josh himself, give him cause.'

Benson was in political overdrive.

None of the five were drinking. Benson put away the revolver which he had been checking and rechecking since he had entered the bar. Not through necessity. Just habit. Old habit. It had been quite some time since he had allowed himself to become involved at this level. Still, this particular situation required that he should.

"You sure the boys are clear on that?" he asked Colby. "No interference. None, We don't want to make a hero out of Feltman."

"They've been well told." Colby showed no irritation at being repeatedly interrogated on the same point. He understood his boss's need for reassurance. "They're out there to plant the seed. An' just in case some of them couldn't resist getting' in on the glory; we removed temptation. Walker can't move for the hardware stacked in his office."

Benson nodded, satisfied. Everything would have to be just right. No mistakes. He turned to the other three men.

"You follow Colby's lead. He decides if and when Feltman goes down. You're only there to add to the firepower, give Colby an edge. You draw only when he draws. Clear?"

It was clear.

"But stay alert. You never know when one of these mealy-mouthed shopkeepers might discover he has a set of balls."

All the tough-looking men laughed. They knew it was unlikely. Benson laughed with them. He enjoyed this. He always had. He enjoyed turning adversity into profit. It really was his forte.

That dumb bastard Dave couldn't just take care of old Joep like he'd been asked. Had to go and kill the kid as well. And leave a big sign pointing back to me.

He couldn't ignore that. But he hadn't had to deal with it. That Feltman, jesus.

No real surprise to find them all gathered round the trough first light this morning. Bye-bye, Dave.

Colby was much more the thing. Intelligent and tough, he carried out instructions to the letter. And he did not get emotional about it. That's what Benson liked most of all.

Colby was going to fit nicely into the scheme of things. Feltman had done him a favour by getting rid of the

McCabe boys. A little messy, perhaps, but better than trying to pension them off.

Talking about pensioning people off, he turned his attention to Judd. "You know what you've got to say?"

Judd nodded. But he wasn't sure he could do it. "I could sure use another one?" He indicated his whisky glass on the counter.

"No, one's enough." God, but this little man was a liability. "Tell you what, Harry," Benson changed his mind, "have as many as you like." He moved down the bar and put a consoling hand on Judd's shoulder. "Archie," Benson summoned the Barman, "the Marshal's money's no good here."

Benson smiled his friendly smile. "You stick around here with Pete over there," he indicated the gunman at the table. "Just leave it all to us. We'll talk when it's done."

Benson glanced down at the butt of the revolver which jutted invitingly out of the worn, black leather holster. He couldn't resist it. His hand swooped down and the gun slapped smoothly into his palm. Judd almost shat himself. But Benson only had the gantry covered. If any of those bottles moved, they were dead.

He smiled, genuinely surprised that he still had the feel for it. But he would have to watch that he did not let his imagination run away with him. If there was any shooting to be done, Colby and the other three would handle it. He broke out of his reverie and re-holstered the gun.

"All right, let's go."

Pete stood and rested his hand on the ornate doorknob. At Benson's nod, he swung it open to an anticipatory buzz from the impatient mob already gathered outside. Benson paused under the hotel awning, drinking it all in; accepting the noise as a note of approval as he anointed the crowd with a Presidential wave.

289

The five men filed down onto the street, where the three gunmen fanned out behind Benson and Colby, cutting a wide swath through the crowd who were pressing against, but not infringing on, the empty rectangle of the Main and Grant intersection.

The ribald comments which accompanied their stiff-legged walk drew a few self-conscious smiles but failed to cut through the tension.

As they broke clear of the crowd at the junction, two of the deputised gunmen moved quickly ahead. They veered away sharply to make for the North side of Grant and climbed up onto the sidewalk outside of 'Ma Kelly's.'

Ma was stood in the restaurant doorway, exchanging pleasantries with Old Don who was tucked safely round the corner on main, ensconced in one of the restaurant's chairs. Ma had specifically supplied the chair for the purpose of keeping Don safe while he soaked up enough of the action to re-tell the tale. Because being in the know meant a lot to Don; it kept him alive. But no point in getting killed to keep you alive. What Don couldn't see Don would make up. And the re-tellin' would be all the better for it.

Ma spared the self-important pricks a sour look as they passed. Behind him, the place was packed with craning heads.

The remaining gunman in the back-up trio immediately lengthened his stride to come abreast of Colby and together they mounted the broad planks of Grant's south side, leaving Benson to turn into the street, symbolically alone.

Limon's new champion of law and order paused briefly, playing to the mob as he savoured the moment. Bar a lone horse, this section of Grant was now deserted, rolling out in front of him until it slammed up against a solid wall of bodies beyond Stonewall.

Above street level however, the story was different. In

addition to those adventurous souls still wandering about the sidewalks as they decided which store would give them the best balance of safety and view, people were hanging out the windows and packing the balconies; the consensus being, seemingly, that bullets whose trajectory veer from the horizontal are rendered harmless.

Benson took a deep breath and let it out slowly, deliberately utilising the tension. He rocked on his heels before moving purposely on, instinctively drifting closer to Colby's side of the street as both pairs of covering deputies matched him step for step on the slow walk towards his destiny.

Doctors Brady and Pardoe glared balefully at Coly and his sidekick as they marched solemnly by. Brady grunted something choice and moved back around the corner into Main where he slumped his body into a rickety chair outside Sammy's, dumping his bag at his feet.

After a brief hesitation, Pardoe followed. But since Brady now occupied the sole chair available – which a tag proclaimed was for buying, not sitting – he remained standing, surveying the crowd.

The whole thing verged on the ridiculous. Was ridiculous. Pardoe had been witness to more than one gunfight since he had come out west – they were hardly uncommon in the frontier territories; but they had always been fought out with rifles, or scatter guns, and with the combatants invariably firing from behind barricades. He had however, both heard and read about these stand up gunfights where men faced each other with six-guns and found them incomprehensible. They bore no comparison with the archaic rituals of Europe; duels where gentlemen adhered rigidly to a code of conduct whilst settling points of honour with a single shot.

Here, there appeared to be a distinct lack of rules, with

one side frequently outnumbering the other - as in the present case. So why the pretence? Why bother? Why not just shoot each other in the back and be done with it?

But what he found the most irritating of all was the arrogant assumption that he and Brady would wait patiently until these morons had finished blasting holes in one another, then rush to use their expertise to patch them up. And even more irritating still, was the fact that their assumption was correct.

"Doctor."

Pardoe swung around at his colleague's summons.

"Let it happen," cautioned Brady. "Have a cigar."

Pardoe accepted the death stick with a polite bow.

"Don't mind if I do, Doctor."

The sum total of the action that had been taken by De Brecco, Hartford and the Judge had amounted to swapping one corner stance for another across the street. The grain store for the bakery.

On seeing the mass exodus from the Lady Anne, De Brecco had temporarily left the other two. It was not the girls led by Bel that he objected to, but the fact that his day guards had followed them out.

Hartford and the Judge watched as he remonstrated with the men, trying to convince them that this was exactly the time when someone would burn the goddamned place down. A promise of a little something extra clinched the argument and the guards trooped back inside, still a little miffed at missing out on the entertainment.

While they were waiting for De Brecco's return, Hartford caught the motion of waved cigars, made in casual greeting from the opposite side of Grant. He managed to stifle the reflex acknowledgement. Stevenson and Bono could stew in their own juice. The fact that their judgement might well prove to be correct only stiffened Hartford's resolve.

De Brecco was having to fight his way back to the corner, shoving his way through the queue at the bakery window. The double entrance doors on the corner might have been firmly shut but business decreed that a steady flow of bread dripping with butter and slices of dried raison and apricot tart were being passed out to smiling spectators who were waiting eagerly for the action to begin.

It was carnival time.

De Brecco spread his hands as he reached the corner. "That would really have put the seal on it. Feltman dead and the Lady Anne burnt to the ground in one day."

But he only had an audience of one. Hartford was staring intently down Grant towards Main. "Here comes Benson," he informed them despondently.

"Feltman's got to have something up his sleeve," said De Brecco, more in hope than firm belief. "The man's not crazy"

True to form, the Judge decided it was time to put his foot down. "I'm going to put a stop to this nonsense," he announced, and strode off down the sidewalk, hell-bent on a collision course with Colby and friend. De Brecco and Hartford set their faces and trailed along behind.

Inside the jailhouse, Feltman wiped the last of the soap from his face with his retrieved shirt and threw it back in the corner. Judd's hygiene regime didn't run to towels. He pulled his saddle-bags across the desk and pulled out his deep blue shirt. It felt crisp and clean. He gave it a snapping shake out and slipped it on. The gunbelt came next, strapped on a little low for some, but comfortable and slick for him.

He reached into the other bag and pulled out his clip

holster with the .38 Remington resting snug in its cushion of soft leather. He attached it high on his left side with the butt facing forward. If he ended up with a gun in either hand he would be losing the battle. One gun at a time. One accurate bullet at a time. And he had twelve. If he needed to reload, he really was in trouble.

He picked up Judd's pitted tin mug and examined the cold tar residue of his morning coffee. Maybe not. He reached for the whisky bottle instead. He took a short, single slug. Just enough to feel the fire in his veins.

He stood for a moment, letting the warmth spread.

Feltman thought that maybe he could still have her. She would be fragile, maybe hate him for a long while. But maybe she would forgive him. In any case, he had to try. If he wanted her, it was the only option. Play it out but change the ending.

He tossed the whisky on to the Marshal's cot. A nice present if Judd were to make it back. He picked up his hat from the desk and placed it firmly on his head.

Too much, too fast. Time to go.

Benson saw the judge and his two pageboys bearing down on Colby and stopped in the street, level with the entrance to Melville's barber shop.

The Judge came down one step and clutched at the hitching rail in front of Colby. He leaned his upper body over the spar, the better to glare fiercely down at Benson. "I thought we had an agreement that this was not the way things were going to get done?"

"And we citizens of Limon thought the town had hired a peace-keeper. Not a crazed lunatic who goes around murdering innocent people." Benson had his public speaking voice on and his carefully chosen words boomed out to the populace, proclaiming that he was one of them.

The Judge was frothing. "Innocent? McCabe? You are claiming that degenerate was innocent?" He was spluttering now, his outrage heartfelt. "The only innocents were Joep ten Dam and young Josh."

"And I, and these few brave men, duly deputised by Marshal Judd, are here today to see justice done." The oratorical quality of Benson's words left Judge Perry's protestations floundering, indistinct and impotent. "If Feltman surrenders to the appointed officers of the law, we are confident that you will ensure he gets a fair trial."

The irony of that statement was not lost on the Judge.

"You are not getting away with this, Benson. I refuse to believe Judd has deputised you." The Judge was snarling now, losing the battle and falling into the trap of anger-inspired irrelevance. He snapped his head up, making a show of scanning the crowd. "Where is Judd? Judd is the man to arrest Feltman if he has committed any crime."

Benson did not look like he was inclined to respond, so Colby answered for him. "Marshal Judd's got a pile of work on this morning, Judge. He's chasin' around somewhere, huntin' down all them escaped prisoners." Colby smiled, "Seems there was a bit of a jailbreak last night."

The Judge stared at Colby, completely bereft of anything to say. Behind him, Hartford found himself grateful that his eminent friend was finally lost for words. His inane prattling had not been helping any. If anything, it had only served to heighten the enjoyment of the rabble, their enhanced excitement tangible as the belligerent confrontation was relayed back through their ranks.

Colby said quietly to Benson, "He's coming now."

The avid murmuring of the crowd ceased abruptly. Then it rose in humming crescendo as the lone figure began to weave his way through the mob. A mixture of awkward glances and uneasy smiles marked his pathway. But most took care to avert their gaze completely. It was not possible to actually root for the man. After all, it looked like he was sure to go down.

In an equally mild tone, Colby spoke to the Judge. "Might be a healthy time for you to invite these gents into Mel's for a shave an' a hot towel. You'd have the best seats in the house."

Benson smiled. He liked Colby.

Judge Perry's scathing reply was stifled as he simultaneously saw Colby stiffen and heard the shocked gasp which rose from the assembled crowd, one of whose number had broken clear of its massed ranks and was now racing down the street behind Feltman, kicking up dust and closing fast.

A cowboy.

They saw Feltman break his stride and turn to face the danger, his right hand a blur as he snapped the colt from its holster, then, extended and steady, line it up on the heart which was pumping energy into the suicidal charge. But the gasp came again when the cowboy ignored Feltman completely, running straight past him to continue his sprint down Grant.

The crowd caught its collective breath yet again while it waited for the dashing cowboy to be blasted to smithereens by Benson's gunmen but, with the amazing subtlety that is the sole prerogative of the massed voice, expelled it in roaring approval as his intended objective became clear.

In an astounding exhibition of balanced, athletic dexterity, the cowboy took off a good five feet from the tethered horse, allowed his left foot to touch briefly on the hitching rail, then hung in mid-air, harnessing the extra impetus, before swinging his right leg over the chestnut's back to fall sweetly into the saddle.

Deftly leaning forward to pull the reins free, he politely raised his hat to the assembled company and with a "'scuse me, gents," wheeled round Benson and tore off down the street with his rescued horse.

Colby smiled at the Judge. "I'd take his advice if I were you."

Hartford did not wait for his friend to answer. He grabbed him by the arm and hustled him into the barbershop with De Brecco following close behind.

Angrily, the Judge shook his arm free as he was propelled through the door. He ignored Mel and his startled expression as he looked up from his reclining customer and turned to the window, his face tormented.

Colby had moved forward a few paces until he was directly in front of the large display window that fronted Truman's haberdashery. His sidekick moved with him, positioning himself just slightly in front of Benson. Across the street, the other pair of gunmen matched their movements so that the five of them formed a shallow, open-ended box, waiting for Feltman to step inside.

Feltman had missed her the first time. When he had broken through the perimeter of the crowd she must have been just outside his peripheral vision. But it would have been hard to miss her as he swung round to assess the danger from the foolhardy cowboy.

As he had re-holstered his colt, he had let his eyes roll across the proud stance Christina had taken up on Bartlett's corner; stock still, erect; imperial in her blood-red dress; waiting for him to die.

Maybe she would get her wish. If she didn't, he would have to deal with her, or she eventually would.

Marie-Louise watched as Feltman scanned the crowd. She did not imagine that he was looking for her. But she couldn't resist bending her wrist back to give a little finger wave of good luck.

Beside her, Bel was shaking her curls in despair. "Marie-Louise, if you ever find out what makes men so stupid, be sure to tell me. I don't want to go to my maker not knowing."

Marie-Louise smiled across at her boss. Bel had been good to her, kindly even, within the constraints of her employment.

And men were stupid. But not as stupid as women.

She had jumped out of one fire straight into another with that piece of shit fiancé of hers. Elliott was one nasty son of a bitch and she was well rid. And when that railway came in she was heading straight back out on the first train down to Cheyenne and all the way to Sacramento.

She would find herself a nice deserving man and fuck him until he thought he was in heaven. She would be faithful and have babies and a house.

And a life.

As Feltman moved steadily on down Grant, across the intersection, the mob jamming the sidewalk on the east side of Stonewall magically opened to leave a deferential pathway for Rachel.

She came striding through between McGarvey and Clancy who had grabbed themselves a pole position. Her face was flushed and set; hate in her heart. Behind her, a worried Carrie, pulling at her, desperately trying to slow her down, calm her. And behind Carrie, the Water Boys; Tomas concerned, Freddy captivated.

Carrie grabbed at Rachel, restraining her before she could dash out on to the street. Tomas moved to help Carrie, his left hand across Rachel's body, propriety precluding him from touching her. Wishing to seem concerned, Freddy put a helpful hand on Carrie's waist.

"You kill him." Rachel was screeching as she struggled frantically, almost bent double in the caring embrace of her friends. "You hear me, Michael? I want that evil bastard dead."

Feltman heard. And he was glad. But now he shut out Rachel's screams as she strived to match his progress from the sidewalk, dragging her escort with her as she continued to issue a stream of invective relating to Benson's fate.

Clancy was looking at McGarvey looking at Freddy. "My friend, if you're gonna kill that boy, can ya wait until he's finished supplyin' water to the hotel? We're talkin' fresh drinkin' water here, Garve, through a faucet."

McGarvey smiled and stopped firing daggers into Freddy's back. "No need. He's got about as much chance as me. Ninguno. I just don't like the long piece of shit." The saloon-keeper eased himself off the bakery wall. "What do you care? I thought you'd sold the place?"

"I might buy it back. I'd give it back if Angie were still here."

"That ain't gonna happen." McGarvey looked back across Stonewall over the heads of the crowd to the grain store where Christina still stood; magnificent in her dignity and grief. "That's a woman who would know something about runnin' your kind of hotel."

Clancy followed McGarvey's stare. Christina was entirely focused on following Feltman's walk to his fate, completely ignoring the Optic's sketch artist as he tried to capture her likeness to add colour to their debut afternoon edition.

Clancy laughed gently, "Yeah, well, a man can dream."

"She'd eat you alive, Clancy."

"I reckon. But there's a lot o' chewin' on me. Might take her a while to get to somethin' vital."

They switched their attention back as Rachel's voice screamed even louder, protesting and distraught. Ritchie's wife had come out of the haberdashery and was insisting they get her out of harm's way. Persuasion wasn't working and eventually, Richie, worried about Rosalin, came out and hauled Rachel into the shop, a relieved escort trailing behind.

In the barbershop, the Judge slammed the side of his fist into the window frame. "Is there nothing we can do?" he asked of no one in particular. Neither did he expect an answer.

Mel stopped sliding the cut-throat razor on the leather strop and advanced towards the Judge, waving the lethal, honed edge in his face. "I told you this was gonna happen," he squealed. "I warned yus. That Feltman's no better'n any'm."

The blade of the razor traced an arc as Mel pivoted and began to wave it in front of Hartford. "Is that what we get for our money? A dead Feltman? Huh? Not to mention Joep an' Josh."

Hartford backed away from the swinging blade. "Shut up, Mel. And put that damned razor down."

"That's uncommonly impolite of you, Andrew."

Mel grinned delightedly at the comical, stunned reactions which the unsolicited comment had evoked from all three men. That startled the bastards. His customer had swivelled in his reclined chair and was now pushing himself to his feet, dabbing at his face with the lukewarm towel.

"Brian." The single, incredulous word was uttered by Hartford.

Judge Perry continued to stare blankly. It was De Brecco who recovered first. "You're here. By god, you're here. But how could he have reached you in time?"

"Your rider? I was already on my way in. I met him on

the trail," Cairns answered with a smile.

"You were already coming in?" asked Hartford, puzzled. "But how could you have known?"

De Brecco had every appearance of the man who had been thrown into the bottomless pit only to find that his fall was short and his landing cushioned by a thick pile of one hundred dollar bills. He peered out the window, his faint reflection mirroring his relief and delight. "No wonder Feltman was pissed with us. Your boys done a good job o' sneaking in." His eyes were searching along the roof tops. "Where are they?"

The door clanged open and two of Limon's finest stormed in, immediately rushing for the window were they took up station either side of De Brecco. They pressed the right side of their faces against the panes, squinting in order to peer out at the street where Feltman had come to a halt, less than thirty feet from Benson.

"Jesus," screeched Mel, "I should've sold tickets."

Needless to say, he was ignored. Limon's citizens were surely entitled to a decent and safe viewing point.

"My boys?"

It would not have been accurate to say that the flames of relief which had flickered with varying degrees in the stomachs of De Brecco, the Judge and Hartford spluttered and died. They were doused; extinguished; tramped on. The smile that had been forming on the Judge's face reached an instantaneous peak and faded. "You don't have your men with you?"

"How could I? I only came in for a shave."

"But our rider?" Hartford tried to fathom it out. "They are coming in?"

"Sure. Half my crew will be here in a little under an hour, I guess."

Hartford nodded his dumb acceptance while the Judge

301

sagged back against the window frame, emotionally weary and waiting for the inevitable. De Brecco saw only his own reflection, engrossed in watching its expression change from delight to dejection.

Out in the street, Benson had already started to set the scene, his orator's voice powerful, carrying to the crowd.

"Look, Feltman. We're gonna be straight with you. We didn't come out here to arrest you. You wouldn't let that happen. An' even if you did, consensus is, his eminence, your friendly paymaster, the Judge, would spring you. An' we, the good people of Limon, ain't gonna stand for that."

Benson was in his element. He removed his cigar for a brief examination. It was nicely chomped and wet from the saliva generated by his speech.

"You're one dangerous son of a bitch, Feltman." The compliment was not in any way backhanded. "So, we know, if you go for your gun, some of us will die here today." Benson included Colby and his henchmen in a magnanimous sweep of his cigar. "But so will you."

Benson held the pause to let that sink in.

"But there's been enough killing in this town. It's time for it to stop. Time for people to go about their business without murder and mayhem doggin' them at every turn."

This was a good speech. Benson was proud of himself.

"So we're going to give you another option, Feltman. Walk away." Benson allowed himself a small, depreciating smile. "Figuratively speaking, of course. Get on your horse and ride out. An' don't come back. Your choice, Feltman. Either way, you're leavin'. If you want to do it in a box, pull that gun."

Benson was standing, relaxed and confident, with his thumbs lightly hitched in his gunbelt and his fat cigar jammed between the fingers of his left hand.

Feltman had thought about interrupting Benson's

speech with a bullet, but, aware that Colby was alert for any sign, decided to lull them with his response – and cut Colby down when they got the impression he was about to accept their generous offer.

Colby's friend would be next, followed by Benson. He would be attracting lead by then, but he would be on the move. He would have to be unlucky to take a serious hit. And Feltman didn't believe in luck – of any kind. The boys to his left would go down. And they would not be getting back up.

Feltman's whole body relaxed, ready to move and he started to work his mouth to give Benson his reply. But the words refused to come. That was because his mind had deserted his vocal chords entirely, to concentrate solely on the urgent, flashing picture which his eyes were sending back to his brain.

A middle-aged man and a young woman had stepped off the sidewalk outside Ma's and were strolling sedately up the street towards the combatants.

Cleery and his daughter.

Colby tensed as he saw Feltman's demeanour change and his focus shift. His hand moved a fraction to hover over his gun but he held off, unsure. Benson lost his relaxed expression and sent his cigar spinning into the dust. The three other gunmen were poised, ready, looking to Colby for a lead.

Feltman shuddered to compensate for the sudden loss of body heat as the steady trickle of sweat from his pores became a gushing torrent erupting from his skin.

Why would any man walk his daughter down the street to a gunfight?

Worse than fear, resignation debilitates. Feltman knew they were walking down the street for him.

Benson saw Colby turn his head slightly to look past

him, picking up Feltman's line of vision. This brought confusion and fear. Behind him? Who? He stared intently at Feltman as if to extract the information from the other man's mind. He could not bring himself to turn round. He switched his gaze to Colby and watched as his expression changed to something close to puzzled amusement. But not fear. No, not fear.

Inside Mel's, De Brecco was practically jumping up and down as he punched Judge Perry repeatedly on the arm. "But look. Just look at them. It has to be something to do with Feltman."

"But what can they do," the Judge asked, the string of recent disappointments holding his desire to be convinced in check.

"*Jesus-H-christ!*" retorted De Brecco in exasperation. "An old man doesn't take his daughter for a morning stroll into the middle of a goddamned gunfight. He'd have to be crazy."

"Maybe he is," said Hartford dryly. He was with the Judge.

Out in the street, Benson was beginning to feel foolish. He knew he would have to turn round. But the difference in reaction between Colby and Feltman to whatever was behind him was more than a little disconcerting. He had just started his head on a slow swivel when all thirty-five square feet of Richie Trumen's pride and joy, his hand-engraved, semi-frosted display window, splintered outward and dissolved into a multitude of light-reflecting slivers and cubes of brilliant glass.

The consensus afterwards was that, had it not been for the large, hard body of the young Mr Henderson suspended in the mist of this flying shower of crushed ice, the overall effect would have been quite pretty.

Colby felt the stinging patter of glass particles against his back and neck, and saw and heard the crashing hail of them as they bounced off the sidewalk on either side of him.

Taken completely by surprise, his reactions were, nonetheless, very fast. His gun was already out and he had started to birl round when Henderson's flexed knees caught him heavily in the small of his back, the crushing weight sending him forward and down, unable even to bring his hands in front of him to break his fall. The bridge of Colby's nose cracked solidly against the top step, then his face scraped messily down the other two boards as Henderson's bulk rode him like a human sleigh.

Colby's partner, who, quite naturally, was staring open-mouthed at the sight of Benson's top gun being bounced off the planking with this giant mounted on his back, realised too late that he was part of the same spectacle and looked up only in time to see the blur of the Winchester as it tore his head off. As least that's what it felt like in the fleeting moment he had before unconsciousness.

As Colby's head ploughed into the dirt, bringing both himself and his rider to abrupt, inclined halt, Henderson rolled back on his heels, perfectly balanced, and brought his rife to bear in an easy, flowing motion. He fired twice, shifting his aim slightly after the initial shot. Neither of Benson's men on the other side of the street had got their guns clear of their holsters. They died without ever realising what it was all about.

Henderson's knees dug deeper into Colby's back as the young giant forced himself up, springing forward to land a dusty boot either side of Colby's head. His rifle came back to rest in a steady bisecting line between Feltman and Benson.

Beneath him, Colby strained and made a feeble attempt to twist his hand, still firmly holding his gun, trying to bring it to bear on the massive body towering above him.

Ruthlessly, Henderson brought the rifle back to the 'port arms' position and drove it down. The sickening squelch of Colby's skull caving in carried clearly to those in the Barber's shop.

It had no effect whatsoever on De Brecco's display of unbounded joy. He was actually hugging Hartford in his delight. "He did it. Hot damn, he actually did it." He reached back and, unmindful of the razor still clutched in Mel's fist, hauled the moaning bastard forward by his waistcoat, shoving his face to the window. "Ain't that the best fifty bucks you ever spent?"

Without waiting for a reply, De Brecco yanked the door open and rushed out to secure his share of the backslapping. The rest followed close behind, Cairns bringing up the rear. Mel chose to remain in his shop, peering balefully out the window.

Benson, his brave decision to look behind him momentarily halted by the explosive appearance and chilling action of Henderson, now completed his turn.

He stared in confused fascination at Cleery and his daughter. He backed away from their presence, clearly spooked; finding them even more unnerving than the young assassin, who had remained standing astride Colby, the stock of the Winchester jammed into the top of his right thigh, relaxed but watchful.

The crowd were enthralled, and now surged eagerly forward in a congratulatory wave. Windows flew up and doors were hauled open and smiling people poured out, convinced they were happy that Benson had finally got his. But, inexplicably to those at the rear, the crest of this human wave began to lose its initial momentum while it was still a mite short of the central figures whom it had intended to swamp and, as those at the front became certain that all was not well, the cheering hushed while the flowing tide of humanity went briefly into ebb, shuddered, and was still.

On the sidewalk, De Brecco had pulled up short, checked initially by the absence of any triumph showing on Feltman's face, then halted completely by the awareness that, for all his apparent casualness, the young leviathan was covering both Benson and Feltman.

Beside him, doctors Brady and Pardoe had come to a halt; their rush to attend the injured stalled, unsure as to whether the mayhem was actually over. The initial exodus from Truman's store had been curtailed almost immediately. Only Rachel was out on the sidewalk, with Carrie and Tomas Hawksley in protective attendance. She was there to see Benson die, and her eyes never left him.

Freddy stayed in the doorway; absolutely certain there was more excitement to come. Ritchie Truman had forcibly prevented Rosalin and her friends from going outside, and they now stood together in a tight group inside the store, framed by the frosted edging around the shattered window. Megan at the front; Rosalin and the Tryst in the middle row with Ritchie at the back, looking for all the world like the baritone in a heavenly choir.

Christina alone continued to move forward through the crowd, leaving the newspaper man trailing in her wake. Clancy and McGarvey elbowed a gap for her as she finally broke through on the crowded sidewalk, her eyes boring into Feltman, impatient for him to die.

The heavy silence which now hung over Grant signified that it was now obvious to everyone that something was very definitely wrong.

Since first casting eyes on him, Benson had never once shifted his gaze from Cleery, who was dressed in a grey suit belonging to some by-gone age the pants of which were tucked into his wide, calf-high boots; the frills on a shirt from the same era mostly hidden under his grey beard. A brown, flat-crowned hat clashed with the rest of his outfit.

Samantha had her left arm hooked through his, clutching a wicker shopping basket, looking very fetching in a green gingham dress. The pair of them could have been on their way to have lunch by the river.

Benson found a version of his voice. "Who are you people?"

Cleery let the question hang for a second.

"Yeah, we can surely get to that, Bramwell." There was nothing of the showman in Cleery's voice. It was hard, gravely and flat. "But don't you reckon it'd be polite to introduce yourself to these good folks first?"

Benson flinched at the use of his given name and started to back away.

"What's happening? What is it?" Judge Perry failed abysmally to summon even a vestige of that commanding imperialism he habitually utilised when bemused. His confusion was markedly apparent in the timbre of his tone and sad lack of specifics in his enquires. None of the others lined on the sidewalk ventured a question but they waited impatiently for answers.

"Allow me to introduce Bramwell Benson Forbes, late of Chicago, and one time candidate for Mayor of that fine city. You never made first citizen, did you Bramwell?" Cleery lifted his eyes to the main gallery and explained, "Got caught with his hand in the wrong till. Very careless."

Seeing the perplexed look in Benson's eyes, Cleery shook his head. "Not me," he said, disclaiming any credit. "I'm only recallin' a bunch o' telegraph messages."

Benson's hand made a futile twitch over his gun, stopped only by the fact that any attempt to pull it out would bring almost certain death in the shape of a bullet spurting from Henderson's rifle.

He had made a mistake. A grave error.

He had celebrated before he had won. If ever there was reason for his men to follow orders to the letter, this was it. They were scattered and leaderless. And they had just watched the clinical execution of Colby and three of his best men.

Benson took another nervous step back, away from this bizarre couple who, inexplicably, knew enough to crucify him.

He had to extricate himself from this. He turned slowly to face Henderson who was staring at him, while covering Feltman with the rifle. He raised his hands chest high, pushing them out to help him back away another step. Even now, like all political thugs, he used the currency he dealt in. He expected others to be reasonable when he was not.

Another slow step back. And another. Moving quicker; and still the rifle was pointing at Feltman. If Henderson altered his aim, surely Feltman would take him? Backing into the crowd, sensing them part for him. Feltman's body shielding him from Henderson's view. Turn now.

And just run.

Cleery sighed and looked at Henderson, giving him the nod, and the lethal young man loped after the rapidly retreating back of Bramwell Benson Forbes, who was now desperately seeking to break free of the crowd, who held him in a prison corridor by defining his route as they parted in combined reflex, fearful of getting in the way of the bullet that was bound to follow.

Throughout all this Feltman had not moved. He remained rigid, the tumbling sweat of seconds before now frozen to his body, his stomach a mass of churning ice. he found he could not think. He did not want to think. It had finally happened. And he was cold.

"Dirty business, politics." Cleery was speaking again. "Forbes got put away for mis-appropriation of party funds. But that was hardly the climax of his anti-social behaviour; was it, Feltman?"

All heads on the sidewalk immediately swivelled, switching their attention to Feltman, who stayed silent, staring sightlessly at Cleery and Samantha.

Cleery obviously did not feel that an answer was essential. "No, Bramwell's main theme was eliminating rival politicians, an' anyone else who was provin' to be a nuisance; a task allocated to his number one man here. And carried out with the minimum of fuss an' maximum efficiency. You might have noticed that about Feltman. He's very efficient."

"Feltman?" Hartford croaked, clutching for support at the Judge's shoulder. "Feltman worked for Benson?"

"Wrong tense. Works for, always has. Number one boy an' chief liquidator."

There was a thump as Judge Perry sat his ass down on the top step, almost bringing Hartford down with him. De Brecco was white and swaying. "But how …. Feltman?" he could not even understand his own question. His words trailed away, his mind rejecting the conclusions it would inevitably reach once the complex emotional barriers were dropped.

"Who are you?" The Judge was deflated and repeated Benson's question with much the same sense of unease.

"James Cleery." The expressions on the faces of his captive audience confirmed that this meant nothing to them. "Johnny Oh sends his regards."

Just puzzlement. Johnny Oh?

Cleery didn't wait for the questions, "Him an' Galbraith have had folks scratchin' around in Benson's backtrail awhile. Couldn't even find him, so nothin' to see. Kinda suspicious in itself, they reckoned. But seems he got a tad careless when they were tuckin' into some fancy chow together a few days back. Dropped a thread, gave them somethin' to pick at." Cleery made a motion with his hands. "An' here we are."

"You work for Johnny Oh." It was not a question from Hartford. More a statement made in capitulation.

Cleery gave an assenting nod. "Deal with problems too hot for the legal boys."

"But what was the point?" the Judge asked, desperately seeking understanding.

"The point was that things were getting' a little too hot for Bramwell in the Windy City, so he had to set his sights a little lower. He settled them on Limon. Only he had gone as far as he could go using the blatant rough stuff an' you people were getting' a little desperate. I imagine you had him worried when you called in those army boys. But, by a stroke of good fortune …," Cleery caught himself, although it was unnecessary. Carrie was as mesmerised as anyone and took no offense.

"I apologise, Miss." Cleery tipped his hat to Carrie and started again. "Unforeseen events meant that you had to ask them to leave. But that still left Bramwell with a problem. It was just a little too early for him to go legit. Or as legit as he ever gets. Too many roughnecks in town. That would have put him in the same position as yourselves. Vulnerable.

On the other hand," Cleery continued, "you good citizens were a determined bunch. Always scratchin' around for an answer to the violence. An' he couldn't be sure he'd be able to handle your next solution."

Cleery found and held Judge Perry's eyes. "So, he gave you one. He gave you Feltman."

"He gave us Feltman." The Judge repeated the words

311

slowly, incredulously.

Cleery nodded. "Clever laddie, our Bramwell. He knew that you'd jump at the chance of hirin' a wolf to see him off. But what you got was a wolf in wolf's clothing. He was eatin' you up an' you couldn't see it. An' there's Bramwell sittin' back, in the clear. How could this come back to him? When it was your own paid employee runnin' around doin' his work for him. And Bramwell, full of community spirit, doin' all he could to help the due process of law."

"But they were going against each other," protested Hartford. "It's absurd. It doesn't make any sense."

"Don't it? You heard the speech play. Nobody would have blamed Feltman if he had backed down in the face of five guns. An' if he high-tailed it outta town, nobody would be comin' after him either. I hear McCabe wasn't that well liked."

"But Benson could have shot him. He wouldn't have risked that." Hartford couldn't see it. " And he still ha…" Hartford stopped speaking. He heard nothing of the disdainful retort from the old man in the street.

"The rest o' his money comin'?" Cleery shook his head sadly at the naivety of it all. "You already dropped him a wad. An' that was only whorin' money. Appears he was on five grand a hit back in Chicago. So his tally was already twenty-five, maybe thirty-five, if Forbes was inclined to throw in a bonus for takin care of the McCabes."

"But …" De Brecco was trying to formulate a question that would stop this being true. "it was a coincidence. I was in the restaurant. It couldn't have been a set-up."

"That wasn't, no," agreed Cleery. "You were so desperate you clutched at a straw that wasn't even offered. But you can bet Bramwell had somethin' lined up. My guess would be the preacher men. From what I hear the town just about had their fill o' them; without anybody havin' the sand to do anything about it."

De Brecco nodded dumbly, acceptance winning the battle with denial.

"An' as for Bramwell shootin' Feltman. Well, reckon that's why he was out on the street. Feltman insisted. Anything slightly off an' Bramwell would be the first to die. An' Bramwell would have thought he was safe from Feltman. Hard to pick up your fee from a dead man."

"Joshua."

The soft whisper of her brother's name had no trouble cutting through Cleery's amiable reasoning. Rachel was motionless, rigid. She was leaning slightly forward now with only Feltman as her focus.

Cleery was glad that she had strong hands around her and a woman beside her. He looked down at his boots, taking a moment, trying to be careful about what he was about to say. "If it's any consolation, Miss, I don't think you could lay the deaths of Mr ten Dam and your brother at Feltman's door. That was sure to be McCabe."

"But the breeds? An' Angie?" De Brecco knew but he wanted to be told.

"An' you, if there had been enough time," was the brutal conformation. "And Ramon and O'Sullivan." A sympathetic hum rose up from the crowd at the sound of the loveable rogue's name. "An' that poor little Mex he set up. Feltman's a killer. That's what he does. An' he does it well."

The full horror of what had been going on was beginning to permeate through to the select group on the sidewalk. The only facial colour going about was burial grey. Aside from Rachel, who looked perfectly serene, a statue staring into Feltman's soul.

Then the single, rolling report of the rifle came back at them, skimming over the crowd to shake Feltman out of his passive acceptance of death.

He would still die, probably. But no need to go easy. This nonchalant old man in front of him, so sure of himself. And so sure of Feltman that he had allowed the boy to take off after Benson. He would die too.

Cleery did not appear to be armed, though he was certain to be packing something, tucked away somewhere. He would never reach it. Cleery wasn't the problem.

When he killed the arrogant old fuck, Feltman would have to chase down the boy. No point in fleeing. Henderson would come after him. And he would keep coming until he found him. Better hunter than hunted. But the boy was lethal. So it was unlikely it would end well. Feltman was sanguine about that. That thing he'd found when he hadn't been looking was gone. And it wouldn't be coming back.

Rachel came down a step, still silent, staring. Carrie clutched at her elbow and Tomas Hawksley, his face set, wrapped his strong arm even tighter around her waist. Propriety not an issue now.

Feltman could not look at her. Preoccupied with thoughts of his own demise, he was getting ready to die.

Cleery had been waiting for the change. "Easy, son .."

"Old man, you talk too much."

" ...ah wouldn't do that."

But it was too late. Feltman was already moving and he was very, very fast. In a blur he had his .44 clear of his holster, thumbed the hammer back and was lining up on Cleery's stomach.

His chest.

His head.

Now that was dumb. Feltman never went for a head shot. Not unless he was finishing somebody off. So why start now? And his index finger had picked a fine time to wander over the trigger guard because he could not get at the trigger to squeeze it.

He realised he had given Cleery the time he needed to hit the dirt because he'd disappeared from view. Only buildings and sky and the sun searing across his eyeballs and more sky and upside down people and his hat.

How can I see my hat?

Feltman heard the sound of his colt going off and hoped to hell he had hit the smug old bastard. Then his head was chasing his hat down the street.

With the exception of Rachel, who was deep in her own world of anguish, those gathered on the sidewalk and the near fringes of the crowd had been startled when Feltman had spoken. He had been quiet and still for so long that he had ceased to exist.

And the speed with which he had went for his gun had thrown a communal stab of doubt into the hearts of the assembled audience, fearful of the final outcome.

It was through awe-struck eyes then, that they watched Feltman rise up on his booted toes from the impact of the .31 calibre bullet fired from the 1851 colt pocket revolver that Cleery's daughter had produced from her wicker basket, and was now holding extended in her elegant, capable hand.

Feltman's feet remained rooted as his body arced backwards, sending his hat flying from his head to land behind him. His gun dropped from his leaden fingers, firing harmlessly under the sidewalk on impact with the dusty street. Then the back of the killer's head hit his hat and ploughed it along the dirt for a couple of feet, before his torso made contact with a soft 'carump', sending up swarming clouds of dust which hung above his body for a moment then settled back down on his inert form, covering it in a filthy shroud.

Samantha released her hold on the tiny weapon, letting it fall back into her basket, her composure belied only by the slight tremor of her hand. Cleery gave her arm a discreet, reassuring squeeze.

On the sidewalk, Christina lifted her eyes from Feltman's corpse. No triumph. No satisfaction. Just vengeance. Her eyes drifted over Rachel. But no sympathy. Having seen what she had come to see, she spun on her heel and disappeared back into the mob.

Brian Cairns eased his way past the Judge and limped down to the street. Crossing over to the young woman, he took her gently by the shoulders and murmured, "Samantha," combining sympathy with fond greeting as he kissed her on the cheek.

Nothing could have reached Hartford now. "You knew," he said, simply, without accusation.

"Not at first," Cairns replied. "I was told. I knew Jim from my time with the railroad. He was doin' some detectin' then for the Central Pacific." Cairns shrugged. "He paid me a visit."

There was a stirring in the crowd and Henderson reappeared. The young man halted beside Feltman's body.

In response to Cleery's silent query, he said, "He was tryin' to get on a horse."

Cleery nodded his understanding and turned to Cairns so that the two old friends were looking at each other over the top of Samantha's head.

They were in agreement.

So Cleery glanced up at the line of ashen faces on the sidewalk. Unlike their audience, who were enthralled and becoming animated as understanding set in, the gallery of principals were drained and lifeless. He was not entirely unsympathetic. "Guess we'll leave you people to bury your dead."

As the young Mr Henderson moved to join them, he stopped and swung a gentle boot into Feltman's ribs.

"Hey, I think this one's still alive."

But Cleery and Cairns had already turned and, arm in arm with Samantha, were strolling off down the street.

"Let the bastard rot."

The New Pretender

The Ultimate Quango does not seek to rule the United
Kingdom. It exists merely to expedite the major policy
initiatives of the government of the day – whatever its
political hue.

The peace process in Northern Ireland will shortly receive
a boost from The Downing Street Declaration. Enough,
perhaps to bring it to eventual fruition; if the right safety
valves are in place.

Independence for Scotland cannot be allowed to coincide
with reunification of the Emerald Isle. For those Loyalists
who will never succumb to Dublin rule must be
encouraged to relocate within the UK – and that does not
mean the English Shires.

The shadowy Mandarins of the Quango view the
shooting-star political career of Iain Morrison with
dismay. They put the SNP's latest recruit into Parliament.
Now they must remove him. But they do try not to be
vindictive. Not even when they resort to using Michael.
It's simply an administrative thing.

*The sweet and sour entree of June in Brooklyn whets the
appetite for the onrush of adrenaline as the chillingly
violent action sweeps through the grit and sophistication
of Glasgow, to London, Quebec and Jamaica – but never
so fast that the relentless tension cannot be savoured and
rolled on the tongue.*

*The New Pretender is Braveheart brought bang up to
date. There remains some doubt, however, as to just who,
exactly, is going to get hung, drawn and quartered.*

The New Pretender

JUNE IN BROOKLYN
(A short love story)

It was an aggressive group that burst out of Benito's pizzeria on Court Street.

Rat-arsed, but tactically aware, Neil Roebach took two clumsy steps to his left and lent his back against the cool sandstone portal. The hot sweetness of the night air had brought him close to gagging. But, with his hands braced behind him and his body arched, allowing the welcome chill from the dressed stone to seep deep into his backbone, he felt ready to handle, what must surely be, the final round of goodbyes.

They had been saying goodbye for an hour.

As the sozzled remainder of the belligerent band stumbled past, Neil put his head back and started to laugh. Stone cold sober, he would have permitted himself a condescending smile. In his present condition, any attempts at stifling mirth would have resulted in the attendance of a paramedic.

Between them, Freya and Eduardo had a grimly precarious hold of young Roberto, clutching desperately at him in a humane effort to keep his bum off the sidewalk while they armed and legged him towards the waiting taxi. Roberto was somewhat lop-sided, mainly because Freya was having more success than Eduardo, who, to be fair, was also having to cope with the mesmerising effect of his fellow carer's amply presented bosom, which was floating alluringly, in and out of his blurred focus.

Roberto's arse suffered as a result. But he would only feel it in the morning. Following close behind, like a majestic, drunken battleship in full flow, Maria had an Amazonian grip on Luciano's collar, towing him along in her wake, forcing her husband's legs to work. The combined objective of this swaying procession was to gain sanctuary within the confines of the yellow cab that had been waiting patiently at the curb for the last twenty minutes.

And if the thought of a New York medallion waiting patiently for anyone, anywhere, seems too ridiculous for words - well, this was family. So, when Vito Tassotti got out of the driver's seat, he was smiling affectionately; mostly at his son. By the time he had relieved Freya of her half of the burden, he was laughing out loud.

Encouraged by Vito's laughter, Neil gave some volume to his own and the bleary lights of the buildings opposite flickered and drifted from his vision as he stretched his head back a little further. Another night, a million pin-pricks sparkling in a deep black sky might have made an impression. Not tonight. It could have been pissing down; slanting torrents of hard rain could have been splattering off the sidewalk. Tonight was beautiful. The day had been beautiful and tonight, this night, Neil felt as good as he had ever felt in his life.

To say that George Nugent was stunned would have been to overstate only slightly. Anyone who glances up from their stuffed sweet pepper to find a complete stranger offering profuse apologies for lateness, prior to taking his place at table, is entitled to experience a little flutter of the heart. Especially when seated in the dining room of one's own home.

Mrs. Nugent was slower to register alarm. She first

looked for explanation from her husband; then a stab of panic as she realised he had none. Only the child was not fazed. To her, strange faces at the dining table were a boring piece of normality.

The uninvited guest did not seem at all perturbed that no place had been set for him. Simply clasped his hands and turned expectant eyes on George.

Waiting.

Initially unnerved, but fast regaining self-control, George turned to his wife. "Darling, I really need to speak to this gentleman alone."

Now the child was upset. The bribe of a desert yet to come had helped the pepper go down. But she knew better than to argue and huffily allowed her mother to usher her from the room.

George managed to swallow the interesting, but superfluous, 'How did you get in here,' and started again. "What do you want?"

"When your wife returns with Bernard and Charlie, keep them calm. Don't allow them to approach the table."

He knew their names.

"They're armed." Defiance.

"I know."

George Nugent was not a man to panic. He lived by crisis; was used to it; generated it in others. But he was not in control now, and reliable instinct told him that he would never be. Not of this one. With a deep bad feeling tearing at his gut, he tracked the padded envelope as it slid across the polished surface of the dining-room table.

He really did not want to open it.

His face. Artistic studies of Evelyn on a shopping spree. Joanne; with her school friends. His face targeted; the cross hairs focused between his eyes.

The sharp click of the door opening brought his hand

up, palm showing.

He had more trouble with his head though, having to force it up from his quartered image to meet the calm, steady eyes of the intruder.

"What is it? Give me those." Evelyn's voice scratching. Puzzled.

An out of focus Bernie behind the stranger, waiting for the nod he would never give.

Bright red fingernails clawing the prints and the list away. No longer his responsibility.

Charlie lurking, glimpsing the photographs over Evelyn's shoulder, interested.

"What the fucking hell is this?" Evelyn's voice going high, her east-end accent surfacing, seriously unnerved by her husband's inaction. Oh, she knew what this was all right, and if Georgie boy hadn't the balls for it …"Blackmail? Fuckin' blackmail? You stupid bastard. You think you can just swan in 'ere with a few photographs an' we're all goin' to pee in our panties?"

Evelyn in full flow. Pointless to try and stop her; leaning right over the table her fists planted, her features twisted in contempt, straining into the stranger's face.

Charlie pleased, waiting for playtime.

Bernie poised, impatient.

Evelyn down, her arms collapsed and splayed like a puppy's, wide on the table. Her head twisted away, an earring scoring the surface.

Quiet.

Unwilling to move, frozen in his chair.

Charlie stunned, unable to believe.

But Bernie, lumbering at the stranger's back. Hopeless.

The chair moved back. Just enough. Bernie colliding, his momentum taking him over and down. The stranger helping Bernie's face into the edge of the table.

Charlie, man of action, leaning into the curve as he scrambles around the far end of the table. Reaching under his flapping jacket. Too late. He should have reached for it first. No difference.

The matter-of-fact 'plutt' as the bullet makes its silenced exit from the stranger's weapon. Charlie's scream greeting its entrance into his kneecap. The stranger asking Charlie to suffer in silence, clipping him on the temple.

Over. Waiting.

The stranger takes his time. Flicking his eyes over the scene; Evelyn looking particularly gruesome, lying over the squashed remains of her stuffed red pepper.

At last, his eyes resting on George, still locked in his chair. "I can see why you're the boss."

Coming over. Close.

What?

"Individual letters, I think. Sincere apologies. It would be foolish to suppose that there could be any accidents. Children crossing the road – that sort of thing. There would be no warning. No police. No debate. Just . . . . . . "

George Nugent's quartered image landed in front of him once more.

The stranger leaving.

Pausing.

"And slip in a family travel voucher. From one of the local agents. Somewhere exotic. Two thousand, two and a half ... whatever. Don't be mean."

Gone.

The New Pretender

THE RECRUITMENT

Sometimes, the sun was too much to bear.

He steeled himself and took a firmer grip on the heavy curtains. A quick 'whoosh' of movement, and there was light. It was not as bad as he had expected.

A beautifully muted, Sunday morning. Not harsh at all. He opened his eyes fully. Nothing but clear, blue sky.

Hiding somewhere to his right, an errant pocket of flimsy cloud had formed a delicate screen around the sun, dissipating enough of its raw energy to prevent the river and the scrubbed sandstone and sparkling glass of the cathedral from sending its blinding reflections screaming through the bay window of his apartment.

The river Clyde looked particularly lovely this morning, flowing gently through the heart of Glasgow, bathed in warm, filtered sunlight, slowing down the early morning walkers on the footbridge, making them dawdle; some of them pausing to go to the rail and stare. Not Port Grimaud, perhaps, but, thankfully, not the London Docklands either.

Fully awake now, he left the view and went back to the sofa. He turned off the table lamp whose cosy light had almost lulled him back to sleep and sipped the last of his coffee. He was feeling depressed. Sundays were for reluctant wakening and snuggling up to warm, receptive flesh. Not for falling out of an otherwise empty bed at some god-forsaken hour to drag yourself off to work.

He glanced again at the sports page of Scotland on Sunday. The Irish World Cup squad were depicted in delighted celebration after their unexpected victory over the Italians. Jack's boys had pulled it off again, keeping the dream alive a little longer.

He flipped the newspaper over on to the front page where other dreams were shown. Shattered; blown to bits in a pub in Co. Down. Six innocent men, one of them eighty-seven years old, blasted to death in O'Toole's bar in Loughinisland.

They had been celebrating a victory for Ireland.

He was depressed. They were dead.

He stood up and slipped on his jacket. The blinking, red light on the ansaphone pricked at his conscience. He did not need to listen to the message to know who it was. The ringing of the telephone had woken him up and in vengeful mood, he had ignored it.

Relenting, he picked up the phone. His call was answered almost immediately.

"David, it's Iain. No, no. Relax, I'll be there. I'm leaving now."

He put the phone down and picked up his briefcase. He was glad that he had called. David Jofre was a very pleasant young man who was in no way responsible for the current darkness of his mood.

His steps resounded on the ancient, varnished pine as he crossed the circular hallway to let himself out. He paused, as he almost always did, on the shared landing of the beautifully restored sandstone tenement to admire the intricate tiling on the walls and the scrolled ironwork and polished hardwood of the banister.

This morning, he also let his eyes wander back into his hallway, taking in its fifteen foot high ceiling and wonderfully decorative cornice. The old merchants knew how to build. A new bachelor's dream pad.

He would sell it. Trade it in for a timber-framed bungalow with lots of grass at the back. Buy a cardigan and a dog. Or pursue for half-custody of Benji.

He slammed the door shut behind him, using more force than was strictly necessary. He was feeling a little bitter this morning.

Divorce? It wasn't worth an extra-marital fuck.

The New Pretender will be published in 2021

Fancy a night out

Then why not grab a drink, find a comfy chair, kick
off your shoes, relax and come down to

The Radical Man.

You won't get to know these people but you will get to
listen as they sound off in alcohol induced passion,
completely free from the self-censorship normally
practised when discussing Politics, Religion and Royalty –
all mixed in with the usual pub-articulated cobblers
associated with Sex and Sport.

Join the **Rad's** clientele and drink in the atmosphere as
they rake over the coals of covid-19 and rehash the tribal
stance of Brexit and Scottish Independence. Absorb the
emotional range – from fervour to indifference – and
maybe even contribute some indignation, a little laughter,
or even a measure of agreement.

And come back again, two days later for the more
congenial and slightly surreal **Warmth Down**

The Radical man will be published in 2021

The Radical Man
(Snippets of Inebriated Exchanges)

Climate Change

"Are you a denier?"

"Whit am I denyin'?"

"You know what I mean."

"Well, I'm pretty sure we live on the crust of a lump of rock which has a furnace for a molten core; burnin' away at six thousand degrees centigrade; two-thirds covered in sea water; sloshin' about as we spin at a thousand miles an hour while hurlin' round the sun at sixty-odd thousand; which big, bright star, I'm reliably informed by that boy who plays the keyboards, is itself skooshin' through the universe at god knows whit speed.

I'm feckin' amazed the climate's so stable."

Culture

"Dae ye think the Scots are less sophisticated than other nations?"

Japanese Saying
(Oxbridge translation,
possibly ignorant of
the nuances of Japanese
humour.)

*To claim humility is to be proud.
Do not claim. Be*

Scottish Saying
(Translated by
 nobody.)

*Picking up ma dug's shite
keeps me humble.*

Covid -19

Don't get me started.